He hated London in the summer

Assumed Virtue
A Sweet Pride and Prejudice Variation

Based on the characters in Jane Austen's Pride and Prejudice.

Victoria Lynn

Copyright © 2021 Victoria Lynn

All rights reserved.

ISBN: 9798487425614

DEDICATION

For the gentlemen in my life: my husband, my brothers by blood, my brothers-in-law, and my brothers of the heart. You have been such blessings in my life.

"Assume a virtue, if you have it not.
That monster, custom, who all sense doth eat,
Of habits devil, is angel yet in this,
That to the use of actions fair and good
He likewise gives a frock or livery
That aptly is put on. Refrain tonight,
And that shall lend a kind of easiness
To the next abstinence; the next more easy;
For use almost can change the stamp of nature."

Hamlet, William Shakespeare

1

Thomas Bennet poured three tots of brandy, handed one to his brother Robert Phillips and another to his brother Edward Gardiner before seating himself behind the big desk in his study.

"So, the renovations have been completed to the Bath property. We can get a larger sum now for leasing it out, but I believe that we will not do so this season. Jane and Lizzy need a wider variety of acquaintances in order to attract suitors. The war and London have drawn too many of our young men away. Fanny feels they need a season in Bath this year." He settled more comfortably in his chair. "What is the prospect for a competent tenant for Netherfield Park?"

Gardiner shook his head dismally. He was the new owner of Netherfield Park, having purchased the estate only two months past. He was leasing it out as he did not plan to take up residence for at least two years as he readied his employees to take over the day-to-day management of his business. "I cannot say I am impressed, Thomas. The most financially sound candidate seems to be a young fellow whose background is in trade, which means he will not know enough to administer the estate properly."

Phillips nodded. "His name is Bingley, he is a chatty young man, quite pleasant but he made it clear he has no experience, he has lived the whole of his life in cities. He is interested in leasing an estate to see if the life of a country landlord is one that would be attractive to him. His father wanted his family to be landed. While he wants to honor his father's request, he is uncertain if it is the right thing for him. The good thing is he has a friend who has agreed to tutor him; I met the friend also, a taciturn and reserved man of some eight and twenty years named Darcy."

Bennet looked interested in that. "From Derbyshire?"

"Yes, do you know him?"

Bennet shook his head. "No, I knew his father quite well in my younger days and I knew his mother a little. They were good people, gone far too young. Lady Anne passed, heavens it must be about 15 years ago now and George just six ago. If he is following in his father's footsteps, young Darcy would be a good one to tutor your tradesman; George Darcy was a wonderful landlord. I wonder if Maddie could find out if their estate still is exceptionally well run."

Gardiner nodded soberly. "She has already written, and it is so. Mr. Darcy has the reputation of being a good and fair landlord, he has not lost any tenants since his father's death and the estate is still quite prosperous. For Mr. Bingley, leasing first is a sensible choice, particularly as his friend is knowledgeable and willing to aid him. However, there is another concern; his reputation is not of the best."

Bennet straightened abruptly. "A rake?"

Gardiner shook his head. "No, not precisely. He is not a man running around compromising young ladies. However, he has a tendency to focus his full attention on a young lady for a month or so, to the point of incivility to all others around him. Anyone observing his behavior would assume he is completely besotted, and of course, often the young lady thinks so too. And then just as suddenly as it began it is over and he is on to the next young woman, again behaving as a young man in the throes of love. He apparently is quite sincere at the time and has no ill intentions; he simply seems to have no concept that his actions leave the young lady possibly broken hearted, certainly pitied and often mocked by the ton. He has gained a reputation for flirtation and inconstancy."

Bennet shook his head in disapproval. As a father with five daughters to protect, he was not sanguine about having such a man in the neighborhood.

"You know I would not endanger my nieces. His fancy always seems to alight on tall, lovely blondes. If she were forewarned, could Jane guard herself against such a man?"

"I would have to discuss it with her. Indeed, I would have to consult with Fanny, Maddie, Phyllis and all the girls. I would not have a daughter heartbroken, nor would I have one pitied or censured due to the inconstancy of this Mr. Bingley. Of course, if it is just the two gentlemen, then there are fewer worries, they cannot entertain ladies."

"No," said Phillips, "there will be more than just the two of them. Mr. Bingley has two sisters. The elder is married to a Reginald Hurst and the younger is single and will be his hostess."

Gardiner nodded, "I have had someone investigate them also; the Hursts are nonentities. His father has a small estate he will eventually inherit, perhaps he is also going to learn something of running an estate. At any rate, nothing good about them is known but nothing too bad either; Mrs. Hurst appears to be rather vacuous, and Mr. Hurst appears to indulge in the pleasures of the cellar too often but that is hardly unusual. Miss Bingley, on the other hand, is considered a fortune hunting social climber with a bent for vicious gossip and is a thoroughly unpleasant young woman from all reports. However, she appears to be completely focused on someday becoming the next mistress of Pemberley, so as long as none of the local ladies catch Mr. Darcy's attention she should not trouble the neighborhood."

"Well, let us rejoin the ladies. You have given me much to think on and I believe we need to discuss this with all involved before we make a decision."

As the gentlemen entered the sitting room to take tea with the ladies of the household, Thomas Bennet paused in the doorway to appreciate the view.

Francis Marie Bennet had been a beauty in her youth; while presenting her husband with five daughters had thickened her figure a bit and age had added some lines, she was still a fine-looking woman. As a child her beauty was all her mother had praised, it was the only thing that was important to her, and Fanny could have grown into a brainless, flirtatious woman quite easily if not for her brother Edward. Six years old when Edward was born, Franny had adored him from the first time he was placed into her arms.

As there was only one son, their well-to-do tradesman father had spared no expense to prepare him for the world. Edward had been a precocious child, so their father had hired a tutor for him by the age of six. And so, Fanny, wanting to spend time with her baby brother, had ended up learning as he did. By the time she was seventeen and out she had had five years of philosophy and geography, math and science, Latin and Greek lessons; not that she showed that to the world at large or even to her parents at home. Even as an uneducated girl of twelve she had possessed enough native shrewdness to know that if her mother had realized all she was learning the lessons would end immediately.

So, she had hidden her quick mind behind a beautiful face and bubbly personality and waited for a man who would try to engage her mind. She was fortunate that Thomas Bennet, attracted by her beauty and her joyful nature, had been wise enough to wonder if there was anything beyond the face and figure.

Their marriage had been a happy one and they had taken great joy in their daughters, in working to better their estate and to ensure that their daughters would not go penniless into the world.

As her daughters began to mature, Fanny had talked to Thomas about her upbringing and how damaging it could have been for her.

She could not stop a neighbor from pronouncing this daughter or that one to be uncommonly pretty, but in the Bennet household what was praised would not be a child's looks. It would be character and knowledge, kindness and responsibility that garnered praise. Looks were all well and good, but as Fanny had pointed out to her daughters, one spent a far greater amount of time married than single and what good was beauty then? Did her daughters want their husbands to sit and stare at them all the evening long but to have nothing more that they valued? What would they talk about, alone on a Sunday afternoon? What would they teach their children? How would they manage a household and an estate?

It was this unusual attitude that shaped the characters of the Bennet daughters; five disparate personalities and appearances, but all of them intelligent and each with their own talents and strengths. It was as natural as breathing for Thomas Bennet to discuss the Netherfield tenants with the women of his household.

Three and twenty years old, his serene first-born Jane; so quick to see the good in others, bright and insightful, with a gentleness of spirit that one could instantly feel. Lively, laughing Elizabeth was next in age and if he were honest perhaps first in his heart; at twenty she had blossomed into an amazing young woman, quick witted, well read; not so universally accepting as her older sister but kind and loving. Mary, studious, musical, with a surprising dry humor, perhaps the most widely read of all his girls; compassionate but clear sighted, she was uncompromisingly honest. The quietest of his girls, at nine and ten she was just out. Her older sisters had helped her overcome her innate shyness and had aided her in learning to soften her honesty with tact and she was finding her feet in society now.

Only allowed at family functions or dinners with close friends, and not allowed to dance with anyone not of the family, Catherine and Lydia were still forming their personalities and opinions of the world around them. Just turned seven and ten, Catherine, called Kitty by her family, had an artistic bent and was a bit dreamy. She would do her lessons, but it took her much longer than the other girls as she was prone to having her mind wander down paths of watercolors and charcoals instead of attending to her math lessons. And bubbly and bright, at five and ten his youngest Lydia, who was still very much a mischievous child in some ways; she had been a handful when younger but was coming out of the most trying years.

Sitting with them were his beloved sisters, Madelaine Gardiner, the granddaughter of a Derbyshire landowner who had fallen in love with a tradesman and never looked back. Their three-year-old twin boys were in the nursery, and it was for them that Gardiner had purchased the estate. He wanted his boys out of the city in the worst of the summer. He did not care which son took over the estate, he was no Peer; he hoped as they got older one would grow to love the country and the estate and one would love the business.

Then dear Phyllis Phillips, the oldest of the Gardiner children. She had not had the advantages that Fanny had had, but marriage to her kindly and erudite solicitor husband had allowed her to spread her intellectual wings and she had taken full advantage of the books and papers and learned conversations around her. What Phyllis had not learned as a young woman, she had made up for as an adult; there were few current events that passed her by and her knowledge of everything from the corn laws to the war was prodigious. Never blessed with children, she and Robert adored the Bennet girls and spent many happy hours at Longbourn.

Thomas Bennet loved his family fiercely and was determined to protect them from harm; now he would need to work with them to see if the Netherfield tenants would pose a danger and if so, how best to prepare his family to meet any challenge.

2

The next morning dawned cloudy and cool, encouraging a sleep in by some of the girls but by mid-morning all the Bennet daughters were gathered in the back parlor, locked inside due to the downpour outside. Jane spent her time sewing while Lizzy read aloud to them; Mary was studying a complicated musical score while lending half an ear to her sister and the younger girls listened while playing backgammon. Naturally they would have to have some conversation about the revelations of the previous evening.

Coming to the end of a chapter, Lizzy quietly closed the book. "What do you think of the concerns about our possible neighbors, Jane? From what papa said it seems most certain that this Mr. Bingley will make you the object of his attentions, at least for some weeks. How do you feel about this? Tell us your thoughts and feelings."

Jane, placidly embroidering a runner for a table in the morning room, remained silent a moment then spoke slowly. "I am not sure what I think or feel at this moment and yet I know I need to make a decision soon so that Uncle Gardiner can move forward with leasing Netherfield. It is a situation I have never had to think on before and I am not sure I am comfortable with the thought of a man paying such obvious attentions to me with no care for either of our reputations. Shall I be branded a silly fool for giving the appearance of believing in one so fickle? If I do not allow his attentions will he move on to someone else, someone who has had no prior warning of his inconstancy? And what of him? What if his heart is touched? I will not encourage him, but I do not want to play the part of a temptress either."

"Jane, if his heart is touched without any encouragement from you, there is naught you can do. As long as you remain cool to him, then it is up to fate is it not? I think Lizzy and I can be of some help with the neighbors," said Mary thoughtfully. "It is certain that if he pays you such attentions there will be many ladies in the neighborhood who will ask if your heart is touched. It would be easy enough for us to make sure that everyone knows that you are indifferent to him."

Lizzy nodded vigorously. "Oh yes, we will be asked and can answer this way. My question is can you guard your heart? Such attentions could cause you to fall in love with him and since we know he is inconstant, that could be heartbreaking for you. None of us want to see you suffer pain, dear Jane, and that includes Uncle Gardiner. If you feel you cannot do this, then you must be firm in rejecting this proposal. We will all understand."

"He may turn to someone else anyway," pointed out Lydia.

Jane nodded, but replied, "That may be the way of it, Lydia, but it seems unlikely. Remember, according to Papa, Mr. Bingley seems to single out tall blonde women and there are not so many to choose from here in Meryton. This is not London, where a dozen women might be said to qualify."

"And even in London your looks would be outstanding, Jane," pointed out Kitty. "I know we are not to focus on it, but I spend much time watching the world around me to better understand how to combine all I see and feel into a drawing or painting, and I can truly say you are a most beautiful woman sister. In my mind it is a certainty that he will focus on you."

Jane laid her embroidery aside and regarded her sisters somberly. "I believe I can easily guard my heart, for how could I love a man who flits from one woman to another so easily, so selfishly? He apparently has no care for the feelings of the young women he pays court to, so no matter how cheerful and engaging Uncle Phillips says he is, I could not love so uncaring and fickle a man. I have two worries: my reputation, for after all, he may go back to London, but I will live here with the aftermath of his behavior; and what of any other women if he does not go back to London? Will he suddenly change his attentions to another who has no idea what type of shallow, inconstant man he is? Is it fair to agree to this, knowing we cannot protect any outside the family?"

"Well, that is easy enough to solve," said Lydia cheerfully. "All we have to do is let Mrs. Long and Lady Lucas know, in the strictest confidence of course. It will be all over Meryton in no time."

Laughing, the ladies agreed with Lydia and put the question aside for now.

Later that day, as the family sat down for tea, Jane announced her decision. "I have thought long and hard on this and have consulted with my sisters also. I believe that I will have no problem remaining indifferent to Mr. Bingley. He sounds too much of a selfish being for me to entertain his attentions with any seriousness. I have worried about his moving his attentions to another lady, but we believe it would be possible to warn the neighborhood of his fickleness; and so, my thought is to agree to the lease."

Fanny nodded. "I thought that would be your decision. I believe that if we let the neighborhood know prior to his arrival, that his attentions are not to be trusted, and we do so subtly of course, and that if you retain your composed demeanor around him, then we can protect your reputation while also having a care for the hearts of the other ladies of the area should he move on from you."

Lizzy added her agreement. "We also may have some help with the Netherfield tenants. If this Mr. Darcy is as good a landlord as his father was, he will instruct Mr. and Miss Bingley in seeing to the concerns of the tenants. That could only be a good thing."

Gardiner nodded. "Very well then, I shall speak with our brother tomorrow and ask him to move forward on the lease with the Bingley family."

Maddie Gardiner sent a mischievous smile toward Fanny, "And Fanny and I will begin organizing a little evening gathering to start spreading the word to be wary of the gentleman."

3

Three weeks later, Charles Bingley bounded down the steps of Netherfield Park towards the carriage that had just stopped under the portico. "Darcy," he cried, exuberantly. "You are here at last! Welcome, welcome my friend."

As he alighted from the carriage, Fitzwilliam Darcy's stern expression lightened at his friend's enthusiasm. "Bingley, it is good to see you. How are you faring as a landlord?" He paused then to bow slightly to Miss Bingley who had joined her brother in eagerly welcoming him.

"Oh, the natives here are quite savage," Miss Bingley simpered. "I do not know if we will survive the experience. Please, come in Mr. Darcy, all is ready for you."

"Nonsense," Bingley replied cheerfully. "The gentlemen of the area have come to call, and they all seem to be quite friendly and welcoming. We did go to a small dinner party at the neighboring estate, Longbourn, and they seem to be a quite charming family."

Miss Bingley sighed theatrically. "Naturally you think they are charming, Charles. Miss Bennet, the oldest daughter, is quite a pretty thing. No doubt you are already enamored. I have been informed of their circumstances by my maid," Miss Bingley continued addressing her objections to Darcy. "They have only a small estate, it is entailed away to some distant relative of the father, and they have no connections or dowries to speak of, so I am quite sure that they will show us only their most charming and alluring manners. You will both no doubt be the object of every fortune hunter in the county, and I count the Bennet chits among them."

"Well, never mind, Darcy, you shall soon judge for yourself. We are going to the local assembly this evening and you will be able to meet all our neighbors. I have purchased tickets for all of us and I know we will have a most agreeable evening."

"Charles, Mr. Darcy has just arrived. I am sure he has no desire to go to some country assembly. I shall remain here with Mr. Darcy while you and our brother and sister entertain the natives."

Darcy suppressed a sigh at her transparent attempt to keep him at her side. Nothing could be more improper than to remain back from the evening's planned entertainment with only his hostess in residence.

"I shall attend the assembly, Miss Bingley. If your brother is to engage in all the activities of a landed gentleman, then it is important that he establish good relations with the neighboring estate holders. He would be remiss to remain behind and certainly you would wish to forward his interests in the area."

Miss Bingley sniffed a bit at that but allowed the subject to die. "Mr. and Mrs. Hurst requested I give you their apologies for not attending your arrival, Mr. Darcy. Mrs. Hurst has not been feeling well and Mr. Hurst attends her. They hope she will feel well enough to join us this evening."

Darcy nodded, then requested leave to retire to refresh himself and rest a little before the night's entertainment. He wished Miss Bingley would not be overly clingy that evening though he had only faint hopes of this. The woman was getting worse as time progressed and he did not offer for her; he would have to talk to Charles again about curbing Miss Bingley's behavior.

Several hours later Darcy paced the front hall of Netherfield, impatiently awaiting the presence of Miss Bingley so they could leave. "It will be considered quite rude by your neighbors that you arrive a full hour late, Charles. You need to speak to your sister about her tardiness. It is unfortunate enough in London; it is intolerable in the country."

"I know, Darcy, but what am I to do? I have told her many times that she needs to amend her behavior and she always promises to do so but she never changes."

"Leave her home," suggested Reginald Hurst. "Your carriage is ready; you and Darcy go ahead. Mrs. Hurst and I will bring Caroline later in Darcy's carriage, if he has no objections."

Darcy gave a faint smile at that. "No, I have no objections. Bingley has an extra pair of horses so mine may continue to recover from the day's journey. Come, Charles, let us go now.; your sister can join us later if she chooses."

"If I choose what," demanded Caroline, who had waited at the top of the stairs impatiently for Darcy to look up and see her gracefully descend. She had finally given up the wait and had flounced down the stairs and now stood behind Darcy.

"To be left behind," said Hurst bluntly, his dislike of his sister ill-concealed. "I have told your brother that he and Darcy should leave on time and Louisa, and I will bring you later in another carriage. We are tired of the delays you cause. You are here now, but it is my suggestion that this will be our plan going forward."

Caroline waved his comments aside. "Nonsense, who are these people that they would expect us to arrive on time to their little dance?"

To Darcy's disappointment, Bingley just muttered under his breath then demanded they all leave now. He had already missed at least the first set and they would be well into the second by now. He was impatient to see his newest angel.

Victoria Lynn

"I know, Darcy, but what am I to do? I have told her many times that she needs to amend her behavior and she always promises to do so but she never changes."

"Leave her home," suggested Reginald Hurst. "Your carriage is ready; you and Darcy go ahead. Mrs. Hurst and I will bring Caroline later in Darcy's carriage, if he has no objections."

Darcy gave a faint smile at that. "No, I have no objections. Bingley has an extra pair of horses so mine may continue to recover from the day's journey. Come, Charles, let us go now.; your sister can join us later if she chooses."

"If I choose what," demanded Caroline, who had waited at the top of the stairs impatiently for Darcy to look up and see her gracefully descend. She had finally given up the wait and had flounced down the stairs and now stood behind Darcy.

"To be left behind," said Hurst bluntly, his dislike of his sister ill-concealed. "I have told your brother that he and Darcy should leave on time and Louisa, and I will bring you later in another carriage. We are tired of the delays you cause. You are here now, but it is my suggestion that this will be our plan going forward."

Caroline waved his comments aside. "Nonsense, who are these people that they would expect us to arrive on time to their little dance?"

To Darcy's disappointment, Bingley just muttered under his breath then demanded they all leave now. He had already missed at least the first set and they would be well into the second by now. He was impatient to see his newest angel.

Victoria Lynn

4

The Meryton Assembly Hall was much like any country Hall. A small entry gave way to a large room, lined with chairs and with an orchestra in a small alcove. Beside the main room, arched openings gave way to a card room and a dining area. Mr. Hurst made a beeline to the card room, not even waiting to be greeted or introduced, while Bingley beamed at all and sundry, Mrs. Hurst was silent, and Miss Bingley made sotto voiced comments about the horrible venue. Darcy stiffened involuntarily as she clutched his arm while muttering insults to the company into his ear, commenting derisively about the heavy-set, jovial looking man hurrying over to them.

"Welcome, dear friends," proclaimed Sir William Lucas expansively. "We are most pleased to have your fine company for the evening."

Bingley returned Sir William's bow. "We are delighted to be here. Let me introduce my companions."

Introductions were completed and if Miss Bingley's silence and abbreviated curtsey were borderline insulting, their jovial host did not seem to notice.

"Allow me to introduce you around the hall. Of course, some introductions will have to wait until the dancers are free to greet you, but please come with me and I will introduce you to your neighbors."

As Sir William led them around the room, introducing lady after lady, along with their sons and, of course, their marriageable daughters, Darcy mood darkened. "It really is intolerable," he thought in concert with Miss Bingley's comments. There seemed to be no one of note here, just a very large group of nobodies. It was in this disgruntled mood that he had his first glimpse of Bingley's newest angel, and his opinion was fixed at that moment of an unfeeling woman as the serenely beautiful blond curtseyed gracefully to him.

"Miss Bennet," he murmured, eyeing her warily. He turned to meet her two sisters and found them eyeing Bingley and himself with guarded interest. "Of course," he thought," no doubt word of my wealth and my estate have already circulated." Before Sir Lucas could continue the introductions, a gentleman strolled up behind the ladies, and suddenly too disgusted to continue what he thought of as an irritating charade, Darcy simply turned and walked away. Thomas Bennet's eyes narrowed at the slight. "So, this is my friend George's son? How very disappointed George would be," he thought sadly. In all the years they had been friends, Bennet could not come up with a single instance of George Darcy behaving in so rude a fashion.

He turned his attention then to Bingley, whom he could hear importuning Jane for two dances; her refusals were calmly and kindly delivered, but no less firm for the gentle tone. One dance she would grant him but not a second, finally securing his agreement when she pointed out that many a lady would go without a partner this evening with the few gentlemen in attendance. He needed to do his duty to all the young ladies.

Thomas and Fanny shared a quick, concerned glance, then moved toward the edge of the room with Lizzy and Mary. "So it begins,' murmured Lizzy. Mary nodded then asked softly, "Have you ever seen the like of Mr. Darcy?"

Lizzy shook her head, keeping her voice low to avoid being overheard. "He is quite well favored, even could be called handsome, I suppose, but his rudeness is appalling. Both he and Miss Bingley seem to feel they are far above the company this evening. And yet, for all his wealth he is not a peer, just a gentleman's child as are most of us here. And Miss Bingley is below almost everyone as the daughter of a tradesman. How can they pretend to be so far above us all?"

"Well, in truth, it gives me some ease of mind," said Bennet softly. "We have conspired against Darcy's friend, and it went against the grain with me to so treat someone who is apparently esteemed by the son of a good friend; now I need have no guilt for this beyond what is reasonable when one plots against another."

Thomas held his hand up to stop his ladies' protests. "No, do not contradict my thoughts, for that is what we have done, and I will not hide behind platitudes or pretend it is not so. We acted thus for a good cause, and I would do it again, but there is no dissuading me from this opinion. Our family set it about that young Bingley was untrustworthy in his dealings with young ladies before he arrived; we made sure our words were heard and more, that they would be widely circulated. That he has fulfilled his part by singling out Jane to the exclusion of all others on half an hours' acquaintance, that Miss Bingley is so unpleasant, well that just confirms what we knew; we were told Mr. Darcy was reticent not that he would be unpleasantly haughty and rude; such an attitude is unworthy of George Darcy's son, his very unpleasant nature eases my conscious."

Lizzy and Mary were engaged for the next set and so they moved to the dance floor with their partners; Fanny went to talk with her friends and Bennet returned to the card room; all were in a thoughtful mood.

It was later in the evening that Darcy exceeded even his most ardent critic's expectations of incivility. Morosely watching the dancers, Darcy's response to Bingley's repeated demands that he dance confirmed the opinions in the neighborhood of a haughty, disagreeable man.

"Come, Darcy," said Bingley, "I must have you dance. I hate to see you standing about by yourself in this stupid manner. You had much better dance."

"I certainly shall not. You know how I detest it unless I am particularly acquainted with my partner."

"I would not be so fastidious as you are," cried Mr. Bingley, "for a kingdom! Upon my honor, I never met with so many pleasant girls in my life as I have this evening; and there are several of them you can see are uncommonly pretty. There is a lovely young miss sitting down just behind you, she is very pretty, and I dare say very agreeable. Do let me ask Sir Lucas to introduce you."

"Which do you mean?" and turning round he looked for a moment at Elizabeth, till catching her eye, he withdrew his own and coldly said: "She is tolerable, but not handsome enough to tempt me; I am in no humor at present to give consequence to young ladies who are slighted by other men. You had better return to the dance floor, for you are wasting your time with me."

Lizzy, sitting next to Mary, was too stunned by the insult to react. Mary paled at the slight and stood quickly, moving between Lizzy and the rest of the room so she was shielded from the sight of the others in attendance. Charlotte Lucas, who had been sitting with them and so also heard this insult was horrified. "Lizzy," she gasped, "well, how could he say such a thing? I am mortified at such behavior, my friend. Though he looks the part, by his words he is certainly no gentleman."

While Lizzy's first reaction was that she hoped none other heard him, her second more reasoned thought was that perhaps this would prove useful to them. Turning her friend's ire to laughter, she proclaimed, "No, no Charlotte. It is all to the good. For now I do not have to scramble about for an excuse to escape dancing with such a man, for if I simply refused him I would forfeit my chances for amusement the whole of the evening." And so, the three ladies jested at Mr. Darcy's expense until they were claimed by their partners for the supper set and parted ways.

It was the tradition of the Lucas and Bennet ladies to gather the morning after an evening's entertainment to discuss the event in detail. The ladies delighted in this, for they spoke much of friends and acquaintances and thus news of births and deaths, of gowns and hairstyles, of babies to come and babies born took up much of the morning. It was well into the visit before the newcomers were deemed of sufficient interest to discuss.

"Well Miss Lizzy," said Lady Lucas cheerfully, "I hear that while all of us were snubbed by that haughty Mr. Darcy, for some reason you received more than your fair share of his disdain."

"I did, indeed," agreed Lizzy, then turning her nose into the air and affecting an exaggerated supercilious air, she continued, "I feel quite singled out for his particular disregard and so am set up amazingly in my own conceit now."

The ladies shared a laugh at Lizzy's jest then Lady Lucas turned the focus to Jane. "That Miss Bingley's disdain was evident from the moment of her arrival, indeed she was quite rude to Sir William you know, and as for Mr. Bingley, well, it was just as predicted. He is importuning Jane already. Staring at her when he was not dancing with another and trying to catch her eye as he squired his other partners on the dance floor." Lady Lucas' disapproval was evident. "What is the man about to be so particular upon so slight of an acquaintance?"

Jane blushed a little but replied with her usual calm, "Indeed, it was most uncomfortable. It was fortunate indeed that there were more ladies than gentlemen present and so it was possible to insist he give others his attentions also." She shook her head. "In truth, although we were warned, I did not quite understand how blatant his immediate regard would be; I thought if I were to be the focus of his attentions that it would be a more gradual thing."

"And what of his conversation?" asked Mary. "Did he have much of interest to convey?"

"Not a thing," sighed Jane. "His whole conversation was empty compliments of how beautiful I am. No subject I introduced was an agreeable topic to him, he simply filled every silence with praises to my looks as if this were some kind of major accomplishment on my part instead of an accident of birth. While he has pleasant and amiable manners, he seems to be a foolish fellow to me, incapable of seeing beyond the surface of person."

Lady Lucas nodded, her curiosity satisfied and her mind already turning over what she would say to her other neighbors and to her dear friend Mrs. Long. The Bennet girls were in no danger of losing their hearts to these newcomers and Lizzy was unbothered by Mr. Darcy's unkindness. She could hardly disguise her impatience to be the first in county with such gossip.

5

The following weeks were busy ones for the Bennet household. Spring planting was behind them, but there were always tenant concerns and like all the neighboring gentlemen's households the Bennets saw to their own tenants and a portion of those who looked to Netherfield Park as no owner had been in residence in many years. Spring was also the time for inventory and cleaning and the final tallies of supplies used for winter. The still room needed to be organized once more and plans made for the spring blossoms that would scent oils and sachets. There was sewing for the tenants and finer stitching to do for gowns and fichus and handkerchiefs as there were far more evening entertainments than was the usual in their corner of the county.

At some point over the summer each of the twenty-four landowners would host an entertainment and naturally the Bennets were included in most of them. So too were the new residents of Netherfield Park. Familiarity, however, did not breed respect between them, at least not for the two eldest Bennet daughters.

"Jane, I know you are trying to be courteous to Mr. Bingley," said Jane's favorite sister one afternoon. "But do you not think you can hint him away more strongly?"

"Lizzy, I have tried. I have tried to direct him to others. I have tried to make it clear that I do not appreciate conversations that are solely about my looks. I have tried to introduce other topics, even if it is just talking about his family, but to no avail."

"Well, in all fairness, if I had the choice of speaking about Miss Bingley or speaking about your beauty, I know which I would choose," laughed Elizabeth. "I have tried to help distract him, you know, but it has been impossible to do so."

"Meanwhile, Mr. Darcy cannot seem to be distracted from you."

"Mr. Darcy? Jane, I am all astonishment. He does not even like me and he certainly does not think much of my beauty."

"I know what he said, but you know that everyone says things they do not mean sometimes. He is often near you listening to your conversations and he watches you a great deal."

"I know, but Jane, trust me, he is only listening and watching to find things to criticize about me. I could feel his disapproval from across the room last evening when I was playing. I know he has access to the finest of entertainments and I know I need to practice more to become truly proficient, but I do not believe my performance was so bad that he needed to glare at me the entire time." She gave an inelegant shrug of one shoulder. "Enough of him. In fact, enough of all of them. Let us go pick flowers and refresh the bouquets, for I noticed this morning that they were looking shabby."

It was into this whirlwind of activity that they received the expected visit of a long-term guest, a gentleman who was the heir to the estate who was now in a most dismaying circumstance.

Mr. Collins, the rector of the parish of Hunsford in Kent, had visited the family twice in the recent past. The first visit had been remarkable for its discomfort when it began, as Mr. Collins had babbled on almost without pause about his noble patroness, the beauty of the Bennet daughters and the wonderful estate for three days complete until Mr. Bennet finally took him aside and requested he desist in his endless compliments.

Mr. Collins was greatly relieved by his cousin's words. While he had been a good student and truly felt called to serve his parish, Mr. Collins was also a man of little confidence, the result of having been raised by an illiterate and angry father who was impossible to please. His appointment to the living in Hunsford was a good one for him financially and he enjoyed his parish work immensely; while he was considerate and well-spoken among his parishioners, his appointment had not engendered this attitude to those of equal or elevated status. It was his unfortunate fate to have received his living from a patroness who was an overbearing woman, whose conceit was immense and whose need for praise appeared to be unending. His relief upon discovering that this attitude was not needed or in fact appreciated by his relatives was palpable and thereon his visit had progressed amicably.

Mr. Collins was, perhaps, not an attractive specimen but his heart was good, and he willingly forewent his former subservient attitudes when he was so kindly accepted. Mr. Bennet had also made it plain to the man that his daughters were free to marry where their hearts led them and that if Mr. Collins were interested in a closer alliance with the Bennet family he would have to woo the young lady properly and gain her affections. While he had thought of the possibility of such an alliance and had in fact hinted at the same in his correspondence with Mr. Bennet, he was relieved that the family was not mercenary and insistent that he marry where there was no affection. A bad marriage was never a good thing and for a parson it was disastrous. Mr. Collins wanted and indeed needed to take time to know his cousins to determine if there was a suitable connection of mind and heart to be found.

The second visit had taken place only a few short months ago and the Bennets had universally claimed it to be a success. This time Mr. Collins dropped his subservient attitude at the door and was accepted in a friendly and familiar fashion at once. He had enjoyed the visit as immensely as his hosts had done and he felt blessed to belong to such a welcoming family; never having been part of a loving family, his acceptance as part of the Bennet clan had been balm to him and he vowed in his mind to be of service to them if ever he could.

Soon after this visit, however, disaster struck the young man. While helping a farmer to unload a cart with a broken wheel, the whole load it carried had become unbalanced and had fallen on the young preacher. Mr. Collins had progressed enough to spend some small amount of time each day in a bath chair and so was no longer confined to his bed chamber, however, he was unable to walk or move about freely; still he could now acquiesce to his patroness' angrily expressed demands that he leave the parsonage so that a replacement might be appointed.

Mr. Collins' latest missive read, in part: *"The apothecary holds out little hope for my recovery beyond the eventual diminishment of the pain of the broken hip joint to a more bearable level. His hope is that eventually I will be able to gain more freedom of movement by employment of the bath chair for more than just an isolated hour once or twice per day. Such a hope is balm to my spirits in my own regard but does nothing to aid my natural dismay at the forced abandonment of my parishioners. I cannot well serve them, though thankfully my curate has been most helpful in visiting those in need and the reading of my sermons.*

"My patroness has been most vocal in her demands that I leave the parsonage, even demanding my removal well before it would have been safe to move me from my chambers. I was most distressed by this attitude of one I have tried to esteem. While I have been grateful for the appointment, it is disheartening to realize that her care for her own selfish interests far outweighs any other. I have succeeded in my determination to remain here until such time as I believed she had appointed as a replacement for me someone whose attitudes toward the parishioners is one of tender care and consideration for them and not just someone who can only flatter her Ladyship with empty compliments while not caring for those he must needs place in the forefront of his concerns.

"Therefore, cousin, I will take advantage of your kindly offer and request that you make such arrangements as you feel are best to allow me to travel to Longbourn, and remain there for the near future, until such time as I can determine a course of action that will not discommode you and your dear family any more than needed

by my current condition."

The Bennet family had been understandably distressed by their cousin's misfortunes and all had been in agreement that any help they could render their cousin was to be offered to him. Many ideas were debated but in the end it appeared only one real solution was viable: Mr. Collins would need to be offered a place in their home for as long as he needed such consideration.

Directly off the gardens at the side of the Longbourn manor house was a room that had long been given over to family entertaining, particularly entertaining the very youngest of their relatives. It had French doors that opened directly onto a lawn, a lovely view of the rose beds that Lydia and Mrs. Bennet tended assiduously and had been furnished with cast offs from rooms so that little ones could spill, and dirt could be tracked in with no need for scolding. Upon deciding to offer a home to their injured cousin, Mrs. Bennet had immediately thought of this room. Cleaned and scrubbed, with a screen hiding a comfortable bed, and a chaise positioned to allow Mr. Collins to comfortably relax and look out of the opened French doors and drink in the beauties of nature, it was hoped this would be a haven for their injured cousin.

The ladies had long since made the needed changes in the household to accommodate their injured guest and so one fine spring afternoon they disposed themselves in the parlor to speak in hushed and shocked voices at the appearance of their injured cousin.

"Do you think he can recover," Lydia half-whispered, not wanting him to inadvertently overhear, though how that would be possible from several rooms away was a mystery.

"I am fearful he will not," replied Mary, her voice soft though not a whisper. "He has such a frail look about him now that I was quite shocked."

Lizzy sadly agreed. "Indeed, I would have hardly recognized him if I had come upon him unexpectedly. His suffering has aged him and has left him much altered in appearance, though in essentials I believe he is much as he ever was."

"We will do all we can to ensure his comfort, girls," soothed Mrs. Bennet gently. "There is no more that we can do; relate to each other your concerns and your shock now, for when he joins us for dinner I would have us all be delighted to welcome him and show none of our worried faces. No doubt cheerful company and kindness will help him enormously."

The afternoon following their cousins' arrival found Mary and Lizzy walking to Meryton. Mary wished to see if the music she had requested had arrived and once this errand had been accomplished, the ladies went for tea in the parlor with their Aunt Phillips and to deliver an invitation to supper and cards two evenings hence; while such entertainments were usually held at the Phillips home, this time all had been in agreement that Longbourn would be the better locale in deference to Mr. Collins' situation. To their surprise their aunt was entertaining several red-coated officers in her parlor; the militia had not long been in the area, and they were unfamiliar with the gentlemen.

Introductions were made, and Lizzy was immediately the focus of the attention of one very attractive gentleman, a Lieutenant Wickham, who was, he informed them, the newest member of the militia. While slightly older than his companions, he seemed most agreeable, asking questions about the family and the neighborhood. Lizzy was interested to note that he reacted oddly to the name Darcy but felt she could not politely question such a new acquaintance. The girls delivered their invitation to supper and cards at Longbourn, and included the militia officers in their invitation, which was eagerly accepted by the gentlemen.

6

On the evening of the card party, Mr. Collin's bath chair was wheeled into the drawing room, positioned near the door for when it was time for him to retire and a chair set on either side of him that would allow the company to sit and speak with him easily. He found himself looking forward to the evening with a combination of pleasure to be in company again and uneasiness regarding his acceptance at the same time. No doubt there were those who would be uncomfortable in his presence. Well, he would just have to do his best to ease their fears.

As more and more people came through the drawing room doors, Mr. Collins was astonished at the easy acceptance he received, but here again, his cousins had served him well. All the locals were well aware of the source of his malady and kindly sympathetic to him, wishing him a speedy full recovery and many of them stopped by his chair to chat briefly. A Bennet family member was usually beside him to perform introductions and see to his needs. Lydia Bennet, who had designated herself as his champion since his arrival now took it upon herself to ensure his comfort in what could have been difficult surroundings.

Mr. Collins' arrival had come at a rather pivotal point in Lydia's young life. The spring season of country balls and picnics and suppers was just beginning, and the youngest Bennet daughter had been keenly aware of the unjust fate that made her the youngest and therefore the last to taste the delights of society. Then Mr. Collins had arrived, gaunt and somewhat frail looking, the uncertainty of his fate having carved a furrow onto his brow and weeks of pain having dug deep lines into his face. Watching this young man, who had gone from a slightly rotund and jolly sort of fellow to a man who could not walk unaided, and one who appeared to be wasting away, had pierced the fifteen-year old's focus on herself, causing her to see someone else as actually suffering as opposed to her own supposed sufferings and she was mortified by her own selfishness.

In penance for her former attitude, Lydia had become his chief comforter, bringing him tea and news of the neighbors, reading to him when he wished to relax in such a manner and leaving him to rest in solitude as needed. This night she eased his way into cheerful conversation with the various neighbors who stopped to greet him, smoothing over the awkwardness of their shock at his appearance as best she could. She was, therefore, in no mood for the improper advances of the militia.

Having briefly meet Lieutenants Denny and Carter at Lucas Lodge some days earlier, Lydia performed the introduction to her cousin then found her eyes widening in surprise as the new member of the group bowed theatrically low and kissed her hand. "Ah, Miss Lydia, how enchanting to see such loveliness before me. Allow me to escort you to the other room for a glass of punch."

"I am sorry Lt. Wickham; I cannot agree to that. I am not out yet, as you can see," she replied, referring to her modest dress with its high hemline and her hair being down in two thick plaits instead of dressed atop her head. "I will remain here with my cousin Collins."

"Surely even one who is not out cannot be denied a stroll in the family drawing room with a friend," replied Lt. Wickham, obviously depending on his charm and ease of manner to convince the young woman to accompany him.

But Lydia, far from being convinced was entirely shocked. Once informed that she was not yet out the gentlemen should have immediately removed themselves; indeed, society dictated that they not even look at her directly and that all conversation was at an end with her announcement. Her eyes flashed with anger as she realized they thought she was a foolish girl, easily led into improper behavior.

Before she could speak up, however, her cousin came to her aid.

"Gentlemen, the young lady has informed you she is not out, which indeed you should have divined from her appearance. All propriety demands that you leave her presence at once and do not return. Kindly move on to others for your conversations and enjoyments this evening." Collins's voice was firm, and it was clear he was not happy with the soldiers.

Although Denny and Carter appeared embarrassed, Wickham directed a look of disdain at Mr. Collins before bowing slightly and moving off with his companions.

"Well," huffed Lydia, "I cannot say that I care for that Lt. Wickham's attitude at all. He professes to be a gentleman but ignores that my hair has not been put up nor my hems put down. I am seriously displeased with him."

"I am not best pleased myself, Cousin Lydia. He makes me uneasy, I confess, and I did not like either the way he looked at you nor his words as he seemed to feel that it was acceptable to flout convention."

"Well, you should not be made uneasy by such a man, Cousin Collins. Let us think no more of the Lieutenants."

Wickham, however, was not yet done with discomposing the Bennet ladies for the evening. While he found Jane beautiful and Mary attractive, it was to Elizabeth that his eye was drawn next, enjoying the sparkle in her eyes and the easy wit she displayed. The Lieutenant decided if the young, foolish Lydia Bennet refused to become prey, then Miss Elizabeth might be induced to succumb to his charms.

Seating himself next to her, Mr. Wickham began his conversation with Lizzy on neutral subjects but soon wended his way to his main objective, asking in a curious manner how far Netherfield was from Longbourn and, after receiving her answer, asking in a hesitating manner how long Mr. Darcy had been staying there.

"About a month," said Elizabeth; then unwilling to let the subject drop, added, "He is a man of very large property in Derbyshire, I understand."

"Yes" replied Mr. Wickham, "his estate there is a noble one. A clear ten thousand per annum. You could not have met with a person more capable of giving you certain information on that head than myself, for I have been connected with his family in a particular manner from my infancy."

Elizabeth could not but look surprised.

"You may well be surprised, Miss Elizabeth, at such an assertion after seeing my reaction to the news of his presence in the neighborhood, for although you were kind enough not to comment on it, I could see that you noticed and were surprised. Are you much acquainted with Mr. Darcy?"

"As much as I ever wish to be," cried Elizabeth very warmly. "I have spent several evenings in company with him, and I think him very disagreeable."

"I have no right to give my opinion," said Wickham, "as to his being agreeable or otherwise. I am not qualified to form one. I have known him too long and too well to be a fair judge. It is impossible for me to be impartial. But I believe your opinion of him would in general astonish—and perhaps you would not express it quite so strongly anywhere else. Here you are in your own family."

"Upon my word, I say no more here than I might say in any house in the neighborhood, except Netherfield. He is not at all liked in Hertfordshire. Everybody is disgusted with his pride. You will not find him more favorably spoke of by anyone."

"I cannot pretend to be sorry," said Wickham, after a short

interruption, "that he or that any man should not be estimated beyond their deserts; but with him I believe it does not often happen. The world is blinded by his fortune and consequence or frightened by his high and imposing manners and sees him only as he chooses to be seen."

"I should take him, even on my slight acquaintance, to be an ill-tempered man."

Wickham only shook his head.

"I wonder," said he, "whether he is likely to be in the country much longer."

"I do not at all know but I heard nothing of his going away when I have spoken with the residents of Netherfield. I hope your plans in favor of the ----shire will not be affected by his being in the neighborhood."

"Oh! No, it is not for me to be driven away by Mr. Darcy. If he wishes to avoid seeing me, he must go. We are not on friendly terms, and it always gives me pain to meet him, but I have no reason for avoiding him but what I might proclaim before all the world, a sense of very great ill-usage, and most painful regrets at his being what he is. His father, Miss Elizabeth, the late Mr. Darcy, was one of the best men that ever breathed, and the truest friend I ever had, and I can never be in company with this Mr. Darcy without being grieved to the soul by a thousand tender recollections. His behavior to myself has been scandalous, but I verily believe I could forgive him anything and everything, rather than his disappointing the hopes and disgracing the memory of his father."

Elizabeth found her interest of the subject increased, and listened with all her heart, for Mr. Wickham's account tallied with her father's memories of George Darcy, but the delicacy of it prevented further inquiry.

Mr. Wickham began to speak on more general topics, Meryton, the neighborhood, the society, appearing highly pleased with all he had yet seen and speaking of the latter with gentle but very intelligible gallantry.

"It was the prospect of constant society and good society," he added, "which was my chief inducement to enter the ---shire. I knew it to be a most respectable, agreeable corps and my friend Denny tempted me further by his account of their present quarters, and the very great attentions and excellent acquaintances Meryton had procured them. Society, I own, is necessary to me. I have been a disappointed man and my spirits will not bear solitude. I must have employment and society. A military life is not what I was intended for, but circumstances have now made it eligible. The church ought to have been my profession; I was brought up for the church and I should at this time have been in possession of a most valuable living, had it pleased the gentleman we were speaking of just now."

"Indeed!"

"Yes; the late Mr. Darcy bequeathed me the next presentation of the best living in his gift. He was my godfather, and excessively attached to me. I cannot do justice to his kindness. He meant to provide for me amply and thought he had done it but when the living fell open, it was given elsewhere with no consideration for my claim on it."

"Good heavens!" cried Elizabeth, "but how could that be? How could his will be disregarded? Why did you not seek legal redress?"

"There was just such an informality in the terms of the bequest as to give me no hope from law. A man of honor could not have doubted the intention, but Mr. Darcy chose to doubt it, or to treat it as a merely conditional recommendation and to assert that I had forfeited all claim to it by extravagance, imprudence, in short anything or nothing. Certain it is that the living became vacant almost five years ago, exactly as I was of an age to hold it and that it was given to another man; and no less certain is it that I cannot accuse myself of having really done anything to deserve to lose it. I have a warm, unguarded temper and I may have spoken my opinion of him and to him too freely. I can recall nothing worse. But the fact is that we are very different sort of men and that he hates me."

"That is quite shocking! He deserves to be publicly disgraced."

"Sometime or other he will be, but it shall not be by me. Until I can forget his father I cannot defame the son."

Elizabeth honored him for such feelings and thought him handsomer than ever as he expressed them.

"But what can have been his motive? What can have induced him to behave so cruelly?"

"A thorough, determined dislike of me, a dislike which I cannot but attribute in some measure to jealousy. Had the late Mr. Darcy liked me less, his son might have borne with me better."

"I had not thought Mr. Darcy so bad as this, though I have never liked him. I had not thought so very ill of him. I had supposed him to be despising his fellow-creatures in general but did not suspect him of descending to such malicious revenge, such injustice, such inhumanity as this."

"I will not trust myself on the subject," replied Wickham, "I can hardly be just to him."

Elizabeth was again deep in thought and after a time exclaimed, "To treat in such a manner the godson, the friend, the favorite of his father and one, too, who had probably been his companion from childhood, connected together I think you said, in the closest manner."

"We were born in the same parish, within the same park; the greatest part of our youth was passed together inmates of the same house, sharing the same amusements, objects of the same parental care. My father began life in the profession which your uncle, Mr. Phillips, appears to do so much credit to, but he gave up everything to be of use to the late Mr. Darcy and devoted all his time to the care of the Pemberley property. He was most highly esteemed by Mr. Darcy, a most intimate, confidential friend. Mr. Darcy often acknowledged himself to be under the greatest obligations to my father's active superintendence and when, immediately before my father's death, Mr. Darcy gave him a voluntary promise of providing for me, I am convinced he felt it to be as much a debt of gratitude to him as of his affection to myself."

"How strange!" cried Elizabeth. "How abominable! I wonder that the very pride of this Mr. Darcy has not made him just to you, if from no better motive that he should have been too proud to be dishonest, for dishonesty I must call it."

"It is wonderful," replied Wickham, "for almost all his actions may be traced to pride and pride had often been his best friend. It has connected him nearer with virtue than with any other feeling. But we are none of us consistent and in his behavior to me there were stronger impulses even than pride."

"Can such abominable pride as his ever done him good?"

"Yes," replied Wickham earnestly, "it has often led him to be liberal and generous, to give his money freely, to display hospitality, to assist his tenants and relieve the poor. Family pride and filial pride, for he is very proud of what his father was, have done this. Not to appear to disgrace his family, to degenerate from the popular qualities, or lose the influence of the Pemberley House is a powerful motive. He has also brotherly pride, which with some brotherly affection, makes him a very kind and careful guardian of his sister and you will hear him generally cried up as the most attentive and best of brothers."

Shortly after this final discourse on the Darcy family, Elizabeth and

Lt. Wickham were interrupted by Prudence Long and so the conversation ended, though Lizzy found herself thinking of it again and again, going over the salient points and wondering at the disagreeable man who had come into their midst. In all the general dislike of Mr. Darcy, he had not been portrayed as dishonorable and this facet of his character distressed her greatly. She could not bear to see injustice done and the tale recited to her by Lt. Wickham caused her much anger.

7

Breakfast at Longbourn brought Lizzy a great deal of confusion for both Mr. Collins and Lydia had lost no time in letting her parents know of Lt. Wickham's improper advances to her and it was much discussed while the family, minus Mr. Collins, broke their fast together the next morning.

Lizzy did not know what to think, for such shocking behavior did not seem to go along with the charming manners of the gentleman who had discoursed so pleasantly with her, so once the family had finished their meal, Elizabeth sought Jane's council. As they put on their bonnets to stroll in the garden, for Lizzy felt the need of privacy to relate her story, Charlotte came to visit so the three young women walked together among the roses as she related this most shocking tale of dishonor and cruelty, charges that were leveled against Mr. Darcy by Lt. Wickham.

The girls were all silent for a time, digesting the information.

"Lizzy, we heard this morning about Lt. Wickham's improper behavior towards Lydia and now I must ask, do you think it was proper for him to tell you this when you had just met?"

Charlotte agreed. "It was not at all proper of him. You are not in a courtship nor engaged that he should be recounting such a personal history to you and to do so in a public setting where anyone might overhear is quite beyond the pale. And while I am not as well-read as the Bennet sisters," she added with a touch of humor, "I do know what defame means. When your Lt. Wickham said he would not defame Mr. Darcy he did so while he was defaming him which has to argue a duplicitous nature from this...this person, for I do not believe he qualifies to be called a gentleman."

"Good heavens," cried Elizabeth, "I did not see that at all. How do we know the truth then?"

Jane sighed, "Dearest Lizzy, if Lt. Wickham truly did not want Mr. Darcy to be publicly disgraced, why would he tell this story and to a total stranger? Charlotte and I know that you would be discreet, but how would he know that? He had just met you; for all he knows you could be like Mrs. Long, who gossips to everyone of all she hears, and then would the story not be known to all in attendance before the evening was done? No, I cannot believe that he does not want Mr. Darcy disgraced, his every action speaks to just the opposite. I am sorry to say that I believe the story cannot be true, based on Lt. Wickham relating it so freely."

"Oh dear," sighed Lizzy, "I have just thought of something else. Our Cousin Collins is a very good man, but even before his injury he was not as charming or attractive or so well-spoken as this Lt. Wickham. If Mr. Collins could find a living then why was Lt. Wickham so completely unable to do so? And what has he been doing all this time, how has he lived? For he said he had just joined the militia. If he had a calling to the clergy, and a promised living had been denied him, surely he must either have found another profession or would have searched to find another placement at some point in the past five years. Was there no opening anywhere in all of England that he could have taken to further his ambition in the church?"

"I doubt very much if he was ever ordained," replied Charlotte. "I was in conversation with the Lieutenant and Mr. Goulding last evening and Mr. Goulding made a Bible reference at one point to support his position in our discussion, and even though it was not an obscure one, it was obvious Lt. Wickham had no idea what he was referencing."

The three women looked at each other in consternation. When she had begun to relate her tale, Lizzy had certainly expected upset and anger but had not thought these emotions would be directed at Lt. Wickham. She cringed inside at her gullibility, acutely embarrassed that she had not realized any of these points while listening to the charming, attractive man.

"Oh Jane, Charlotte, I am a wretched creature indeed," she cried. "Do I know myself at all? Am I so vain that all a man must do is flatter me with his attentions and I will believe anything he says, no matter how absurd? Does an insult from a man I had not even met prejudice me so firmly against him that I will believe any infamy of him?"

"No Lizzy, do not be distressed that you did not realize all of this at the time," consoled Jane. "Distrust is not in your nature so why would you disbelieve what he told you? Indeed, he seems to have played the part of a man sorrowed by injustice very well; I met the Lieutenant only briefly and his charm was nearly overwhelming; discovering his true motives would be very difficult to do while being the object of such charm and flattery as he so effortlessly dispenses. I believe he is a very practiced liar and so his ability to deceive is well-honed."

"Well, I believe we need to speak with our fathers," announced Charlotte. "I do not trust this Lt. Wickham at all. There is such a thing as being too charming and there are a lot of foolish girls in the world, as we know, and I include my younger sister in their number."

"Do you fear seductions, Charlotte?" gasped Jane.

As Charlotte nodded grimly, Lizzy replied, "Jane, I think she is correct, I truly believe there are many foolish young misses who may be in danger from him, and that is particularly true as he importuned Lydia despite her obvious appearance of not being out and then being directly told thus. There are many young girls who will not be so proper nor so well protected and so are at risk. One cannot expect an inexperienced girl of ten and five summers to be proof against his charms and I fear for the youngest of our community."

"I will go home and speak with my father, and do you go to yours. I do not think this should be delayed." And Charlotte hurried away down the lane toward Lucas Lodge.

Some thirty minutes later a stern Thomas Bennet regarded his two eldest daughters. He agreed the tale they told did not bode well for his community.

"Yes, I see that something is going to have to be done. I will need to think of exactly what and no doubt I will hear soon from Sir William; I will send a note to him requesting a meeting."

Thomas paused a moment for a sip of coffee, then continued, "There is another salient point, one that you girls would not be aware of but has a bearing on this. Lizzy, you say he recounted that the wording in the will was just informal enough so there was no legal recourse. In reality, when a great estate changes hands, nothing in the will is informal. Even regarding an estate as small as Longbourn, when the time comes for it to be passed down, the livelihood of many, many people will depend on a smooth transition. Not just the family, but the servants, the tenants, the people of Longbourn village, even the merchants in Meryton, they all will be affected and so everything must need to be very clear, with no possibility of misinterpretation. Pemberley is many times the size of Longbourn; the elder Mr. Darcy was a careful and very thoughtful man, and his will would have reflected this. Nothing about it would have been informal, nothing would have been left to chance."

"Was nothing the man said truthful?" Lizzy asked somewhat mournfully.

Mr. Bennet replied thoughtfully, "Probably some few parts are true. The best kinds of lies are a mix of truth, half-truth and falsehood. It would not surprise me, for instance, to discover that the elder Mr. Darcy left a living to Mr. Wickham, on the condition that he was ordained. Not having done so would naturally disqualify him from being the recipient of the living. This would not make the younger Mr. Darcy a villain or a cruel man; he could not grant a living to someone not ordained, nor could he leave the living vacant indefinitely waiting on this to happen. The parishioners need their spiritual advisor and not to appoint someone would have been wrong. Nor could he appoint someone and then take the living away at a later date. That would not be fair or just. I have to wonder also if Lt. Wickham did not receive some renumeration to replace the lost income from the living. It would not surprise me at all, for the estate is a rich one and a goodly sum could have been given to him. That could well answer your question of how he has lived this past five years."

"I feel like such a fool," Lizzy lamented, "I pride myself on being a good judge of character and being intelligent. And I failed utterly to see through this man's falsehoods, yet now I see them so clearly."

"Lizzy, do not be so hard on yourself. I believe that both of these are true of you in general, but you must also realize that you girls have been greatly protected by growing up in a small community where most everyone is known to you," consoled her father, his tone kindly. "There are many types of scoundrels in the world, and I am thankful that few of them have come into our orbit. This is a very good lesson indeed. Now, should you encounter this situation again, you will take the time to dissect the conversation carefully, noting discrepancies and seeing the falsehoods. This will serve you and your sister very well in the future."

Mr. Bennet bade them leave him then so he could pen a note to Sir William Lucas; in addition to being a longtime friend, he was the local magistrate for their community, and he also had daughters to protect. Bennet had a bad feeling about this new Lieutenant; Fanny and the girls would warn the other gentle families in the area, but he was not sure any warnings would be enough to protect all the maidens in their town.

8

For the next several days no officers arrived at Longbourn to disturb their peace. Mr. Bingley, however, arrived daily, sometimes accompanied by Miss Bingley and the Hursts, sometimes alone and sometimes, as on this day, with Mr. Darcy. Only Jane and Lizzy were present to receive the gentlemen; the sweet strains of a harp were heard as Mary practiced in the music room; Kitty was with her father for her morning studies, Lydia was reading to Mr. Collins and Mrs. Bennet was visiting a Longbourn tenant who had a son who had fallen from a tree and broken his arm. Commiseration was not needed. In fact, according to his father what was needed was a firm dusting of the young lad's trousers; but Mrs. Bennet enjoyed the company of Mrs. Brown and so took some of Hill's broth and biscuits and had settled in for a comfortable chat.

As was the gentleman's habit, Mr. Bingley immediately attached himself to Jane's side, speaking to her in low voiced compliments in a non-stop babble oddly reminiscent of the early days of their acquaintance with Mr. Collins. Jane, pasting a look of polite interest onto her face, heard him out in near silence, as always offering him courteous attention but no encouragement.

Mr. Darcy, after granting the ladies a silent, disapproving bow of greeting, moved over to stare out the window in silence as was his unsocial habit. On most occasions Lizzy tried once or twice to courteously draw the taciturn man into conversation then gave it up. Today, though, she was determined to have a conversation with him regarding the tales that Lt. Wickham would no doubt be spreading about him throughout the community.

Gathering her courage, Lizzy fixed him a cup of tea and then moved toward him, offering it to him politely. He nodded his thanks, still not speaking, so Lizzy took a deep breath and spoke softly to him.

"Mr. Darcy, I know we do not know each other well, but a distressing and false tale has reached my ears regarding you, and I have no doubt portions of it, at least, are being spread through our community."

Mr. Darcy's mien grew more forbidding, but his voice was polite enough as he requested she continue.

"Recently we made the acquaintance of a certain Lt. Wickham, newly come to our area to join the militia. He has quite the fairy tale to relate in regard to his dealings with you. I will not test your patience with a recitation of all his accusations but will simply relate that it is quite an unbelievable and fantastical story, painting you as dishonorable and, indeed, the verist blackguard. No one at Longbourn believes his tale of woe, but I did feel it would be only courteous to let you know that he is blackening your name; there may be others in the community who accept his words as truth and so I felt you would wish to be aware of the situation."

To her surprise, while Mr. Darcy's eyes had looked shocked at hearing Wickham's name, as she made it obvious that she did not credit Wickham's version of events, his demeanor changed to one of curiosity.

"It is good that you do not believe him, for I have at times been accused of unseemly behavior by those who should have been sensible enough to judge his stories as false. I am interested to hear that you do not believe such slanders."

Lizzy sighed, "Well, on first hearing I did," she candidly confessed, "for he is very charming you know, giving every appearance of being a true gentleman, and he makes quite an interesting and thrilling tale of it, so one can hardly help being caught up in it. Indeed, one is left quite breathless with anticipation to hear what he will say next. But afterward, when one is actually looking at the details, it is clear that there is much of the story that is false, for he even contradicts himself while telling the tale. We assume it was not entirely false, for as my father pointed out the best of fabrications have some truth incorporated to lend a certain verisimilitude to the whole."

Mr. Darcy nodded thoughtfully at that. "Let me guess, he told you he was denied a living that was left to him in my father's will."

At Lizzy's surprised agreement, he continued. "That is true in so far as it goes, however, the facts bear little resemblance to the tale he usually relates. Instead, the truth is that after he learned of the bequest he came to me and stated he had no interest in the life of the church but would prefer to study law; he wished to have some funds granted to him to support him while he studied and to this I readily agreed. As a result, I gave him the thousand pounds left outright to him and another three thousand pounds to compensate him for the loss of income from the living."

Mr. Darcy's displeasure at the tale was clear as he continued, "The living came open only a few months later and naturally I gave the living to someone else; I am pleased to say it turned out to be an excellent choice as this man is a kind and caring shepherd to the parishioners who fall under his care. When Wickham later requested that he be given the living as he had wasted all the monies he had received, I did indeed deny him; so your father is quite correct, there is a kernel of truth in among the distortions."

He shook head at his childhood friend's behavior. "And you should also be aware that even when he returned with his demand for the living, he had not taken orders; had I been so unjust as to wish to rescind the living from one who is so well suited for it, I could not have done so for a man who had not been ordained in the church. It is well though, for while I have some care for the man as we were once great friends, I am not such a fool as to be believe a man like

Wickham should be entrusted with the spiritual well-being of any persons."

"Four thousand pounds? And only five years ago? How could he waste such a sum in so short a time? It is beyond my comprehension."

"He is a gambler, Miss Elizabeth, and not a very good or lucky one. And no doubt there are other unsavory habits for him to support also." Mr. Darcy regarded her keenly then. "I must again express my surprise that you and your family so quickly discerned the truth for he cannot long have been in the neighborhood, or I would have encountered him." Mr. Darcy was silent a moment, then with seeming reluctance he added, "I would have hoped he was turning over a new leaf by joining the militia but if he still spreading that tale, then I am afraid it may be a vain hope."

"I do not know how long he has resided here, but I met him a few days ago only, while visiting my Aunt Phillips in Meryton. He then joined some others of the militia at a small gathering here Tuesday last and it was then he related the story to me." Lizzy's beautiful eyes, usually dancing with joy, now flashed angrily as she had a sudden revelation, recalling the Lieutenant's querying her if she would only speak against Darcy in a family setting or if she would do so in other houses. "I have just this moment realized from something he said that he fully expected me to carry his tale to the rest of the community here. How base indeed!"

"Certainly it can be considered improper for him to have told a mere acquaintance such a personal history."

"Improper, and not his only impropriety of the evening for he importuned my youngest sister, despite her very appearance proclaiming she was not out; even when bluntly informed of this circumstance and taken to task for requesting her company he persisted in his attentions and did not desist until called to order by my cousin." Her mouth set in a firm line of disapproval, but then another thought occurred to her.

"I wonder if his circumstances have perhaps become more difficult? For he is rather older than the other lieutenants, he is beginning his career in the military far later, I think, than is generally done. I am not aware of what kind of renumeration is given to lieutenants in the militia, but I doubt it is enough to support a dissipated lifestyle."

Darcy nodded thoughtfully, "Yes, that could be. No doubt he thought to make himself an object of compassion to those in the neighborhood. That could make it easier for him to obtain credit."

"My father and Sir William Lucas have taken it upon themselves to warn the local merchants to be cautious in extending credit to him; I do not know how seriously they will take this warning, but Sir Lucas was once in trade and my father felt his presence would carry much weight when they delivered their warning."

It was then they were joined by the cheerful Mr. Bingley, pointing out they had reached the limits of time allowed for a call and so must be on their way. The gentlemen bowed and left, leaving behind a thoughtful Lizzy and an exasperated Jane.

"Oh, good heavens, Lizzy, I simply do not know how much longer I can endure Mr. Bingley's ridiculous attentions."

"Is it truly so bad, sister? I know you said he is not very interesting, but I would think by now you would have found a subject of mutual interest to enliven your time together."

"There is no such subject. Certain it is that I have lost track of the number of topics I have tried to introduce, Lizzy," Jane replied sadly. "If I have to hear him compare me one more time to an angel or listen to him rhapsodizing endlessly about how beautiful I am, I shall not be responsible for my actions. I have never before in my life entertained such a thought, but this morning my mind actually wandered to dropping my teacup onto his lap to make him go away."

Lizzy burst out laughing. "Oh, dear Jane, he must be frustrating indeed to have you thinking of committing violence. That is the most unforgiving I have ever heard you speak."

"Jane is being unforgiving?" asked Mary, who had finished her morning's practice on the harp and come to find her sisters. "I am all astonishment."

"She is going to pour hot tea on Mr. Bingley when next she sees him," teased Lizzy.

"Jane, I never would have believed it of you. Now had you told me Lizzy was going to throw hot tea on someone I would instantly believe it to be true," Mary teased back.

Lizzy laughed again and agreed. "Indeed, we all know that Jane has the patience of a saint and I have no patience at all."

Mary chuckled at this, then a sudden thought occurred to her. "If Mr. Bingley was here I must wonder, was Mr. Darcy here also?"

Lizzy nodded. "He was and I had a chance to warn him about Wickham's slander. He said father was correct, there is a kernel of truth to the story as he did deny Wickham the living, however, it was after Wickham had first declined the living and been handsomely compensated for it. Mr. Darcy had given the living to another, who he says is an excellent man, well suited to caring for the needs of the parishioners. After Wickham wasted *four thousand pounds* in less than five years, he came back to ask for the living; but as he had already been paid for the living and he had not taken orders, Mr. Darcy had no hesitation in denying his request. Wickham is a blackguard indeed to spread such a false tale."

Mary gasped at the amount. "Four thousand pounds? How could a single man with no family or obligations possibly spend all of that in so short a time?"

"Mr. Darcy related to me that he is an unlucky and apparently not very skilled gambler and so the money must have run through his fingers like water. And Charlotte may be right about the other dangers he presents for Mr. Darcy mentioned other "unsavory" habits, which sounds quite dire to me."

9

Although only Darcy being an early riser in their party, both Bingley and Miss Bingley had conformed to his habit, Bingley so they could go over estate needs early in the day, freeing his time later for his social life; and Miss Bingley so she could display her excellence as a hostess to Darcy. Bingley's presence was welcomed by Darcy, as he was as silent a companion as one could wish in the early morning. Miss Bingley, however, was another matter entirely. There were times when he truly felt she was made as uncomfortable by silence as he was by crowds.

"Really, Charles," she declared after serving herself from the overfull sideboard the next morning, "I do not see why you must visit Longbourn nearly every day. You are giving rise to expectations there that can never be fulfilled."

Charles sighed, feeling unequal to having this same conversation again and particularly so early in the day.

"Caroline, as I have told you before, nothing has been decided. If, however, Miss Bennet is my choice it can be nothing to you."

"It is everything to me, brother!" she cried. "You will lower our prestige as a family, you will make us a laughingstock in the ton with such a connection. Mr. Darcy, I beg you, represent to my brother the ills this could bring upon us."

Darcy laid down the newspaper he had been perusing and regarded her impassively. "Miss Bingley, it is true the Bennets have no connections to the peerage; however, Miss Bennet is a gentleman's daughter. You and your brother are from the ranks of trade. Therefore, it would be a step up for him to marry Miss Bennet." He ignored her gasp of outrage at this blunt assessment and continued on with his appraisal, "I cannot agree with you on the presumed ills of such a match. My only hesitation in forwarding such a marriage would be my doubt of her affection for your brother; I cannot see any such emotions in her demeanor and in fact, I have felt from our first meeting that she is of a somewhat cold disposition; and yet here I would have to defer to your brother's knowledge of the lady. I have spent no time in conversation with her and so cannot presume to divine her feelings. Perhaps she is merely very reserved."

"Cannot divine her feelings? How can you make such a claim? Obviously she has no feelings for him; her only thought would be to secure an advantageous match for herself." A look of cunning crossed her face before she schooled her expression to one of mournful commiseration. "Indeed brother, she has told me herself that her hopes are to secure a fortunate match to aid her family."

Charles looked at her in astonishment. "She said this? When? Why would she have told you such a thing if she is hoping for such a match with me? Caroline, I do not know what you are about, but if I should question Miss Bennet on this I must ask, would she tell me she has formed such a close friendship with you that she would confide these feelings to you?"

Caroline blushed but was determined to carry her point. "Well perhaps she did not say this so explicitly, but her feelings were clear enough in relating her purpose."

Darcy shook his head, both at her machinations and at Charles' evident confusion over his sister's motives. While he would prefer to decline to involve himself in their dispute, he had to agree in principle with Miss Bingley. He could not believe Miss Bennet would marry to disoblige her family nor did he think she entertained any warm feelings for his friend. Before Miss Bingley could once again appeal to him, Bingley abruptly switched topics.

"Caroline, I am going to hold a ball."

"What? A ball? Why would you hold a ball?"

"The neighbors here have been most welcoming. I want to return their hospitality, but there are many of them and only one of me. So, I have been considering and I believe a ball is the answer. I spoke with Mrs. Nicholls, who spoke with Cook, and they believe they could have all in hand to hold one in ten days. So that is what I am going to do."

"If I am not mistaken, there is one in our number for whom a ball will be wholly unpleasant, Charles. We would not wish to make any guest uncomfortable."

"If you are speaking of Darcy, he can go to bed if he does not choose to attend. I wish to repay the welcome of the neighborhood and I wish to do so by holding a ball," stated Charles with unusual firmness.

"I cannot put on a ball in ten days, Charles."

"Can you not? I would have expected someone with all of your hostessing skills to be able to do so but if it is too much for you, I will ask Louisa to be my hostess."

"No, no, that is not at all necessary," Caroline replied hastily, with a quick glance at Darcy. "I am sure that I can put something together for you in that amount of time."

"Good, I am glad to hear it. Come to the study after breakfast and we will get everything sent off to London to have the invitations printed at once."

Before they could continue their discussion, a disturbance in the hallway caught their attention. A moment later, a tall, well-built, pleasant looking gentleman in a red coat followed Nicholls into the breakfast room.

"Richard! I did not expect you so soon," welcomed Darcy, rising to greet his cousin. "How good to see you. You remember Bingley, of course, and Miss Bingley?"

Colonel Richard Fitzwilliam bowed politely to the Bingleys then smiled in genuine pleasure at Darcy. "I came as soon as I received your note, cousin."

Bingley, ever gregarious, immediately offered the Colonel lodging at Netherfield.

"Thank you Bingley, I am grateful for the accommodations." Richard acknowledged genially. "Indeed, I was hoping you would offer, though I saw an Inn in the small town near here that could no doubt offer me adequate housing if it should be inconvenient for you to host me."

"No, no, we would not hear of it," declared Bingley. "You must stay with us. Caroline, are we not pledged to visit Lucas Lodge this evening? I will pen a quick note to Sir William that we will have another guest with us; I am sure of his agreement, he is a most generous and kind host."

"Perhaps we should remain at home this evening, Charles. I am sure the Colonel must wish to rest from his journey."

Richard secretly amused that Miss Bingley would think a four hour journey through the English countryside in one of Darcy's luxurious coaches would fatigue the battle-experienced warrior, declined to rest that evening. "I thank you for your consideration, Miss Bingley, but there is no need to change your plans for me. I am quite able to recover before this evening's entertainment, I assure you."

"Of course you can," enthused Bingley. "Please, be comfortable Colonel. And can we offer you breakfast? You can see there is much left to tempt you."

Richard smiled at Bingley's enthusiasm, thanking him and moving to the sideboard to fill a plate with some of the offerings still on display. "Thank you, Bingley, if you do not object to my sitting down in my travel dust, I would be delighted to join you. I did break my fast much earlier, but as a soldier I never turn down a good meal and this looks uncommonly good."

Darcy laughed at Richard. "Well, there is no gunfire or mud, and plenty to eat so if your past claims are to be believed, you are now in perfect heaven."

The rest of the meal passed in pleasant conversation, the presence of the Colonel of necessity curtailing the Bingley siblings' disagreements. Charles then went to pen a note to Sir William, and to work with Caroline on the wording for the invitations and on the guest list for their ball and Darcy and Richard quit the breakfast room and strolled in the gardens.

"So, Wickham has finally deigned to show himself? What is he doing in this little hamlet? There cannot be much here to tempt him."

"He has joined the local militia, though how he could afford to purchase his way in is a mystery to me."

"No doubt some cowardly second or third son purchased it for him. Do you know who the commanding officer is?"

"A Colonel Forester is in command here."

"Hmm, if it is who I think it is, he is a good man. Of course, there is not much he can do to curtail Wickham's activities as long as the man is doing what he is ordered to do. It is not against regulations to gamble using vowels with the others in the regiment or to use credit at the local merchants; it is only dishonorable to do so if one has no intention of eventual repayment, and there is no proof of that of course. One cannot discipline someone on suspected future dishonor."

"Then there is nothing to be done?"

"I would not say nothing, cuz. First, I will speak with Colonel Forester, to inform him of some of our past dealings with Wickham. I will need your copy of his receipt for this. Then the merchants must be warned so he does not run up debts that cannot be repaid. Then I scare the wits out him. Then I return here and try to convince you once again to use the debts you have purchased to see the man in Marshalsea where he belongs."

Darcy's lips twitched in amusement as he contemplated Richard confronting Wickham. Their childhood friend now disliked him, but he was terrified of the Colonel and with good reason. "There is no need to warn the merchants, they are aware. And the estate holders here have also been warned to have a care for their daughters."

Richard gaped at him. "You actually forewent your blasted pride and spoke out against him? Who are you and what have you done with my cousin?"

Darcy gave a sardonic laugh. "No, my friend, you are quite out. My pride still will not allow me to speak of my private concerns with others. In this case, Wickham set himself up by telling his tale to the wrong person."

"Someone declined to believe him based on his winning looks? I am astonished as he usually relates it to some pretty young miss who takes it as truth and proceeds to blacken your name for him."

Darcy nodded and related his conversation with Elizabeth to his cousin, ending with, "So yes, he told his tale to a 'pretty young miss' but she declined to believe him and, in fact, when she realized from something he said that he expected her to disseminate the story was quite enraged by his presumption. It is her father along with our host this evening, Sir William Lucas, who took it upon themselves to warn the merchants and the fathers in the neighborhood, and 'twas done before I even knew of his presence."

Richard nodded his approval. "Good men, I am pleased to hear that they take the protection of their community seriously. I will leave you now; I need to see Forester and have a chat with Wickham if he happens to be available."

10

That evening Charles Bingley expressed his displeasure with his sister in a tangible fashion for the first time that Darcy was aware of and in a way that would no doubt cause her much frustration. He took his brother Hurst's recommendation to heart and ordered Darcy's carriage made ready to leave at seven in the evening and his own to be readied at eight. Then, when Caroline did not appear when the rest of the party was ready to depart, he and Darcy and Colonel Fitzwilliam left for Lucas Lodge while Mr. and Mrs. Hurst remained at Netherfield to await Caroline's appearance.

Richard found the situation hilarious, while Darcy's amusement was tempered by the knowledge that Miss Bingley would no doubt make them all pay for what she would consider an egregious insult. As far as the two men could discern, Bingley never thought of her again once in the carriage, his sole focus being spending an evening in the company of his latest angel.

Sir William's genial welcome was matched by Richard's equally genial acceptance of such; his experiences on the battlefield had long since taught him that the true measure of a man was not a matter of birth and that the lowliest of circumstances could produce the highest of results. As the second son of the Earl of Matlock he outranked everyone present, including his haughty cousin, but no one would have discerned this from his ease of manner and genuine interest in his company.

He welcomed the introductions to all and sundry and soon found himself in an extremely interesting discussion of the war and the policies the government was promoting with Bingley, a solicitor's wife, the lovely daughter of a neighboring estate and a disabled parson. So intent was he that it took several hints from Bingley before he realized that they were interrupting Bingley's plans to spend time with the gorgeous blonde woman who had an amazing grasp of tactics and strategy. As Bingley led her away, he was surprised to see his companions wearing almost identical expressions of resigned distaste. Taking a chance, he asked softly, "You do not approve?"

The parson, who had been introduced to him as William Collins, shook his head slightly while the solicitor's wife, Mrs. Phillips, directed a shrewd look at him. "I do not know how well you are acquainted with Mr. Bingley and from our discussion it is easy to discern that you have spent much of the last years on the battlefields so perhaps you are unaware of his reputation?"

Richard's surprise was genuine. "I was unaware that he had a reputation."

Mrs. Phillips nodded in satisfaction that her assumption had been correct then she elucidated, "Mr. Bingley attaches himself to a beautiful blonde, he showers her with attention and compliments, then he deserts her for another without hesitation. It is his pattern; one he seems to have perfected over the last few seasons in the ton. Everyone here is aware of this and no one takes his interest in Miss Bennet seriously, including herself. She would have far preferred to remain here and continue our fascinating discussion, but she would never be rude or unkind to another and so she tolerates his attentions."

Richard looked over at the couple and saw that if appearances were to guide his conclusion, Mrs. Phillips was correct. While they had been conversing Miss Bennet's gorgeous face had been warmly animated and interested, her eyes had sparkled with intelligence and her arguments had been well reasoned and cogent. Looking at her now, he saw a beautiful woman whose entire aspect was cool; she was neither engaged nor interested, but simply politely responding. Bingley, on the other hand, appeared utterly besotted.

Thinking of their conversation, Richard realized that Bingley had not contributed at all; his only interest had been in staring at Miss Bennet, hinting that they were interrupting his pursuit of her, then leading her away. He wondered what Bingley was saying to her that prompted so cool a response and was startled at the tolerant amusement in Mr. Collins voice when he said, "He is no doubt comparing her to an angel."

Richard gave him a questioning look and Mr. Collins responded in a gentle tone that spoke of mild disapproval and resignation, "It is all he does you see. He seems to have no conversation to offer her except to speak of how beautiful she is. No doubt there are many women who would find such to be satisfying but you will realize if you come to know the Bennet women that this will not do for them. Thomas Bennet married a woman of great beauty but more she is one of uncommon kindness and strength of character and unusually educated as she attended tutoring sessions with her brother." Mr. Collins gave a soft laugh, and added, "My cousin told me he began being infatuated with her beauty, but he fell in love with her when he discovered she spoke Latin and read Greek."

Richard found himself chuckling both at the wry tone and at the notion of discovering such intelligence behind a beautiful façade. Mr. Collins continued, "Mrs. Bennet decided long ago that her daughters would be raised to always value real qualities that matter over such an unimportant consideration as physical appearance. Kindness, intelligence, compassion and good character; these are the qualities my cousins value."

Mrs. Phillips added, "It is fortunate for Mr. Bingley that it is Jane who is blonde and beautiful; Elizabeth and Mary are equally lovely but are dark of hair and eyes. And so, his interest alighted on our dear Jane, whose patience is legendary; had he tried to court Mary with empty compliments, she would be hiding in the shrubbery to avoid him and as for my niece Elizabeth she would have sent him about his business in five short minutes."

By the time the evening ended Richard's mind was awhirl with all the impressions and conclusions he had reached at Sir William's gathering. While he was not a gossip, he knew the value of knowing your ground and had been interested to note that many of the general impressions were ones he could wholly agree with.

He had, over the course of the evening, heard the commonly held story of the nefarious Lt. Wickham. No parent was going to allow a daughter near him; by extension it appeared to have made them wary of the militia men in general, an attitude that Richard could only applaud. There were too many rogues in the militia; better safe and than sorry.

He heard how well liked and respected were the Bennets, parents and daughters alike, sometimes with a direct remark, such as Miss Bennet's forbearance with Bingley; or by extension as when he heard Miss Elizabeth and Miss Mary discussing with Sir William and Mr. Bennet the situation with a tenant on Netherfield property who was in need of aid due to an illness and noted the obvious respect for their opinions both their father and the elderly knight displayed.

He heard the story of Mr. Collins' accident and the compassionate care the Bennet family had extended to him, along with some rather disgusted views of his former patroness whom Richard had quickly identified as his own aunt, Lady Catherine de Bourgh. The general opinion of her as a selfish, interfering busybody, lacking in compassion and needing constant praise was sadly accurate.

He confirmed that the general view of Bingley was that he was a flirtatious and inconstant man, as he had been told by Mrs. Phillips; Bingley was tolerated for his happy manners, but no one took him seriously; the term he heard used most often was that he was a puppy; Richard felt it describe him rather well.

It was no surprise to him that Miss Bingley was universally despised and again there was good reason. She had stormed into the room in front of the Hursts, an hour late, ridiculously overdressed and obviously furious. She had been rude to her hosts and unpleasant to everyone except for himself, as he had completely avoided her, and Darcy, who she had fawned over relentlessly. Since the company seemed unsurprised and indeed, generally disinterested, her behavior this evening must not have been much different than it had been during their other interactions with her.

The general opinion he heard that bothered him was that his cousin Darcy was haughty, unpleasant, and universally disliked; that his behavior was not that of a true gentleman. Richard heard that he had insulted Miss Elizabeth Bennet loudly and even cruelly during his first appearance in the neighborhood. He heard how Darcy always refused to dance, though gentlemen were scarce, and many ladies were forced to sit out when there was dancing due to a lack of partners. Apparently Darcy had attended several events in the neighborhood, but rarely spoke to anyone outside his own party once his hosts had been greeted, he was called overly proud and disdainful of all of them; in short, Wickham did not have to blacken Darcy's name, he was doing a fine job on his own.

What was not mentioned, but that he noticed, was that Darcy was obsessed with Miss Elizabeth Bennet. He could be found close to her, listening in on her conversations, staring at her when she was conversing with others. Twice during the evening, he even briefly engaged her in conversation and Richard could not call to mind anyone else so honored by his cousin. No one else seemed to see it, but to Richard it was glaringly obvious: Darcy was besotted. Equally obvious was that she was oblivious to his attention. He wondered if her opinion were in accord with the others and if so what it would do to Darcy when he discovered the only woman Richard had ever seen affect him disliked him.

It was a long time before Richard slept that night.

11

What was wrong with this town, Lt. Wickham wondered irritably. He had always been able to charm small town merchants into extending credit to him and, as a member of the militia he had thought it would be even easier. Instead, the merchants were wary of extending more than a tiny amount of credit to any of them. Why just this morning he had been refused credit and had to turn over hard earned coin for his new gloves. The mercantile had refused to allow him to pick up some pretty ribbons to ease his way with the ladies until he settled his account. And even the tavern wench he favored had demanded to see his coins before she would agree to a tumble. He had never seen anything like it.

Disgruntled, he left the shops of Meryton and stalked back toward camp; before he could reach his tent he was summoned to Colonel Forester's office. Wondering what else could go wrong in this cursed town on this cursed day, Wickham strode ahead of Denny into the commander's office then stopped short. Sitting at his ease in the one guest chair in the room, Colonel Richard Fitzwilliam chatted easily with Colonel Forester.

"What are you doing here?" Wickham, blurted out, frightened and furious.

"Lt. Wickham," barked Colonel Forester. "You will not speak to a superior office in such a manner. Come to attention, Lieutenant and wait to be addressed."

Wickham followed his Colonel's order and tried to control the shaking of his hands. The last time he had seen Colonel Fitzwilliam he was being restrained by Darcy as he declared his intention of killing Wickham on the spot. So close, he thought now resentfully, he had been so close to eloping with Georgiana Darcy and her thirty thousand pounds, when they had ruined it all. He had wasted weeks on the boring girl, progressing from family friend to courting gentleman by slow stages; agonizingly slow stages, as the shy girl, just turned five and ten, had never so much as had her hand kissed by a gentleman.

Finally, after weeks of wooing the chit, he had convinced her that eloping to Gretna Green would be a wonderful, romantic adventure. Had convinced her that her brother and cousin would welcome her and her new husband with open arms.

When the two gentlemen, worried by the paucity of letters from their ward, had decided to pay a surprise visit, the stupid girl had confessed it all, starry eyed and sure of their approval. Darcy had been furious but controlled. The Colonel, equally furious, had simply declared his intention to run him through and George had escaped only due to Darcy's intervention.

Now the man who wanted him dead eyed him like a cat watching a particularly tasty mouse.

"Lt. Wickham, you told me a story about a bequeathed living. I remember it quite clearly. Do you also remember it?"

"Yes, sir."

"Hmmm, well what I do not remember is hearing you state that you had refused the living; nor do I remember any mention of the three thousand pounds you were given when you refused it. And yet, I have here in my hand your signed receipt for the monies and your statement that you were voluntarily refusing the living in exchange for the funds. Can you explain that to me, Lieutenant?"

Wickham felt sweat pooling at the small of his back. He had considered his options for explaining it away should Darcy contradict his story, but he had not once thought that his receipt would be produced, that his Colonel would have it in hand, that Fitzwilliam would be eyeing him smugly, that Denny would be on the other side of the open office door no doubt avidly listening. He opened his mouth, shut it again, then decided the only thing he could do was to brazen it out.

"That may be the case, sir, but—"

"*May* be the case Lieutenant?"

"Well, yes sir, it is the case, but I changed my mind and requested the living and Darcy refused to give it to me. So, it is truth that he refused me the living that his father intended for me to have."

"Were you ordained, Lt. Wickham?"

"No sir, but I would have done so had Darcy granted me the living."

"Did you offer repayment of the funds, since you changed your mind and wanted the living after all Lt. Wickham?"

Wickham had to forcibly stop himself from grinding his teeth in frustration. "Well, I would have repaid it out of the payments from the living once I received it, sir."

"So the answer to my question is no, you did not offer to repay it, would that be correct, Lieutenant?"

Wickham's resentment burst forth at that. "Why would Darcy need me to repay it? He has more money than he will ever need. I was raised to be a gentleman, and I should have been supported by Darcy, but he has refused to help me time and again."

"You were raised as a gentleman? Was your father not a steward?"

"My godfather, Mr. George Darcy, sent me to the same schools as his son, he treated me like another son. I should have had an estate granted to me, not some paltry living."

"So, you were given a gentleman's education to allow you to better yourself in the world and granted a living also, but instead of being grateful for these advantages, you squandered your education, refused the living and wasted the funds, then demanded the son of the man who had given you so much give you more? And when he justly declined, you blackened his name by telling the tale in such a manner as to make it appear you were robbed of something you had in fact refused. Would that be an accurate assessment, Lt. Wickham?"

Wickham stood sullenly before Colonel Forester as the silence stretched on.

"As of right now, you are confined to camp, Lt. Wickham. You will do your assigned duties and when you are not engaged in them you will be in your tent. You will not gamble with your fellow officers, in fact, when you receive your next pay you will redeem your outstanding vowels; if there is anything remaining you will pay your accounts with the town's merchants. There will be no exceptions, Lt. Wickham, and no second chances if you do not follow my orders to the letter. Lieutenant Denny."

Denny strode in briskly and saluted, avoiding looking at Wickham. "Sir?"

"You will escort Lt. Wickham to his tent and will remain there to ensure he does not leave said tent until I send someone to relieve you."

"Yes, sir."

"Dismissed. And close the door behind you."

After the door closed, Col. Forester gave Fitzwilliam a sardonic glance. "He will run you know. His kind always does."

Col. Fitzwilliam nodded soberly. "Yes, I believe he will. Have you the men to spare to watch him, obviously watch him, for a few days? I will send a missive to my General requesting the loan of some few of my men who have worked well with me in the past. Dressed in civilian garb or militia garb, they will not garner Wickham's attention. When a few days have passed, your men can be instructed to give the appearance of easing their attention from him, just enough so that he can slip out. When he runs, my men will follow."

"You know that we do not usually hang deserters in the militia, Fitzwilliam."

Fitzwilliam rose, giving the other Colonel a tight smile. "I do know. But we all hang horse thieves, Forester, and I do not see Wickham running on foot. He is lazy and feels entitled to whatever he wants or feels he needs; he will take a horse, without thinking of the consequences, and when he does, we will have him."

Assumed Virtue

12

As Mr. Bingley, Miss Bingley and Mrs. Hurst entertained Mrs. Bennet and her three eldest daughters with tea in the drawing room, Richard requested the loan of Bingley's study for a conference with his cousin.

"You plan to see Wickham hanged?" Darcy was appalled, he could not help it. His father's godson, his childhood playmate, a man he had tried to save more times than he could count, was being set up to be hanged and it tore at him. "My father—"

"No, Darcy, I will not listen to your excuses any longer," Richard snapped, incensed at his cousin's attitude. "What do you think your father would have done, how would he have felt if he knew that his godson had tried to elope with his daughter? His shy and innocent daughter who was just turned five and ten? Wickham would have been lucky if all your father did was horsewhip him. You have dragged your father's feelings into this for years, but the fact is that Uncle George would have had no hesitation in condemning Wickham if he had known the kind of man he has become. You know that is true."

Still angry, but feeling some sympathy for Darcy's obvious distress, Richard placed a hand on his cousin's shoulder. "Will, I know you want to honor your father's memory and that you feel a responsibility to old Mr. Wickham as well. But Wickham is a rotter. He has had multiple chances to change his life for the better and has refused to do so. *You* have honored their memories, *he* has not. It is time to end this."

"Surely transportation would be punishment enough? Perhaps he could forge a new life for himself in Canada or the former colonies."

"Are there not women in Canada and America who will be despoiled by this man, their lives shattered? Who will support his bastards there, who will try to aid them as you will not know of it? Are there not merchants who will be unable to feed their families because Wickham has charmed them into giving him credit and then walked away? You will not be there to repay them, to see their families clothed and fed. No, Will, the answer is not to allow him to continue to ruin lives so long as he does so out of your sight. The answer is to stop him."

Richard gave his cousin a wry grin. "Besides, it might not happen. Wickham could do what he should do, what he is supposed to do: stay in camp, accept his punishment, behave as the gentlemen he pretends to be. Even if he refuses to do so, if he deserts on foot, he will not be hanged, and you will get your wish and see him transported."

"You know that will not happen. He will steal a horse and be hanged as a horse thief and a deserter!"

"That is what I believe will happen, yes. But it is not certain. He is being given another chance here. One he does not deserve, but it is a chance. All he has to do is behave and he will be free to pursue a career in the military, or to complete his first term of service and sell out. I do not believe he will do it, but I could be wrong. But for good or ill, what happens will be his choice alone. You cannot save him from himself, nor can I nor can Colonel Forester. Wickham can save himself; he is the only one who can do so. It is time for you to accept that he is a man grown, he makes his own choices and must bear the consequences. After last autumn, your father would not have continued to protect him," and here Richard's voice gentled, "and it is time to be honest with yourself, Will, it is your feelings you are protecting, not your father's and not his father's either."

Darcy sat with a sigh, dropping his head into his hands. Richard was right, he knew that Richard was right, he could accept it with his head but not his heart. That organ ached with unshed tears, with the memories of a laughing, charming boy who had been a friend to him. How could he turn his back on those memories?

"You are allowed to mourn your friend, cousin, to feel sorrow for the lad he was," Richard said gently. "I, too, remember our playmate, remember the good times of childhood when the three of us roamed Pemberley and were united in friendship. But that boy is gone, long gone and in his stead is a vicious man who leaves heartache and chaos and ruin wherever he goes. This is what he has become, and he must be stopped now."

The two men sat in silence, Richard watching his cousin, his brother of the heart, with compassion but there was no regret in him; Wickham had bedeviled Darcy for years and his attempted seduction of their ward was the last straw for him. He would not tell his cousin, he would not tell anyone, but if Wickham ran on foot and was sentenced to be transported, he would take it upon himself to make sure that the blackguard did not live to set foot on any ship. He had kept military secrets for years; he would keep this one if needed. The short, unpleasant life of George Wickham was coming to an end, one way or another.

Darcy ran agitated fingers through his hair, then sat up, and although his face reflected his misery, he stiffened his spine and met his cousin's eyes. "Yes, you are correct, it is time and past time. He will have to face the consequences of whatever choices he makes. I will not attempt to dissuade you from your course any longer, nor will I intervene to save him from his fate if he comes to trial as a deserter. It is his life and what he makes of it is his to own."

Richard nodded, but before he could say anything further, they heard a disturbance from the hallway then Miss Bingley's shrill voice. Moments later a knock on the door revealed their hostess with an express which she handed to Richard. "I do hope there is nothing amiss with your delightful parents, Colonel."

"I will not know until I read this, Miss Bingley. If you would excuse us please?"

Miss Bingley hesitated, obviously searching for an excuse to stay, but finding none, she curtseyed with ill grace and left them.

As soon as the door closed again, Richard slit the seal on the express from his father.

Matlock House, London

July --, 1811

Son,

You informed me you would be staying some few days with Darcy, and I wanted to get this information to you both quickly. Be assured your mother and I are well; at least as well as we can be given that my sister descended on us in all her regular fury last night.

She was and is furious that I have taken over seeing to the finances of Rosings. She was and is furious that Darcy did not arrive at Rosings for Easter. She was and is furious that Anne and Darcy will not wed.

Anne was quite ill when they arrived, your mother tended to her and then demanded that our physician be brought in. He has told us that while Anne's heart was permanently damaged by her childhood illness, there is no reason for her to be as weak and sickly as she is. Apparently the apothecary that Catherine has had treating her daughter is a quack who prescribes tonics for everything and when added together there was so much mercury in them that it was poisoning Anne. The doctor feels that once she is off the medications and able to moderately exercise herself and eat a more varied and healthier diet that she will be able to live a comfortable if not necessarily energetic life. This is much better news that I had thought to receive as she looked deathly ill when they arrived.

After the physician left, Anne asked to speak with me and your mother. It was a long and very interesting discussion, but the end result is this: Anne is giving you Rosings Park, along with the de Bourgh townhouse in London.

I know this is a shock to you Richard, it was to us also, but when she explained her reasoning it makes sense. She is never going to marry, son, and she likely would not survive childbirth. Anne was quite clear that she does not have the interest, the knowledge or the energy to administer the estate and that she is adamant that it go to you. Forgive me, I should have told you that she actually became the owner of the estate when she turned five and twenty, but she has not had the stamina to stand up to her mother and has been biding her time until the right opportunity presented itself. Her mother dragging her to Derbyshire and then to London in order to find and berate me was the perfect chance for her and she seized upon it at once.

I know you said you were on a mission, but London is close. When you can, please come home long enough so that we can begin to settle matters for you. And once whatever it is you are doing is *accomplished I would like to see you resign your commission and take hold at Rosings.*

Yours, etc.

Henry Fitzwilliam

Dazed, Richard handed the missive to Darcy to read and went to the sideboard to pour two tots of brandy.

"Richard, congratulations! Oh, this is excellent news. We have all respected you for your dedication, but we cannot help but worry about you whenever you are called to battle. Now you can resign and be safe."

"Darcy, she cannot do this. It is her heritage; it is not right. And I know nothing about managing an estate."

"Richard, you read what I read and once you are past the shock you will see that Anne is making a wise choice, the best choice for her and the correct choice for Rosings. She has not been educated to run the estate either and you know how little it takes to exhaust her. Besides you have been responsible for the lives of your men for years and I would wager you remember more than you think of what your father was teaching Hill when you were a boy. It takes stamina and energy and focus to run an estate well Richard; the doctor feels she will never be an energetic lady, but she can be a happy one."

"But Darce, what will she do, where will she go? With her health issues it cannot be good for her to be in London and besides father writes she is giving me the house in town."

"Well, at a guess I would say she will go to Bath. You may not know this but Sir Louis always preferred Bath to London and purchased a home there years ago. I only know about it because the income from leasing it is part of the annual accounting. And Sir Louis knew what Lady Catherine was like. He protected Anne's dowry by placing it in a trust administered by both of our fathers. I took my father's place at his death; it has been invested all these years and is now worth close to forty thousand pounds. She can live very well indeed on the interest from that Richard. And since we will still be administering it, she will be able to live largely without any kind of stress at all. Given that her heart is weak, I believe that is important. Administering an estate is obviously not a stress-free proposition. I do not think her heart could stand the strain; if she is forced to take hold there it could very well hasten her death."

Some of the tension left Richard's face at that blunt assessment. "I had not considered that. Given how anxious I feel about taking up the reins there I can only imagine how hard it would be on her."

"And you know that I will help you. So will your father and so will Hill. We will probably give you so much advice you will be wishing us all at the devil in no time."

Richard laughed at that, rose and set his empty glass aside. "I will count on you Darcy. I know you have made Pemberley more prosperous than it was even under your father's steady hand; and you know Rosings well from trying to browbeat our Aunt into running it properly for these past five years." He moved over to the desk and drew parchment and ink into place. "I will ask father to come here. I cannot leave while the situation with Wickham is unresolved."

Assumed Virtue

13

The Earl of Matlock was an unhappy man. He hated London in the summer and was only in residence to handle looking over the ledgers for his sister's estate and to handle a few legal items with his solicitors as long as he was in London anyway. His plan was that he and his wife would be in London for a week only before they would return to the cooler weather and sweet breezes of Fairwinds, their estate in Derbyshire, and the week was nearly at an end. He had enjoyed a good dinner with his dear wife and now was hearing a voice that would no doubt ruin his evening and probably would ruin his digestion too. He was in no mood to deal with his difficult sister, who had been a thorn in everyone's side her entire life.

Her arrival at Matlock House would upset the entire household. He and his wife both took deep breaths, bracing themselves to meet the dragon who was Lady Catherine de Bourgh.

"Why are you here, why did I have to travel all the way to Derbyshire only to find you in London?" Lady Catherine raged, her voice rising to a shriek. "Things are all in upheaval. Why did Darcy not come to Rosings at Easter as he supposed to do? Why must I search you out? I have been forced to leave Rosings Park and travel in haste to this horrid place, where I find you living in luxury while you are demanding I curtail my spending and live in poverty like a peasant. What are you thinking to treat me so badly? What would our dear mother say to you trying to force me to live like some nobody?"

As Catherine raged on, the Earl and Countess simply watched in silence, letting her complaints roll on until she finally wound down.

That changed when Anne, leaning heavily on Mrs. Jenkinson, shakily entered the parlor. The sight of the young woman, pale and shaken and obviously not well, galvanized the Countess, who promptly rose and went to her, gently escorting her out of the room.

The Earl, who normally took his sisters rants with composure, was infuriated by the thought of his obviously ill niece being dragged around the country by her selfish mother.

"Enough," he roared at her. "I have had enough of this. You are supposed to be a lady and yet you come here shrieking like a harridan and disrupting the household, insulting everyone and everything. I have had enough, madam."

"How dare you," cried Lady Catherine, but her brother had indeed reached the limits of his patience.

"No, how dare you, Cathy," he snapped back. "Your behavior is appalling. If you have something you wish to speak of to me, I will hear you but not while you are shrieking in such an ill-bred manner. You will come fully into the parlor and sit and speak like the gentlewoman you are supposed to be, or you will not speak to me at all."

Lady Catherine gaped at him, thrown off her course by his anger at her. Henry never yelled at her. He might be angry, but he was always controlled. She stalked to a chair and sat, then seemed to draw into herself as if she did not know what to say next to him.

It was into this charged atmosphere that the Countess arrived, her face set in lines of disapproval but her movements brisk and controlled.

"I have settled Anne in the green guest room on the northeast corner. We could open the windows there to keep the room cool while settling Anne out of any drafts. She is quite ill, both from whatever malady has been ailing her and from the movement of the carriage which always is unsettling for her. Cook is preparing beef broth and bread and butter for her which is all she can stomach right now. I have prepared some items from my stillroom to help settle her so she can eat and to help her sleep."

She regarded Lady Catherine grimly for a moment before turning back to the Earl. "She needs a competent physician to see her, Henry. She has quite literally a dozen different medications she is taking. Many of them contain mercury and I believe the amounts, when added together, are enough to poison her. It would explain many of her symptoms. She also has two tonics that contain heavy doses of laudanum, but fortunately she had a bad reaction to the drug the first time she was given it and so she has refused to continue to take them. One of the items I have given her is willow bark tea, which will allow her to rest without the ill-effects of laudanum."

"I will send for Dr. Howard. Do we need to get him here yet tonight?"

She shook her head. "Tomorrow will be fine. She is not in immediate danger, but I do not believe that whoever has been attending her has been helping her much and he may in fact have been harming her."

She directed another scathing look at Lady Catherine then continued. "There are two other things to be discussed directly. First, it sounds as if Lady Catherine may have pushed her team to the point of foundering. Anne is not certain, but she believes it may be the case." She spoke over her husband's outraged cries at that news. "The other issue is that Anne has asked that you keep her mother out of her room and that she not be forced to see her at this time. I have stationed a footman outside her door and arranged for another to relieve him so there will always be someone to keep her from entering the room and bothering Anne."

This last broke Lady Catherine's silence, and she immediately informed them of her affront. "You are speaking of my daughter, Audrey. I make the decisions for her not you. There is no need for a physician or for my brother's interference and you cannot keep me from her room. She is my child, and she will do as I say."

"She is nearly six and twenty, Catherine. She is not a child but an adult and this is her request. There is no reason that I can think of to deny her."

"I demand that you take me to her at once. Do not think to gainsay me."

"Do not think that you can order anyone in this house, Catherine; most particularly you have no authority over me at all. You are an uninvited and unwelcome guest in my home. You do not rule here. Henry, I am going to sit with Anne for a little while, then I will see you in our sitting room." She left then her back stiff with outrage.

"Well," huffed Lady Catherine, "she is quite rude is she not?"

"She has displayed far more courtesy than you deserve, Catherine. You arrive here with no notice, shrieking insults and demands. I will tell you this once and will not repeat it nor give you a second chance: if you expect me to host you then you will behave like the gentlewoman you are supposed to be. You will not rail at me, my wife or the servants. You will behave, Catherine or you can open the de Bourgh townhouse and stay there. Now what is your current cause of outrage?"

"Henry, you cannot expect me to curtail my expenses. I am the daughter of an Earl therefore I have no need to be prudent with my funds."

The Earl regarded her with astonishment. "Cathy, your parentage has nothing to do with your finances."

"Of course it does, Henry, I must have what is my due. And I do not understand why you are having my steward come here and looking over the ledgers. That is my nephew's job, after all the estate will be his once he marries Anne."

"Let us deal with this as the two separate issues it is. First, Darcy is not and never has been under an obligation to help you with Rosings; he did so at my request as a favor to me. He will not be coming to Rosings again. He came directly to me after he left Rosings at Easter a year past and he related the conversation he had with you. He told you that if you did not take his suggestions for changes in the way you administer the estate he would no longer waste his time with you. You did not follow through on any of the suggested changes, and so he is finished. I will attend to the estate books now. As the head of your family and a trustee of Sir Louis' estate I can compel you to invest into the estate instead of only taking from it and if you do not comply of your own volition, I can force you to cease administering the estate altogether.

"As for Darcy and Anne, they are not going to marry, there is absolutely no chance that this will happen, Catherine. No, do not speak. Just listen. They are not going to marry. Darcy needs an heir; Anne is unlikely to ever be healthy enough to give him a child. They care for each other as cousins, but they do not have the kind of fondness between them to marry."

"But if he would only marry Anne," Lady Catherine began, but the Earl interrupted her, speaking with dispassionate coldness.

"But he will not. We are not fools, Catherine, we are all aware of why you wish them to marry. You have long thought that you could force them to wed, send Anne to Pemberley with Darcy and rule Rosings without oversight in their absence. And you have desired to get your hands into Pemberley's deep pockets. Since we all know these are the reasons you want Darcy to marry your daughter, you may now desist. You can console yourself with the thought that even if they had wed

Darcy would never have let you drain Pemberley's coffers to fund your profligate spending or to prop up Rosings Park. You will never get your hands on Pemberley's wealth, so you may now quit scheming to do so and turn your attention to your much abused tenants."

The Earl rose and pulled the cord to summon a servant. "You will go to your rooms, Catherine. We will discuss anything more tomorrow, including if you have foundered your horses, for I will not be purchasing new ones for you nor will I allow you to waste Rosings funds on horses you are simply going to mistreat. Go to bed. I will see you at breakfast."

By mid-afternoon the next day, Henry Fitzwilliam, Earl of Matlock, was at his wits end. He had run his family's estates competently for years, he had helped raise two fine sons, he was a powerful and respected member of Parliament, and he was unable to talk any sense of any kind into his sister. No matter what was said her only topics of conversation were Darcy and Anne getting married and getting her hands on more funds to throw away. Horses almost foundered? Why did Darcy not betroth himself to her daughter? Anne's health? Why could she not have unlimited access to Rosings' funds? She was obsessed and he was unsure how to get through to her.

Fortunately, he had an excuse to avoid her for at least part of the day. He had received the doctor's report and was both dismayed and relieved. Anne's health was not as bad as her appearance the previous evening would suggest and, according to Dr. Howard, once she had recovered from all the tonics he had summarily tossed out she would be much better. The childhood illness she had suffered had indeed caused some permanent harm, but that did not mean she could not live a much better life than the one she was living now. She would not be robust, and it was unlikely she would ever be strong enough for marriage and childbirth, but she could be healthy enough if she was allowed a proper diet and some moderate exercise. He was relieved she was not at death's door, which he had truly thought possible when he had first seen her; he was dismayed because as the head of the family he should have stepped in sooner, should have done something to rescue his niece.

Now she had requested his presence, and that of the Countess.

Seated in the pretty sitting room attached to Anne's bedchamber, the Earl and Countess greeted their niece then patiently waited for her to gather her thoughts and address them. The quiet young woman had answered their questions on her health somewhat shortly, reiterating what the doctor had told them, then requested they leave it be for now.

She began somewhat hesitantly. "Uncle, before I speak of the plans I would like to put in place, I need to ask some questions. First, I believe that instead of being the heiress to Rosings Park that I am actually the owner now, is that not correct?"

The Earl looked surprised but admitted this was so. "Your father's will was explicit. Once you married or turned five and twenty, the estate devolved to you."

"And Lady Catherine, she has the use of the dower house but no rights to the manor home or the monies from the estate, correct?"

"That is also correct. Lady Catherine has life tenancy to the dower house unless she voluntarily gives that up. Her income would derive from her dowry, though she has spent so much of it she would have to greatly reduce her spending to stay within her income."

"And my dowry, has she run through that also?"

"No, she had no access to your dowry Anne. According to your father's will, it has been held in trust for you. George Darcy and I were the administrators and with his death, your cousin Darcy replaced him. We have invested some in funds and some in other ventures. It has grown quite nicely from the original five and twenty thousand pounds to more than forty thousand. I do not know the exact amount, but it is a goodly sum."

Anne nodded, thinking deeply. "Lady Catherine can live somewhere else if she wishes, can she not?"

"Yes, she could but I do not see her easily leaving Rosings. It has been her home for thirty years."

"The manor has been her home," corrected Anne, "and she will be leaving it whether she goes to the dower house or to another home."

The Countess smiled broadly at that. "Are you planning a coup, Anne?"

Anne laughed softly. "Well yes. But my plan is rather complicated. Let me lay out what I would wish for, and we will see what you think can be done." She drew a deep breath then began. "First I would like to see Lady Catherine leave Rosings entirely. She will never allow anyone else to peacefully and properly administer the estate if she remains. She will always be disputing any decisions made and demanding more funds. Some other solution must be found. I do not have one as yet, but I am hopeful that between us we can find another place for her. Second, I do not wish to run the estate. I do not have the experience, I do not and will likely never have the energy to do so and frankly I have too many bad memories there. I know that Rosings is not my only property, that I own the house in London and also a house in Bath. I believe I would like to leave Rosings and live permanently in Bath."

"If you are to live in Bath, then why is it so important to you that Lady Catherine leave Rosings?" asked the Countess.

"Because I do not want her to run the estate into the ground; because the tenants deserve better treatment than they have or ever would receive from her; and because I want to give the London house and Rosings Park to Richard, and I do not believe he should be forced to deal with an angry Lady Catherine every day as he tries to bring the estate back to what it should be."

The Fitzwilliams exchanged stunned looks. "Anne, that is wonderfully generous, but you cannot do that," protested the Earl.

"Of course I can. Oh, I could give the estate to Darcy instead I suppose, but then it would just be one more obligation to him. He would run it well I have no doubt, it is what he does, but he would not love it, he would not live there, he would never turn it into the home it could and should be. You need an estate for Richard. His luck is going to run out eventually and his death in battle far from home will devastate so many people, myself included. A quiet life in my house in Bath can easily be supported by the income from my dowry. I do not need more and as I said I do not wish to administer the estate. Richard is the obvious choice for many, many reasons."

"But Anne it is your heritage."

"It is, Aunt Audrey, but it is not what I want or need. I do not say it would be impossible for me to transform the place where I have been imprisoned into something resembling a home, but I do not want to do it and for the first time in my life I am going to do exactly what I wish to do. Nothing about Rosings Park suits me. Lady Catherine has turned the manor house into a museum of bad taste. It is overloaded with gilt; it has become an unremittingly formal and gloomy and dark place to live. It needs energy. In fact, it needs Richard's unbounded energy. It needs someone who will marry and raise a family there and again, that is Richard. Rosings Park has been a prison, it has been a house, but it has not been a home since the death of my father. It is time for it to live again and I truly believe Richard is the perfect one to do it. I will not yield on this. The question remains, what do we do about Lady Catherine?"

For long moments there was silence as everyone thought deeply on what Anne had told them. Then Lady Fitzwilliam spoke decisively. "She will live in the Dower house at Matlock."

"What?" gasped the Earl. "We do not want her."

"Well, no we do not, but we can control her, indeed we are the only ones who can. Anne is wholly correct that if your sister remains at Rosings she will be a thorn in Richard's side. Leaving will not be her first choice but it is the practical one. At Rosings she will have to pay her own servants and bear the other expenses of the house, which she cannot afford to do. If she lives at Matlock, she can live there without bearing the expenses, and while the income from her dowry may not allow for all the luxuries she will want, it is still enough to make her comfortable. Matlock can afford this, while at the moment Rosings cannot. And I am correct, am I not, in my understanding that once she takes up residence elsewhere, she loses the right to return to Rosings' Dower house?"

The Earl rather grudgingly admitted that this was true.

"Very well then. Oh come Henry do not be so gloomy. The Dower house is far enough away that we do not have to see her often and we do not need it. Think on this, my dear. Having our own staff in place at the Dower house means we can control your sister to a great extent. She will not be allowed to run a team into the ground to go interfere in other people's lives if we hold the purse strings. And you may fully trust me when I tell you that I will have no hesitation in letting the staff know they do not have to take any abuse from her."

She added cheerfully, "And Anne is right, if she is anywhere near Rosings she will contest every decision Richard makes, she will interfere where she has no right or reason to do so and she will make the lives of everyone around her pure misery. More, if we do not take her, then where will she go? She has no other near relations so it must be us."

The Earl nodded glumly. "As always, dear wife, there is much sense in what you say. We can keep her under control, it is true, but it goes sorely against the grain with me that she will not have to suffer the lifestyle of want that her unrestrained spending has earned."

"Well, I am not thrilled with it either," admitted Anne, "as I should dearly love to see her suffer the consequences of her abuse of the estate, but if you and my Aunt are willing to take on the burden of her presence it would greatly relieve my mind. Richard will have enough to contend with in trying to undo all the harm she has caused; he does not need her harping at him while he does so. By the way I have also thought of how to finance some of the repairs he will need to make. First, lease the London house. It will be his also, as I cannot ever live in London; the smells, the noise, the whole atmosphere is one I cannot bear. Richard does not need a London home at least until he marries as he can stay at Matlock or Darcy house when in town. And another thing: he must sell the furnishings she has purchased for Rosings."

"He cannot sell Rosings' furnishing," argued the Earl, "that would not be right."

"Of course, he should sell them. There are no doubt many people with taste as poor as hers; and Lady Catherine spent huge sums of money to furnish the place. Get rid of all that junk. The attics are stuffed full of timeless, lovely pieces that she replaced with the gaudy, gilt laden atrocities she spent so many pounds on. And you should know also Uncle that she has purchased large amounts of equally gaudy jewelry over the years. The jewel safes at Rosings are overflowing with the stuff. They are not part of the de Bourgh or the Fitzwilliam heritage. Much of it could be sold back to the jewelers. Between all of this it will give Richard funds to begin investing into the estate instead of draining every last penny and more out of it."

Sounding buoyantly happy, Anne beamed at the still reeling couple, "Oh Aunt and Uncle, I cannot wait to someday visit and see the changes Richard will make. It makes my heart lighter to know that Rosings Park will become a wonderful place to live again."

After sending missives to the bank and his solicitors and an express to his son, the Earl escorted the Countess to Lady Catherine's sitting room. She had not been out of her rooms since her last altercation with the Earl who was convinced she was just biding her time, plotting to somehow get her own way.

In this he was mistaken. Although she had not been able to force the match yet, Lady Catherine had told herself and everyone else that Darcy and Anne would marry for so long that she had convinced herself of it; she had also been certain that if they refused her brother would support the match; he was the head of the Fitzwilliam family and could force the match for her. Her failure to bend Darcy and Anne to her will and Henry's forceful declaration that she was alone in demanding their marriage had shaken her badly. Lady Catherine had found herself oddly unable to focus, to concoct a plan, a situation she was totally unfamiliar with as always she had known precisely what to do.

So she had returned to her rooms, not plotting or planning but simply brooding. Instead of an angry, shrieking termagant, the Earl and Countess found an unexpectedly quiet woman; always a force to be reckoned with she seemed today to be just a tired, brittle and old woman.

"So, you have decided to see me and disagree with me once again? I do not understand why you are here when you will support nothing I have to say, but if you wanted to speak with me why were you not here earlier? No doubt you feel you had more important things to see to," complained Lady Catherine.

"In fact, I did," replied the Earl calmly. "I wanted the physician to see Anne and to get his report as soon as may be. My niece's health is my primary concern."

"No doubt she is much as she ever is," muttered Catherine, "sickly and weak and a continuing disappointment to me."

"I am sorry to hear that opinion from you Catherine. I wonder, would it surprise you to hear that she is at least equally disappointed in you?"

"Hah, I have done nothing to earn her disapprobation."

"You mean nothing except encourage your apothecary to give her so many tonics you were poisoning her? Or perhaps you feel that denying Anne her inheritance and running her estate into the ground are nothing?"

The Earl waved an irritable hand at her. "It matters not. I have come to discuss your future Catherine and I will tell you now your choices are limited, very limited indeed. Anne is taking charge of her inheritance and you will not be allowed into the de Bourgh homes in London or Bath, nor will you be allowed to return to the manor house at Rosings; you will no longer have a say in running the estate and you are cut off from Rosing's accounts. You will no longer fund an extravagant lifestyle off your daughter's inheritance and the work of her tenants. You will have to accept that your days of ruling Rosings Park are over."

"Ha! No one can keep me from my home, or from any of my homes Henry, so kindly do not spout such nonsense at me."

"Ahh, but they are no longer your homes, sister. They belong to Anne and you know that Catherine. You were there when Sir Louis' will was read so it can be no surprise to you that they belong to her as of her birthday almost a year past. The Dower house is available to you, of course. Your income is going to be reduced to the interest on what is left of your dowry and since you have run through much of it and will be responsible for paying the servants and for the upkeep on the Dower house, you will be living in very reduced circumstances going forward."

Lady Catherine stared at him shock, her mouth opening and closing more than once but no words coming forth. Finally, she shook her head and stated, "I am the daughter of an Earl. This is simply not acceptable."

"You will have to accept it, Catherine. Frankly, Anne does not want you in her homes, she does not even want you in the Dower house, and it is only available because Sir Louis' will decreed it to be so. Given the choice, you would be abandoned to starve in the hedgerows by the daughter you have injured so severely. No one in the family will allow you to live with them, you have alienated everyone with your selfish determination to order everyone's lives to align with the decisions of your choosing while ignoring their wishes."

"If you are determined to enforce this ridiculous idea of Anne's then I shall reside at Pemberley. Darcy will not refuse me."

The Countess actually burst out laughing at that. "Catherine are you really so foolish as to think that is true? Have you not noticed that he will no longer even pay you the compliment of acknowledging you as his aunt but calls you Lady Catherine? You will not find shelter at Pemberley, no nor anywhere else either. He has related his last conversations with you to us and if you will think on it, you can see that he will not abide having you in his home. Can you honestly think of anyone who will give you houseroom? Does anyone ever visit you at Rosings that is not purely doing so out of duty? Surely you must see that your behavior does not invite people to enjoy your company?"

Lady Catherine flushed an angry red and for a moment Henry thought they would be treated to her fiery and unrestrained temper as so often in the past. But then she sagged in her chair, looking haggard and slightly ill.

"Is not duty enough anymore? I believe the world has gone mad around me, for no one sees the benefits of the old ways, of the proper ways to do things. I do not understand this world any longer nor do I know what to do and I always know what to do. I cannot live in the Dower house at Rosings, Henry you must see that it is impossible. I cannot afford it and I cannot live as a pensioner where I have ruled for so long."

Her brother nodded. "We thought that might be the case, so we offer you one other choice. You can live in the Dower house at Matlock. The estate will cover the costs of the servants and the upkeep on the home. You will still be living on considerably less than you were, but you will have enough for a comfortable lifestyle if not a lavish one."

"You just said no one would have me, why would you make that offer?" she asked bitterly.

"Because you are my sister, because I would prefer you not bedevil the younger generation any longer and because my wife is a saint. If not for these things, the offer would not be open to you. Now we will leave you, Catherine but we will expect your decision by tomorrow so we can begin making the necessary arrangements."

"There is no choice, not really, and you know that. I will go to Matlock but first I must return to Rosings to gather my things."

"No, Catherine, you will not be allowed back into the manor, not at any time. Your clothing and personal items will be packed and sent to Matlock for you, but it will be done by Matlock servants, and it will not include the jewelry you have so recklessly purchased. That will be sold, and the funds will be reinvested into the estate. In fact, much of what you have bought so extravagantly will be sold. The estate must be put back on a sound financial footing and you are not going to loot the contents to hoard or to sell for your own selfish pleasure. I will make the arrangements to have what is truly yours brought to you, but not one extra item will you receive."

Lady Catherine directed a hard and bitter look at the couple. "So, you will watch all my efforts to make Rosings the envy of all dismantled; now I know I could never live in the Dower house at Rosings. I will not watch the work of 30 years destroyed. Leave me now. There is nothing more to be said between us."

As they went back to their suite, the Countess cocked an eyebrow at the Earl. "You did not mention that Richard is going to be the new owner of Rosings."

"No, and she will be installed at Matlock without access to transportation before I do so. Right now she is content to sit on her past schemes and mourn them. If she knew of her daughter's plans I do not think the whole of London would hold her rage. We do not want her demanding to be at Rosings out of spite, nor do we want to fight her to keep her from descending on Anne in Bath. And it really is no longer her concern. Rosings is not hers anymore and that is really the material point. All else will wait."

14

At Netherfield Park, Richard was quietly awakened at dawn by his batman who had been awakened by his groom. The General had come through and six soldiers in civilian dress were awaiting instructions at the White Horse Inn in Meryton. Forty minutes later Richard was drinking truly vile coffee with his men in an otherwise empty taproom, softly detailing their mission. By the time most of the residents of Meryton were sleepily greeting the day Richard was on his way back to Netherfield, while Colonel Forester was reading a note that Richard's men were in place and the plan to entice Lt. Wickham to desert was in motion.

Richard was sipping a cup of excellent coffee and trying to determine if he should have something more from the groaning sideboard when his father's answering note was delivered. Waiting for Miss Bingley to stop chattering at Darcy about a ball Bingley was determined to hold in less than ten days hence, he finally jumped in to give her the news.

"Miss Bingley, I am sure you must be tired of the Fitzwilliams imposing on you however, I would ask your indulgence to accommodate another uninvited guest. My father will be traveling here today, and it is possible that my mother and a cousin will travel with him or will follow him in a day or two. Would it be acceptable for them to stay here, or shall I make arrangements for them at the Inn in Meryton?"

"Stay at that dreadful little Inn, sir? I should say not. Of course we will be delighted to host the Earl and Countess! I shall make arrangements at once. When are they expected to arrive?"

"I am afraid I can give you no real assurance of the arrival time except that it will be today around afternoon teatime I would think."

To Richard's amusement and Darcy's relief, the news caused Miss Bingley to rise and bustle out of the room, calling for the butler and the housekeeper as she rushed to prepare the house for such elevated visitors.

"She is going to be disappointed you know, Richard. Your parents are nowhere near haughty enough for Miss Bingley's taste."

Recalling his cousin's reputation in the neighborhood, Richard leveled a disapproving stare at his cousin as he rose from the table. "No, nor am I. We leave that kind of pretentious behavior to others."

Darcy's mouth set into an angry line. He was not pretentious. Certainly, he was aware of his worth, of his station and his wealth and connections. His reserve had never bothered Richard before; this must be because he had not fallen under the spell of the Bennets. Had Richard fallen under their spell? He had seen no sign that Richard was enamored of Miss Bennet. His heart seized as the thought came unbidden that Richard might be attracted to his Elizabeth. Before he could follow him, Bingley broke into his thoughts.

"I say, Darcy, do you think I should remain at home in case the Earl and Countess arrive? I am quite sure Miss Bennet is expecting me, you know it is my habit to call at Longbourn. I would not wish to disappoint her for she is very gentle you know, and her feelings could be easily hurt. And I wished to inform her about the ball we are to host. I want to make sure I secure the first set with her and perhaps the supper set also. But I would not wish to slight the Earl and Countess in any way, and I am sure Caroline would expect me to remain here. What do you think I should do?"

Darcy looked at him blankly, his mind taking a minute to process his friends' questions, then he replied impatiently, "Of course you should remain here Bingley. Any guest would expect you to greet them upon arrival. No doubt you can see Miss Bennet tomorrow."

To Darcy's surprise, when he left the breakfast parlor, his cousin was nowhere to be found, nor was Miss Bingley. He fully expected Richard to be waiting for him, his cousin would have known Darcy would want to address his veiled insult. And why was Miss Bingley not much in evidence, trying to impress him with her arrangements for the Earl and Countess or boring him to tears with her arrangements for a ball for the "savage company" in Meryton? And that got him thinking about the Hursts, who had not been in evidence yet this day. Where in blazes was everyone? Were they all avoiding him? And if so, why?

Bingley was not avoiding him, in fact Darcy wished his friend would go wherever everyone else was if only to stop his chattering. How many times must he repeat that the Earl and Countess would be gracious guests and Miss Bennet would be fine, she could not have given her dances away, did he not realize no one else even knew about the blasted ball yet? Were they going to go round and round with the same questions and answers all the day long?

It was infuriating. Darcy's temper, already frayed from the situation with Wickham and Richard's annoying attitude, finally snapped.

"Bingley, for heaven's sake, I will tell you once again, you are obliged as the host to be here to greet the Earl and Countess. They will be gracious guests because they are gracious people. It will not matter to Miss Bennet, no one else will have asked for any dances as no one else even knows about the ball yet, so you will still be the first whether you visit today or tomorrow. She will not care if you are not there this morning. Why are you so worried? You fall in love at the drop of a hat; you will not even remember her name a month after we leave here."

Bingley drew himself up. "That is not true, Darcy. I know I have fancied myself in love in the past but my feelings for Miss Bennet go far beyond what I have known before. I have never met, no nor ever even seen, a more beautiful woman. She is serene and gracious and never says an unkind word about anyone, not even about Caroline. She calms me, Darcy. When I am with her, no one and nothing else matters and when I am away from her I crave her company."

Darcy grew more and more worried as his friend spoke. "Do you know if she shares your feelings, Bingley? Do you not think you need to give some consideration to Miss Bingley's words that she only wishes to marry you to oblige her family? What if this is the case?"

"I know her family situation is not good and that she will bring no dowry, but that does not automatically make her mercenary Darcy. You want to marry where there is money and good connections. Does that make you mercenary?"

"That is different, Charles, you know it is. I would not marry *only* for money. I have no need to do so. If all I wanted was a fat purse, I could have married any time in the last eight years. So yes, I will not marry someone who would shame the Darcy legacy, but no, it is not mercenary as I expect there to be some mutual regard, some true esteem between us."

"So, if Miss Bennet does not love me, but she esteems me, will that satisfy you? Will you then agree that she is not mercenary? I do not believe I am the first man to fall in love with her, so perhaps she is not so grasping as you think."

"Or perhaps no one else had a big enough bank account to satisfy her? Bingley, I am not saying it is so, I do not know the woman at all. But surely you must own that this is something to be considered before you make a decision to marry. Marriage is for life and if you make a mistake it cannot be undone. Such an important decision cannot be made in a month. It must be carefully thought out and the feelings of both parties must be taken into account."

"I am not planning to propose this day or tomorrow or even this week. And please do me the courtesy of assuming that I have taken thought to this. I have thought of little else since I first saw her. I will not make the decision now, I will wait, but I do not know how much longer I need to wait. Love does not have a timetable, Darcy. It just happens and there is nothing more to be done."

Bingley strode off then, leaving Darcy prey to a great uneasiness for his friend. He could not rid himself of the idea that Miss Bennet was a cold woman. But perhaps Bingley did not care? Miss Bingley was a cold woman, and Bingley seemed able to tolerate it easily. Of course, Miss Bingley did not bring with her a host of predatory women, all of whom would have a claim on him once they were family. Did Bingley not see that he was only trying to caution him, to save him from a loveless marriage? Deciding that he had borne enough, he went to his room to change into riding clothes. Perhaps a brisk ride would settle his mind, for right now he was quite certain the world was spinning out of his control.

Assumed Virtue

15

In the militia encampment just east of Meryton's main street two plays of very different kinds were taking place. Wickham had been furious when he had heard Colonel Forester's accusations and restrictions, so angry that he had been unable to try to come up with a convincing tale for Denny to explain away what he had heard. Now that Wickham had slept on it, he had concluded that it was just as well. Certainly Carter, perhaps Sanderson and one or two others would soon hear the story from Denny; it was too juicy a tale to keep to himself; there would be no regaining lost ground with them, and it would be a waste of effort to try.

His so-called friends would desert him, he thought resentfully, but he could spin it for the other Lieutenants and Captains, he could make it seem that they were taking Darcy's part because he was rich and well connected. A word dropped here or there, a long-suffering sigh, and his obvious forced confinement within the camp could work to his favor.

It should not have to be for very long. At least once or twice a week some sort of entertainment was planned that included at least some of the officers. No doubt, as time went on, the focus would shift away to him and back to the society of Meryton.

Right now he was being watched closely, but eventually the men set to guard him would grow bored. Oh, they would still stand at the tent flap, but they would not be so attentive, so quick to wonder if he was there if too long a time passed in silence. They would be listening for the return of their friends, hoping someone would be charitable enough to stop by and gossip before turning in.

For now, he would bear himself with obvious forced cheer, a man determined to return unkindness and injustice with courtesy and forbearance; there would be many who would find it plausible, and he only needed one, one sympathetic guard perhaps distracted by a good tale, and he would be gone.

While Wickham played his part for his compatriots, six men who could in no wise be called sympathetic had their own parts to play. Two new stable hands checked hooves and curried coats; a lowly new orderly strolled into Meryton on an errand for Colonel Forester. Two travelers took a room under the eaves at the White Horse inn that happened to have an excellent view of the militia camp and a certain Lieutenant's tent. And the cooks gossiped about the Colonel's increased appetite for lunch, for who would expect that someone had bedded down in the attic of the old house that served as the militia's headquarters?

The six watchers, though young, were battle hardened veterans, men who had little respect for the rank and file of the poorly trained and undisciplined militia. They had been through fire, storm and battle with their Colonel and had appreciated but not needed his explanation of Wickham's perfidy to agree to their assigned tasks. Wickham could count on the officers of the militia to grow bored and careless; the Colonel could count on his officers not to fail him.

In a London ballroom or the drawing room of a minor knight in a small English town, Richard Fitzwilliam would charm with his ease of manner and cheerful acceptance of all those around him. His kindness, his intelligence and his ready smile were genuine. He was the son of an Earl, but he had no improper pride, and his acquaintances enjoyed his company in part because he so obviously enjoyed theirs.

On the battlefield, he was not Richard Fitzwilliam, charming and genial son of the Earl and Countess of Matlock. On the battlefield he was the Colonel, and he was justly revered by his men. A strong and fair leader, a man who would fight with his men when guns were fired and for his men when the enemy was vanquished, he had earned the loyalty of those who served under him. They had seen too many good men die and too many scoundrels live to be concerned with abstract ideas of justice and they neither knew nor cared about Darcy. For them it was a much simpler equation: The Colonel wanted Wickham, so Wickham he would have.

Assumed Virtue

16

The residents of Netherfield gathered in the drawing room to await the arrival of the Earl of Matlock. As they waited, Richard watched the company more out of habit than interest. He was preoccupied on many fronts this day and he occupied himself in ordering things in his mind so he could set them each into a compartment to be pulled out and examined when necessary.

Wickham he could leave be for now. His men were in place, they knew their jobs and would do them well. Since there was nothing more he could do, he put it away.

Anne and Rosings Park could also go into its own compartment for now; he would discuss things in detail with his father so there was no need to worry about it now.

Darcy, however, was another matter. Richard was worried about Darcy; he was fairly sure his cousin was enamored of Miss Elizabeth and also that he had never been in love before; to fall in love with someone who did not meet his lofty standards of what was due him in a bride must be a confounding experience for him. Did Darcy even know he was in love? He might not, thought Richard. Darcy was so shielded that few ever touched him emotionally. He must be in a state of confusion and distress, but Richard had no idea how to bring up such a subject with his reticent cousin.

And, if he was being honest, Richard would have more sympathy had he not realized that the Meryton gossips were right. Darcy's shyness and reserve had turned into haughtiness and excessive pride, causing him to treat people disdainfully, ignoring them or speaking down to them in turn. He had been genuinely shocked when he had heard of his cousin insulting Miss Elizabeth, for it was certainly not the behavior of a gentleman; he knew how difficult it was for his shy cousin to make friends, but he felt that Darcy needed to take a long look at the effect his association with the Bingleys was having on him.

Bingley was far too dependent on Darcy's advice, setting his cousin up as the final arbiter of virtually all aspects of his life. Miss Bingley's malice and unwarranted hauteur seemed to bring out those same qualities in his cousin. Spending so much time with those who disdained all who they met while bringing neither intelligence nor character to the relationship was having a disastrous effect on Darcy. This was something he would have to think on carefully, for he cared deeply for his cousin and knew it would be a difficult conversation but one that they would have to have.

In contrast to the Colonel, Darcy, as was his habit, observed little of his companions, sitting in brooding silence. He had ridden hard, hoping to blow away the cobwebs and find some peace, but in the end he had done no more than tire himself and one of Bingley's horses. His mind seemed to run in circles; he was unsure of himself, and since it had been years since he had doubted himself or questioned his conclusions, his essential rightness, he had no experience to fall back on to understand what was happening and so floundered in his thoughts from one thing to another.

He did not condemn the Bennet women for wanting to make prudent matches or at least he did not condemn them much. Even though the heir was disabled, he would be the first to encourage one of the daughters to make a match with him to secure their futures. In fact, it might be the best match any of them could make for their lack of connections and dowries would surely limit their choices. This was really not a criticism; it was simply fact so how could that be wrong to say?

Did he look down on the company here? Of course he did. But did that make him haughty? Of course not. The people here were not members of the ton, their manners were unsophisticated, unpolished and sometimes even improper; although some few had no doubt attended university, their return to and immersion into such a limited society no doubt soon made them forget much of what they had learned. They had no wealth, no connections, nothing that would place them on an equal footing with a man such as himself who was a wealthy, well-connect, well-educated gentleman. Again, these were simply the facts. Was it really so wrong for him to acknowledge this? Why would anyone be offended by something so obvious?

Of course, there were always exceptions. Certainly, he would not wish to encourage Elizabeth to marry the parson. No matter that he was a good man, he was certainly not her match in intelligence, wit or zest for life. She needed a whole man, one who could show her a wider world than just this little corner of Hertfordshire. She was so completely above the rest of the company here that he could not fathom how everyone could not instantly see it. It was a shame that her fate would likely not be to marry such a man as he.

Then there was Wickham. Darcy could not stop his mind from returning again and again to his memories of his childhood, before time and vice had stolen his friend from him. He had had so few real friends in his life; his natural reticence, the isolation of Pemberley from any elevated neighbors, his own high standards; all of this had made it difficult for him to make friends and those he did make, he cherished. He knew Wickham's faults; his own beloved sister had suffered, still suffered from his avarice. There had been more years of contention between them than there had been of true friendship but somehow the earlier memories seemed to carry more weight, and so even though he knew that a strong man, a just man, would condemn Wickham he hesitated and was lost.

Richard had the clearer sight there. He had divined what Darcy could scarcely admit. It was not his father's memory that had stayed his hand; it was his own feelings that somewhere under the avarice and greed, somewhere buried beneath the jealousy and the profligate habits, his childhood friend still existed and that if somehow he could reach that child he could change the man.

Bingley had only one weighty matter on his mind, his latest angel, and as was his habit when distressed he fidgeted, in this case wandering to the windows to gaze mournfully in the direction of Longbourn then pacing back to his chair to stare vacantly at the company before rising to go once again to the windows. He was hesitant to go against the wishes of his sister and his friend. He had no confidence in his own judgement and had long depended on others to point out the correct course of action to him. But his feelings for Jane were more that they had been for any other of his many flirts and he was torn between his desire to make this beautiful creature his wife and his fear that his friend and his sister were right, and he would be making a horrid mistake. So he wandered and fretted and came to no conclusions.

The Hursts, complacent and perhaps a little sleepy after an evening of connubial bliss, also had little to say, but it went unnoticed in the ever flowing words that poured from Miss Bingley.

Miss Bingley was in high alt. Nothing could destroy her good mood this day. She was neither generous nor gracious, but she had a firm grasp of the mechanics of being a good hostess, so chambers were readied, menus created, possible entertainments planned. She had spent a large part of her morning penning short notes to her acquaintances in the ton, explaining her brevity with the excuse of all the work that needed to be done to prepare to host the Earl and Countess of Matlock at her brother's estate. Really, could it get any better?

Well, actually it could. She had already started her preparations for the ball her brother had decided he would host. Now if she could convince the Matlocks to remain at Netherfield long enough for them to attend it would be a coup worth boasting of for years. Equally important, if Darcy's noble relations were to attend, surely he would finally see her as a worthy mistress of Pemberley. The very thought sent a thrill of delight through her and so she spoke long on all the hard work that had gone into preparing for their guests, the work she had done and had still to do for the ball and noticed not at all that none of her companions were listening to her.

If the Earl's quiet arrival was anticlimactic for Miss Bingley, she did not show it. Curtseying and fawning her welcome to him, tossing orders to staff to make sure all knew she was in control she was the picture of satisfaction as she poured tea for everyone.

"How long will we have the pleasure of your company, my lord?" she simpered at him.

The Earl gave a faint smile and replied courteously. "I believe I will only be here for this one evening, Miss Bingley; however, if it is not too much of an inconvenience, I will return in a few days with the Countess and possibly with my niece."

"Of course not, my lord, we would be happy to host you whenever you are in area. I am sure no one could object to hosting you and, of course, your lovely wife, the Countess."

The conversation continued, Miss Bingley fawning and the Earl pleasantly responding with polite nothings until they could finally disperse.

By prearrangement, the two Fitzwilliams and Darcy repaired to Bingley's study after tea.

"Father, I am very grateful that Anne wishes to give me Rosings, and Darcy has pointed out how much it will benefit Anne's health, but still, I am hesitant to accept it. It does not feel right."

"I understand, son. It is not in your nature to accept anything you feel you have not earned, and this is a huge gift. But Darcy is correct; the doctor has seen Anne and will continue to see her every day while she is at Matlock House and he feels she will gradually recover but it will take time, perhaps as long as a year before she is truly feeling well. And even then, she is going to need to be wise in what she chooses to do to protect her energy as she is never going to be truly robust. She and your mother were discussing it and Anne pointed out that since she is unlikely to marry she would have made you her heir anyway. By doing this now she allows herself to live the life she wants instead of trying to force herself to be Mistress of Rosings and possibly damaging her health further. She cannot leave her mother in charge of Rosings any longer. And Darcy cannot really administer two such major estates as Rosings and Pemberley unless it is all he does. Accept it graciously my son. The world is not fair, and sometimes we are lucky enough that it is unfair to our advantage."

Richard nodded reluctantly, accepting his father's advice as sound but he knew it would take time for him to truly be comfortable with Anne's decision.

The Earl then spoke in more detail about what Anne had said, including her suggestions for funding repairs to the estate.

"I cannot sell the furnishings," argued Richard, appalled at the thought. "It is ghoulish to even think of it."

"Can, will and definitely should," disagreed Darcy firmly. "Richard, think man. You know what that place looks like. It is not only ugly, but also truly uncomfortable furniture. If Anne is correct and the attics are filled with the furniture that was there when we were boys, think what an improvement it would be. And you will need the funds, Richard. Lady Catherine has not put one groat into the estate that she could spend elsewhere. If you did not need the funds I would suggest burning it all in a grand bonfire but at this point monies are more important than fun."

Richard laughed a little at that, then settled in at the desk with a sigh. "Alright then, let us go over the paperwork you have with you and get things started. I cannot yet leave, but it should not be too much longer before I can do so."

"I will leave tomorrow morning but will return in a couple of days and I will bring your mother with me and I think we will bring Anne with us also. I do not wish to leave her at Matlock house with no one to protect her from her mother. I doubt she will be able to socialize once here, but she can rest here in the country as well, or perhaps even better, than in London. Our staff can handle Catherine at Matlock House for the short time we will be here. The sooner this is completed the sooner you and Anne can start your new lives."

The next day, after the Earl's departure, Charles announced his intention of visiting Longbourn. Richard enthusiastically agreed to accompany him while Darcy did so reluctantly.

As had happened occasionally in the past, only Jane and Elizabeth were available to greet their guests. Bingley promptly claimed Jane's attention, Darcy bowed shortly and stalked to the windows and Richard took a chair next to Elizabeth. Since both were sociable and friendly people, they were soon chatting easily though Richard glanced over at Darcy often enough to engage Elizabeth's curiosity.

"Is something amiss with Mr. Darcy?" she asked quietly.

"I was wondering the same thing. He has not moved from the window since we walked in," Richard replied, equally quietly.

That brought Lizzy's delightful, gurgling chuckle out. "Well, if that is all you are worried about then there is nothing wrong at all. It is what he always does."

Richard looked confused at that. "I do not understand."

"Mr. Darcy disdains us all," Lizzy replied to her voice cheerfully indifferent. "He generally refuses to speak with anyone not of his own party. And every time he accompanies his friend on a visit to Longbourn he stalks over to the windows, stares outside for the entire visit and never speaks or notices any of us. We are quite used to it, I assure you."

Mrs. Hill stepped in with the tea tray and was closely followed by Mary pushing Mr. Collins in his bath chair. Richard rose as they came in bowing to Miss Mary and giving Mr. Collins a friendly greeting. Still Darcy had not moved from his place at the window. Jane moved to the tea service and began dispensing cups, and Richard watched in some annoyance as Lizzy took a cup to Darcy which he accepted silently with only a curt nod.

As the conversation moved on around them, Mr. Collins caught Richard's eye. Moving next to the parson, Richard asked if he could be service. "Would it be possible for me to speak privately with you Colonel?" the parson softly requested. Richard nodded slightly then asked softly if he would like to meet then or sometime later?

"I have been in the chair for a couple of hours now. I will be returning to my rooms in just a few minutes, if you would not mind volunteering to conduct me to my room we could speak freely there." All went as planned and soon they were in the pleasant room with the doors open to the sweet scents of the rose garden.

Richard helped Mr. Collins out of the Bath chair and settled him reclining on a chaise comfortably. After exchanging some small pleasantries, Richard's curiosity could no longer be contained. "How may I be of service to you Mr. Collins?"

"I have a rather odd request of you, sir, and I will bear you no ill will if you cannot acquiesce, but I feel I would be remiss in not taking an opportunity presented to me." Mr. Collins paused in thought, staring out the at riot of blossoms just beyond his door, then directed a somber look at the Colonel.

"When my cousin Thomas was so generous as to send his coach to convey me here, he also arranged for me to stay for two days with his brother Gardiner in London and there to consult with a physician experienced in my form of injury. He was kind but adamant that little recovery beyond what I have already achieved is likely. He also stated that many times, the shock followed by the long inactivity is wearing on the heart; I could literally die at any time." Mr. Collins favored Richard with a wry smile. "Of course, that is indeed the human condition is it not? We live our lives refusing to admit that we know not when God will call us home; the difference of course is that for me there is no hiding from the knowledge.

"Mr. Bennet is in excellent health, but he too could die at any time, and it has been in my thoughts that more provision than he has already planned could be made for my dear cousins. I would like to repay their kindness to me. As I was praying on this, it came to me that I cannot go out and see to the tenants; indeed, there are days when the pain is too great for me to leave this room or even to sit in the bath chair or recline as I do now. How would I be able to do what is needed for the people who depend on this estate? So when Bennet offered to tutor me in running the estate, I proposed instead that we work together to break the entail; it is for three generations only, and I am the third one so between us, Mr. Bennet and I can petition in chancery court for this to be done with some hope of success. Longbourn then could be left to whichever daughter married a man willing to take the Bennet name and to administer the estate."

Richard nodded thoughtfully. "Yes, I can see that your injury would make it difficult; it is a kindly thought."

Mr. Collins nodded. "We have worked with Mr. Phillips and have the petition ready for the courts, but they need not only our signatures but that of two witnesses who are neither from the solicitor's office nor of the household. Sir William Lucas has agreed to be one of the witnesses. We could have another neighbor sign, we are surrounded by good men who would see the need; however, when Mrs. Bennet mentioned at lunch that your father was visiting, I instantly thought to request that you ask if he would consent to be the second signature. These things can linger in the courts for months or even years. The signature of the Earl of Matlock would give them good and sufficient cause to hear the case in a timely manner."

Richard regarded the parson with interest. It was true, the disposition of a minor estate near an unknown town would likely languish unheard for quite some time. That it was being presented by a solicitor who was no doubt a stranger to the court was also a drawback. The Matlocks were a powerful family, not just in society but in government and his father's signature would likely cut months if not years from the wait for a decision.

It was a selfless act on the part of Mr. Collins for he would be well within his rights to remain the heir. That he had decided to put aside his rights in favor of what would most benefit the estate and his cousins spoke volumes about his character. He thought of his cousin Anne doing the same thing and felt humbled.

"Yes, I will ask. And while I cannot guarantee his response, I believe he will agree to do it. He is a thoughtful and generous man and will recognize those same qualities in you, sir."

Mr. Collins shook his head. "No Colonel, do not credit me with more than I have earned. It is of no great matter to me, for as I said, I could never administer the estate; nor will I marry or father an heir of my own. I would like to see the Bennet line remain at Longbourn, they have been here for many generations and they are such good people. I do not slight my cousin, for he and Mrs. Bennet economized greatly when the girls were young so now they will not go dowerless when they wed. While they have provided as much as they could for their daughters, to know that they will be allowed to remain in their home after they lose Mr. Bennet must be of comfort to them."

There was a soft knock on the door and Jane, hearing Mr. Collins' bid her enter, came in bearing a tea tray and a kind expression. "Colonel Fitzwilliam, excuse me, Mr. Bingley and Mr. Darcy are preparing to return to Netherfield Park. Cousin I know you were weary earlier and did not stay in the drawing room for more than just a single cup of tea. I thought to bring you another cup and the lemon biscuits you particularly like."

Richard had risen when she came in and politely took the tea tray from her; he saw her settled in the chair, a genuine and pleased smile gracing her features as she served her cousin. Miss Bennet, he thought, was much too good for Bingley.

Assumed Virtue

17

The next week passed swiftly for the residents of Meryton and the surrounding estates. It had been a decade since the big ballroom at Netherfield Park had been used for its stated purpose. It had housed a family or two in the spring flooding several years ago and had served as a makeshift infirmary during the influenza epidemic back in '05. But no ball had been held there since the death of the older generation who had held Netherfield. The son had never been interested in returning and the estate had been promptly let. That the Bingleys were to host a ball was thrilling.

Excited mamas and daughters descended on the shops of Meryton in search of new shoe roses and ribbons and even, for some few, the purchase of a new ballgown. Amused papas practiced dance steps with anxious daughters and tried to dodge the whirlwinds that were their female relatives.

At Netherfield Caroline's shrill voice could be heard at all hours of the day, chivvying the servants, complaining about the lack of supplies and intelligent help, demanding her sister and brother attend to her and take on task after task. When he could, Bingley escaped to visit Jane, but it was a rare occurrence that week.

As they had planned, the Earl had returned and brought his spouse and his niece with him. Anne, of course, had had to rest upon arrival for travel was still difficult for her, but even so she was not looking so washed out as Richard had expected. The Earl and Countess were preoccupied with Anne and with the smooth transition of Rosings, so except for the Colonel, the Fitzwilliams were not much in evidence in the neighborhood; the family crisis precipitated by Anne taking hold of her inheritance and then promptly passing it on engendered an enormous amount of paperwork that needed to be dealt with and hours of conversations hammering out details. Correspondence between the Earl and his solicitors and the Rosing's solicitors flew back and forth and the Earl's grooms were pressed into service as express riders.

The Rosings Park steward had been informed of the changes to come and he was in almost daily communication with Richard who met with Anne, his father and Darcy daily going over the missives and learning what was needed to begin taking up the reins of the estate. The Countess spent long hours with Anne, sometimes walking with her and encouraging her, sometimes just listening as the young woman who had been long neglected poured out years of hurt and heartache and loneliness; the Countess felt she needed to come to terms with her past before they could begin truly planning for her future in Bath.

While the Colonel's days were filled with details on the estate, his evenings were more pleasantly spent. He had explained the Longbourn situation to his father, and while the Earl might not have agreed under other circumstances, like Richard he was immediately struck with the similarities to what Anne was doing, both of them giving up their inheritances for the sake of others and so he affixed his signature to the petition to dissolve the entail and even included a letter authorizing his solicitors to be of aid to Mr. Phillips in presenting the petition. The Colonel had returned the papers to Longbourn and had found himself warmly welcomed by Mr. Collins and Mr. Bennet.

Thomas Bennet, Richard had discovered, was a most interesting man. Like himself he was a second son, and not expected to inherit. Unlike himself, Mr. Bennet had been included with his older brother in the training to run the estate; he had just begun to teach at Oxford when he lost his father and brother and returned to the estate, a well-educated neophyte. He was fortunate in his marriage for not only did he and Mrs. Bennet clearly esteem one another, she had been in full agreement with him that economies while the children were young would be felt less by them and allow the Bennets to invest in the future of their offspring.

Another fortunate occurrence from the marriage was his brother Gardiner. Taking a small inheritance, Edward Gardiner had invested it in business and had become so successful that he now, only twenty years later, had been able to purchase Netherfield. Along the way he had grown the Bennets' wealth significantly. There were few fathers with such a small estate who could dower five daughters adequately, but from what he gleaned there would be more coming to the daughters than was generally known. And, if the petition to break the entail was granted, one of them would bring Longbourn to her marriage.

So, while his family was not keeping company, the Colonel, a gregarious man by nature, saw no need to spend his evenings going over everything they had done that day again. Instead, he accepted an invitation from Colonel Forester to dine with the officers, attended a musical evening at the Gouldings and twice visited Longbourn late enough in the day to be invited to remain to sup, which invitations he gladly accepted. He found he enjoyed the company of this family and as they grew comfortable with him they felt free to include him in spirited exchanges on books and poetry, on the latest news and on estate concerns and one evening, heaven help him, he even found himself in an involved debate regarding the nature of man.

It gave him much to think on both for himself and for his cousin. The more time he spent with Miss Bennet, the more intrigued with her he became. And the more time he spent with Miss Elizabeth the more he was convinced that she would be perfect for Darcy. She was kind but strong, witty and intelligent, well read and at ease in company. She could soften Darcy's hard edges, while he could open up whole new worlds for her, allowing her to indulge her curiosity without hinderance. And he had discovered that Mrs. Bennet had been a fine teacher to her girls; no estate would suffer at their hands like Rosings had under his aunt's reign. They knew what the mistress of an estate should do, and they were kind and generous women along with it.

Darcy had never been easy in company and was even less so if women were part of the group. Richard wondered if his cousin saw how excellent a match Elizabeth was too and was simply too shy to try to come to know her better or if his hesitancy was based on his burgeoning hauteur.

Finally, two days before the ball was to be held, the Fitzwilliam family gathered for a private supper in the smaller, generally unused breakfast parlor to discuss their progress. There was no doubt Caroline was offended by their request for privacy, but she had acquiesced and made the arrangements though with no good grace.

"Well, we are well on the way to winding ourselves out of this maze at last," Lord Fitzwilliam said wearily. "The petitions have been filed and it will be another week, I think, before everything is finalized but the solicitors are finally satisfied that everything is in order for the transfer of the property to Richard. Have you resigned your commission son? I keep meaning to bring it up but then another letter arrives and it flies from my mind."

"No sir, not yet. In all the confusion surrounding us, I believe it has been easy to forget that I have a mission to accomplish here. It will not take much longer, only another two to three days, I think. After that, I will gladly put off the red and become a landlord."

Darcy fixed his cousin with a rather grim stare at that, but Richard only nodded slightly at him, indicating they would discuss Wickham later.

"Tell me, Father, have you heard of a man of trade named Edward

Gardiner?"

"I have indeed, son. He is very well respected by those of us who are wise enough to know that owning land is not enough, that diversity in investing protects our estates; he seems to have a great talent for finding the perfect investment at the perfect time. We have some of our funds placed with Gardiner Enterprises and have had a great success with him; Darcy I believe you also have invested there. Why do you ask?"

"Mr. Gardiner is brother to Mrs. Bennet. She kindly wrote to him for me explaining some of the situation at Rosings Park and has received his reply. He has suggested sending two trusted men to Rosings Park with me once I can come there myself. We will inventory what is to be sold and for a very reasonable fee they will pack and transport everything to London for me; Gardiner will arrange an auction which is what he recommends. He tells me that this will likely garner the most funds from the sale."

"That is wonderful, Richard," exclaimed the Countess. "I have known the Gardiners for years and they are trustworthy and discreet."

"You know this tradesman, Aunt?" asked Darcy, astonished.

"Indeed. They are not guests in my ballroom, but I have taken tea with Mrs. Gardiner more than once and I know she would not be out of place should I invite her. She is a charming woman, the granddaughter of a gentleman from Derbyshire and has been kind enough to escort me to visit her husband's warehouse when he has a shipment of fabrics she feels I would be interested to see. It has saved me a substantial sum over the years. And the income from my dowry has been invested with them also." She smiled lovingly at her younger son. "I have never needed to draw on my dowry of course; since we cannot sever any property for you, I have long been investing the interest for you so you have also been the recipient of

Mr. Gardiner's talents. I do not have the exact figures but some five and ten thousand is going to be available to you as an emergency fund as you take over Rosings."

"Mother, I had no idea!"

"No, we did not discuss this with you son. It was not enough yet to support you in the lifestyle of the son of an Earl, and clearly not enough to purchase an estate of any size. I know you have been frugal with your allowance, so we felt that with your savings and our investments at least you could have a comfortable lifestyle once you chose to retire. With an estate in hand, the funds will serve you well."

"Now on to other pressing matters," she continued. "Anne and I have been writing to Mrs. Bates at the house in Bath. Because it has been leased regularly, everything has been maintained in good repair there. She feels some updating of furnishings will be desired but nothing that would need to addressed immediately. Apparently Catherine's opulent tastes were not given full reign in Bath so while it may need some changes, they will not be onerous nor immediately needed. The staff there are preparing everything for Anne and Mrs. Jenkinson's arrival and they are looking forward to having a de Bourgh in residence again."

Anne nodded enthusiastically. "Her letters have been most informative. I am excited about this new adventure. I do not know how much longer we will be at Netherfield, Aunt, but I was wondering now that I have some returning energy and strength, would you be willing to work with me on what I need to know to manage a house in town? I am amazing ignorant about the duties of the Mistress of the house."

The Countess beamed at her niece. "I would be thrilled Anne. And I will not bore our gentlemen with talk of lace, but once we are ready we will need to discuss your wardrobe. Your mother has been locked into the fashions of a decade ago and really, her color choices suit her far better than you my dear. Mrs. Jenkinson will also need new things as she is going to be your companion and will need to be dressed as a gentlewoman and not as a servant. We will address that later, for although I do not want to pander to our men's concerns, they are quite correct that all these other necessary arrangements must take precedence."

The gentlemen laughed at the Countess' gentle tease. "Where are we in the process of relocating Lady Catherine?" asked Darcy.

"We are moving along quite briskly there, too, Darcy. The Dower house is well maintained and furnished of course. The housekeeper at Fairwinds has overseen a thorough cleaning and is now both arranging to transfer some staff and to hire more as needed. Hilliard has someone seeing to the grounds, though again it has been basically maintained; he felt the gardens needed updating and refreshing and that preparations for an expanded kitchen garden for the household needed to be put into place. Several of my senior staff from the London house have traveled to Rosings and are in the process of packing Lady Catherine's personal items. I should be receiving an inventory of jewelry shortly and I have requested the inventory of the de Bourgh pieces be sent to me. They will stay with the estate, and some pieces I will allow my sister to keep. Anne, however, will have first choice of any she wishes and then we will consign the rest to be sold."

They were silent awhile, enjoying their dinner then Anne, who had been thinking over everything she had heard asked quietly, "So you believe we should be returning to London very shortly after the ball?" At the Earl's nod, she continued, "Then shall we all be going to Matlock house? When will you be transporting Lady Catherine to Derbyshire?"

"I believe we can all travel together as far as London. Then Richard, and Darcy if he wishes, can escort you to Bath and Audrey and I will take my sister to Derbyshire."

"I will inform Miss Bingley and have my dresser prepare a ballgown and my jewelry for the ball," said the Countess. "I assure you, our attendance at her function will more than compensate her for the inconvenience of our stay. She will be thrilled that you and I attend my dear."

The Earl nodded. "Not perhaps my preferred way to spend an evening but not too bad a price to pay."

"Actually sir, I think you will enjoy it more than you imagine now. These are country folk, it is true, but there are some very highly educated people here and you will, I think, enjoy meeting and conversing with many of them. And even those who are not so very interesting are pleasant and welcoming."

Darcy pursed his lips in disagreement.

"You do not think so Darcy?"

"I do not. I have seen little here that would inspire such praise. Miss Bingley is not far off in her appraisal that the company is quite savage."

And with that the ladies retired for the evening, the Earl went to the study and Darcy and the Colonel sought their entertainment in the billiards room.

18

Darcy and the Colonel played the first game without much conversation, but then William decided he was ready to address his concerns with his cousin.

"So you think Wickham will run in the next couple of days?"

Richard nodded. "I do. In fact, I think he will run the night of the ball. My men in the stables report that he has briefly stopped by daily for the last three days, being overly friendly with the hands. And Perkins, my lead man, says there is an air of anticipation about him. Nothing overt, it is subtle but if you are watching for it, the change is plain to see."

"Is that all you have to go on? That he visits the stables and seems like he might be anticipating something? Even if true, perhaps it is something else altogether."

"Darce, think about it. What would he be anticipating? More restrictions? Fewer funds? No, he is going to run and it is going to be soon. The night of the ball is the perfect opportunity for him. Normally only a few of the officers are at any event, but all of the officers not on duty have been invited to attend the ball and that will include all the senior officers; they are the ones who are least likely to be swayed by Wickham's demeanor of a man wronged and bearing up under injustice. He is going to be guarded by someone likely to have bought into his latest fiction."

"So, you are setting him up?"

"I thought you were reconciled to our course, cousin? And yes I suppose you could look at it that way, but it would be the case regardless. The junior officers are going to be left behind with perhaps one senior officer to be in charge of the camp and that would happen Wickham or no Wickham. We are not in enemy territory, there is no danger to the camp, so there would not be a reason to leave the senior officers on duty. Wickham is cunning but he is not smart. He will see his opportunity and never consider that it is our opportunity also."

"What do you mean cunning but not smart? I have always considered Wickham to be intelligent."

"But he is not. Put aside your feelings and look at it rationally Darce. He is the son of a steward, with neither a livelihood nor any connections. He is a terrible gambler, yet he continues to game more than he can afford. He has enemies everywhere he has ever lived, indeed most places he has lived he would be hunted like a rabid dog should he return and yet he does not change his ways. He has tormented a man of many times his wealth and power for years, even plotting to bring disgrace to the family name, thus destroying what could have been a connection of merit. How can that be anything other than stupid? A man of even moderate intelligence would have realized how little success his current course has brought to him and would change his ways."

Richard gestured at Darcy with his glass. "He was your friend Darcy. How much better would his circumstances now be if he had remained your friend? If he had not let envy eat him alive, he could be comfortably established somewhere; if he had just had the intelligence to cease bedeviling you and retained your good will, what could he have become? He would not even have had to work hard for you as you have always been very forgiving of him. He could be an under steward at one of your smaller estates if he had not wanted to take orders, or he could have asked for your advice and help with the funds you gave him and be successful in some other field by now."

Darcy frowned, "I never thought of that, never looked at it from an outside view."

"I know; it is hard to do when you are enmeshed in it, but worth the effort I believe. It struck me rather forcefully when I was dining with the Bennets last evening."

At Darcy's look of distaste, Richard snorted. "Darce, you are letting your feelings interfere with your thought processes. Do not try to tell me you are not intrigued by Miss Elizabeth Bennet. And it is causing you to convince yourself that she and everyone else here is worthless. But that is wrong, you know that it is wrong." Richard waved aside Darcy's protest. "That is a discussion for another time. We are discussing Wickham. And what struck me was this: Edward Gardiner and George Wickham had basically the same start in life; one is now a landed gentleman and wealthy, one has nothing."

At William's astonished look, Richard continued. "Look at the parallels Will. Both men are not of gentle stock but have ties to a gentleman. Both men were well educated. Both men received a bequest that was meant to help set them up in life. Gardiner took his inheritance, invested it, worked hard and many very long days to build a business and he has now purchased an estate; he has married the granddaughter of a gentleman and has twin boys to carry on his legacy both in business and as a landowner. Wickham took his inheritance, wasted it, and is now a lowly militia lieutenant, starting a military career at his late age and not working at that either. By the time Gardiner was Wickham's age he was already successful. Wickham has accomplished precisely nothing."

"I understand what you are saying but I see him still, I think, as the bright and charming lad he was, my friend who could always make me laugh and enjoy life. Perhaps you are right, it is past time that I stopped seeing him as such and look at who he is today." Darcy sighed. "I have let my memories and the wishes of my father, and his father guide my thinking in this too long."

Darcy meditated on it for a little time then asked, "What do you think he will do?"

"I will not say it will be precisely this way as I cannot always understand his thought processes, but I know what kind of a man he is and have enough experience with his kind to give you a good estimation. What I think he will do is this: he will take the opportunity as everyone is leaving to slip out of his tent. Once everyone is gone his best bet would be to sneak off into the night directly, but I do not believe he will do so. Colonel Forester garnished his check to pay his debts, so he has no funds to speak of and he is too lazy to leave on foot. I think he will sneak into some few tents and steal what cash and small items he can, then I think he will hide near the stables until the hands leave for mess; he will steal a horse and run toward London as a large city is easiest to hide in and it is so close. Three of my men are going to be stationed with their mounts near the road, three will remain in camp. Two of each threesome of my men will follow him and the third will report back to me. I will have a horse loosely bridled and ready to ride after him and we will have him in hand that night."

"So not just a horse thief. He will steal from the men in his unit, men who he has lived and worked with every day." Even as he grieved the loss of his boyhood companion, Darcy could not help the disgust he felt at that realization.

Richard nodded somberly.

"That is what I think. And although it may not feel like it to you this betrayal is even worse than his attempted seduction of Georgiana. He will steal from men he has sworn an oath would be his brothers; men who he should be willing to protect with his very life. It is the essence of military life, Darce, that you are not only fighting for King and Country, but you are also fighting for the man beside you, your brother in arms. And he is going to betray those men, betray that trust, without hesitation or remorse."

He sighed and placed his empty glass on a side table. "For that betrayal, hanging is literally too good for him."

Assumed Virtue

19

The day of the ball dawned sunny, with a promise of some heat in the afternoon. Everyone breathed a sigh of relief that no clouds were sighted and in homes all over the neighborhood preparations began early in the day.

At Netherfield, the final blooms were placed in vases, every polished surface was checked again for perfection, the kitchen staff ran ragged to do both the final preparations for the supper for the ball and to make sure all the residents were fed during the day. In most houses, breakfast would be limited, and the midday meal would be cold meats and cheese and bread to allow the kitchen staff the time and extra hands needed. No such consideration would be allowed by Miss Bingley.

At Longbourn, baths started early in the day. It was too hot for fires, so hair had to be washed and slowly brushed dry early in the day; the new dresses were carefully scrutinized for any loose thread or pulled seam. The Bennet ladies were lucky indeed that Mrs. Gardiner's seamstress had their measurements and Mr. Gardiner had just received a shipment of gorgeous silks. The new gowns had arrived only two days before the ball and had been accompanied with matching threads for adjustments after final fittings and matching shoe roses. Mrs. Bennet looked elegant in lavender and silver; Jane was stunning in icy blue. Lizzy and Mary, so alike in coloring, glowed in cream and jade for Lizzy and muted yellow for Mary.

Kitty and Lydia rushed from bedroom to bedroom, helping with ribbons here and lacings there. Their excitement was contagious and by the time the four ladies and one gentleman were boarding the coach the two girls had well-nigh exhausted themselves from sheer giddiness. The ladies who were out shared a little gentle teasing at the expense of the younger two, but it was affectionately done and whiled away the short carriage ride to Netherfield.

Every window in the great house seemed to shine with candles and footmen were stationed to aid the ladies in descending their carriages and gaining the main doors without mussing their gowns. Cloaks and hats were handed to waiting servants and the Bennet party joined the short queue to the receiving line. There Charles and Caroline and the Hursts greeted the guests, each according to their personalities. Charles was ebullient, Caroline coldly polite, the Hursts indifferently courteous.

The ballroom did not disappoint. Ribbons and flowers adorned the room, candlelight reflected from crystals hung in the great chandelier and in mirror backed sconces along the walls of the room. As they moved out of the receiving line the Bennets were greeted by a smiling Colonel Fitzwilliam and a somber and silent Darcy. The Colonel begged leave to present the party to his parents and led them to where an elegant older couple stood, the gentlemen slightly portly but dressed in a finely cut suit; the woman shining in silk and lace with costly jewels glinting in the candlelight. The Earl and Countess had dressed to honor the company that night and were a sight such as no one had seen in a Meryton ballroom.

Introductions were made, and the Bennets were unsurprised when the Earl stared hard at Mr. Bennet. Finally, Mr. Bennet took pity on him and said softly, "Surely you have not forgotten George's friend Bennet from Oxford, my Lord?"

The look of concentration vanished from his face, and he gave a chuckle, "My good heavens, it is Tommy Bennet all grown up and the father of a bevy of beauties. I could not place the face though I knew I had seen you somewhere."

Bennet laughed along with him. "The years bring vast changes, my Lord. Even your vaunted memory for faces must bow sometimes before father time. And yes, a bevy indeed, and two more waiting in the wings at home, though none in my eyes can match their mother for loveliness."

"Mrs. Bennet, I understand that my sister's parson, Mr. Collins, now resides with you. Will he not be joining us this evening?" asked the Countess.

"No, my lady, this type of evening would be too difficult for him. You may know that he uses a bath chair to get around due to an injury. An evening of music or conversation in the home of one our neighbors who understand his situation is within his capabilities, for we can come early to get him comfortably situated and leave once his energies flag or his pain is too great. He is content to remain home with my two youngest for they will read to each other, play chess and backgammon and enjoy each other's company this night."

"Yes, I understand," replied the Countess sympathetic. "Well, I am sure we will all enjoy a lovely evening, and your other daughters will have much to relate to their younger sisters."

Mrs. Bennet agreed, then curtseyed and moved on to make way for others to be introduced to the noble couple but both the Earl and Countess determined to speak more with the Bennets once the dancing started and the older couples took their places on the sidelines.

The Colonel asked Jane for her second set, Elizabeth for her third and Mary for the fourth, explaining that since his father would not be dancing he would be responsible for opening the ball with Miss Bingley, even though, he added with a droll look, he was probably not her first choice of partner. The second son of an Earl, with no wealth or estate that she knew of, was not someone Miss Bingley would waste much civility on. But even Miss Bingley's ambitions must bow before protocol; after his parents, Richard was the highest ranking person in attendance. Besides, Darcy never danced the first dance because it was considered a significant one and he did not wish to raise expectations.

Of course, being Darcy, he did not just sit out the first dance; he asked no one to dance, staring at Elizabeth then tearing his eyes away to gaze around the ballroom, then watching her again, entirely unable to resist drinking in her beauty. The green of the silk gown seemed to enhance the green and gold flecks in her chocolate eyes, the riotous curls were caught up high on her head then two thick curls had been allowed to cascade down over one shoulder. She seemed to Darcy to be the embodiment of beauty and grace and her joy at being there brought an added glow to her beauty. Bingley might think Jane the pinnacle of beauty but for Darcy no one shone brighter than Elizabeth.

As neighbors and friends began to fill the ballroom the Bennets were caught up in conversation and greetings with all. The Colonel was kept busy bringing the county's notables to his parents for introductions, asking various daughters to dance and presenting a carefree appearance. In the back of his mind, as with Darcy, the thought of George Wickham hovered, waiting like a villain in a play for his cue to come onstage.

As the red coats of the officers began to fill the ballroom, at the militia encampment George Wickham ran through his plan again and checked his supply sack carefully. He did not think he would need to stop anywhere in his flight this night, but he had taken some thought to the possibility of a thrown shoe or bad weather and secreted some bread wrapped in a linen square his bag. His few coins were in his purse, and he had replaced the distinctive red coat with dark blue to blend in with the dark.

He had listened carefully during the shared meals with his fellow officers and so knew who had won at cards and dice most recently. He had planned the shortest route to various tents to relieve the men of their excess coins then on to the stables where he would wait for his chance to borrow a mount. London was only a little over three hours if he pushed his horse and he had decided to make for Mrs. Younge's boarding house. She would have forgiven him for the failure of the autumn by now and even if she was still a little angry, she had never been proof against his charms. By morning he would be a free man again.

Assumed Virtue

20

Charles Bingley was a happy man. Held captive by his sister and her demands this week past, he was finally in company with the angelic Jane Bennet for more than a few minutes. He would swear his heart had stopped when he had taken in her beauty in the receiving line and, once his guests were all welcomed, he had led her to the place of honor to open the ball with him. Surely that must make his attentions plain to her.

He drank in her beauty, murmuring compliments to her eyes, her hair, her gown, her smile each time they came together in the figures of the dance. Jane Bennet bore it all with serenity, kindly allowing him to babble on. No one would guess that the thought that surely this set would end soon, and she would have a more congenial partner next was the true reason she could tolerate his silly conversation with calm composure.

Lizzy opened the dance with her dear friend and childhood partner in crime John Lucas. She and John had never had a romantic inclination for each other but were fast friends and so spoke easily and freely to each other. And Thomas Bennet had honored his third daughter with the opening dance, declaring that since it was still her first season and certainly her first grand ball, the honor must be his to lead her out. Father and daughter moved easily through the steps, having practiced together many times and so Mary was able to overcome any vestiges of shyness and simply enjoy herself.

Later in the evening Darcy finally succumbed to his unspoken desires and asked Elizabeth to dance. He knew it was unwise, he had danced only with Mrs. Hurst and Miss Bingley as their family was hosting the evening and so propriety dictated that as their houseguest he dance once with each. He should not single her out in this way. He had spent the evening prowling the edges of the dance floor, scowling at Elizabeth's dance partners and speaking to no one; but there was only so much even a man of his iron control could take. He had to have one dance with this beautiful siren; just one dance to remember with fondness after he left Hertfordshire never to return.

They danced at first in silence, Darcy looking forbidding and Lizzy contemplative. Finally she broke the silence.

"Come Mr. Darcy, we must have some conversation."

"Do you generally converse while dancing, Miss Elizabeth?"

"Some effort must be made at civility do you not agree, Mr. Darcy? It would be very odd I think to spend fully half an hour in company in silence. It need not be much, just general observations. I could comment on the number of couples and you could respond with a memory of a similar ball from your past."

"I am quite certain I have never been to a similar ball, Miss Elizabeth. Balls in London are rather different than a country ball, no matter how elegant the appointments."

"Do you indeed find it so? People are just people anywhere are they not? Some good, some not, some interesting, some not. All the varieties can be found in almost any setting I would think."

"I cannot agree with you. The style of company, the educated and elevated conversation of the highest society cannot be replicated in such a setting as this. Perhaps had you experienced this you would understand."

Lizzy's eyes flashed at the implied insult, but she would not make a scene, nor would she allow him to ruin her enjoyment of this night. Insufferable man. She wondered why he had asked her to dance just to insult her. "Perhaps you have the right of it Mr. Darcy. Silence is not such a bad thing in some dance partners."

Darcy, having no idea he had just greatly insulted her and thinking she too wished to just enjoy their limited time together, nodded gravely and they completed the set without speaking again; he escorted her back to her mother, bowed to both ladies in silence and moved away quickly, certain that his heart was beating so loudly it could be heard above the noise of the crowd.

"Lizzy, you look a little distressed my dear."

Lizzy shook her head. "Oh mama, I do not understand that man at all. He asks me to dance, does not wish to speak with me, insults my intelligence and leaves without even the courtesy of thanking me. How is one to understand such a taciturn and haughty person?"

"He insulted you again?"

"Oh not so egregiously as at the Assembly mama. But he made it clear that the company is so far below that to which he is accustomed that there is no enjoyment to be had in this night for him."

"Well my dear, obviously there is only one thing to be done," replied Mrs. Bennet with a smile. "You must enjoy every single moment from here on out for someone should benefit from all of Miss Bingley's hard work and take enjoyment from it; since Mr. Darcy refuses to do so, we must be sure to be more than pleased."

Lizzy giggled at her mother and agreed, then moved off to speak with her friend Charlotte who was standing nearby.

"Well my dear friend, apparently you are tolerable enough to dance with this night."

"I have no idea why he wished to dance with me Charlotte; he certainly gets no enjoyment from my company."

"Really, have you no idea? It is in my mind that he watches you a good deal."

"No doubt to criticize me in his mind for impertinence or ignorance or heaven knows what. Really Charlotte, he can barely open his mouth without making it clear how far below him we all are, and I assure you he includes me in his disapprobation." Lizzy shook her head then smiled at her friend, "Enough. Enough time wasted speaking of that impossible and unpleasant man. How have you fared for partners this night, dear Charlotte?" And so, Lizzy turned the conversation, determined that Mr. Darcy would have no place in her thoughts again.

It was after the supper set that a footman discreetly approached Colonel Fitzwilliam and spoke in a soft murmur, letting him know that a person had requested he be told that this was the summons he had been expecting. The Colonel nodded then softly asked him to let Colonel Forester know and turned back to continue his conversation. Then, with a kind word here and a genial comment there he made his way unobtrusively out of the ballroom. Once out of sight of the company the genial manner vanished, the gentleman giving way to the soldier. Moving quickly he headed for the stables and there met with one of his watchers.

"Just as we thought, sir. He left his red coat, went into three tents, then waited behind the stables until mess was called. We left then Parker doubled back. He did not just take a horse, sir, he took the Colonel's horse. Forester is not going to be happy to hear that!"

Richard smiled grimly, "No, it is just another sign that he does not think things through. If he had taken the oldest nag in the stables there might have been some small consideration given to him.

Forester waxed almost poetic about his new steed; he will be livid that Wickham took him."

As they spoke the men had been readying and mounting their horses and they moved quickly toward the London road.

"Is he armed?"

"I checked his tent; his sword and pistol were left behind, but I would assume he has a pistol that is his own and not one that is a service issue. No way to tell until we come upon him."

Thirty minutes later they found their men and a disheveled Wickham, hands bound behind him and sitting a horse on a lead coming toward them back to Meryton.

On seeing them, Wickham immediately appealed to the Colonel. "Richard, thank heavens you are here. These miscreants have intercepted me as I was on my way to London on an errand for Colonel Forester. It is quite urgent; they need to release me at once."

Richard shook his head. "An urgent errand for Colonel Forester? Well, Lieutenant, the obvious solution is for us to return to camp and let your Colonel handle disciplining the men, would you not agree?"

Wickham squirmed at that. "Well, no, I do not think there is any reason to disturb the Colonel, if you would just have these men let me go, I will be on my way."

Richard laughed at that. "I am sure you would be, Wickham, I am sure you would. You would sell your Colonel's horse and disappear into the bowels of the city an hour after arrival. No, Wickham, we will return to camp and discuss this in detail with your Colonel." Then as the men began riding back toward Meryton he moved his horse closer to Wickham's to say softly, "We hang horse thieves you know Wickham. Think on that as we ride." And took a dark satisfaction at the terror on Wickham's face at his words.

Colonel Forester was indeed livid that Wickham had stolen his horse. The steed had been paid for from his own funds and had been carefully selected; when it was discovered that Wickham's travel sack was loaded with coins and small items belonging to other men in the unit that could be easily pawned Forester's rage was awesome to see. After castigating Wickham thoroughly, he directed the men to place him irons and led him to the small building that served as a jail for the community. There were no amenities, just a chamber pot, a straw pallet and a stout door to the windowless room.

"Well, it is done now. He will hang and good riddance I say," muttered Forester "He stole my horse, Fitzwilliam. And he stole from his brother officers."

Richard nodded, "Yes, it is past time for justice to catch up with him. My men and I will leave at first light tomorrow and convey him to London to face the military courts. Can you write up a statement including all the stolen items for me? Military justice is quick, they will probably try him and hang him before the week is out."

21

Darcy slept poorly that night, his thoughts consumed with the dark haired beauty who haunted his dreams and woke tired and grumpy. His mood went from bad to worse when his valet handed him a note from Richard.

Darce,

Our suppositions were correct. W stole his Colonel's new steed, stole coins and small goods from his fellows and fled toward to London. My men intercepted him, and we returned here for what remained of the night. I will not accompany the family to London today but will leave at first light to convey W to London.

I will have Forester's statement and my men will bear witness to the thefts and the capture of W as he deserted; however, I intend to be there at least through the trial. I need to see that done. If Anne has not yet journeyed on to Bath, I will escort here there after W is dealt with; if she is already gone I will visit her then go on from there to Rosings.. As long as I am in London and will be able to return my men to their unit, I will take the opportunity to resign my commission.

I would suggest you send an express to Mrs. Annesley so she can inform G. Militia desertions have been climbing and they will no doubt publish an account to try to deter others. They may not mention him by name, but then again they may, and it is better that G learns of his fate from someone who can break it gently to her than for her to come upon it in the paper.

R

His message to Bingley was in quite a different vein and was delivered to the company as they gather to break their fast in the late hours of the morning.

Charles,

Please accept my apologies that I could not take my leave in a more traditional manner, but my duties demanded my immediate return to London. I thank you and your sister for your gracious hospitality. Please convey my sincerest regards to your kind sister and the Hursts.

Yours, etc.

Colonel Richard Fitzwilliam

"Well," huffed Caroline, "what does he mean by all this rushing about? He certainly never mentioned that he would have to leave so abruptly. Why would he not wait and escort us to London?"

Darcy answered in unemotional tones. "His family was aware that he had a mission to accomplish while here Miss Bingley. That does not take away from his enjoyment of the company. The mission was successfully completed, and he must return to London to report. No doubt there is paperwork to do. There is always paperwork to do when dealing with the government."

Caroline sniffed disagreeably, but let the matter drop as she was anxious to supervise the closing of the house and returning to London. Now that she had experienced it, she realized she hated living in the country as opposed to being a guest at someone's estate.

And Netherfield was close to London, to Meryton and to the neighboring estates. Pemberley was far more isolated than Netherfield. Once she was Mrs. Darcy they would need to spend only a few weeks each year at Pemberley and would have to be sure to invite a large group of guests for entertainment during their short stays. No doubt Darcy would oblige her once they were wed. But he would never offer for her while in Hertfordshire; Miss Elizabeth Bennet, as brazen a flirt as ever lived in Caroline's opinion, was just too distracting.

Assumed Virtue

22

When the Netherfield Party left in a caravan to London, Caroline Bingley entertained hopes that they would stop at Matlock House before continuing on to the Bingley town house. Surely the Countess would offer refreshment when they arrived. She longed to be able to tell her friends that she had arrived in London with the Matlocks and then had tea with the Countess. Alas, had she consulted her brother perhaps he could have suggested it but when Darcy said that he planned to go directly home and would be leaving the party once in London, he naturally decided to do the same thing. They barely arrived in the city itself before the Bingley carriage and wagon turned away from the Matlock and Darcy carriages.

Long inured to Caroline's complaints, Bingley ignored her anger at his arrangements and simply stared out the window and thought about Jane Bennet. She was truly so beautiful, and he thought she liked him. Were Caroline and Darcy right about her? That she would only marry him for his money. Well, what if they were right? She would be his wife and she had never shown any sign of ever being unkind so perhaps that was enough. But what if it was not enough? Once he was married there was no going back, Darcy was definitely right about that.

They arrived hot, tired and dusty to an unprepared household. In her anxiety to get them out of Hertfordshire Caroline had forgotten to send ahead to alert the London servants that they were on their way. That it was her fault for not informing them did nothing to assuage her fury or rudeness. It was what her family expected from her, but it did not make it easier to bear.

The Earl, the Countess and Anne arrived to a peaceful and prepared household. The Countess, an experienced mistress, had informed Mrs. Nicholls of their plans, secure in the knowledge that she would see to notifying the Matlock house staff. Cool baths were already waiting, and the party immediately went to their suites. It had been a short journey, but it was dreadfully hot that day even in the country; in London the heat was enervating, and everyone was looking forward to baths and naps. Anne declined to join them for dinner as did Lady Catherine, so the couple were able to relax in their sitting room and finalize their plans.

"I am unsure about leaving Anne on her own in Bath, Henry."

"She is almost six and twenty, she wants to do this right away Audrey, and we cannot simply leave my sister here while we get her set up. We need to settle Catherine at Matlock. With the two of them staying in the same house, they are bound to run into each other, and I do not want to subject Anne to an unpleasant scene. And we need to take some time for the estate."

"I know, but I think there are things I can do to make this easier for Anne and so less worrisome for me. If you give me a few days I can introduce her to Mrs. Gardiner. She will be able to guide Anne in purchasing a new wardrobe and it would keep Anne busy enough without exhausting her."

"Whatever you think she needs my dear," sighed the Earl, "though the sooner we can leave the better I believe."

23

At Longbourn, Thomas and Fanny held a family meeting to discuss their plans for the upcoming season with their daughters and Mr. Collins.

"Jane and Lizzy, I would like you to be ready to leave for London by Monday next. And you will not be returning until spring so you will need to begin planning and packing without delay. Pack the best of your wardrobes, but you will not need all of what you have for you will both be getting new gowns once you are in London," Fanny said, fanny herself vigorously in the afternoon heat.

"But mama, what about harvest?" asked Lizzy. "Surely Jane and I need to be here, particularly if Mr. Bingley does not return to supervise the Netherfield harvest."

Her father shook his head. "Not this year, Lizzy. It is time for the other girls to begin learning what you and Jane already know. Mary will be their leader and Kitty and Lydia will be lending a helping hand wherever they are needed, just as you and Jane once did. And your Uncle Gardiner is going to clear as much time as he can to come learn about harvest-time for himself."

"But are you sure we should not be here, just in case of need?"

"Lizzy, my dear, I know how responsible you are but that is precisely the reason you and Jane cannot stay. It is very difficult to teach someone to do something when you are used to doing it yourself. You and Jane would no doubt end up taking on your regular duties, and your father and I believe we would be hard put not to allow this as we are also used to it. No, it is for the best that you go to London, gather your new wardrobes and await your papa. Once harvest is done he will join you in London and you will travel to Bath together for the season."

Jane's eyes shone at that. "We are going to the house in Bath? Oh, I am so glad, I have wanted to see the improvements with my own eyes instead of only hearing the reports."

"Of course you do," laughed Lizzy. "Oh Jane, only you could hear that we are spending the season in Bath and be far more excited about plumbing than about a new wardrobe and possible suitors."

Lydia bounced in her chair with excitement. "This is wonderful for us too. It means you think we are old enough to take responsibility. How grand to be involved and not just be watching out the windows as everyone else bustles about. I can hardly wait."

Fanny laughed at her youngest's exuberance. "Well, I believe you will all three do well. It is exhausting work, and I warn you now there will be days when you will want to simply stay abed and let someone else worry about your tasks, but it is worth the effort and weariness when all goes well. And Mr. Collins, we thought you should consider where you would like to spend the winter. You may, of course, live here with me and the three younger girls, or you can go to Bath with Thomas and Jane and Lizzy. There is plenty of time to decide, but please know that whichever course you choose we will do everything we can to make things comfortable for you."

"I do not know that I am comfortable with the thought of leaving only the ladies here," replied Mr. Collins.

"If you do decide on Bath, the Phillips will remove here for the duration of my stay in Bath. It is close enough to be no real difficulty for my brother's business and they will be both protection and company for my ladies," answered Mr. Bennet.

"And Jane, Lizzy, I believe we should consider inviting Charlotte Lucas to accompany us," he added. "There is no one at Lucas Lodge to take her place during harvest, but once it is over I believe she could be convinced to journey with us; I could bring her to London with me when I come to take you on to Bath in October."

Lizzy nodded thoughtfully. "Yes, that would be good I think. We all know why we are doing this, there is no one here in Meryton for us, not for me and Jane and not for Charlotte either. Perhaps in Bath we will have more opportunities."

And so, three days later, Lizzy and Jane saw their trunks tied to the coach and after a somewhat tearful leave-taking from their family they set out on the road, arriving at the Gardiner home in London in time for tea.

"My dears, tomorrow we will be visiting Edward's warehouse and we will have guests. Lady Audrey Fitzwilliam, Countess of Matlock, is bringing her niece Miss Anne de Bourgh who needs a whole new wardrobe."

"Colonel Fitzwilliam's mama?"

Jane blushed as Lizzy and her aunt regarded her quizzically. "I do not know why you are surprised that I remember. We met them at the ball at Netherfield less than a week past."

Lizzy eyed Jane in a way that made her sister aware that she would not be sleeping until she had been thoroughly quizzed but she did not comment for now, contenting herself with professing pleasure at meeting a relative of the pleasant Colonel and asking their aunt about their dressmaking appointments.

Once in their bedroom, Lizzy plopped down on the bed, looked up at her sister and said, "You know I am not going to let you sleep until you tell me all, Jane."

Although a faint blush stained her cheeks, Jane protested, "There is nothing to tell, Lizzy." At Elizabeth's raised eyebrow, she repeated, "There is nothing. I just happen to have danced with him and spoken with him several times; I will admit I found him an interesting man to converse with and that is all."

"Jane, you could never be a gambler. You would blush if you tried to bluff."

Jane laughed, but it ended on a sigh. "It does not matter, Lizzy. We did not have a lot of time to get to know one another because Mr. Bingley was always there. And now we are to go to Bath, and I do not know where he is; certainly, I have no right to ask. Perhaps you and I will both meet the right gentlemen in Bath. I confess, I would like to be married, Lizzy. I have lived as a daughter long enough; I want to be a wife and have a home and children." There was a world of longing in her voice, and it found an answering echo in Lizzy's heart.

"Yes, I have felt something of the same, an impatience to get on with the rest of my life. I know I would miss my family and friends but still, I would like to meet someone, to be mistress of my own house or even a small estate. But you know us, Jane. We cannot just marry someone for security; I know Charlotte says she would, but I think that she would not really do so. And I know we would not."

"I think you are not making allowances for differences in personalities; I confess that I would understand if she did so, but for myself I should so very much like to marry for love."

The sisters were quiet then, quickly preparing for sleep and sliding in under a sheet only, for it was too warm for anything more than that. Although neither of them spoke again, it was long before they slept as each tried to sort through the tangle of thoughts and emotions their discussion had brought to the surface.

24

By the end of the next day, Lizzy was sure they had made a new lifelong friend in Anne de Bourgh. When Anne had met the Bennets, she had somewhat shyly asked if they knew Mr. Collins who had been the parson at Hunsford. When they told her their cousin was living at their family estate she had been delighted to hear that he had been warmly welcomed to their home.

"I thought that I recognized your names; when Mr. Collins returned from visiting you he would always be so very complimentary about your hospitality to him. When next you write, could you please give him my greetings and tell him I asked after him? His parishioners miss him, and many prayers are often offered up for his recovery. I am so terribly sorry I could not do more to keep Lady Catherine from berating him, but I shall always be grateful that I did manage to get his preferred candidate accepted by the bishop before she could block it; I know how important that was to him and to those whom he had cared for so diligently."

"No one blames you for anything your mother did," Lizzy assured her. "You did what you could, and I promise you he has often mentioned how grateful he is that his successor is a good and caring man."

"Well, Lady Catherine is retiring to the Dower House at Fairwinds, the seat of the Matlock estate in Derbyshire, so the new man will have an easier time serving his flock now."

After a light tea the Countess, Anne and Mrs. Jenkinson, along with Jane and Lizzy were shepherded through Gardiner's warehouse by Mrs. Gardiner; she first took them to a huge room filled with crates of fabrics from all over the world. Lady Fitzwilliam stopped just inside the doorway, surveyed the room and drew a deep breath of satisfaction. "This may actually be my favorite part of ordering up something new. The adventure of finding exactly the right material."

The ladies all laughed and began to move further into the room and soon cries of delights and calls to each other echoed thought the room.

At Mrs. Gardiners' direction two small rooms had been prepared for them. In one the curtains had all been thrown open. In the other room the drapes had been tightly closed and candelabras were placed to light the room. On a table that had been placed along a wall in the hallway, bolts of dozens of fabrics rested, neatly divided by which woman had chosen them. And so began a long morning and early afternoon of choosing fabrics for several new gowns for each of the Miss Bennets and dozens for Anne, whose entire wardrobe had been deemed unsuitable by the Countess.

While Anne was surprised by the arrangements, the Bennet ladies were familiar with the process of choosing the most flattering fabrics. As Jane began, first holding fabrics to her face and looking into a mirror in the hallway and then in each room while accompanied by Mrs. Gardiner and Lady Fitzwilliam, Lizzy explained in a soft voice to Anne that fabrics looked different in different lights, and they reflected on the skin differently. "As you can see that particular shade of pink looks lovely against Jane's skin in the hallway and in sunlight but in candlelight it is too pale and makes her appear washed out. So it can be used for day dresses and perhaps a walking dress but not for evening wear. That is what they are discussing and what we will discover when it is time to choose colors and fabrics for you."

Anne nodded thoughtfully. "I know that none of the colors Lady Catherine chose for me become me; Aunt Audrey agrees that nothing I have will be kept." She eyed Lizzy shyly. "Is there something I can do with all the dresses she has purchased for me? I have so many and none of them become me, neither the colors nor the styles."

Lizzy pursed her lips in thought, examining the walking dress that Anne was wearing. "I might have a suggestion. We have a good friend who will be joining us after harvest. Charlotte Lucas and her family live at a neighboring estate. Would you consider offering them to Charlotte? Your coloring is very different, I would not be surprised to find that the colors are quite becoming to her. And she is very talented with her needle; so are all the Bennet ladies. We could do a much-expanded wardrobe for her if you would consider it."

Anne's eyes lit up with pleasure. "Oh, I would love to do that. I now know how expensive all of these fabrics must have been, I would hate for them to go to waste and I would love to give these to her."

When applied to for her opinion the Countess promptly agreed with the suggestion. "Miss Elizabeth I heartily approve. When you come to know us better you will find out that with few exceptions we are a very frugal family. I am not one of those women who purchases their entire wardrobe new each year to impress society and when I shop with my niece Georgiana Darcy, I make sure to order all her gowns with extended seams and a deep hem. She is just turned six and ten and is still growing and I see no reason to completely replace her wardrobe each year. It is wasteful and unnecessary. If Georgiana's coloring allowed it I would have already claimed Anne's wardrobe for her; if your friend's appearance will be flattered by these colors, then by all means, let us pack all of these away for her."

"Please can you call me Anne? Can all of you call me Anne? I would be very pleased. And I am not just thinking about this dress or what I brought with me for your friend Miss Lucas, I have trunks and trunks of dresses that Lady Catherine purchased for me based on what colors become her and not what is flattering to me. Once enough of my new wardrobe has been delivered I would be pleased to gift them all to her. And when we are in Bath, I will send to have my wardrobe from Rosings Park packed up and delivered to her." She reached over to take Elizabeth's strong hand in her own much frailer one. "Do you know that Lady Catherine has ordered three ballgowns for me every year since I turned 18? And she has never hosted a ball nor were we ever invited to one. I do not exaggerate when I tell you I have two dozen ballgowns that have not been worn since their final fittings and that do not become me. Aunt Audrey is correct, it is wasteful to leave all that expensive fabric sitting in my wardrobes at Rosings where they will never see the light of day."

"Good heavens," cried Lizzy, "two dozen ballgowns? Whatever would she do with all of them?"

Anne laughed at her. "Well, I assume she would wear them," she teased, drawing chuckles from everyone.

The ladies all agreed to use first names, even Mrs. Jenkinson asking that they call her Maude when in a private setting. "Since I will be responsible for chaperoning Anne, I would prefer Mrs. Jenkinson when in public. It gives me an authority that I hope not to use but may need."

It was an exhausted but satisfied group that gathered for their afternoon tea in the Gardiner's drawing room. "Well, this was a very productive day! Now, I have made an appointment for Anne at Madame Lorraine's shop tomorrow, Madelaine. I love what she does with your wardrobe, and I see no reason to go to the added expense of using one of the Bond Street modistes. Anne is going to be in Bath, not London and so it will not harm her in the ton to be using an unknown seamstress. And the best are not necessarily the most fashionable. When choosing your dressmaker in Bath, Anne, you are going to want to try more than one and see who works most comfortably with you. You want to look your best; you also want to feel attractive without being inappropriate in the styles they choose. And even though we will order the majority of your wardrobe now, it is important that you purchase some of your gowns locally. You want to support a good dressmaker who is convenient to you."

"Well, that explains why I could not take Madame's entire day tomorrow," Maddie said with a rueful smile. "I had asked for it and she is closing the shop except for at ten when she told me she has a client she cannot refuse."

Anne beamed at them and said, "What fun then. We will all be together again tomorrow, and I can begin learning about lace and ribbons and styles and all the fun things that will go into making me a dress I actually want to wear."

"Madame Lorraine will be thrilled that you are part of our party, it will make it much easier for her. And she is truly talented. Do not worry that she will force you into the latest of fashions. Good heavens, they have bodices now that are little wider than ribbons. I cannot see any of us being comfortable going out dressed like that."

Anne blushed. "No, if that were the case, I would not leave the house."

"Garish colors are also the rage right now, but you will note we avoided them. Choose what becomes you, my dear, and then a good dressmaker will work with that to incorporate those parts of current fashion that will work with your style and not against it."

Arrangements were made to meet at the seamstress' shop the next day and the ladies parted for the evening, all of them too weary to want anything more than a lie down before dinner. Then it was dinner with the family and off to bed so everyone could be up early and out the door directly after breakfast the next morning.

As they ended the next day at the seamstress, the Countess drew Mrs.

Gardiner aside. "I am afraid that I am going to be leaving London for Derbyshire in just a few days. I would like to ask if you can include Anne in some activities whenever it is convenient for you? The friendships she is forming with your nieces will serve her well, I think, as they are far more comfortable in social situations than Anne will be. I have noticed that Miss Elizabeth in particular is able to draw her out and make her feel at ease."

Madelaine nodded. "Lady Audrey, we will definitely include her, and we will be with her for her appointments for final fittings and we will help her find the accessories she will need," she said reassuringly. "You do not have to worry about her being lonely while my nieces are here."

"Thank you so much. I know that my son has said that the mission he was on is to be completed today and then he will be available to spend time with her and to ensure that she is safe. He will be escorting her to Bath once her wardrobe is completed, or at least enough of it is completed to allow her to be well dressed upon her arrival in Bath."

"Lady Audrey, my nieces are to stay with me until the harvest at their father's estate is completed. Then he will travel here and will be taking Lizzy and Jane and their friend Miss Lucas to Bath for the season. If it fits in with their plans, your son and Anne would be welcome to travel with them I am sure," suggested Mrs. Gardiner. "They would be a welcome addition. The Bennets own a house in Sydney Place; it has just undergone a series of renovations and while they have leased it out for many years, Mr. and Mrs. Bennet have decided that their girls need a season in Bath this year."

The Countess' smile grew wider. "That is where the de Bourgh house is located also, so they will be neighbors. That will make Anne feel welcome from the day she arrives. The Earl and I have to be in London much of the time during the season due to Parliament, but whenever possible I would like to be in Bath for Anne."

Richard was waiting for them when the Countess, Anne and Mrs. Jenkinson arrived back at Matlock house.

His mother greeted him cheerfully and began to discuss possible travel plans with him when she stopped abruptly and studied him as if truly seeing him for the time. "Richard, you are in civilian dress! Have you resigned? Are you truly never going to war again!"

He laughed at her eager joy. "Truly, mother. I am now a gentleman of property, and I will not wield a sword again unless the tenants of Rosings stage an uprising!"

"Oh my dearest son, I am so very, very happy. This is the best of news."

"I am rather pleased myself. Now who are these wonderful friends who will be helping our Annie adjust to being a social butterfly."

Anne giggled at Richard. "Now that would be something to see indeed. They are wonderful and they know you."

Richard looked at them with eyebrows raised in question. "The Bennets, Richard, you know them from Hertfordshire."

"The Bennets are traveling to Bath for the season?"

Anne nodded vigorously. "They have a house there and it is also in Sydney Place so we will be neighbors. I am so pleased; I like them so very much. They have helped me, particularly Miss Elizabeth, to find the right colors and fabrics and to feel comfortable in the new styles I will be wearing. Perhaps we should talk to Darcy about bringing Georgiana to Bath this year. I know she is not out, but I believe she will like Jane and Elizabeth as much as I do."

"I liked them too, I had some very interesting conversations with them and Mrs. Bennet sets a wonderful table. I wonder if their cook is going with them."

His family laughed at him. "Do you suppose that in years to come you will cease judging people by the quality of the food or is that a soldier's habit that will always be with you?"

"Well I cannot imagine disdaining good food or a comfortable bed. I spent too many years without either one. As for the travel plans, my next duty is to take up the reigns at Rosings Park, and I can arrange my own travel plans to suit you Anne."

"Well Jane and Elizabeth will be in London until after harvest in Hertfordshire so I imagine it will be a month complete before they will be ready to leave. But they have promised to keep me company and their aunt, Mrs. Gardiner, has said she will help me to learn what I need to know to run the house in Bath so if you wish to go to Rosings now, you can do so with a clear conscious. And if you are not quite ready to escort me to Bath when they are ready, I have been invited to travel with them, so make what arrangements will suit you and Rosings best Richard."

25

Darcy had arrived at his London home in a somber mood; he knew that sometime in the first few days he was in London Richard would be bringing him the news that Wickham had been tried and hanged. He knew it was right, it was the consequence of the decisions his childhood friend had made, but he had hoped up until the last minute that Wickham would not desert, or at least not steal from his comrades and then steal a horse while deserting. But no, Wickham had done just as Richard had predicted.

At least he had plenty of correspondence to distract him. And he could congratulate himself that Bingley had been removed from the influence of Jane Bennet. It was good, too, that he no longer had Elizabeth Bennet to trouble his thoughts. It was a shame she was so ineligible, but now that they would no longer be seeing each other he could consign her to a fond memory, something pleasant from the past that had no power in the future.

When Richard arrived with the news that they were done forever with Wickham, Darcy poured them both a generous measure of brandy and they sat in silent companionship for a time, Darcy consumed by thoughts of the childhood friend who had somehow lost his way so badly there was no redeeming him and Richard quietly respecting his cousin's need to process his news.

"Well, enough wallowing," sighed Richard. "There is good news on some fronts. Anne is so much healthier, Darce, you would scarcely know her. Mother has taken her shopping for new gowns and introduced her to a couple of young ladies who are also going to be sojourning in Bath for the season." Richard hesitated a moment but knowing that his cousin had a strong prejudice against the Bennets he decided not to mention the ladies by name. "And I am no longer in the Army and will be taking up the reins at Rosings."

Darcy nodded somberly. "I am happy to hear that Richard; it is particularly good news that you have resigned your commission. Are you going to Rosings immediately?"

"Quite soon. I need to see my banker, my tailor and take a look at the London house as long as I am here. I do not plan to be in London for the season, so I would like to see what needs to be done to make the house ready to be leased. Once harvest is over, I am planning to take lodgings in Bath and spend the season there. I can escort Anne to various functions and help make her comfortable during her first season. And it is a short journey, Rosings to Bath, so I can return regularly to the estate. I do not want my people there to believe that I am going to be an absentee landlord."

Darcy agreed. "I think that is a fine plan. Are your parents going to be in London or will they too be in Bath?"

"London, of course. Father needs to be here while Parliament is sitting and mother is not likely to want to leave him here alone, she knows he does not pay enough attention to his health if she is not there to watch over him. And he counts on her as a political hostess you know. I am sure they will visit Anne, but they will not be staying there for extended periods. I owe Anne a lot, I do not think it is too much to ask that I be available to help her get settled into her new life. Not that she did ask or would ask, but it is something I feel I should do."

"I agree. I wonder if I should speak to Anne about having Georgiana stay with her? It is fine for my sister and I to reside together alone in the country but a bachelor residence in town is no place for her; I had thought to have her stay with your parents again but perhaps I should consider the two of us going to Bath also."

Richard shook his head. "I do not think this is the time to do that, Darce. Anne needs to concentrate on herself, on her new life and I cannot think it would be a wise decision to ask her to take a girl not yet out into her home. She is embarking on a brand new adventure, her first ever adventure really and I believe she should be allowed to do so without asking her to be responsible for someone else right now."

Darcy sighed, "Yes, I suppose that it might be best to wait to introduce someone else into her household."

Richard rose then, setting his glass aside. "Thank you for the brandy and the company cuz. Until father and mother head back to Derbyshire with Aunt Catherine I will stay at Matlock house I think; I want to spend time with them and with Anne. Once they leave, if you are agreeable, I will take up residence here again for the short time I will be in London."

Darcy rose and clasped his cousin's hand. "Thank you, Richard, for everything. And of course you can stay here. I will not be here much longer of course. You know I need to get to Pemberley before harvest begins and I need to spend time with Georgie. I will not be staying in London more than a day or two, just long enough to tie up a few loose ends but come when you need to and stay as long as you like."

William spent the next day meeting with his solicitor and his man of business; he was ready to get out of London. He felt he should see Bingley one last time before his journey but had no desire for Miss Bingley's company, so he sent a message to his friend to meet him at his club for dinner that night as he would be leaving for Pemberley in the morning.

When they met that evening it struck Darcy that Charles did not seem his usual jovial self. "Charles, it is good to see you," he greeted him, then added, "are you doing well my friend?"

Bingley sighed. "Honestly Darcy I do not know. I find that rather than being relieved to be back in London, that I liked living in the country and miss it. I enjoyed the sport and the gentlemen and how accepting everyone was. I surprised myself by even enjoying the slower pace. I am not sure I am ready to tackle another season in town."

As they sat down and ordered, Darcy thought about his friend's statement. It was unusual for Charles not to be delighted to be back in society. Was he missing Jane Bennet? Or was he truly missing the experience of being master of an estate and living a country life? Darcy did not want to blurt out such a personal question and was wondering how to approach the subject when an idea occurred to him. If Bingley took a house in Bath for the season, he could stay there with Georgiana instead of leaving her in London with his aunt and uncle. It would give Charles something to look forward to and be very convenient for him. And he knew how easily led Bingley was.

"Well Charles, you know me well enough to be unsurprised when I say I never look forward to a season in London. And this year, I am thinking I might not have one."

"Are you going to stay at Pemberley all winter?"

"No, I am considering doing the season in Bath."

"Bath? Why? What is in Bath?"

"Not what but whom. Anne de Bourgh is going to be having her first season there. She is six and twenty and has never really been in society; she owns a home on Sydney Place and is planning on making it her permanent residence. Richard is going to stay in Bath for the season to help her acclimate and I was thinking I might prefer a season there to one in London. There are far fewer match-making mamas in Bath and as I understand it, the pace is much slower; I might actually enjoy the season or least I might find it tolerable. My only hesitation is Georgiana. I cannot have her live with me in a bachelor household, but London is close enough to Bath so I could have her stay with our aunt and uncle and visit often. Richard is going to take lodgings there and I could do so also."

"Stay a moment Darce," said Bingley, sounding excited. "What if I take a house there? With Caroline and the Hursts in residence it would be perfectly acceptable if both you and Georgiana stay with us. You could have her company for the whole of the season. And of course, Richard would be more than welcome. I think I would like it very much."

"Well, if you think your sisters would not object, it will certainly make it easier for Georgiana and myself. I do not know Richard's plans for a certainty, I am sure he does not either at this point, as it depends on the harvest at Rosings and Anne's plans also, but I know that Georgie and I would be very pleased to accept your invitation if you do take a house."

"Then let us consider it settled. I know you are leaving for Pemberley tomorrow so once I have everything readied I will write to you and give you the details."

Darcy smiled at his friend's enthusiasm and teased drily, "Perhaps you should have your man of business send me the details, you know how awful your handwriting is, I would hate to have to scour all of Bath to find you because I could not read the address."

Assumed Virtue

26

The de Bourgh house in town had been unoccupied for years, but Lady Catherine's perception of what was due her because of her elevated status meant that the house had been regularly maintained and fully staffed. While it had been financially unsound to keep putting money into the establishment and never using or leasing it, it was serving Richard well today.

He had gathered up Anne and the two eldest Bennets daughters and they embarked on a journey of discovery. To his relief the house was meticulously kept, the furnishings no more than ten seasons old. Fortunately, this was just prior to the ghastly Egyptian influence that had permeated the ton and so no alligator tail table legs or fake sarcophagus cabinets or artist's renderings of Cleopatra had been given house room. If the furniture was deemed too heavy and bland for current tastes, then that was all to the good as Lizzy pointed out. It would offend fewer people who might be looking for a fashionable address for the season.

The staff was delighted to learn that someone would be residence for the season, even if it was only renters and not family, and the tour of the house took on an almost festive air as they investigated the house from attics to cellars.

At Gunter's, celebrating with ices and pastry after their tour, Lizzy pointed out that their uncle had been arranging for the lease of the Bennet house in Bath for years. "He could probably be of much use to you, Colonel."

"Oh yes," agreed Jane. "And he and Uncle Phillips arranged for the Bingleys to lease Netherfield. I am sure he could be of much help even if it is just to tell you what to beware of and what you might want to specifically request."

"Ladies, I believe that is a wonderful suggestion. Let us go to my parents' home and I will pen a quick note to Mr. Gardiner for you to deliver for me if you would be so kind. I will make myself available to him whenever he can find a few minutes for me for I wish to do this right."

Two hours after Richard and Anne had arrived at home, a messenger delivered a note inviting them, along with the Earl and Countess, to dine at the Gardiner home two nights hence. An acceptance was sent off post haste; the Earl and Countess would be leaving for Derbyshire the morning after this planned dinner and there was much to do to prepare; giving the kitchen staff the final night with only Lady Catherine to serve would be a blessing.

The servants that the Earl had sent to Rosings had returned, bringing with them many trunks of personal items for Lady Catherine along with a stunning amount of gaudy jewelry that would be sold back to the jewelers; the Earl, Richard and Anne sat down together to determine which stones would be kept and which would be taken to a reputable jeweler on the morrow. The representatives from Mr. Gardiner's organization would be available to journey to Rosings once Richard gave them a date he would be arriving there to pack and transport all the furnishing that Richard did not want to the London auction house. Once Richard took care of all his concerns he would be well on the way to placing the estate on a sound financial footing.

The next day Richard and Anne arrived early at the Gardiners then after he escorted all of the ladies to Madame Lorraine's shop, he met with his father at Rundell and Bridges to dispose of the jewels that had been brought from Rosings.

The gentlemen went from the jewelers to the bank then on to their club. Seated in a private room, the two men spoke of desultory subjects until food and drink had been brought and the doors securely closed.

"For the love of heaven father," said Richard softly, "has my aunt run completely mad? How in the world could she think an estate such as Rosings could afford that kind of expense? I doubt the Royals have spent as much on useless finery."

The Earl's sighed wearily, "I truly had no idea how bad it had gotten. No wonder Rosings has been teetering on the edge of collapse. Darcy has been telling me for years that the books were inaccurate, that there was no way she was spending the money in the places she was recording, the estate simply did not show the kind of prosperity that investing would have produced. I have been looking for other accounts, but we may have just found most of the missing monies." The Earl stared at his glass, absently turning it in circles on the table. "Matlock is a prosperous estate but there is no way we could handle this kind of outlay, not even spread over the years. At least you now have the funds to invest into the most needed repairs. That was a concern, that there would not be enough garnered from the sale of the jewelry and the furnishings to make a dent in what has to be invested. Now we know that you can begin the process of bringing the estate back at once; there will be things that need to be done over time, of course, but this is a good start, a very good start."

"Well yes, that is good for the estate and for me; but it makes me wonder how much has been stashed away in the other accounts we know my aunt has. There cannot be much, not with all she has spent."

"My man of business has found two, but you are correct, there is not much in them. It all adds up of course, but in a very real way we are lucky she was so enamored of gaudy jewelry. It is easily resold. The furnishing and paintings and such would have cost less, of course, but the estate will be lucky to see a return of even fifty percent of the initial cost. The stones she purchased, no doubt we lost a little on some but for most of them they have appreciated in value."

"Since there are many ways she could have wasted the funds that would be unrecoverable I am grateful I suppose, though likely I will feel it more after the shock has worn off; for now, let us speak of other things. I am going to collect Anne after I leave here, her energy is better all the time, but she still tires more quickly than someone who is in full health. I know the Bennets and the Gardiners would allow her to rest as needed but I worry about her."

His father nodded agreement. "Besides the family connection and affection, we owe her much son. I will be interested in spending some time with Gardiner that is not a true business meeting, though I know we will be touching on several things. He has always struck me as a sensible and interesting man, but we have never had a chance to speak outside of business and investment concerns."

Dinner with the Gardiners and the Bennet daughters was as enjoyable as Richard had anticipated. The food was excellent, and the conversation flowed easily from topic to topic and Jane Bennet was as charming, intelligent and beautiful as always. He could not mention it to Darcy, and his explanation that he would be in Bath for Anne was truth, but it was not the whole truth. He wanted very much to continue to get to know Miss Bennet.

Gardiner was very knowledgeable about what to look for and what to avoid when leasing. He explained that he had refused to lease the Bennet's Bath home to any single gentlemen no matter their reputation, unless they had family who would be residing there also.

"The last thing you would want is for the reputation of the house to be damaged by a rake or a gambler. It is odd, and not sensible, but there is no doubt that if just one or two in the course of a decade had been in residence the house itself would become harder to lease. Whoever rents the de Bourgh townhouse needs to be above reproach and generally speaking you will protect the reputation of the home by leasing it to a family. Your man of business should be able to tell you what kind of monies are being asked for similar homes and once you have that figure you are going to want to have any applicant's finances investigated to make sure their income is roughly triple what you are asking. For many landlords that is all they ask, but as I said, I investigate also to make sure we have people of quality."

Richard nodded thoughtfully, then asked, "Did you investigate the Bingleys before leasing Netherfield to them?"

Gardiner smiled wryly, "We knew of Bingley's proclivities yes, but he is not a rake after all. His younger sister is incredibly unpleasant and unpopular, but the perfect people are not out there. We wanted to make sure that no one would be a threat to the neighborhood and were hopeful when we heard that Mr. Darcy would be mentoring him that he would be a good estate manager, though that turned out to be a forlorn hope. Still, he has paid his rent, the servants were irritated by Miss Bingley but not abused; the tenants are not happy that apparently he will not be returning for harvest, but Bennet is used to overseeing Netherfield's harvest and I will be there this year also."

The Earl had frowned upon hearing that. "I cannot understand what Darcy was thinking not to insist that Bingley be there for harvest. Even if my nephew returned to Pemberley, the harvests are far enough apart that he could finish the harvest in Derbyshire and still be able to help Bingley through his first harvest in Hertfordshire. To not be there at all is inexcusable."

"I do not wish to be overly critical," put in Lizzy, "but the fact is that other than riding around the estate I saw little real effort at estate management. They had virtually no contact with the tenantry, though to their credit the issues that were spoken of to the steward were generally addressed. But there seem to be no plans in place to be there for harvest. We know the steward well of course and he has said that there is nothing set up for spring planting."

"I think that Mr. Bingley is not quite ready for the responsibility of being the master of an estate," said Jane in her gentle voice. "He is not serious about the duties he simply wants to live as a guest on an estate not as the master; perhaps Mr. Darcy recognized this and decided it was not a good investment of his time to do more than they did."

"That is possible," agreed Richard thoughtfully. "And Darcy may have advised him to return for harvest and Bingley decided not to do so. After all, Darcy has no real authority over Bingley, they are simply friends."

Lizzy agreed somewhat grudgingly, and the conversation moved on to other topics. Once the gentlemen separated, Gardiner asked the Fitzwilliams for their word that the news he was to speak of would be kept confidential. Assured they would tell no one, Gardiner began by thanking the Earl.

"Without your aid, this would not be news. The entail on Longbourn is broken. Mr. Phillips received notice this morning and sent word by express. Thomas wants to inform his daughters himself so Maddie and I are keeping it quiet, but it has happened, and we all know this could have dragged on for months if not for your intervention Matlock."

The Earl beamed at Mr. Gardiner. "I am glad I could help. I was impressed with the generosity of your Mr. Collins, with his determination to do what was best for the estate and for his cousins. This is excellent news indeed."

The next morning the Earl, the Countess and Lady Catherine began the journey to Derbyshire. Richard removed to Darcy House as it would cause talk and be improper for him to remain at Matlock house with Anne in residence and his parents gone. He remained in London another week, escorting Anne and the Miss Bennets to the park, to the museum and, once Anne's wardrobe had arrived, to a dinner party hosted by a family friend. She had been a bundle of nerves, but Richard had been proud of how she handled herself. Anne truly was a young woman with hidden reserves; no one who did not know her well would have seen anything but a gracious and poised young woman.

He also spends several afternoons working with his man of business to lease out the London house, reminding himself that he needed to stop thinking of it and referring to it as the de Bourgh town house. It was the Fitzwilliam town house now, as odd as that might seem to him.

Then once he was comfortable that Anne would be fine with the Bennets for company and Mrs. Jenkinson to aid her, he decided to leave London for Kent. He would return to London the first week of October to escort Anne to Bath even though she would be safe traveling with the Bennets. Once she was settled there he would return to Rosings for harvest.

Assumed Virtue

27

The journey to Matlock for the Earl, the Countess and Lady Catherine de Bourgh went far more smoothly than anyone had anticipated. They all had expected Lady Catherine would be rude, insulting and overbearing at every stop, filling the air with her incessant complaining and her ridiculous demands. Instead, she made the trip almost in silence, taking her meals alone in her room, stepping out of her coach only to briefly refresh herself at stops then returning immediately to sit in silence.

By tradition, their final stop was the Red Lion Inn, some two hours from Matlock. Some of the servants always went ahead from there to ensure that those at the estate were aware that the Earl and Countess were within a few hours of arriving. This time it was also to ensure that everyone was aware that the Dower House was about to receive its new mistress.

Arriving at the estate, Lady Catherine's coach went directly to the Dower house while the Earl and Countess made the longer journey to the manor house. Their daughter in law, Marjorie, greeted them cordially, explaining that the Viscount, their son Hilliard, had gone to the Dower House to greet Lady Catherine and would join them shortly. Marjorie related to them, with a twinkle in her eyes, that Mrs. Byars was at the Dower House to introduce Lady Catherine to her new housekeeper and to ensure that all went smoothly.

Of course, the Earl thought, amused, Mrs. Byars had been the Matlock housekeeper for decades and she would not take any insults from Catherine; he would not have thought of it, but he should have realized that the ladies of the house would ensure that his sister was made aware that the Dower house staff had the full support of those at the main house; it was a subtle but firm reminder that the staff was not really hers to command; she could request but her power over the people who served her was no longer absolute.

He went to his study, ostensibly to look over his mail but in reality to simply take a small amount of time for himself; he slowly sipped his brandy and relaxed fully for the first time since his sister had bullied her way into his London house. There had been so many details to see to, so much that had to be accomplished quickly, that he had not truly had the time to reflect on how his family's circumstances had changed radically from just a fortnight ago.

First and foremost, his son was safe. He had found that one phrase, my son is safe, had been repeating in his thoughts often, as if his mind had to keep reminding his heart. He had spent so many years with an unspoken dread as his constant companion that he felt it might have become a permanent part of him. Now that Richard was safely out of the military, the relief was almost bewildering; to be able to go to sleep without his last thought being a fearful prayer for his younger son's safety, to wake and not start each day with the desperate hope that today would not be the day where word was brought to him of the injury or death of his boy; it would be an adjustment to be sure, but one he was delighted to make.

That Richard now had an estate, that he could marry for affection and not fortune was a secondary blessing; one that he welcomed but that fell far short of his relief at the safety of his son. He hoped Richard would be able to marry a woman who cared for him, but he had seen plenty of marriages that were ones of convenience that had turned out well enough. Still, he hoped that Richard could follow the examples of himself and Hilliard in marrying where his heart was engaged.

Audrey, who missed very little where her boys were concerned, had thought there might be something, a bit of a spark, between Richard and the eldest Miss Bennet. He had met her at that country ball and had remembered her certainly as a lovely woman; he had spoken with Bennet enough to know that all the daughters were well educated in more than just the more traditional subjects; Audrey had spoken a little with the young ladies then and from her impressions felt they would bring intelligence and heart to their duties when they wed.

He had had a chance to speak with her when they had dined with the Gardiners and agreed with his wife that she and her sister were impressive. Miss Elizabeth was more to his taste as he had enjoyed her wit and quickness; but he could see that with the life Richard had led Miss Jane Bennet's serenity might be a better match for his son.

And, unless he missed his guess, there would likely be more of a dowry there than others might think. The Earl was a shrewd judge of character and it struck him that no matter the rumors of their situation, Thomas Bennet was an intelligent man, he would not be likely to let his connection to Mr. Gardiner be for naught. And with his influence, the entail on the estate had been broken and Longbourn would be a fine dowry for one of the girls.

Then there was Anne. What a wonderful surprise she had been for them. Intelligent, courageous, generous; she had decided what she wanted to do with her life and her estate and had planned and waited and finally grasped the chance to see it through despite ill health and no guarantee that he and Audrey would support her. He was so proud of her; she was reaching for the life she had long envisioned, and he hoped that she could find joy in these upcoming years. She had spent too much of her life in a miserable existence under her mother's thumb.

Well, that was for the future. Audrey would keep him informed of the progress of the friendship between Anne and the Bennet ladies. They would help her more than he and Audrey could in learning to navigate in society; having friends of her own would be a confidence boost that family could not really provide. And it would naturally place Richard in company of Miss Bennet. Time would tell if anything was going to happen there.

28

By the time the Earl and Countess were settling Lady Catherine into the Dower House, Darcy had already thrown himself into the myriad details that had awaited his return to Derbyshire. He arrived at Pemberley on a lovely evening; this far north, the hot days were already giving way to gentler temperatures at night so that unlike those suffering in London, here sleep was comfortable once more. By traveling longer days Darcy could make the journey in only two days though it meant arriving too late to do anything more than bathe and have some bread and cheese before sinking into his familiar mattress in the Master suite at home.

Home. Pemberley had always been home, far more than the London house or any of the smaller estates he administered. But oddly, this time, it failed to work its magic on him. He was glad to be home, of course he was, but the calm contentment he had always felt was missing this time. He had never been so restless here and he found it disconcerting. He could hide it from his sister, from his staff but he knew it was there and he knew the cause too: Elizabeth Bennet had followed him in his mind and invaded his space as surely as if she had followed him in person.

He had assumed that he would not think of her again once he left Hertfordshire. That had not happened, but he had been comfortable with the idea that the stress of London and then the boredom of travel encouraged thoughts of her, and he assumed she would be banished once he arrived home. But again his assumption proved faulty.

He wanted her here. He could picture her so clearly, curled up in the massive library with a book, wandering the rose garden, exploring the trails through the woods. She would love Pemberley; he knew that with clear certainty. He could see her in the music room with Georgiana, could picture her in candlelight in the dining room, in moonlight in his bedchamber. He had always been a man of iron control, and yet her image laughed at his determination to quit thinking of her. A moment's inattention and she was there again, eyes radiant with joy, invading his mind, destroying his peace.

He could bury himself in the satisfying tasks that kept Pemberley and her people safe and solvent and for a while he could pretend that he was not missing Elizabeth. He could ride hard across his estate and pretend he did wish her to be riding beside him. Through his meetings with his steward, his rides out to see tenants, his planning for tallying the harvest and setting up for next year's planting, she was in the back of his mind; he was haunted by the thought of what it would be like to do each of these things then go home to Elizabeth, how it would be if he could find her and they could talk over his day; he was certain they would be in perfect harmony with each other; and as for when he retired each night, retiring with her as his wife was something he tried not to think on too often, he was a gentleman after all. And if his dreams were not what a gentleman should be thinking, well, he had no control over his sleeping mind, he could not be blamed for dreams.

Even listening to his beloved sister play for him in the evening could not banish her image.

And here again, another assumption proved faulty. He apparently could not hide his abstraction from his sister.

The soothing sounds of Mozart gave way to silence, then his sister's soft voice broke into his thoughts.

"Brother?"

"Brother?"

He came into the present with a jerk. 'I am sorry Georgie I must be more tired than I thought. What do you need?"

"Brother, can you tell me what troubles you?"

"What makes you think I am troubled?"

"You have not been yourself since you returned. I know you are busy but I know that whatever it is, this is more than the normal rush and hurry of harvest. I have seen that too often to be mistaken."

"Nonsense," Darcy replied briskly, "there is nothing amiss at all."

Georgiana's face fell and her voice dropped to a whisper. "I am afraid you do not trust me any longer, not after *him*."

"Georgie, truly I am well."

"No, you are hiding a grave trouble from me, but I shall not press you further," she replied sadly, her posture drooping. "I will leave you now."

He could not bear to see her so downtrodden, so he held out a hand to stop her. "I am not unwell or even troubled my dear. I am afraid I foolishly allowed myself to become infatuated with someone quite unsuitable to be the next Mistress of Pemberley. It is disconcerting, but I am sure it will pass."

"Is she not a gentlewoman, Will?"

"She is a gentlewoman, my dear, I have not fallen so low as to be attracted to a dairy maid. She is a bright and kind and joyful gentlewoman. But she is one of five sisters, all mercenary, all hoping to marry to better their positions. Her father is a country squire with an estate that is entailed away from his daughters to a cousin. They have little to recommend them beyond their charms."

"In all my life I would never have believed you would be enamored of a fortune hunter, brother. I am so sorry."

"I am sorry too and I never would have believed it myself. I try not to blame her, after all it is not her fault that she has no dowry, but I wish so much that she was part of my social sphere, that she came from a family of fortune and connections."

"But you would not be happy with a woman who threw herself at you for your fortune, you know that."

"Well, I would not say she actually threw herself at me. She flirted with me certainly, but it was charmingly done. And she met Wickham, he tried to importune her with his tale of my mistreatment of him, but she was not fooled. She even warned me that he was spreading what she called a fairy tale about me." Enjoying being able to speak of her, he warmed to the topic quickly. "I would see her and her mother or sisters sometimes when riding; they would be going to visit tenants, always carrying a basket or two of goods with them. She loved walking the countryside too, you could see her love for it when she spoke of it. And she was always so easy in company, she made it possible to actually enjoy being surrounded by people."

"That all speaks well of her. So far, I do not see what is so unacceptable about her."

"As I said, her father is a country squire, and she has no dowry or connections."

"Hmmph. Brother, you have been in society for years without ever meeting someone who you even could consider as Pemberley's mistress. We have connections and I believe we have no need of more money. And even if her sisters are mercenary, if she did not pursue you then why do you accuse her of being a fortune hunter?"

"Well she does not seem to be mercenary," he admitted. "It was her sister who was prepared to marry Bingley for his money even though she did not care for him. Elizabeth never showed any signs of being a fortune hunter."

"Elizabeth Bennet?"

Darcy stared at her in astonishment. "Why yes, how do you know of her?"

"I have had countless letters from you Will, and the only time you have mentioned a woman in an admiring way was in your letters from Hertfordshire. You would write how she had turned Miss Bingley's insults back without losing her poise or temper or how she had helped someone find a dance partner or, oh, I do not know, a dozen different little things you liked about her. I had thought sometimes that she would make a wonderful sister."

"I think you are right that she would be a wonderful sister to you, but it is not to be my dear. I am sure once I have been away from her long enough she will no longer be in my thoughts as anything but a pleasant memory."

"Brother, is that what you want for me then? Am I to marry for money and connections? I would so very much like to marry for affection."

"Georgie, I am sure when the time comes you will meet someone whom you can esteem who will also not bring shame to the Darcy legacy. It is not necessary to choose one or the other, you know."

They did not discuss it again, though Darcy noticed her eying him thoughtfully from time to time and hoped that he had reassured her. When he received a letter from Bingley he decided it was time to give her something new to think on.

"Georgie, you know that Anne is going to be living in Bath do you not?"

"Why no, brother, when did Aunt Catherine decide they would be going to Bath? Is she not still importuning you to marry our cousin?"

"I am afraid that in the press of all my other business, I have not brought you up to date my dear." Darcy proceeded to tell her about Anne's inheriting Rosings, her trip to London with Lady Catherine, Anne's rebellion and her giving Rosings to Richard and Lady Catherine's exile to the Dower house at Matlock. Georgie listened wide-eyed to his tale.

"Oh my heavens, Will, this is wonderful, astonishing but wonderful. So Richard does not have to go to war anymore and Anne can live the life she wants. And our aunt can no longer trouble any of us. I cannot believe you did not think to tell me."

Darcy winced a little, aware that he had been so taken up with his infatuation with Elizabeth Bennet that he had not given his other relatives much thought since his return.

"Well, now you know dearest and here is my plan: I believe we should spend the season in Bath. Richard is going to be there most of the season and I have just heard from Bingley that he is taking a house there for the season also. With Miss Bingley and the Hursts in residence it will be perfectly proper for you to stay with me. Bingley is going to ask Richard to stay with us also."

As he was looking down at the letter in his hand, he missed the grimace of distaste on his sister's face at the mention of Miss Bingley; by the time he glanced up again her face was serene once more. "So we will all be there! I should like to get to know Anne a little better. We have corresponded now and then, but she warned me that she could not often write what she wished and that I needed to be very discrete because her mother read all her incoming and outgoing mail. She could only tell me that much in a letter she had smuggled out by

Mrs. Jenkinson. They did not dare do so very often for our aunt watched both Anne and her companion very closely."

"I wish we had known sooner what the true state of affairs was for Anne, perhaps she would not have had to wait so long to begin her new life."

"Brother, do you believe she would have left? It seems to me that she gave Rosings to Richard because she wanted what was best for the tenants and she probably would not have wanted to leave the estate while her mother still was in charge there. So even if you had known I do not believe there would have been anything you could do until she inherited. I do not feel you have cause to feel guilty."

"You may be right poppet and it is past praying for now. I think I also would like to know our cousin better. For so many years I was unwilling to spend time with her because if I did so Lady Catherine would have jumped to the conclusion that an offer was imminent, and it would have made things difficult. Now that is no longer a problem."

"Will we be in Bath the entire season?"

"I believe so, at least that is what I plan right now. It may be that once we are there we find it is not where we wish to be, but from what I hear about it, the season is slower paced, there are far fewer fortune hunters, and the lending library is supposed to be particularly good."

"Well as long as you are with me and there is a music room in the house that Mr. Bingley leased I believe I will be content. Shall I inform Mrs. Annesley?"

"That is not necessary, I will inform her myself. Just let your maid know so she can pack for you. We will be leaving approximately one week after the harvest celebration for the tenants."

The meeting with Mrs. Annesley was as uncomfortable as Darcy had anticipated. He had been impressed with Mrs. Annesley's credentials, impressed with the woman when he met her, he knew Georgiana liked her and was beginning to trust her, but he disliked that she disagreed with him about what his sister should be learning. He felt she was too young and fragile to take on the responsibilities of running the household or visiting the tenantry; these were things she could take on later. He also felt that the aborted elopement was entirely the fault of Wickham and Mrs. Younge. Mrs. Annesley strongly disagreed and although she bowed to his wishes she clearly did not approve. Perhaps when they were in Bath he would find someone to replace her. No doubt Georgiana would be unhappy for a time, but she would adjust. Really, he could not have employees who did not agree with how he wanted to have things done.

29

The trip to Rosings was an easy one for Richard as he traveled in the large de Bourgh road coach and broke the journey once to rest the horses.

He had no nerves regarding meeting his tenants or working with his staff. He had spent his military life working with everyone from Generals to raw recruits, with all manner of men from varied backgrounds; he had interacted with the native populations in half a dozen countries, and he had come home and balanced his duties in London with his mother's demands that he attend balls and routs and dinners.

No, he had no qualms about being able to meet and run his staff; his nerves were of a different order. He was used to making hard decisions and making them quickly under pressure, but he had years of battles, years of tactics, years of being trained and, in turn, training others to enable him to make the best choices. How would he know how to make the correct decisions when he had no hands-on experience to guide him; when he had mostly the memories of harvests of long ago on his father's estate? How did he compensate for not having a mistress for the estate? Were there things he should be doing that neither he nor Darcy knew about? How would he find the time to connect with his tenants, finagle his finances, make sure the surrounding small communities were supported? All the myriad details ran circles in his mind.

Richard's arrival at Rosings was subdued as he had not informed anyone of his exact plans for arrival. The last thing he wanted was for everyone to be lined up and waiting for his arrival. The staff was aware that he was the new Master, and they were familiar with him from his Easter visits with Darcy, but he had had little interaction with most of them beyond that of any guest and he knew they were unsure what to expect from him.

Richard was courteously welcomed by the butler, Simmons then followed the housekeeper upstairs where instead of his normal room she led him to the Master suite, rooms that had been unused in almost twenty years, since the death of Sir Louis. Everything had been prepared, including a new mattress and bed hangings, but the heavy, old-fashioned furniture remained. He did not mind. He preferred the solid and comfortable to the fashionable, uncomfortable and often too delicate furniture his aunt had preferred. He felt lucky that she had never felt the need to update and redecorate the suite that would now be his.

Once free of travel dust and refreshed, he made his way to the small dining room where a light luncheon had been set out for him. He rang for the housekeeper, deciding to speak with her while he made his meal.

"Thank you for preparing the suite for me, Mrs. Simmons," he said in a friendly tone of voice to the woman standing stiffly before him. "I assume that you have been in communication with Miss de Bourgh?"

"I have sir. Also, the Countess has written to me."

"Ahh, that explains the light lunch," he said with a smile.

Mrs. Simmons gave him a tentative smile in return. "She did mention that the heavier meals that Lady Catherine preferred were not really to your taste, sir."

"They are not, nor is dining alone in the formal dining room to my taste. As long as I am alone I would prefer my meals either here or on a tray if I am working in the study. I do not know if either lady mentioned my plans on refurnishing the manor house?"

"No sir, nothing was said of that." He saw a flicker of unease in her eyes, and her tone was cautious as she responded, "Do you have a place to start sir or is there something the staff can do to forward your plans?"

"You would not happen to have an inventory of what is stored in the attics, would you? As I understand it they are filled with more serviceable and far more comfortable furniture. Can you give me an idea of what would likely be available, Mrs. Simmons?"

"I can sir," the relief plain in her voice. "and I have an inventory that not only has a description of the pieces but their original room placement in the manor. Also, should we need more or different pieces than are stored, the Dower House is furnished in much the same style and period as what used to be here in the manor house." She hesitated a moment then asked, "Do you plan to store all the current furnishings?"

"No, I do not. Tomorrow two men from Gardiner Enterprises will arrive and we will go through each room creating an inventory of what will be sold, they will pack and crate everything and transport it back to London where it will be offered at auction. I have not the smallest idea of what we will fetch from the sale, but I am quite adamant that if there is something that simply would be nice but not needed, it will not be purchased. I would by far prefer to use the funds to repair tenant cottages or do needed maintenance than to invest it into something that is not needed to create a functional home."

He paused a moment to review what he had told her, then continued, "I do not expect the staff to be able haul everything down at once.

We will concentrate first on what is needed in the study, this smaller dining room and the library. Once they are ready to use, we can begin gradually bringing down the furniture to furnish the public and private rooms here and then we will move on to the bedchambers. I do not plan to be entertaining any time soon so there is no need to exhaust the staff by doing the other rooms immediately."

He saw some of the stiffness leave her stance as she realized that he was not planning on demanding the impossible from the staff as his predecessor had so often done. "Until we have a mistress, I do not plan to do anything further than this; wall coverings or new pieces and carpets can wait for when that eventually occurs. I also would like to know from you and from Simmons if we need more staff and what should be done to ensure the staff is as well cared for as possible, keeping in mind that there will likely be some changes there once a mistress takes charge of the manor."

Three days later Richard sat in the same room and looked around with a feeling of satisfaction. The overly ornate and overly large rectangular table and uncomfortable chairs had been replaced with a smaller round table and chairs that did not hurt a man's back. The garish carpet had been replaced with one of a more restrained pattern; the heavy dark drapes were still in place and the wall covering was still eye-searing, but those details could wait.

His study now had a large and serviceable desk and chairs; the hideously ornate library furniture had been replaced with large leather chairs and sofas that encouraged a man to sink down with a book, and tables that were large enough to hold a candelabra and snifter of brandy instead of being tiny, decorative and useless. All in all, he was very pleased with the progress even though most of the rooms were now empty of furnishings.

He and the steward, a genial and knowledgeable man named Palmer, had spent every morning riding the estate visiting the tenants and

Richard had been pleased with his reception which he attributed to his Easter visits with Darcy when they had done the same rounds. He now had a better idea of what repairs were urgent and what could be delayed, although he was certain that from the tenant's point of view they were all equally important.

He spent his first afternoons with the men Gardiner had sent; they took their notes and then the next morning packed and crated and hauled furniture out of the house; the afternoon would then be spent in the next series of rooms while all the evenings were spent on the ledgers. Richard felt intense relief when he discovered that Palmer had kept copious notes on the suggestions that Darcy had made over the past three years. Although Lady Catherine had not instituted them, he could see the direction Darcy had been trying to push her to take and studied carefully the notes on crop rotations and the newer more efficient planting equipment.

Darcy had also recommended that some of the men who thatched the cottages be trained in installing and repairing slate roofs and to begin that transition. Fire was always a hazard, and the newer roofs would not burn if sparks from a chimney landed on them. Their upkeep was easier and less expensive also and the stone roofing promoted better health in the tenants by doing away with the pests and the damp that were inevitable with thatch. It would not take an entire crew of men replacing thatch each year either which would eventually be a savings for the estate. This would be an expensive investment, but Darcy had suggested only doing one or two at most each season. That would keep the expenses down and allow time to gradually find places for the workers who would be displaced once everything was done with the new roofing. He noted that Darcy had included roofing the parsonage in the suggestions.

There were other notes too; his cousin was nothing if not thorough and Palmer, who Darcy had actually chosen and hired for the estate, had taken careful notes hoping that the time would come when they would be used. So, among the notes on crop rotation and roof repairs were items like the icehouse needed to be cleaned and repaired, there was repointing to do on the stables and there were windows on the main house and the dower house that needed reglazing.

It was a lot to do, an enormous amount of work would be needed, but Richard had never been afraid of working hard for what he wanted. His comfort level had increased by leaps and bounds as he began to amass the knowledge he would need to administer the estate properly, to care for the tenants as he had once cared for the men under his command. His cousin had been right, his military experience was serving him well. He and Palmer worked well together, and he would be completely comfortable leaving Rosings to escort Anne to Bath.

30

Lizzy thought that when she was old and gray and hopefully was surrounded by a bevy of grandchildren, she would while away a rainy afternoon by relating the story of this day to them. Her father had arrived that morning with her dear friend Charlotte Lucas and their cousin and friend Mr. Collins.

It was obvious the travel had taken a toll on Mr. Collins, but he insisted on staying in the parlor with them long enough to see their reaction when he and Mr. Bennet shared the news that the entail was broken. Lizzy positively glowed with joy and Jane shed happy tears at the news. They had not been afraid Mr. Collins would demand they leave upon the death of their father but to know that the estate would remain in the family, that the legalities were in place for them to always have their home brought joy and unexpected relief. The news given, Mr. Collins retired to the main floor room Mrs. Gardiner had arranged for him and the others gathered for a happy afternoon tea.

"Well Thomas, where is my wayward husband," teased Mrs. Gardiner. Mr. Gardiner had been at the Longbourn estate learning about harvesting for the past fortnight.

"He is remaining until the Netherfield harvest is completed and will represent the family at the celebration. Knowing that we need to get our three girls to Bath," replied Mr. Bennet, cheerfully including his friend's daughter as one of his girls. "we concentrated on Longbourn and Lucas Lodge first. Netherfield is still at least a sennight, possibly longer from completion."

"And how is he adjusting to estate management," questioned Lizzy. She adored her Uncle Gardiner and would hate for him to feel a failure.

"My dear, your Uncle Edward's good sense and years of handling customers, suppliers and employees is standing him in good stead. He has been reading about estate management for much of the last two or three years as he knew he would be purchasing an estate soon; all he needed was a little practical experience and he was happily bustling all over both Longbourn and Netherfield. When he comes to visit in Bath we will go over what I have in place for spring plantings on both estates and why I planned each field and crop; I believe he would benefit from being present in the spring but he may need to be in London and if so there will be time once they have taken up the reigns there to learn; I have no fears for him, he is a natural leader which is an important but oft overlooked trait a good master needs."

"I am so glad," said Lizzy with a sigh of relief. "We know how good Uncle is as a businessman, but I will confess to a little worry about how he would take to this whole new career."

Charlotte smiled at her friends. "You do not have to worry Lizzy. I know it is natural for you and Jane to be anxious for him, but your father speaks nothing but the truth. The tenants could immediately sense that he was a good man, that he was interested in them and also that he had the habit of command, though in truth he always requested never ordered. He listened to them too and that is something that many a landlord neglects to do. He will do very well."

Mrs. Gardiner beamed at this praise of her husband. "He is an excellent man and I am so very pleased you think he will do well; more I am pleased that from the way you speak of him he was interested and engaged. I have worried that being a landlord might be onerous for him and knowing how he has loved business all these years I would not have him do something he dislikes every day. You know we do not care so much about society, and I would love to raise my boys in the country. The city has its blessings to be sure but those we can partake of with visits. I want them to be able to have some years when they can roam freely and explore and just be boys. They will be going to school soon enough and these years will be precious to us."

Thomas nodded his agreement. "I understand Maddie. You know that Fanny and I made the decision to live on the estate year round even when we had the Bath house available. I wanted my children to grow up without the noises and lack of freedom that comes with living in a city."

"We feel blessed to have grown up in Hertfordshire with our friends about us. I agree that raising a family in the city must be difficult," Jane said thoughtfully.

Lizzy looked much struck also for a moment, then she deliberately put that thought aside for contemplating later and smiled over at her father affectionately. "Well, we very much appreciate that you have come as soon as you can papa. We have loved our time with Aunt Gardiner, but we have such gorgeous new gowns hanging in our closets just begging to come out and play. We need to go to Bath and dance at the first ball we can!"

That drew everyone into laughter and harvest talk was put aside for the moment.

"So papa," quizzed Lizzy, "what exactly happens now that the entail is broken?"

"Well, the most important thing was already done and just waiting for the date and the signatures. And that is my Will."

"Oh papa, I do not want to contemplate losing you," Jane's voice was soft and almost pleading.

"I do not want to leave you dear children, but it is the natural order of things that I shall predecease you and I would have it no other way. When that time comes, the estate will go to one of you girls and all kinds of contingencies are allowed for. The best outcome for the estate is that one of my girls marry a man who would be a good estate manager and is willing to take the name Bennet. Failing that I will leave it outright to one of you and trust that you will administer it well and pass it along to a child of your own. I will not demand that the next heir be male. We know how much damage that has done. I have set up an entail, but it is just one that keeps the property together, not one that determines who inherits."

Lizzy nodded thoughtfully. "And of course mama would have life tenancy."

Thomas nodded. "The dower house is leased but it is part of the lease agreement that when I die they will have one year to vacate the property if they are asked to do so. Your mother may want to stay at Longbourn, or she may prefer to move to the dower house. You never know how these things will go so I have left her what options I can. She also has the right to choose to live in Bath instead of either Longbourn manor or the dower house."

Lizzy nodded thoughtfully. "I can see her visiting in Bath but I do not think I can picture her leaving Meryton. She has so many friends there and a lifetime of memories."

Charlotte laughed. "Heavens, my own mother and half the ladies of Hertfordshire would band together to stop her. There is no doubt she is the highest lady of the county, but she is never condescending and most respected. They would not wish to lose her."

Maddie rang the bell for fresh tea. "It sounds as if you have it all arranged."

"I could not help wondering over the years what I would do if the entail were broken. Then once my cousin brought the proposal to me I have thought of little else, jotting notes and going over scenarios in my mind and on paper too. Phillips and I had everything prepared within days of sending the petition off, particularly since we knew this would happen quickly."

"How would you know that?"

"Well Lizzy we had not told everyone the story but now that we do not have to worry about disappointing everyone's hopes, I will tell you. We were worried about how long it would take; these things can linger in the courts for months or even years. And then Matlock came to Netherfield. Collins took the opportunity to ask the Colonel to speak to his father about being one of the signatories on the petition. He not only did so, but he also directed his solicitors to present it jointly with Phillips. Once the Earl of Matlock's people presented it and they saw his signature on the papers everything went through with astonishing speed."

A soft blush spread over Jane's cheeks. "Oh, that is very kind of him."

"Kind of the Earl to sign it or kind of the Colonel to ask?" teased Lizzy.

"Both," replied Jane promptly. "Oh this is the happiest of days."

"It is odd," said Lizzy reflectively, "that it feels as if a weight is off our shoulders. I know that Cousin William would never abandon us or treat us with less than the utmost respect, but I had wondered if I would feel a guest at Longbourn. Now if I am living there, it will be as Lizzy Bennet of Longbourn. I do not explain it well," she finished, frustrated that she could not articulate all she felt.

But the others all nodded at her. "It is a relief, a weight off the heart," said Jane. "I think my mind knew it would be alright, but my heart was unsure. Now we know."

"I wonder what prompted the Earl to sign," mused Charlotte. "I know he is a rumored to be a good man but for someone of his stature to agree with this request is very unusual I think."

"I wonder if it was Anne?" said Lizzy.

"Anne de Bourgh?" said Charlotte.

Lizzy nodded. "I know I wrote to you of our friendship and of course we sent you all those outfits that did not become her. We do not know everything that happened, but from what has been said I think Anne de Bourgh gave Rosings to the Colonel."

Jane gasped. "How would you know that? I did not hear anyone say anything of the kind."

"No, no one has said anything directly. But think of this Jane: Lady Catherine has retired to Derbyshire. We went to the de Bourgh townhouse, not so Anne could see it but so the Colonel could. He is the one who went to Uncle for advice on leasing it. And he is in Kent right now. He is returning to escort Anne to Bath then he is going back for harvest. Anne has health problems, she would not likely be able to administer the estate and she has made it plain that she plans to live year round in Bath. And even though it is her childhood home, it struck me that she has never once mentioned returning to Rosings Park. Add to this that the Colonel has recently resigned his commission." Lizzy paused a moment to let them absorb her observations.

"I think all of that is related. Think of it from the Earl's perspective: at the same time that your niece has given up her estate to your son because of ill health, that same son comes to you and asks you to help a good man do what he perceives is the right thing by giving up his estate because of his health. The parallel is very clear."

"Yes," agreed Maddie, "the similarities seem obvious and would have struck him too I would think."

"Well, whatever the reason, there will be Bennets at Longbourn and for that we can only be grateful," said Charlotte cheerfully.

The next day the Bennets remained close to home. There was much to catch up on and Mr. Collins would be unable to get around well that day. Travel for even short distances was very difficult for him. They did not forget about Anne though; Mrs. Gardiner penned an invitation to lunch for the following day.

"I am surprised our cousin decided to come to Bath, papa. The journey will be very difficult for him."

"It will be, even taking some days to rest in between will not make the journey to Bath easy for him. But the plumbing may prove to be very beneficial for him."

"The plumbing?"

"Hot baths, my dear. You know how a hot brick helps to relieve his pain. What if he could spend time in a hot bath every day? It may not be beneficial, but he felt it was worth the pain to see if it would help. And Bath is not as cold as Meryton. The cooler days are already taking a toll on him."

"I will check the stillroom the first day we are there papa. We may have to ask one of the grooms to ride to Longbourn for some supplies, I do not know what might be available in Bath. But I want to have enough willow bark to brew him a tisane any time he needs one."

Lunch with Anne was delightful. She was a little diffident with Mr. Collins but once past the initial discomfort of being with someone her mother had wronged had passed they conversed easily. And Anne was astounded to see that the pretty morning dress worn by Charlotte Lucas was obviously remade from one from her own closet and that it became Miss Lucas very well. Once lunch was finished and Mr. Collins was wheeled down the hallway to rest by Thomas, the ladies gathered in the sitting room.

Anne's eyes were shining with delight. "Miss Lucas, you must call me Anne please and I know this is not something I am supposed to bring up but I cannot help it, you look so very lovely in that dress which was one that never became me. Oh, I am so pleased."

Charlotte's cheeks had pinked a bit at the beginning of this speech, but Anne's obvious good will along with her equally obvious delight that Charlotte looked lovely dispelled her embarrassment. "I cannot thank you enough. I have a dozen day dresses and several dinner gowns with me that should be easily remade. I did not have a lot of time due to harvest but now I will have both time and several friends to help me."

Anne looked at her thoughtfully a moment then asked, "I know Mr. Bennet said we were to leave tomorrow but I wonder if we could stay a little longer. Richard will be here on Friday so we can travel on Saturday, and I would love to travel together. And if we stayed, we could get a lot of your wardrobe done. My aunt left her seamstress here in London. Mrs. Markham usually travels with them, but she has a grandchild due to be born and asked to remain here. She has been over every day or two to check my wardrobe and confided that she was itching to do some fine stitching. She has been sewing for the babe for months but there is little left to do now. She is very fast, a fine seamstress, she has been with Aunt Audrey for years you know, because sleeves change, and necklines change, and Aunt Audrey simply will not toss out a whole closet of clothes because sleeves are longer this year and shorter the next. She could probably do several gowns over in that period of time."

Charlotte's face light up with delight. "Oh Lizzy, Jane do you think Mr. Bennet would agree? I should so very much like to arrive in Bath with more than one lovely day dress and the few older things I brought with me are going to be relegated to working in the garden or the stillroom as they are not fine enough for Bath."

"I think that is an excellent idea," enthused Lizzy. "If Mrs. Markham can do even a couple of gowns it would be wonderful. And with me and Jane and Aunt Maddie all sewing on your things, we could have several day dresses and dinner gowns for you. I think Mr. Collins could use a couple of more days rest before he is jolted about for another day."

Mr. Bennet readily consented to the change of plans as long as Mrs. Gardiner did not mind them imposing on her. Maddie had laughed at that and told him to take his silliness elsewhere, the women of the house had serious wardrobe issues to discuss.

Assumed Virtue

31

The trip to Bath was accomplished in great comfort, for not only did they have their own coach but when Richard and Anne joined them they brought both the de Bourgh town coach and the large and luxurious de Bourgh road coach. Knowing Mr. Collins' situation, Richard had caused a large and heavily padded board to be placed spanning the seats on one side to allow Mr. Collins to recline more comfortably for the journey. "It will still not be a comfortable journey for you," Richard had told him with a rueful smile. "I have traveled injured so I know that there is nothing that will really make it less than painful, but at least we can mitigate it to a certain extent."

Richard and Mr. Bennet had joined him in the de Bourgh coach and whiled away the journey conversing easily. The ladies had gathered in the Bennet coach to give the gentlemen plenty of room to stretch their legs during the short journey.

"I will be keeping the town coach, while Richard will take the road coach to Kent with him. Once there he will have the de Bourgh coat of arms taken off the coach and replaced with the Fitzwilliam's." At her companions curious looks, Anne continued, "Forgive me, I have been planning this for so long that I believe I have forgotten to explain, I have given up Rosings Park to Richard."

"I confess I had wondered if that was the case. But does not your mother own Rosings?" asked Lizzy.

"I inherited Rosings on my birthday a year past but I simply was too tired and ill to fight Lady Catherine for my rights. So I bided my time and when she decided she had to confront my uncle about his insistence that she curtail her spending, I made sure to go with her." Anne sighed, gazing out the window pensively. "It was an awful trip; I was being made ill from all the medications I was taking, the journey made me worse and we began by traveling three days to Derbyshire then turning around and traveling two and a half days to London. But it was worth it. Once I was safely at Matlock House, my aunt and uncle supported me against Lady Catherine, even before they knew I was going to give up the estate to Richard."

"Forgive me for asking, but why would you give up the estate?" queried Charlotte.

"It must seem odd, but I do not have the knowledge or the energy to run it properly, nor do I have any interest in it. The doctor is very optimistic that I will continue to improve in energy and health, but I had an illness in childhood that damaged my heart, and I will never be robust, can never risk having a child. I had determined to make a will that left the estate to Richard, but I had also decided that if I could find a way to do it I would give it to him before then. He will make an excellent job of it and it allowed him to freely give up his commission. For me, I have been an observer of life only; now I will become a participant. I may not be able to do everything, but I am anxious to see how much I can do. Now, you tell me, I have heard several comments about renovations to your home in Bath. Why is everyone so excited about them?"

Lizzy blushed a little but explained. "Well it is a difficult subject to bring up in company, but my father and my uncle have invested in a company that produces fittings for new bathing and refreshment chambers."

Anne's face lit up at the news. "Oh, oh I can hardly wait to see. I have read of them, where servants no longer have to haul water for baths and that chamber pots are replaced. There is a pump, is that correct?"

"I defer to Jane on this," chuckled Lizzy.

Jane also blushed a little but answered readily enough. "Yes, a pump and a small cistern; there is also a boiler so hot water is available for bathing and of course the pump brings colder water up. I know plumbing is not a subject to discuss generally but I am very excited too; I worked closely with my father and uncle and with the builder in designing the new chambers and I am particularly excited to see them."

Lizzy gave her a mischievous glance and added, "The original plan was for one, but by the time Jane was done with them, they had to expand their plans significantly. There are four in the house, one on the main floor, one to be shared between the mistress and master chambers, one for the rest of the suites on the family floor and even one for the servants."

"Well I can hardly wait to find out how this works for you; I know I would be interested in a similar renovation if all works as planned."

Lizzy chuckled at that. "I think that is why Uncle did not want Aunt Maddie to come with us just yet. He is afraid she is going to demand that he renovate their house and really, from everything we have heard, it is almost impossible to live in the house while the renovations are taking place."

Assumed Virtue

32

Anne wondered if people would think she was a little mad if they knew that some mornings she surreptitiously pinched herself to prove to herself that this was not a dream, that her life was real. Her prior, long held daydreams of what her life would be like seemed colorless and flat compared to the reality and she had no hesitation in acknowledging that it was due to the Bennet family.

She and Maude Jenkinson had settled in that first night, taking a light dinner in Anne's sitting room and retiring early. Anne had awakened unsettled. She was excited about being on her own, she was happy to have found her first real friends, but she honestly had no idea what to do next. Fortunately, her friends had worried about precisely that reaction. Charlotte Lucas along with Jane and Elizabeth had walked across the square to join her for morning tea.

"Anne, please know you can talk to us about whatever you wish. Are you feeling good after our journey, or do you need more time to recover?"

"Lizzy, I am feeling very good, but I confess I am unsettled. I want to live this new life but now I realize I do not really know what to do, how to go about it. At Rosings I knew exactly what each day would look like and in London Aunt Audrey organized everything, even though she was gone much of the time she still had so many things scheduled that I knew what was to happen next. My time is my own but what exactly do I do with it now that I have it?"

"Well, I know that Aunt Gardiner worked with you on running a town home and so did your own Aunt. Perhaps you need to start there."

"I do know, in theory at least, what needs to be done but now that I am actually in charge of the house I am not completely sure of exactly what I need to do, what would simply be nice to do and what can be left to others."

"I have been running Lucas Lodge for my mother for years, Anne. In your situation, the choice on what to do and what to leave to others is going to be completely your decision. But do not decide too quickly, that would be my advice. You need to know the responsibilities and the possible repercussions of allowing someone else the authority to make decisions on them before you can decide."

"For instance," supplied Lizzy, "think of budgets. You do not necessarily need to be the one to compile the ledgers, but you do need to be the one who reviews them. Before we left Longbourn, mama posed this question: what does flour cost in London? So, I will ask you what does flour cost in Bath? It will be more than at Rosings, you are not working with your own mill here. And how much do you really need each week? A cook or housekeeper can easily cheat an employer who does not know these things, though of course I would not suggest that this is happening. I am just pointing out how easily it can be done. The ledgers could all look good, but even reviewing them to make sure the mathematics are correct does not ensure that all is as it should be."

"Some people look down on those like our Uncle and Aunt Gardiner for being in trade, but if you think about it, running an estate or even a house involves a lot of the same skills needed in business," remarked Jane. "And no one is suggesting that you need to know everything all at once. Mother has been training us to run the estate for years, so we know what things we are most interested in and what we would oversee without a great deal of involvement. Lizzy has the best hand in the stillroom of all of us, Mary is good at it and I am hopeless. But I know what needs to be there, what supplies are necessary. So even though it is Lizzy who would be the one to fix a tonic if someone falls ill, I know what needs to be stocked, what will spoil, what herbs and blossoms and bark need to be harvested and when to do so. When we have our own homes, I would assume that Lizzy will be in the stillroom often, while I will only be there for inventory and overseeing things to make sure we have the proper supplies."

"You are welcome to join us any time, with questions or concerns or just to be in company. We would not stand on ceremony," invited Lizzy.

And that had started two weeks that would always rank as one of the most wonderful times of her life. Each day she and Maude walked over to the Bennet house and broke their fast with their friends. It was wonderful to be part of a cheerful, relaxed group. She was able to spend time with Mr. Bennet and Mr. Collins and found herself able to easily relax in their company. Her questions to her friends about running the house were answered kindly and without condescension, there was so much more involved than she had realized. Three days after they arrived, her old wardrobe arrived from Rosings and they all gathered to turn the creations that had made her look sallow and ill into creations that made Charlotte look elegant and refined. Their work in London had given her a basic wardrobe, but now it could be greatly expanded. Mr. Thomas offered that he would be pleased to hire a seamstress to help the process along and after some hesitation Charlotte was induced to agree.

Being in society was going to be all new to Anne and a new place for the Bennets and Charlotte so they decided to begin slowly. Mr. Bennet signed their names in Mr. King's book and decided the Pump Room would be the first place they visited. "Do not worry about remembering everyone," Mr. Bennet had counseled. "One of the reasons we go to the Pump Room first is so that everyone knows we are new to Bath society. They will understand if you do not remember who they are after a single meeting. Now after a second they will not be quite so understanding. I would suggest that you record this morning's meetings in a journal."

"I do not understand why we are doing that?" asked Anne, honestly confused.

"To fix people in your mind. If you will try to picture each person you met and note their name, then perhaps you can add something about what they look like and if you conversed, you could note if there was something that seemed to spark their interest. For instance, do you remember meeting Mr. Meyers? He was a slightly portly, blond gentleman who was quite polite until Charlotte mentioned something about horses and then he became animated and more interested in conversing. So you might note that. The time will come when this is not necessary, but it is a good exercise for all of you to begin to know people in Bath."

Mornings that were not spent at the Pump Room were spent in the shops on Milsom Street or Godwins Circulating Library or sometimes just in the cozy drawing room with her friends. And regularly, they were escorted by her cousin Richard. She could not be surprised that he was often found in the company of the Bennets or that he and Mr. Bennet enjoyed each other's conversation, but it did initially surprise her that he seemed to have formed a firm bond with Mr. Collins.

"I like him, Anne," he had replied when she quizzed him on it. "I do not know if we would have been quite so friendly if I had only known him as the parson at Hunsford. But I have been injured, have faced waking up every day in exhausting pain, have been forced to depend on the kindness of those around me to accomplish the most mundane of tasks; admittedly for me this was not a lifelong situation, but nevertheless I believe I have an idea of what he is going through. And like you, he knows that his physical situation will prevent him from being the kind of administrator Longbourn needs and was willing to give up his inheritance for the good of the tenants and his cousins."

Anne shook her head at that. "You give me too much credit, Richard. I will not deny that those concerns informed my decision, but there was certainly a selfishness at play for me. I wanted to live the life I am discovering here. I want to take charge of my life and to make decisions, yes, but I also want to do it without the weight of responsibility you have assumed. I am not afraid I cannot do it so much as I am afraid that I would not do it; I would try not to allow my energy and illnesses to be an excuse, but I am no fool Richard; I have rarely had to do the hard things."

When he disagreed with her, she would have none of it. "Do not romanticize my life, Richard. The truth is that just the responsibilities of running the house here are more than I ever had to do at Rosings, and I find that even as few as they are that sometimes I want to allow myself to use being too tired as an excuse to abrogate my responsibilities. It is best for me and for you and for the estate that you have taken charge of it, cousin. For certain I would not do it as it should be done."

Richard was thoroughly enjoying his sojourn in Bath. He had assumed he would, as he generally found a way to be pleased no matter the company. But he rarely had had such an opportunity as the one he now had. He had been in the military since he was seven and ten. With his thirtieth birthday only months away, he was discovering how different his life was now that he no longer had the possibility of dying on the battlefield as a concern. It was odd to realize that he would not have to be alert not to begin something that could not be finished quickly as no one would be sending an express demanding that he be halfway across the channel in mere days. While he had certainly had responsibilities, had been making decisions of major importance for years, to be doing so without a general looking over his shoulder was oddly disconcerting. Enjoyable, but disconcerting.

He found that he truly liked and enjoyed his cousin Anne. She was discovering who she was, and he found it intriguing to watch. He felt they were setting a foundation for a good, strong friendship over and above their family connection.

He was also forming a genuine friendship with Mr. Collins, whom he admired for how he was handling the difficult role life had handed him. He enjoyed Mr. Bennet's company, Miss Lucas was pleasant and Elizabeth was a truly interesting young woman. And then there was Jane. He was attracted to her beauty, certainly, he could not imagine how anyone would not be bowled over by her appearance.

But he was finding now that his initial impressions from Hertfordshire fell far short of the mark. She could indeed hold her own in conversation on any number of topics, she was kind, she was gentle. All that he had seen. What he had not seen was that her intelligence was as keen as that of Miss Elizabeth, just not so quickly displayed.

He had discovered one aspect of how much was hidden when he had experienced the refreshing chamber at Bennet House. The plumbing had fascinated him, but he was a well brought up gentleman and certainly would not speak of it with the ladies present. So he had waited and when the opportunity came to discuss it with Mr. Bennet, that gentleman had told him what little he knew, then confessed he had invested in the company at the insistence of his brother Gardiner, but that if Richard wished to know the details, he needed to talk to Jane. So he had. And had been stunned. She had a breadth of knowledge that spoke of hours of research which she displayed without conceit; and she had laughed a little at herself for demanding that her father and uncle allow her to design four of them for the house.

"It is too much," she admitted candidly, "but each one posed its own unique problems and I felt we needed to have that information in hand when the builders want to know what to do if they run into something they do not know how to handle." She gave him a rather cheeky grin and added, "I know that I am not known for my stubbornness, but that is because there are so many things where I truly do not have a strong preference. But when it is something I do have a strong feeling on, I can be very stubborn about doing it the way I think it should be done."

He had ample time to get to know her. While Mr. Bennet escorted his daughters and Miss Lucas to the public balls on Monday and Thursday and to the concerts that were held each Wednesday, he escorted Anne and Mrs. Jenkinson to the same functions and naturally they all arranged to meet upon arrival or even traveled together.

He was often included in family dinners at the Bennet home as they knew he was staying alone in lodgings so was told to consider their house a second home instead of spending lonely dinners in his chambers at the Edgar Building. And he dined at Anne's, with Anne and Maude hosting him along with Miss Elizabeth, Miss Lucas and Miss Bennet. Anne needed the practice she pointed out as she wanted to be able to host dinner parties and having her cousin and her friends to practice on was allowing her to gain confidence in her hostessing skills.

It had been an interesting time, but tonight was one of the rare evenings he would be spending home alone. He had deliberately not accepted any invitations for this evening. Something was nagging at him; he had had this feeling before and he knew that there was some decision he needed to make. He felt the need to take stock, to look at where he was and where he wished to be and formulate a plan.

He had the housekeeper bring him a tray of meat and cheese and bread in the study; no need to put the staff to the trouble of setting up the dining room just so he could eat a lonely dinner. Then he settled in a big chair, poured himself a small measure of brandy and began organizing everything that had been floating around busily in his mind.

First Rosings and Anne. Rosings Park was his now, his responsibility and one that he did not intend to take lightly. His cousin had given him the gift of choice in his life. He had been able to sell his commission, he was going to be able to live the kind of life that he had never expected, and he did not plan to fail the tenants who were now his people, nor would he fail himself.

By now most of the rooms would be set up. He made a mental note to be sure not to rush off to ride the estate but to stop and see the interior changes first. The staff would need to be thanked for their hard work. He had to return in a couple of days as he wanted to be there for his first harvest. He would return to Bath once it was completed.

There was something going on with his cousin Darcy and he was unsure what was troubling him. Richard had noticed some differences in his letters from his cousin; nothing overt but just enough so that a keen observer would note that something had been bothering him. He wondered if it involved Miss Elizabeth; if that was the case then Richard was afraid he would be decidedly unhappy when he discovered that her family was here and that the Bennets had become close friends with the Matlocks and with Anne. Was he still infatuated with Miss Elizabeth? Distance certainly could make the heart grow fonder, but in Richard's experience that was not often the case; more often distance simply made feelings wither. It would be shame; in his opinion Miss Elizabeth could be the making of his cousin but it was not his decision after all.

Then there was Jane. He had saved the most pleasurable topic for last. He was seriously thinking that once the harvest was in and he returned to Bath he would request a courtship with Miss Jane Bennet; he knew her enough now to know that she would not grant it if she were not genuinely interested. But was she? His mind drifted back to their first meeting, and he remembered how her eyes had sparkled as they had debated some point of politics. And how her whole being had cooled while she tolerated Bingley's attentions. Thankfully he had never been subjected to that withdrawn and icy beauty; with him she appeared interested and engaged. He knew he sported a rather ridiculous grin, but he could not help himself. Interested. Engaged. And quite possibly enough so that there was a chance for him. Should he ask now, before he left for Rosings? He did not want to miss his chance, to find that she had been expecting more and despaired of him. But he did not want to limit her choices either. He knew Mrs. Bennet had wanted this season in Bath so her girls could come in contact with more possibilities than they had in Hertfordshire.

He let his head drop back against the chair. This was it then, the decision that had been nagging at him. He needed to think this over carefully; what was best and fair for himself and for her. He had been a poor matrimonial prospect for so many years that he was not sure how to assess himself now. He had an estate albeit one that needed much attention and investment before it was worth more than merely making him a landed gentleman. He would not have to leave his wife, not have her waiting and wondering as he served. That was all to the good. But without that automatic dismissal of his eligibility, he was not sure what to ask. What would a woman like Jane Bennet want in a husband? And could he be that husband to her?

He no longer served but the memories and nightmares were there, would probably always be there. Could she, could any woman, be happy with someone whose soul was scarred with the deaths of so many and whose dreams rarely allowed for a full night of sleep? Was he ready to make a whole-hearted commitment to her? And was she ready to consider him as a possible husband?

He would not decide tonight, but now that he had defined the questions he needed to answer his mind would let him rest more easily. And he would try to be more aware of her reactions and carefully assess what clues he could discern from her conversation and demeanor.

33

At the Thursday night ball, Richard seized his chance to talk to Jane as they waited for their dance set to begin.

"I am going to be leaving for Rosings tomorrow morning; harvest is beginning, and I need to be there."

Jane nodded her approval. "Yes, it is always important for the master of the estate to be available during harvest, and particularly now when you are so new to them. The tenants need to see you there, to see that you care."

"They do. I will be returning though, and I plan to spend the rest of the Season here. No doubt I will return to Rosings regularly, but it is only half a day's journey, so it is easily accomplished. I want the tenants to know that I will not be an absentee landlord."

Jane was silent a moment then said shyly, "I am glad to know you will be returning."

"Are you?" he asked, regarding her intently. "I will be honest Miss Bennet and tell you that I would like to know you better and to have you get to know me."

"I should like that too."

Richard took her hand to lead her to the dance floor. "Good. I will not be gone long and then we shall have an opportunity to see if we are both going to be interested in a possible future."

When they arrived at home, Lizzy followed Jane into her bedchamber. "We do not share a room here, Lizzy. Have you lost your way?"

Lizzy gave her older sister a completely unrepentant look. "I am exactly where I planned to be Janie: sitting in your room until you tell me what you talked about with the Colonel."

As she took the pins from her hair, Jane met Lizzy's eyes in the mirror. "What makes you think there is anything of interest to tell you?"

Lizzy laughed at her. "Jane, I was watching you as we were waiting for the set to start, and you were blushing red as a rose when you reached the dance floor."

"Perhaps I was just flushed from all the vigorous dancing."

"Or perhaps you had a very interesting conversation with your beau."

Jane set the brush down on the table and turned to face her sister. "He is returning to Rosings to oversee the harvest. Then he will return to Bath."

"That does not seem to be a reason to blush as you were."

"He made it clear that he is interested in me, Lizzy. When he returns he wants to get to know me and to let me know more of him. I believe he is serious Lizzy and that he let me know so that when he returns I can either encourage him or let him know I am not interested in anything but friendship."

"And are you? Interested in more than friendship?"

"I believe I am, Lizzy. I have liked him from the first and the time we have been able to spend together since arriving in Bath has only deepened that feeling. He is strong and kind and good, and Lizzy he does not mind that I am educated and interested in things like plumbing, he actually enjoys it and would, I think, encourage me to pursue those subjects that interest me. That is very enticing."

Lizzy rose and embraced Jane. "I believe you would do well together if liking becomes love. I know mama is hoping we meet good men to marry this season Jane but remember that our parents married for love and want that for us too."

The Monday following Richard's departure saw Mr. Bennet escorting his daughters, Miss Lucas and Anne to the ball in the Upper Rooms. He had assured Anne of her welcome, laughingly pointing out that none of the ladies he was escorting were foolish or flighty young girls. "You are all sensible and intelligent young women, so I do not really have to do aught but be there to show society that you are all protected. Nothing more is required."

As the second set started Mr. Bennet was surprised to hear Miss Lucas' soft exclamation, "Oh dear, oh no, this is unfortunate."

Following her gaze Mr. Bennet had to suppress a groan of dismay; this Monday Mr. Bennet discovered that his presence was indeed required. Coming toward them was Mr. Bingley, along with Miss Bingley, the Hursts and Mr. Darcy. Mr. Bennet sighed. "Well if the two gentlemen are as poorly behaved here as they were in Meryton I am going to have to step in. I do not wish to do so but I will not allow them make my daughters the talk of Bath."

The other party had reached them by now and Bingley greeted Mr. Bennet with a beaming smile. "Mr. Bennet, sir, it is wonderful to see you again. How is your family? Are they all here with you?"

"I am surprised to see you here Mr. Bingley," replied Mr. Bennet, refusing to actually say that he was glad to see the younger man. "I am here with two of my daughters and Miss Lucas, I am sure you remember her?"

"I do indeed, it is good to see you Miss Lucas. Could I have the next set if you have it available please?"

"Of course, Mr. Bingley, I would be happy to dance the next with you."

While Bingley had been greeting them, Miss Bingley had deliberately looked away, watching the dancers, apparently so absorbed she was unaware of Bennet and Charlotte. Darcy had nodded to them but did not speak and Mr. Hurst had departed abruptly to find the card room. Mrs. Hurst, however, stepped forward to greet both of them pleasantly.

Surprised, Mr. Bennet returned the greeting and he and Mrs. Hurst spoke for a few moments until the set ended and the dancers began leaving the floor. Mr. Bingley waited until Lizzy and Jane had joined them so he could ask Jane for a set; when she explained she had nothing available, he bowed and then offered his arm to Charlotte, and they moved toward the dance floor.

Again, Mrs. Hurst had greeted them courteously while Miss Bingley ignored them, and Darcy simply regarded them solemnly but as Bingley and Charlotte moved away he abruptly asked Elizabeth for her next set.

"I am sorry Mr. Darcy, I do not have an open set left this evening, though I thank you for asking," Lizzy replied then turned to greet Mr. Warwick who had come to claim her hand. She politely introduced him to the Bingley party then they left while Jane and Mr. Bennet also joined the dancers.

"I am so glad that I saved this dance for you papa," whispered Jane. "I do not want to dance with Mr. Bingley or Mr. Darcy."

Bennet nodded. "I know you do not, and I doubt Lizzy does either. Charlotte has Mr. Bingley as a partner now. Do you have any open dances?"

Jane shook her head. "Not only this one; and I know Lizzy has none open either."

"Well, I do not believe Mr. Darcy will request a dance from Charlotte and since Bingley is now dancing with her we can hope that we can avoid them for the rest of the evening. When the dance ends we will leave the floor away from wherever their party is. And I will try to keep moving away from them each dance so you and Lizzy can safely retreat to my side without having to deal with them. Be sure to let Charlotte know of our plan if you speak with her. Have you seen Anne?"

"She is dancing with Mr. Richardson. I will inform her too, or you can do so once our dance is finished." She was silent a moment then said, "I have just this moment realized, Anne is cousin to Mr. Darcy. I do not know how close they are but perhaps we should avoid mentioning that we are trying to avoid him also. After all, he is not going to ask any of us to dance, only Lizzy and he has already been refused for the evening."

"You are correct my dear, though I am afraid we are going to have to let Anne know at some point there is no reason to do so this evening. Be sure to warn Charlotte and I will make sure Lizzy is aware."

And so began a dance within the dance for Mr. Bennet, one which he found remarkably amusing to engage in despite his irritation with Bingley and Darcy.

Each time a dance set was coming to an end Mr. Bennet found reason to make sure he was nowhere near Bingley. By the time Bingley reached him both of his girls were leaving with their partners for the next set; Charlotte had her share of partners also as did Anne; Bennet managed to avoid Bingley so well that they were never introduced. In this manner Bennet managed to keep Bingley from importuning Jane for the entire night.

Once Anne was safely delivered home, Mr. Bennet and the ladies under his protection all gathered in the sitting room to discuss the evening.

"What wretched luck," complained Lizzy. "I cannot believe that they are here. Why are they not in London? All Miss Bingley spoke of the entire time she was in Hertfordshire was how she longed to be back in London and now here they are Bath. I do not understand it."

"Nor do I, my dear, but I will handle this on the morrow."

"What do you plan to do papa?"

"I will pen a note to each gentleman, explaining my expectations for their behavior if they wish to spend time with either of my daughters. It is not a task I relish, but I will not have this season ruined for the two of you by their ridiculous behavior."

"Can you forbid them to approach us?" asked Lizzy hopefully.

Her father chuckled at that. "There is my all-or-nothing Lizzy! No, I cannot honorably do that. But I can limit how much time they can spend in your company and in the case of Mr. Darcy I can demand that he dance with other young women outside his party. You were the only one so honored in Hertfordshire and the neighbors there ignored it; we cannot expect the matrons of Bath to ignore such a sign of favor from a man situated as high in the ton as Mr. Darcy. He must either not dance with you or he must dance with others to gain you as a partner."

"Well, it would not surprise me at all if he refuses to do so, so that is all to the good," said Lizzy decisively. "I am quite sure he will not approach me if he can only do so by being pleasant to other young ladies."

Mr. Bennet bade his daughters and Miss Lucas good night and settled behind his desk to sketch out what he wished to say to the young men. He would do clean copies the next morning, but he wanted to get the main gist of his thoughts down now even though he was aware he would probably soften what he was writing on the morrow. At the moment his disgust was so high that he could not trust himself to address them with any courtesy at all.

It was just shy of ten the next morning when the butler presented Darcy and Bingley with missives written in a strong masculine hand and marked confidential. The gentlemen exchanged surprised glances and retired to Bingley's study to read the missives.

Bennet House, Bath

October --, 1811

Mr. Darcy,

I regret having to send such a missive to the son of the man who was my close friend for many years, but your behavior in Hertfordshire was such that I feel I am forced to do so.

Your rude and ungentlemanly behavior during the entire time you stayed in Hertfordshire was tolerated sir as we are a small community and it affected no one's good opinion of my daughters or my family to allow your behavior to go unremarked.

Here in Bath it is a different situation.

I can do nothing about your ridiculous habit of stalking the sidelines of a ballroom with a forbidding and cold expression on your face. I can do nothing about you making a fool of yourself by alternately staring at my daughter Elizabeth and glaring at her other dance partners.

I can, however, forbid her to dance with you and if, as you did in Hertfordshire, you single her out as the only lady outside your own party with whom you will dance I shall not hesitate to follow that course. I allowed it in Hertfordshire since everyone was aware of your insults to her and indeed to our family in general and simply found your subsequent interactions amusing. We are no longer in Hertfordshire and I will not have either of my daughters be the subject of gossip or inuendo because of the poor behavior of the members of your party.

If you are going to request a dance with Elizabeth you will only do so after you have danced with at least two other eligible young ladies who are not of your own party. This is a simple and easily followed requirement, sir. If you do not wish to dance with my daughter then there is no need to follow this course. If you do wish to do so, I will expect you to comply.

Sincerely,

Thomas Bennet

Postscript: Sir, if you do not wish Miss Bingley to be privy to this missive I would suggest you either burn it or lock it securely away. I have had a wider experience than you, I believe, with her sort of woman and I guarantee she will be desperate to know what was written and will not hesitate to read this should she gain access to it. I would not trust a locked door as she is your hostess and has keys to every room at her disposal.

TB

On the other side of the room, Bingley was reading his own missive from Mr. Bennet.

Bennet House, Bath

October --, 1811

Mr. Bingley,

You are perhaps unaware of your reputation in the ton and in Hertfordshire as a fickle and inconstant man who will shower his attentions upon a young woman and then abruptly desert her when someone new catches his attention.

My family, however, is not unaware and I will not allow you to make Jane uncomfortable or to place her in the position of being gossiped about as your latest flirt.

I will allow you one dance per evening with Jane sir, and one only. When the set is completed you will return my daughter to my side and you will depart our presence for the remainder of the evening. You will not monopolize her company; you will not demand more attention than any other casual acquaintance. You will not refuse to leave her side nor will you stare at her while she is dancing with others. I will reiterate, you will dance with her only once, sir and as soon as she has gained my protection or moved to another partner your time with her is at an end for the evening.

If we are in company during a concert, dinner or other evening's entertainment that does not involve dancing you may spend no more than thirty minutes monopolizing her. Then you will seek other company for the remainder of the evening. You may call upon her in my home once per week and no more than that and you will remain no longer than any normal morning caller.

I have brought my daughters to Bath to allow them a wider acquaintance and I will not have what should be an enjoyable season for them ruined by your unceasing attentions to my eldest. There will be no gossip about my daughter nor will you be the reason for any other gentlemen to decline to get to know her because of your unguarded attentions to her.

These are not difficult demands and they are ones I expect you to honor. If Jane ever requests more time with you I will inform you of this.

Sincerely,

Thomas Bennet

Postscript: I will give you the same advice I tendered to Mr. Darcy. If you do not wish for your sister, Miss Bingley, to be privy to this letter, burn it or lock it securely away. She is the kind of woman who snoops in everyone's private business. I would not trust a locked door only; as your hostess she has keys to every room and I guarantee you she uses them.

TB

"Good heavens, Darcy, do you think Caroline actually snoops into everyone's private business when we are not about?" gasped Bingley, the final words of Mr. Bennet's missive being the last he had read they were the first to be addressed. "She would not really do such a thing would she?"

"I should not be at all surprised, Bingley. I keep my correspondence and all my personal papers securely locked in cases in my room so she cannot gain access to them; you will recall I advised you some time ago to always keep your important papers locked in your desk. She has access to your study but not what is locked away."

"But, but that is unforgiveable Darce. She cannot do that. If anyone ever found out she would be ruined, and no one would ever wish to be my guest again."

"That is true. This is something you should discuss with her Bingley. I do not know if it will actually do any good, but it might," replied Darcy impatiently. "I assume Mr. Bennet has warned you away from Miss Bennet?"

"Yes," replied Mr. Bingley glumly. "He says I am inconstant, and a flirt and he will not have Jane gossiped about. I do not wish her to be gossiped about but how can I fix her interest if I cannot spend more than thirty minutes with her? I am not even allowed to visit daily, only one time each week. I do not understand this Darcy. I am a good prospect for her, why would he want me to stay away from her?"

"You keep forgetting how mercenary the Bennets are, Bingley. Your attentions were welcomed when you were the only possible suitor for her hand, there was no one else of interest in Hertfordshire. But now that there are other eligible men around Mr. Bennet is making it clear that she is no longer going to be pursuing you. You should be thankful that you have discovered her true nature before you were trapped into marriage with her Charles."

Bingley looked at him in surprise. "I did not see that she pursued me Darcy. I was pursuing her and it is true she encouraged me and was always welcoming and kind, but I do not believe she was trying to trap me."

"You are sometimes naïve my friend. I watched her closely as I was concerned about you and while she may have been encouraging and welcoming to you with her words, I believe her eyes told a different story. She seemed cold and indifferent to me, Charles. I do not say this to wound you, but I do not believe she ever cared for you."

Bingley paced the room in agitation. "I cannot believe it of her. I cannot. I believe if there is a mercenary motive it is on the part of Mr. Bennet, not on Jane's. I believe that it is Mr. Bennet's intentions that she marry for advancement not Jane's." Bingley stopped then and squared his shoulders, looking at Darcy with surprising determination. "Well, I will not allow her parents' mercenary intentions to destroy our felicity. I will take what he has given me and make the most of every moment I am allowed to be in her presence."

Darcy shook his head grimly but said no more as he knew he would not be able to convince Bingley of Jane's coldness to him, not now. Perhaps the seeds of doubt had been planted and Charles would see for himself now that he knew what to look for.

"What of your letter? Surely he is not asking you to take me in hand? Why would he write to both of us? Is your letter more of the same?"

Darcy hesitated. He would not lie to his friend, but he did not want to disclose what Bennet had said about him and Elizabeth. "It is basically the same yes. He believes that while our party's behavior was tolerable in Hertfordshire, that same behavior is not acceptable in Bath."

"I do not see where he is a judge of our behavior," argued Bingley. "He is not of the first circles; if no one in London disparages our actions why does he think he can do so?"

"I have no idea. Certainly he has no experience with which to judge, but he does have the right to dictate who will spend time with his daughters, that we cannot deny."

"I cannot go against his wishes it is true, but he did say that if Jane wants to spend more time with me he will allow it. I believe he has not told her the true situation and while I would not want to come between them I will be informing her of her father's decree. I have no doubt she will ask him to change his mind about how much time we are spending together."

Before he could go any further, there was a knock on the door followed immediately by the entrance of Miss Bingley.

"I am informed you gentlemen received what appeared to be urgent correspondence this morning. Is there a problem? What is the issue?"

Bingley, with Mr. Bennet's admonishment in mind, eyed his sister with disfavor. "You did not receive any missives so why would you think this is something that would concern you?"

Miss Bingley waved that aside. "Really Charles, as mistress of the house I have the right to know what is going on with the other persons here. How else will I know how best to make everyone comfortable?"

"Well there is nothing in our correspondence that has anything to do with you or with making us comfortable so you may go to breakfast, Caroline." He saw her eyeing his letter speculatively and added, "I will expect you to respect my privacy, sister. After all, I honor yours and I actually do have the right to read anything written by you or to you."

"There is no need to be offensive. I am certainly capable of handling my own letters without any interference."

"As am I, Caroline. Go to breakfast, there is nothing for you here."

She sniffed disdainfully and stalked out of the room, radiating displeasure.

Bingley watched her somewhat grimly then strode around to his desk and dropped the letter into a drawer, locking it once he had done so.

"I may find it difficult to believe but I will not risk it," he muttered.

"A good decision," said Darcy drily. "If you will excuse me, I will take my letter to my room."

Bingley nodded distractedly then followed him out of the room, locking the door behind him. He would not confront her now as his letter was safely locked away, but he would watch and see if she did indeed try to sneak into his study. He had tolerated a lot from her over the years, but if Mr. Bennet's estimation of her character was correct this behavior would truly be beyond the pale.

Darcy strode quickly up the stairs grateful to gain the privacy of his rooms. Once there he read the offensive letter again, feeling his fury rise anew at the impertinence of Mr. Bennet. Claiming a friendship with his father, as if that was something he would simply take on faith. Accusing him of showing himself as foolish, ridiculous, even! Dancing with his daughter could do nothing but increase her consequence; was he really so uninformed as to discount the Darcy name and influence? Why he could ruin them all with no more than a word. To be sure he was reticent but to accuse him being rude and ungentlemanly! Darcy paced the room more and more rapidly as his anger increased. Who did this minor squire, this country bumpkin think he was to take a Darcy to task?

Well, he would certainly not be dancing with a series of unnamed young ladies simply to secure the hand of Elizabeth Bennet for a dance. No doubt she would be disappointed when he did not ask for a set, but he was certain that Bingley was correct, and Elizabeth at least was unaware of her father's machinations. Of course, he could not say anything outright, but they would be in company many times over the course of the season here and he was sure he could find a way to inform her of her father's restrictions.

34

Georgiana Darcy peeked around the corner to make sure Miss Bingley was not lying in wait for her. Once she saw the corridor was clear she hurried to the stairs and down to the music room. If she could be engrossed in her music before Miss Bingley was aware of her presence she could be spared the woman's fawning for a while.

While she would deny it if asked, Georgie was not enjoying her time in Bath so far. She and Will had not talked a lot about it, they were both naturally quiet individuals and her brother had always preferred to be on horseback and not in the carriage when travelling. So they had not had a lot of time to speak of his plans. Somehow Georgie had assumed that a season in Bath would involve her getting to know new people and being allowed some social engagements to prepare her for coming out in London in two or three years.

Instead she saw no one outside their party; naturally no one was visiting them yet as they had arrived such a short time ago, but Georgie had thought that the Bingley's would have enough acquaintances here that they would be busy. Even if she was not included she could have some hours every day without having to deal with Miss Bingley. And so far that had not been the case.

She had her lessons, of course. But while she like Mrs. Annesley and appreciated that she had a wide range of topics that she could teach to her, she also seemed to be disapproving of some of Georgie's cherished routines. She wanted her charge to be up much earlier, to basically keep country hours even though they were in town. She wanted Georgie to express an interest in things like running a household or even, heaven forbid, an estate. Georgie had no interest in budgets and inventories and all the many details that the housekeepers had to remember. She was content with her lessons and her music and the occasional company of her brother.

She sighed as she thought of Will. She loved her brother, and she knew he cared for her of course but he was so perfect. It made her feel inferior to always be with someone so much older and wise and who never seemed to make a misstep. Her own faults seemed so glaringly obvious that it made her shyness worse. She wished she could be more like him, confident and composed and always knowing exactly what to do next.

Well, she could not do anything about any of that, so she would immerse herself in her music, grateful for the time she could spend when she did not have to deal with anyone at all.

Mrs. Annesley meanwhile was pacing her own sitting room, unaware that she was mimicking her employer's steps as her pace increased with her frustration. She simply could not seem to convince Mr. Darcy that Georgiana needed to learn more than French and the pianoforte. She needed to know how to run a house and an estate since she would certainly marry a landed gentleman. She needed to learn how to be gracious and overcome the shyness that led her to drop her eyes and murmur a greeting instead of meeting others with kindness and openness as she should. She needed friends in her own age group and to start mingling with others so she could get comfortable with the idea of society. And no matter how reasoned her arguments, how clearly she laid out the problems, Mr. Darcy responded by denying the need as Miss Darcy was so young.

But she was not so young. There were young ladies her age coming out already. At six and ten she was already well behind where she should be in terms of education that was not to be found in the pages of classic literature or imparted by a master of one of the arts. She had tried to interest Georgie in some of the things she would need to know but Georgie evinced no interest in the practical or the useful. She was young enough not to understand that she needed practical knowledge, but Mr. Darcy was old enough to know better and Mrs. Annesley was at her wits end on how to educate her charge properly.

Unfortunately, there was little she could do right now. Perhaps she could convince Mr. Darcy to escort his sister to the Pump room. She would not know anyone, of course, but she could get the feel of a crowded room of society people and perhaps if they saw some younger ladies Mrs. Annesley could discover who they were and facilitate a meeting. Meanwhile, she knew that the Darcy's cousin, Miss Anne de Bourgh was in Bath and believed she was only a decade or so older than her charge. Perhaps she would know of some younger ladies who would be good friends to Georgiana.

Yes, that was the tack to take first, a visit to their cousin. If Miss de Bourgh was active in society in Bath there was a good chance she could engineer an invitation for Georgiana and herself to accompany Miss de Bourgh to the Pump room; then even if Mr. Darcy was not interested in going, his sister would have the opportunity.

Unfortunately for Mrs. Annesley's plan, Darcy had left the house, determined to ride until his bad mood left him. Bingley was wandering around the house morosely. Mr. and Mrs. Hurst had retired as Mr. Hurst was not feeling well. And Miss Bingley was shrilly deriding everything about Bath and some family named Bennet who had apparently offended her by having the temerity to be in Bath at the same time as herself. She gave Georgiana no more than half an hour in the atmosphere before gently suggesting that it was time they retire for lessons. Though Miss Bingley protested the loss of her audience, Mrs. Annesley remained firm, and she and Georgie retired upstairs, both relieved that they had an excuse to eschew their hostess' company for the afternoon.

Wednesday dawned blustery, with rain showers and strong winds, a completely unpleasant day that tempted no one to go out of doors not even for the weekly concert. Thursday and Friday were more of the same; by Saturday Mrs. Annesley seriously wondered if she would be able to bear being locked in the house with the Bingley's one more day. To her delight, the sun was shining. It was a little chilly to be sure, but at least they could walk out to the park and give themselves a rest from the constant tension that seemed to permeate the Bingley household.

"Mrs. Annesley, could I ask you something please?"

"Of course, Georgiana, you may ask me anything."

"Do you think there is something wrong with my brother?" Georgie hastened to explain. "I do not mean is there something wrong with his health, but it seems to me that there is something more bothering him than just being locked up because of the rain. He seems to be angry all the time right now."

Mrs. Annesley nodded at her charge. "I believe that is very perceptive of you. I too have noticed that he seems to be upset about something, not to the point of losing his temper with the people around him but enough that it is affecting his mood, perhaps making him a little impatient."

"That is what I observed too," said Georgie, relief coloring her voice. "I thought perhaps I was imagining it or that it was just because of the weather but I do not believe that any longer. My brother has always been able to lose himself in a book or to work on estate business no matter the weather."

The two ladies walked a little further in silence then Georgie said thoughtfully, "There is a great deal of tension in the house right now. I think part of it is just Miss Bingley, she seems a very tense person and a strong personality and since she is the hostess that makes the feel of the house tense I think. But Mr. Bingley is used to his sister, and I have never seen him so morose, he is always cheerful. And my brother is used to her too; I do not believe he has ever mentioned any problems with her so he must usually be able to tolerate her quite well. I am not explaining this very well, but I think you understand me?"

"I do. Any home where Miss Bingley is the hostess is not going to have a restful feel to it because of her personality. But I agree, something is going on with the gentlemen that is causing them some kind of distress. We cannot know what it is, of course, but we can hope that is short lived and that soon they will be back to a more sanguine disposition."

Darcy and Bingley were indeed difficult company. The weather had kept them close and Bingley was chafing at his lack of contact with Miss Bennet. Mr. Bennet's letter had wounded him and while his immediate concern was spending more time with his angel, when he reread the letter it was the first paragraph that struck him. Did he indeed have a reputation for being an inconstant flirt? Would his attentions to Miss Bennet harm her? He had never been a particularly introspective man but having had a mirror forcibly placed in his hands he had no choice to but to examine his behavior and he was not sure he could reasonably refute Mr. Bennet's accusations. He would have gone to the Wednesday concert and the Thursday ball despite the weather, but his confusion about his behavior made him easy prey for Caroline and so he had been convinced to stay in.

Darcy was as uncomfortable as Bingley, but his discomfort took the form of an astonishing amount of rage. He was not a cheerful man by nature and perhaps he could be too easily angered at times but this burning desire to demand satisfaction of Mr. Bennet was extremely unsettling. He would have said he was an introspective man, one who examined his motives and actions to ensure they were correct, but in truth that was a far more accurate assessment of himself as a very young man than it was now.

It had been years since he had truly looked at his behavior or judged himself at fault. He was unused to having his behavior corrected and to be judged wanting by Mr. Bennet was galling. He was aware that if it were not for his attraction to Elizabeth he would have been irritated by Mr. Bennet's letter, but he would not have been so outraged as this. It had been years since anyone had attempted to direct his behavior and this fostered an unreasonable desire to deliberately ignore the gentleman's demands. That he could not do so without placing himself in the position of being a cad infuriated him even further.

Once he had seen his sister and her companion off to the park he found himself restless once more, needing some outlet for his pent-up energies. Pacing the library, where he had retreated to avoid Miss Bingley, he was suddenly struck with the realization that they had been in Bath a week and he had yet to call on Anne. This would be the perfect time to do so. Asking a footman to prepare the coach in case it came on rain again, he ran up to change his coat and then descended to let his hosts know where he was going. Naturally Miss Bingley was unable to leave it alone.

"I believe I should love such an excursion. Surely meeting your cousin would be lovely, there are so few persons here of real refinement or good taste that I long for company such as that of Miss de Bourgh."

"I believe you would like her, Miss Bingley, but I do not believe this is the appropriate time for you to meet her. I will see her alone today, to inform her that Georgiana and I are in Bath and to speak with her about meeting your family."

"Surely your cousin would not object to having us accompany you on a morning visit?"

"Perhaps not Miss Bingley, but I will stand by my stated assertion that it is not appropriate at this time. I am not even bringing Georgiana with me but am going alone. My cousin's health has not been good, and I will not impose a group of people on her when I do not know if she is strong enough to host such a group."

Darcy bowed slightly to her then and turned to leave, ignoring her shrill voice following him down the hallway. He was not going to spend the morning in her company; his control over his temper was precarious enough without deliberately placing himself in the company of someone who had a deleterious effect on his attitude.

Examining the façade of the de Bourgh townhouse as he descended to the sidewalk, Darcy found himself nodding in approval. The house looked sturdily build, the strong lines and symmetrical style appealed to him as both tidy and just intimidating enough. One needed to maintain an aura of authority in society and the house projected both wealth and strength.

He was admitted by a butler who looked to have been there for decades and handed his hat and coat to the waiting footman. "I am Miss de Bourgh's cousin, Fitzwilliam Darcy."

The butler bowed and replied, "Miss de Bourgh had mentioned that you might be residing in Bath for the season sir. She has two young ladies here with her this morning. She is upstairs at the moment, but the ladies are in the blue sitting room. Would you like me to announce you Mr. Darcy?"

Darcy hesitated a moment, not really pleased that he would have to keep company with two unknown misses but then decided he could simply not talk to them if needed. "Yes, that will be fine but please keep the door open and station a footman in the hall."

The butler inclined his head in agreement, then stepped in front of Darcy to open a door and announce him to the occupants. Darcy strode into the room and stopped abruptly as he saw Miss Bennet and Miss Elizabeth Bennet rising to their feet to greet him, both ladies displaying expressions of surprised consternation.

Notwithstanding their surprise, Jane and Lizzy politely curtseyed and Jane welcomed him in her kindly way, "Mr. Darcy, how nice to see you again. Anne should be down momentarily. I am sure she would be pleased if you would join us for tea."

"I am sure she would welcome me also; what I am not sure of is what you think you are doing here," Darcy replied harshly.

Jane's eyes widened in alarm at his tone but she replied calmly enough, "We are waiting for Anne, of course. She—"

Jane got no further as Darcy coldly interrupted. "That is obvious madam," he snapped. "I want to know why. You threw yourself at my friend Bingley and now you are battening on my cousin? I will not have it, do you hear? You will leave this house at once and you will not return." He turned a bitter look onto Elizabeth. "I would expect such behavior from your sister but from you, Elizabeth? I expected better of you."

Lizzy voice shook with force of her rage as she answered strongly, "Do not EVER use my name again, you have no right to use it, nor will you ever have the right to do so. And how dare you stand there spouting such viscous lies? Your friend pursued Jane, and never once did she encourage him in any way. How dare you say such a thing? Anne is our friend, and we will continue our friendship unless she asks us to cease."

"Which will never happen," snapped Anne, who had entered unnoticed and stood behind Darcy. "Who do you think you are, coming in here and demanding that my friends leave?"

"Anne, you do not understand, I know these ladies. They are mercenary fortune-hunters. Miss Bennet would have married my friend Bingley without caring a jot for him if his sister and I had not gotten him away from her. Now they have worked their wiles on you. They must leave now and I forbid you to see them again."

"You forbid me? You forbid me?" Anne's voice rose in volume with her feelings of outrage. "What authority do you believe you have over me Darcy? I am of age and perfectly capable of making decisions about my life and my friends without regard to your uninformed opinions. Just because you order everyone else you know, do not think for one moment that you may do so with me. My friends, who I invited here, will stay. You were not invited, and you will leave here and will not be welcomed back until you apologize sincerely to all three of us for your stupid and rude behavior."

Darcy opened his mouth to protest, but before he could form the words, Anne had stalked to the door and told the footman waiting in the hallway that Mr. Darcy was leaving and would not be welcomed to return. She then stood glaring at him until he gave her a short bow and stalked out of the room.

The three ladies simply stared at each other a moment, then Jane moved to take Anne's hands which had begun to shake. "Anne, come, sit. We are all overwrought I believe."

As Jane led Anne to the sofa, Lizzy made an inelegant sound of disagreement. "I am not overwrought Jane I am justly furious, and I believe the same can be said of Anne. Why you are not is more than I can fathom. Chasing Mr. Bingley indeed. Anyone with eyes in their heads could see that he bored you silly and that you only entertained his presence to be polite."

Jane, who had poured a cup of tea for Anne and fixed her a small plate of the biscuits she particularly favored, gave Lizzy a reproving look.

"He was wrong yes, but there is no need to speak with such heat

Lizzy. How many times did I hint Mr. Bingley away only to have him ignore it? Neither he nor his friend ever seemed able to realize what was going on right in front of them. They are not very observant men you know."

Anne made a huffing sound. "Well what I observed was an officious and rude boor castigating my friends and tossing around orders he had no right to give."

Lizzy nodded vigorously, "That is what I saw also. And using my first name! Never have I given him permission to do so, what was he thinking?"

"Well that is a surprise except I spoke to you before that I thought he might have a tendre for you. If such is the case, then Papa's letter would have hurt his feelings quite badly you know. He is generally rude and haughty, but he is not so improper as to use your name without permission. He must be perfectly aware of the implication of doing so."

Lizzy's jaw dropped open. "Good heavens, what if someone had heard him? Rumors of an understanding between us would fly through the ton. What in the world is the matter with that man?"

"And why would he think you are fortune hunters?" asked Anne.

"That I cannot tell you," admitted Jane. "except I think perhaps he believes every woman he meets is after his fortune."

"Well, I cannot blame him for that," Anne admitted unwillingly, "because almost every woman he meets in the ton really is after his fortune. Well, look at Lady Catherine. She has been trying to force a marriage between Darcy and myself since Uncle Darcy died. And she knew we did not wish it, she just wanted to get her hands on his money." She sipped her tea, brooding on her cousin's actions. "You think he is infatuated with Lizzy? And what letter?"

The Bennet ladies exchanged glances, then Lizzy said ruefully, "Oh dear, this is not quite what I was envisioning when I tried to think how to explain this to you. So I will just be my usual blunt self. When we were all in Hertfordshire several things happened. Mr. Bingley monopolized Jane to the point of incivility to any other persons in the room. He would not leave her alone. And Mr. Darcy insulted me more than once but for some odd reason he also asked me to dance; since I am the only one other than the ladies of his own party who was so honored it was very confusing to me because he insulted me before he met me, he insulted me when we danced, and he glared at me virtually every time we were in the same room." Lizzy paused then to gauge Anne's reaction. Seeing her friend nodding thoughtfully, she continued. "When we were at Monday's ball, they were there and it appeared they were going to do the same thing, with Bingley importuning Jane and Mr. Darcy asking me to dance and then not dancing at all once I told him my card was full. So papa sent a letter to each of them the next day. He told Mr. Bingley that he could dance one set with Jane or if there was no dancing he could spend half an hour with her but then he had to leave her alone. And he told Mr. Darcy that if he wanted to dance with me he would have dance with two other ladies not of his party first. He told them both that their behavior in Hertfordshire was terrible, but it was a small community of friends, so no harm was done. If they behave here as they did there it will cause gossip and could be ruinous for us and that he would not allow it."

Anne was silent for a few minutes. "Well, I think your papa did exactly the correct thing. Darcy is very well known in the ton and if he singled you out it would fly around Bath and then London in hours. It would be mortifying. And I believe Aunt Audrey mentioned that Mr. Bingley has a reputation of being inconstant and of setting someone up as a flirt and then deserting her. So I do not see that your father could have done anything else. And I wonder if Jane is not correct."

"About his infatuation with Lizzy?"

"Yes. As I think of it, I believe it may true. Why else would we ask you to dance Lizzy?"

"I have no idea. If you had heard the things he has said to me you would not think he was infatuated. He cut me and Mary when Sir William was trying to introduce us to him. He said I was tolerable but not attractive enough to dance with before he had met me. During our dance at the Netherfield Ball he said that there was no comparison between that ball and the ones in London because of the elevated company and conversation to be had there and that if I had ever experienced it I would understand."

"Good heavens, you never told me that Lizzy!"

"I know Jane, I told mama at the time but after that they left, and I never thought we would be in company again, so I did not see any reason to dwell on it."

"Well I do not know what his problem is," said Anne energetically, "but he is not going to be welcome here until he apologizes. To both of you. And to me because he has no business thinking he can order me around and I will not accept it. I spent my whole life having to ignore what I wanted to do in favor of whatever Lady Catherine was demanding I do and if he thinks I am going to allow that to happen to me again, he had better think again because I will not have it."

Although the ladies tried to speak of other subjects it seemed impossible to leave this morning's contretemps for more than a few minutes before one or another brought it up again. Finally, Jane and Lizzy decided they would go home, that their papa needed to know what had happened and frankly they were all a little weary from the excessive emotions.

Darcy rode back to the Bingley residence in a state of confusion and fury. He could not believe that the Bennets were imposing on his cousin. How dare they? And Anne. What had happened to her? She had been unforgivably rude to him, virtually throwing him out of her home. He had never been treated so in all his life. Of course, it was true she was of age and that he was a cousin not her father or brother and so he did not have any authority over her, but he was older and wiser and a man and Fitzwilliam Darcy for heaven's sake. No one treated him in such a manner.

He banged on the coach and told the driver to go through the park, he was not quite ready to face the company at home and wanted some time to think and regulate his emotions before facing the inquisition he would have to endure from Miss Bingley.

By the time the coach had completed the circle of the park and was trundling toward the Bingley's residence Darcy had come to a decision. He needed to be away from Bath. He could not possibly remain in his current state. He could go to his London house but there would be no peace there during the season. And he would have to leave Georgie with the Bingleys or take her to Matlock house. So he would go to Rosings. He would take Georgie with him, and he would be out of reach of everyone so he could think.

: Assumed Virtue

35

When Darcy's coach pulled up to the front door at Rosings Richard was standing on the steps to welcome them.

"Darcy, Georgiana, I had no idea you were coming! Mrs. Annesley, I have heard much of your accomplishments, but I do not believe we have met. You are all very welcome of course, but tell me is aught amiss?"

"No, Richard, all is well," said Darcy reassuringly. Feeling unaccountably relieved to be in the presence of his cousin, Darcy was able to speak calmly and convincingly. "I wished to assure myself that all is going well with the harvest and that the cold and windy weather Bath is experiencing has not hindered your progress here."

"No, our weather has been clear, a little windy perhaps but not enough to slow us down. Come in, come in and let us see where Mrs. Simmons has placed you. We do not yet have furniture in all the rooms and in truth I have left much of this in her capable hands as I have been more focused on the outside than the inside." Richard led them inside to where the butler and his wife awaited them. "Have we guest rooms available Mrs. Simmons? My cousin, his sister Miss Darcy and her companion Mrs. Annesley have come to visit."

Mrs. Simmons curtseyed to them. "Mr. Darcy your regular suite is refurbished and ready; Miss Darcy and Mrs. Annesley if you will follow me we have a suite with a shared sitting room that I believe will be comfortable for you."

The three travelers refreshed themselves, changing out of their traveling clothes and in a short space of time they were sitting down with Richard in the small dining room for luncheon.

"I admit I did not think of it when we left this morning, but I realize now that I am a little surprised to see you in the house, cousin. I thought you would be out in the fields."

Amused, Richard replied cheerfully, "You are lucky today was your choice to make your journey. It is the first time I have returned to the house before sundown since harvest began. But the builder who is training a few of my people in installing slate roofing wished to meet with me and he had just gone off when your coach was sighted."

"Is all well?" asked Darcy.

"Very well indeed my friend. We have more funds to work with than we had originally assumed, so with two cottages completed we are going to go ahead with the new slate roof on the parsonage. That will be all for this year, for the harvest is not going to be overly large. We are planning now for next spring's planting though and Palmer and I are hopeful that we will see a large increase. I do wish to ride out this afternoon again, perhaps you would like to ride with me Darcy?"

"I will definitely do so Richard. It is gratifying to hear that all is going well."

"And what of you Georgie? Will you rest or do you wish to ride with us also?"

Georgiana's voice was almost inaudible as she answered, "I believe I would prefer to rest cousin."

"Perhaps she can join you another time," suggested Mrs. Annesley, her normal speaking tones sounding overly loud after Georgiana's whispery tones. "Forgive me for asking as I know you are not completely set up yet, but is there a pianoforte that could be made available for us?"

Richard had directed a puzzled look at his ward when she answered so softly and without meeting his eyes but responded to her companion readily enough. "The music room was one of the few rooms where most of the furnishings were allowed to stay Mrs. Annesley, so Georgie can practice and there is also a harp available."

The week was balm for Darcy. He was always happier in the country than in any town and to be able to ride a familiar estate with his cousin, to watch the harvest in progress but not to have to shoulder any responsibility save that of experienced sage allowed him to shed tension with every stride of his horse. He retired each evening with the gratifying feeling of a day well spent and rose the next morning ready to face the day.

For his sister however, the visit was not as pleasant. Certainly her aunt had purchased an expensive and lovely pianoforte that she could use, and the harp was serviceable. She was able to maintain the schedule she preferred, sleeping late and breakfasting in her sitting room then studying and practicing. But dinners and their evenings as a group were tortuous for her. Richard insisted on speaking with her and not just directing comments to her but asking questions and expecting her to respond. She revered her cousin for his sacrifice in going to war, she was awed by his ease of manner and easy geniality, but she did not know him well. She had spent little time in his company over the years and she felt he was not willing to allow her the time she needed to become accustomed to him. His very ease of manner made her feel inadequate, to feel shyer and more insecure, and so her responses were often inaudible mumbles, and she was very grateful for those times her brother intervened and answered for her.

As the harvest wound down, Richard and Darcy began discussing their return to Bath and the decision was made that they would rest on Friday and then make their journey on Saturday morning.

Although both gentlemen were accustomed to country hours, they had been leaving earlier because of harvest so both felt as if they had slept in when they met in the breakfast parlor at only seven of the clocks on Friday morning. After silently sipping coffee and perusing the newspapers they finally felt congenial enough to converse; the feeling was not destined to persist.

"We have had little time for general discourse Darcy, so perhaps today we can speak of things other than Rosings. Do you know what is wrong with Georgie?"

"Georgie? Nothing is wrong with her that I know of, why would you think there was something wrong?"

"Darce, she can barely speak in company, and I am her cousin albeit one with whom she is not very familiar."

"She is shy yes, but she has always been thus."

"But Darce she is six and ten. She will be coming out in a couple of years, and she certainly will need to be able to converse with more people than yourself and her companion. Surely she needs to overcome this?"

"She is young yet Richard. I am sure that as she matures she will be able to overcome her shyness."

Richard directed a skeptical look at him. "How? I have not spent my evenings simply trying to draw her out you know; I have watched you and Mrs. Annesley, and I can state that every time her companion tries to allow her to speak for herself you jump in and answer for her as if she is still a child."

"Well, she is still a child."

"No she is not. She is six and ten Darcy. Six and ten. She was willing to elope not that long ago which must mean she considers herself an adult. At that age you were well on your way to being able to manage Pemberley, you were chess and debate champion at Oxford and were chafing at the bit to be able to be on your own without adult supervision. I cannot see that Georgiana has any accomplishment besides her music. She is well educated in terms of a basic education but if she cannot hold a conversation with me in safe surroundings with no actual stress involved how in the world is she going to come out in two or three years and hold her own in the ton?"

Darcy flushed angrily at his cousin's implied criticism. "Mrs. Annesley and I have been in discussions about expanding what she needs to be taught."

"And have you come to any conclusions?"

"I do not believe we need to go into this right now Richard."

"Very well, I will leave it for now cousin, but while she is your sister and ward, she is also my cousin and ward, and I will not let this linger undiscussed forever." He rose to refill his cup of coffee then changed the subject. "Did you enjoy making use of my lodgings? And how did you leave Anne? Is she finding her way? Did you escort her to the balls and concerts?"

Darcy stared at his plate, wishing not to discuss this either, wanting to avoid taking up the mantle of tension he had shed but knowing he would have to address it.

"I thank you for your generosity in offering your lodgings, but the Bingleys decided to spend the season in Bath and so Georgie and I stayed with them. He has also extended an invitation for you to join us when you return to Bath. And I did not get a chance to escort Anne anywhere; we saw each other only once and I am afraid we did not part on good terms."

Richard eyed his cousin suspiciously. "Why would you and Anne be at odds, Darce? You did not try to order her about did you?"

Darcy replied in a stern tone, "Yes I did, but it was for her own good."

Richard shook his head at his oblivious cousin. "Really Darce, you have to have realized that after spending her entire life being ordered to do what her mother wanted and unable to live her own life that ordering her around was going to raise her hackles."

"She is being taken advantage of by some unscrupulous people, Richard. I did not think telling her she was mistaken to befriend them was going to cause her to become so very angry."

Richard knew without asking who Darcy was speaking of and closed his eyes and took a deep breath to calm himself. "I would guess that Mrs. Jenkinson, Mr. Bennet, the two Bennet daughters and Miss Lucas are all perfectly capable of defending Anne should she need it."

Darcy surged to his feet. "It is the Bennets from whom she needs protecting Richard!"

"Nonsense Darce. They are respected and respectable people, why would Anne need to be protected from them?"

"They are fortune hunters, Richard. Miss Bennet threw herself at Bingley while they were in Hertfordshire."

The Colonel was so surprised by this ridiculous assertion that he burst out laughing. "I knew you were generally unobservant Darce, but did you really not see what was going on there?"

At his cousin's uncomprehending look, he elaborated. "When Miss Bennet is in company with people she esteems, who interest her and with whom she is comfortable she is perfectly proper but has a warm and sparkling look to her. When she is in company with those few persons with whom she is not comfortable and does not wish to spend time with she is cool and reserved. Bingley always brought out the latter response from her. She had no interest in him and no desire to be in his company. Did you truly not observe this?"

"I observed her coolness to Bingley, yes but I did not see that she was warm to anyone. She is a cold woman, and she would have married him for his fortune."

This blatantly ignorant view of a woman he esteemed above all others incensed Richard. "She is cold to you perhaps but who not be? She has no need of a fortune Will. Why are you so convinced that the Bennets are fortune hunters?"

"Their estate is small and entailed away and there are five daughters to dower. Of course they are fortune hunters."

"First the estate is not entailed any longer, one of the daughters will inherit it. Second Edward Gardner was Bingley's landlord at Netherfield, so even if the estate were entailed it is not as if they would be homeless, they could move to the neighboring estate. Third, the Bennets economized greatly when their daughters were young and invested the proceeds with Mr. Gardiner. They may not have dowries to match Georgiana's, but they are hardly dowerless. So I ask you again, why are you convinced they are fortune hunters?"

For the second time that morning Darcy found himself flushing as his pronouncements were summarily disputed.

"Miss Bingley informed me of their precarious position before I had even met them. What makes you think that all you have said is correct?"

"I listen Darce. I listen and I observe, I do not make uninformed judgements and then refuse to change my conclusions if new information comes to light," replied Richard drily. "My father helped them with the petition to the courts to break the entail and I was there when Gardiner thanked him for his aid and informed him that the petition had been granted. Since he has been instrumental in leasing their home in Bath out for years and negotiated the lease with Bingley for Netherfield, I requested his aid in leasing the London property. I have spoken with all of the Bennets and am well aware of their circumstances. I observed the difference in Miss Bennet's behavior the first time I was in company with her at Lucas Lodge, how she went from interested and engaged when speaking with her cousin and her aunt and myself about the war effort to bland and cool when Bingley claimed her attention and began blathering on about how beautiful she is. She was bored, Darcy and I would guess that was obvious to everyone save yourself and your friend."

Richard joined Darcy on his feet then, carefully placing his coffee cup on the table. "I would suggest you begin to re-evaluate your attitudes cousin. You are willfully blind to what your sister needs and if you continue this course she will be thrown onto the battlefield that is the ton unprepared and unarmed. You have quarreled with Anne because you refuse to acknowledge her right to conduct her life as she chooses. And you are going to be at outs with me and my parents if you continue your blind prejudice against the Bennets as we all esteem the family."

Richard strode out of the room then, leaving Darcy confused, angry and oddly ashamed though he could not say why. He avoided his cousin the remainder of the day, spending his time with his sister or striding briskly around the gardens and the home wood but he was unable to rid himself of the uneasy feeling that he was wrong somewhere while simultaneously firmly holding to his opinions that Georgie was a child and Anne should have listened to him and the Bennets were fortune hunters. By the time dinner rolled around he had worked himself into a monumental headache and sent word that he would not be down for dinner. He got headache powders from his valet and laid in bed trying to read until he fell into fitful slumber.

He awoke grumpy and groggy and still unhappy with his cousin. So when Richard suggested that Mrs. Annesley ride with him so that the two Darcys could be alone he coldly agreed, handed his sister into their coach and settled into the corner of the coach to try to doze on the journey to Bath. It never occurred to him that Richard had an ulterior motive in requesting Mrs. Annesley's company.

"Mrs. Annesley are you a good traveler? No sickness or anything of the kind while on a journey?"

Mrs. Annesley regarded the Colonel with amusement. "I am Colonel, excuse me, Mr. Fitzwilliam. Did you have something you wished to discuss?"

"I do indeed. First, you may continue to address me as Colonel. Although I have sold out, my rank allows it, and I am used to it so do not think I will take it amiss. Second, what is going on with my ward?"

"Your ward?"

"Miss Darcy's guardianship was left jointly to Mr. Darcy and me. While it may seem as if I have been uninvolved, it has been a result of my profession not disinterest and Darcy has kept me informed of what is happening in her life including the Ramsgate incident."

Mrs. Annesley's eyebrows rose in surprise. "He told you about Ramsgate?"

"I was there with him Mrs. Annesley and it is only through Darcy's intervention that Wickham walked away alive. I was also the one who suggested you inform Georgie of his fate since I was unsure if Darcy would think to do so."

"He did inform me and I broke it to her gently. She was shocked I think, but I do not believe her heart was actually touched by Mr. Wickham. Her pride and her self-esteem suffered from his callous dismissal of her but I believe that is all."

"If she was not in love with him why did she agree to the elopement?"

"I cannot say that I have received an adequate response to that question. In fact, any time I ask her any question she does not wish to answer or to do anything she does not want to do, she simply bursts into tears. She can cry for hours at a time."

Richard regarded her with astonishment. "Really? She can cry for hours?"

Mrs. Annesley nodded. "Indeed, I have seen her make herself truly ill from non-stop crying."

Richard mulled that over, then decided to set that aside for the moment. "Well, I am interested to know that, but it is not what I wish to discuss. Mrs. Annesley, I do not believe my ward is well prepared for adulthood. And I also do not believe the fault is yours."

Mrs. Annesley sighed. "I do not wish to be critical of Mr. Darcy, but he has a blind spot where his sister's maturing is concerned. It is not unusual as he has acted in a parental capacity to her for many years and there are more than a few parents who are reluctant to concede that their children are growing to adulthood. And her appearance does not help; she is delicate looking and appears both frail and younger than her years."

She shifted a little as if uncomfortable with her thoughts, then confessed. "I have asked Mr. Darcy many times to adjust what he feels is appropriate for her to learn. She should be conversant by now with the basics of running a house and an estate, and yet she knows nothing about either. She should be regularly exposed to others so she can begin to have a comfort level with strangers. And yet I cannot convince him that she needs this and when I have tentatively broached the subjects with her, she has expressed no interest in them at all. She is content to live as a child in the home, rising whenever she wishes, practicing her music and studying lessons but never moving beyond this."

"Yes, I can see that. And of course, confronting her would be very difficult. If she bursts into torrents of tears whenever she runs up against an uncomfortable situation, then discussing a problem and reaching a solution becomes almost impossible."

Mrs. Annesley nodded. "Yes. And because her appearance is fragile and she is so timid, no one ever addresses a harsh word to her. She also needs to know that her brother makes mistakes."

"What? Why would we need to tell her that? Everyone makes mistakes."

"She does not believe it. I truly think that one of the reasons she is insistent that she is not at fault in planning to elope is because she is convinced that her brother never makes a mistake and so she cannot allow herself to make one either."

"Good heavens," said Richard, visibly astonished, "how can he have allowed her to believe that? Of course she will not be able to live up to that, no one could."

Richard noticed the odd expression that crossed Mrs. Annesley's face. "Now what about what I just said struck you, Mrs. Annesley?"

When she was silent and obviously uncomfortable, Richard pushed. "Mrs. Annesley, we both want what is best for Georgiana. I am a man of my word. I will not betray your trust, but I do need to know what it is that you are worried about."

"Colonel, Mr. Darcy has allowed her to believe it because he believes it."

Richard was silent a moment, considering his cousin, his words and his actions, carefully. "You believe then that Darcy feels he cannot make a mistake?"

"No, not precisely that. In fact, I am sure if you asked him he would disclaim perfection immediately. But he is so absolutely convinced of his own superiority to virtually everyone that when he does make a mistake instead of saying, you are right, I should have done this differently or I should have made a different decision and then correcting it, he justifies his behavior and refuses to admit fault. Naturally then that is Miss Darcy's reaction also; she is young, younger than her years in many ways and she has had this behavior modeled to her for years. But it is not how I wish to see her behave and it inhibits her ability to grow. If she never has a behavior that needs to be corrected, then there is no reason for her to change."

"Very well then Mrs. Annesley, we will need to speak with her and with Darcy. I do not remember seeing her at breakfast, but then except for yesterday I was up with the dawn. When does she usually get to the breakfast parlor to break her fast?"

"She does not, Colonel. She will lie abed, dozing and doing nothing until late morning then request a tray in her room."

"Well that is going to change. Bath runs on country hours, and she needs to adjust to that."

"I would suggest we discuss this with Mr. Darcy, he is the key. If he does not support us then even though you are also her guardian I do not believe we will make any progress with her."

"You do not think she would respond if I were to speak with her? I would not try to change everything at once, but I will confess I want to know why she agreed to the elopement."

"Well, once we are settled, if you wish to speak with her in our joint sitting room you are one of her guardians and you have every right to ask."

Richard nodded, then told her he would think on it, and they moved on to more general and pleasant topics. As they reached the outskirts of Bath Richard made his decision. "I think I agree with you that Darcy is the key, but I would like to at least try. If she will not respond I will not push it but perhaps she will agree to speak with me."

They had left early and so were arriving at the Bingley residence by mid-morning. While Richard was not particularly fond of their company, he felt that he needed to be present in Georgiana's life right now and so accepted Bingley's cheerful invitation to stay with them instead of going on to his lodgings. Once he was settled, he sought out Mrs. Annesley and Georgiana in their shared sitting room.

"Georgie, I want to talk to you about Ramsgate and Wickham."

Georgiana fixed him with a look of horror and her voice dropped to a whisper as she answered, "Why? Why should we talk about this?"

"Well I have my reasons but before I continue I would like to ask you why you are whispering?"

Georgiana blushed and looked down at her hands, but her voice was still almost inaudible as she answered, "I do not know exactly but you seem angry, and I do not wish to discuss this."

"Well I am not angry at all, Georgie. Stern perhaps but not angry. And I am sorry if this makes you uncomfortable. But you are not a child, you are six and ten and I would expect you to be able to speak in a normal voice even if you are discussing something uncomfortable."

But Georgie seemed unable to raise her eyes or her voice. "You think I should be to blame for Wickham and Mrs. Younge, do you not? How could I have known how evil they were?"

"You could not, and I do not blame you for their part in this. But Georgiana, you were raised by governesses who taught you right from wrong. You were raised to know that an elopement is wrong from both a moral and a societal point of view. You were raised to know that when Wickham started calling on you, you should have denied him until your brother had been informed and had approved the connection. You knew better and you ignored the teachings you had been given and even your own conscious and pursued a potentially ruinous course."

She rose then to leave the room, but Richard emphatically told her to sit back down, their discussion was not over. True to Mrs. Annesley's warning, she began to cry hysterically.

Although it went against everything in him to sit calmly discussing his failure to be able to speak in an adult fashion to Georgiana with Mrs. Annesley while his young charge was in distress, he followed her lead and did so, wondering as they spoke if Georgie was even hearing them or if she was too involved in her tears to listen. Perhaps they could talk until she stopped, and he could try again? How long could she go on, after all? Too long, he discovered. The girl could cry endlessly. And loudly. Dear heavens in her own way she was as annoying as Caroline Bingley.

Finally admitting defeat, he morosely left the two ladies in their sitting room and sought his own chambers, changed into riding gear and left to visit his cousin Anne and the Bennets.

36

While Darcy and Georgiana were sojourning in Kent, Bingley was beginning his campaign to win over Mr. Bennet and spend time with Miss Bennet. In pursuit of his goal, he decided to visit the Pump Room, reasoning that the Bennets were likely to be there and also that his sister would refuse to accompany him. To his delight he was correct in both assumptions.

However, to his dismay Miss Elizabeth refused to leave her sister's side. Since Mr. Bennet had deliberately pulled his watch out of his waistcoat pocket and checked the time as Mr. Bingley approached them and as he continued to pull it out and check the time periodically, Bingley found himself distracted and was able to make only the most mundane observations.

Finally Miss Lucas took pity on him and asked for his escort to greet some friends on the other side of the room. He agreed before he knew what he was about then found himself offering his arm to her and moving away from the Bennets.

"Mr. Bingley," said Miss Lucas, her tone kind and gentle. "I know that you wish to spend time with Miss Jane Bennet; perhaps you could indulge me and tell me why."

"Why?"

"Yes, why do you wish to spend time with Miss Jane Bennet. Tell me what you know of her."

"Well she is beautiful. She is kind and gentle."

"Yes, she is all of those things. They are also observations that anyone who had spent ten minutes in her company could tell you. You have spent hours with her, so I will ask you again to tell me something about her Mr. Bingley."

Mr. Bingley looked at her blankly. She held in a sigh and said softly, "Mr. Bingley if you are going to try to fix your interest with her, you should come to know her do not you agree?"

Charles nodded vigorously.

"Then I am going to suggest you use what little time you have wisely sir."

"I plan to," he told her firmly. "Meanwhile, I appreciate that you rescued me from an uncomfortable situation, I was not prepared for how distracting being timed would be."

"I could see that," replied Charlotte. "I am usually in company with the Bennets as they are hosting me and Mr. Bennet is acting in loco parentis for me. If you find yourself needing rescue you may call on me to aid you. However, I have one condition Mr. Bingley. We will not talk about my friend. I am willing to be a friend to you as well as to Jane, but I have known her all her life and she has my first loyalty. If we are in company we will speak of other things."

Bingley nodded thoughtfully. "I can understand that. I do not wish to hurt her, and I certainly would not ask you to break a confidence. I do appreciate your help and your offer of friendship. Thank you Miss Lucas, I will return you to your party and will see you all on Monday next."

At luncheon on Monday Bingley told his family that he planned to attend the public ball that evening. When everyone agreed to go he took a deep breath, squared his shoulders and said, "Caroline, remember the gathering at Lucas Lodge in Hertfordshire?"

"I remember it well, you left me!"

"Yes, and I will do so again this evening if you delay us. My coach is leaving at thirty minutes past five of the clock and you will either be in the carriage or you will stay home. I will not ask the Hursts to remain this time to escort you and we do not have Darcy's carriage to have ready for you. We will leave promptly. I will not argue this with you or discuss it further, but you may believe I am completely serious Caroline. Balls here end at eleven and I will not lose half the evening pacing in the entryway waiting for you to make an entrance."

"Charles," she shrilled, outraged, "you cannot mean that. I will be ready as soon as I can be but if you have to wait then that is just how it is."

"No, that is not how it is Caroline. I will not wait. If you wish to accompany us, then you must be ready when we are, or you will stay home alone." With that last pronouncement, Charles rose, bowed to them and left the room.

At four o'clock Louisa and Caroline were sitting together in the music room where they had partaken of a delicious tea then Caroline had played while Louisa embroidered. Hearing the chime of the hallway clock, Louisa put her sewing away and stood, interrupting her sister's performance. "I am going to ready myself for the ball, Caroline. I think you should come away now too."

Caroline shook her head and continued to play. "Charles was not serious Louisa he will not leave me behind."

For a moment Louisa thought about arguing with her sister then decided against it. She wished to go to the ball; unlike her sister she wanted to find friends in Bath, and she liked the Bennets, she would enjoy their company. She had no intention of spending the evening at home with an angry Caroline when she could be with her much more pleasant sibling surrounded by cheerful people who had gathered for companionship and dancing.

Promptly at five thirty the Bingley carriage pulled up in front of the door and Charles, Louisa and Mr. Hurst boarded the coach for the short ride to the Lower Rooms where tonight's ball would be held. Hurst was chortling as the carriage pulled away from the house. "Your younger sister is going to be angry Charles. She did not believe you were serious."

"Well I told her I was serious so if she is upset she has no one except herself to blame," said Bingley unrepentant, and promptly changed the subject. He was determined that he would have an enjoyable evening and Caroline was not going to ruin it for him.

As soon as they arrived Bingley looked around the room and spotted Mr. Bennet standing with Miss Lucas and another young lady he did not recognize. By the time the Bingley party arrived at Mr. Bennet's location, Miss Lucas had been escorted onto the dance floor leaving only Mr. Bennet and the unknown young woman.

"Mr. Bingley, I do not believe you have met Miss Anne de Bourgh, a resident of Bath and a dear friend our family."

Bingley bowed. "I am pleased to meet you Miss de Bourgh. May I introduce my brother Mr. Hurst and my sister Mrs. Hurst?"

Anne curtseyed to them. "I am very pleased to meet you. My cousin, Colonel Richard Fitzwilliam, has mentioned you to me."

Mrs. Hurst smiled at her. "I have heard of you; I believe you are Mr. Darcy's cousin from Kent?"

"I was living in Kent, yes, but now I am a full-time resident of Bath now."

"Are you enjoying it? I ask because we have not spent a season here before now and I must say I find it very enjoyable."

Anne beamed at Mrs. Hurst. "I am enjoying myself also. Do you prefer Bath to London then?"

"I do. I like it that entertainments start earlier and end at a reasonable time. I never have adjusted well to being up until four in the morning then starting my next day in the afternoon. Perhaps it is provincial of me, indeed I have been told it is, but I find that I prefer country hours."

Mr. Bennet, who had been studying Mrs. Hurst with interest, joined their conversation. "That is also one of my preferred things about Bath, though I will say that I find it amusing that even if you are in the middle of a dance once it is eleven o'clock the music stops even if the dancers are in mid-step."

The company laughed at that, Mr. Hurst finding it particularly amusing. "I hope then that I am present when it happens for this would be something to see."

As the first set had now ended, the other three ladies of the Bennet party approached, escorted by their previous partners.

Introductions were made and Bingley seized the opportunity to request Miss Bennet's next open set, which happened to be the second set. He then asked Miss Lucas, Miss Elizabeth and Miss de Bourgh for dances, thus filling up much of his evening. Mr. Hurst escorted his wife onto the floor, and the other ladies were collected by their partners, leaving Mr. Bennet watching from the sidelines where he chuckled a little at Bingley's strategy. Perhaps he thought that by dancing with members of the Bennet party he would be able to spend time between dances with Jane, but they had already discussed this possibility and they would work in concert with each other to prevent it.

When Bingley returned Jane to her father's side, his next partner was Miss Elizabeth, and she promptly claimed his attention. Once on the dance floor she steadfastly refused to discuss Jane and twice called him sharply to order for inattention when Jane's presence on the floor distracted him. The second time she had to do so, she told him such incivility was simply insupportable. "No one wishes to dance with someone who is not paying attention to them Mr. Bingley. If you cannot converse with me and give me your attention for the short space of time we are together on the dance floor then I must ask you not to request another dance from me at any time."

Bingley blushed at this, unused to be being taken to task by any young, single lady. Eligible gentlemen, even those from trade, were usually treated with far more deference than Miss Elizabeth was showing to him.

"You are absolutely correct Miss Elizabeth. I will not allow my attention to stray again." And he did not. He was far better behaved with Miss de Bourgh, with whom he chatted amiably about Darcy and the Colonel. By the time he was dancing with Miss Lucas he was surprisingly comfortable with not obsessing about Jane while on the dance floor with someone else.

As they finished the first dance of their set and were waiting for the music to begin for the second one Miss Lucas complimented him on his courtesy to her. "When we were in Hertfordshire it was a complaint I heard often, that while you seemed perfectly amiable you also were not attentive to your partners. I am proud of you for doing so well this evening Mr. Bingley."

Charles unconsciously straightened his shoulder with pride. "Thank you Miss Lucas. Miss Elizabeth rightly took me task and I realized that she was correct. I am endeavoring to amend my manners."

Charlotte chuckled a little at that. "There is little that needs amending

Mr. Bingley for as I said everyone praised your amiable manners. Now that you are also attentive I would say you are an ideal partner."

Charles and Charlotte found themselves chatting easily through the second dance and they joined the Bennets and Anne and their escorts in the small room set aside for lemonade and cakes to enjoy a small treat before they all resumed their excursions on the dance floor. Mr. Bennet introduced Mr. Bingley to Mr. Burnside and his daughter Angela and Mr. Bingley left with Miss Burnside on his arm to resume dancing.

The evening had been so enjoyable for them that they had completely forgotten about Caroline, who had been furious when she descended the staircase shortly after six to find herself alone and with neither escort nor transportation for the evening. The Hursts and Bingley came into the front parlor for a last cup of tea and some treats before retiring to find Caroline pacing furiously surrounded by broken bits of china.

"Oh for heaven's sake Caroline," said Louisa completely exasperated. "Did you have to destroy the figurines? They were particularly fine in this room, and you know nothing here belongs to us; now they will have to be replaced."

"Well if you do not want things destroyed perhaps you should not slight me and treat me so poorly," Caroline snapped.

"No one slighted you Caroline," replied Mr. Hurst coldly. "You slight all of us every time you make us wait on your convenience to depart. It is time you learned how to behave."

Charles held up a hand to forestall her as Caroline began to retort. "Enough. I will not tolerate this behavior Caroline. Not anymore. Stop breaking things. Start treating those around you with courtesy and that includes being ready to leave at the appointed time. I am going to bed and I suggest you all follow my example. Bath runs on country hours you know."

While Caroline refused to rise before eleven, Bingley and the Hursts breakfasted early then Bingley went to handle some correspondence but told his sister and brother that he would be visiting the Bennets this morning if they wished to accompany him. Both of them agreed so at ten they left the house for the Bennet residence in Sydney Place where they were admitted to the drawing room to find Jane, Anne and Charlotte Lucas all working on various sewing projects.

There was an open chair between Charlotte and Jane that Mr. Bingley promptly appropriated. Mrs. Hurst sat on the other side of Anne with Mr. Hurst beyond her. Jane asked the butler to send in tea and a few minutes later Mr. Bennet strolled into the room to greet the guests.

To his surprise, while Bingley was seated next to Jane he was currently courteously listening to something Charlotte was saying to him. The gentlemen rose to their feet when he arrived, but he waved them back into their seats and took a place near the Hursts where he could speak with them while keeping an eye on Bingley.

Jane, Charlotte and Mr. Bingley continued their conversation, Anne and Mrs. Hurst appeared to be striking up a friendship so Mr. Bennet decided he might as well get to know something of Mr. Hurst. They had an enjoyable conversation about politics, enhanced by a delicious tea and the time flew by. When Elizabeth finally appeared, the company was just preparing to leave.

"I am so sorry I could not come earlier," she apologized to them. "I was in the stillroom."

"Are we well enough supplied child?" ask Mr. Bennet.

Lizzy shook her head. "We are fine for the moment Papa, but we need to send to Longbourn for willow bark. The stuff the apothecary has here is not dried properly and I do not trust it. I would prefer to have some sent from our stores."

Mr. Bennet nodded. "I will write to your mother and make sure that we can get enough from home."

"Why willow bark?" asked Bingley who had never heard of using willow bark for anything.

"When Mr. Collins has trouble sleeping it helps him as it is both a mild pain killer and a soporific. And unlike anything containing laudanum it is not addictive. Of course, it is also not as strong, but when someone is going to need help managing their pain in the long term, laudanum is simply not a good option."

"Really?" said Mrs. Hurst surprised. "I have often heard of laudanum being prescribed but I confess I have not heard of willow bark."

"Well if you ever have a chance to speak of it, ask Colonel Fitzwilliam what he has seen of soldiers who end up addicted to the stuff. It is worse than the injury it is supposed to help with. Short term it is useful, long term it is not," replied Anne firmly. "When I was ill, the apothecary prescribed laudanum for me, but it gave me such nightmares I refused to take it. Once I arrived in London, my Uncle's physician said it was a very good thing, that if I had been taking it as directed I would certainly be addicted by now."

"Oh Anne," cried Lizzy, "I had no idea. How fortunate that you could not tolerate it!"

"I have not seen Mr. Collins with you, I did not realize he had accompanied you," interjected Bingley.

"Yes, he is here to experiment with some things to see if the pain he is in can be managed more comfortably for him. We have some hopes that he can become somewhat more comfortable in his everyday life."

The Bingley party took their leave and the Bennet party all settled themselves again. "I was unaware of a new treatment for Mr. Collins. Do you hope for him to be able to walk again?"

Lizzy shook her head. "That is unlikely though it is possible he could be able to move around using a cane if things progress well."

As Anne was obviously curious and they all knew she cared about Mr. Collins, Lizzy continued, though it was too personal to speak of with most people. "When he was in the greatest pain in Hertfordshire we would use a hot brick to help ease the pain. You know about our plumbing here, of course. It makes it easy for him to take a hot bath which is even more helpful than the hot bricks. We have found that if he takes one in the morning he sometimes has as much as several hours where the pain is not as debilitating. We are hopeful that in time he might be able to move around a little more freely but even if that never happens, to have time that is far less painful, even though it is only a matter of a few hours, has been wonderful for him."

"Oh I am so very glad to hear of this! It is one more reason for me to consider renovating my home."

"Well, when the time comes we would be happy to provide what aid we can," said Lizzy, "but if I were you I would not consider it before summer. Then you could visit us or go to Rosings to visit the Colonel while it is being done because I do not believe you want to be there while it is being constructed."

"Actually, it might not be that bad," said Jane cheerfully. "There is a great deal of difference between doing four of them on different floors and doing one or even two to service the entire house."

"It was certainly a headache," said Mr. Bennet, "but the end results are worth it I think. I had not realized how much more pleasant it is to have dinner served by servants who have recently bathed. And I enjoy the convenience myself. I am strongly considering bringing the whole family here after spring planting next year and putting a modern convenience or two into Longbourn."

Jane's eyes lit up at that pronouncement. "Really papa? Because I have thought about it of course, but I have not drawn up plans because I did not know if you would be interested. But if you truly are considering it I will think on it and begin sketching some plans out."

Mr. Bennet laughed at Jane's enthusiastic response. "Well, you may go ahead and draw up some plans with my blessings. I believe I can assure you that your time will not have been wasted."

The rest of the week was filled with enjoyable outings for the Hertfordshire natives and Anne. Mr. Bennet had sent for the willow bark and the groom had returned with the requested supplies and Lizzy's mare. Since Jane's horse had been brought into Bath earlier the girls were thrilled to be allowed to ride. Mr. Bennet rented a lovely mare for Charlotte and helped Anne choose a placid tempered one so she could begin to learn to ride. Lizzy spent several mornings with Anne, patiently helping her but when it was time to ride out Anne was paired with Charlotte who was a far more cautious rider than either of the Bennet daughters. In particular Lizzy loved the feel of racing along with the wind pushing against her and the world seeming to fly by the hooves of her steed. She could be patient when needed but was the first to admit that her preference was for speed when riding.

The four ladies arranged to ride late morning on Saturday as the weather was turning colder and Anne wished to get as much time in as she could before cold, rain and even snow arrived and curtailed their outdoor activities. They had an enjoyable morning and were just arriving back at Sydney Place when they realized the horseman they saw approaching was none other than Colonel Fitzwilliam.

The ladies greeted the Colonel with welcoming smiles. Anne was delighted to see her favorite cousin, Miss Lucas had always found him pleasant, and Lizzy joyfully greeted a man who had become a friend and maybe would someday be a brother. Jane knew she flushed but she found she did not care; she was so very glad to see him. The Colonel greeted them all and if his gaze lingered on Jane's pink cheeks they all kindly pretended not to notice.

"Come in dear Richard, and we will all have tea."

"Oh dear Anne, I do not think we should all invade your drawing room," objected Lizzy. "I am terribly afraid it would smell of the stables for days if we are all to come in."

Anne blushed then; she had forgotten the unmistakable aroma of horse would linger as they had been riding for hours. Charlotte reached over and patted her hand. "Perhaps you should change and come over to the Bennets. Mr. Fitzwilliam can speak with Mr. Bennet and Mr. Collins, and we can all change also."

Jane had looked accepting but disappointed at Lizzy's laughing assertion but now she threw a grateful glance in Charlotte's direction and agreed at once. "Oh yes, that would be lovely I think. Papa and Cousin William would be so sorry not to see you." The Colonel accepted at once and Anne dismounted and handed the reins to her groom and rushed up the stairs. The other proceeded at a slightly more decorous pace to the Bennet house; once there the Colonel was deposited in the study where Mr. Bennet and Mr. Collins were both engrossed in books.

Conversation was easy and congenial between the three and the Colonel was very interested to hear about the success of hot baths, a little gentle moving around and willow bark tea. "I have to say you look far healthier," said the Colonel studying Mr. Collins closely. "I am pleased to see it and doubly pleased that you look to be in less pain."

"It is not permanent," replied Mr. Collins "but it is far less painful for longer now even in such a short time. The immediate relief is there of course, but the first few days that is all it was. Not that I was not grateful for that," he added with a wry smile. "But I cannot deny that I am more pleased than I can say that I now have some few hours in considerably less pain. Not pain-free, by any means, but it is still an enormous blessing. If I continue to improve it may be possible for me to move about with a cane and not have to use the bath chair all the time."

"That is excellent news," enthused Richard. "I wonder if I should not consider such an innovation to Rosings. Once I am more settled I would imagine some old comrades in arms may visit and many of them have lingering injuries. It would be of great interest to me if this is something that could help with some of their injuries."

Mr. Bennet looked intrigued at that. "I did not look at this in the broader context, though I cannot imagine why I did not do so. I will be interested to know if it turns out it is helpful."

There was a brisk tap at the door then Lizzy's smiling face peeped around the corner at them. "Gentlemen would it please you to join the ladies of the household for tea?"

Mr. Bennet laughed at her. "What you mean is that we are ordered to appear."

Lizzy laughed merrily at her father. "Well, I would not say ordered precisely. After all, if you wish to miss the raspberry torte that Cook has baked for our tea, then it would leave extra for us, and I do not know that I would strongly object."

"Ah, blackmailed with threats of withholding sweets. I see through your machinations miss. You hope to tease us into staying and thus have all the raspberries to yourself."

"Well, I can admit to having occasionally eaten more raspberries that would be considered wise," Lizzy smiled ruefully as she and the Colonel preceded her father who was pushing Mr. Collin's bath chair. "I cannot remember the first time; I was so young that all I have is the story from mama, but it was not the last time. Normally I am a great believer in learning lessons from such hardship, but I am afraid in the case of raspberries I am sometimes compelled to ignore what I know."

And with that the four of them entered the drawing room laughing to find Charlotte welcoming, Anne warmly smiling and Jane glowing.

37

In Laura Place Miss Bingley frowned at her mirror. She had dressed carefully for dinner in Darcy's company only to find that none of their guests were present. Georgiana was apparently ill, and Mrs. Annesley was tending her, the Colonel had sent a note apologizing and stating he was dining with friends and Darcy had requested a tray in his room saying he was fatigued from the journey.

Miss Bingley snorted at that. Fatigued from the journey. It was scarce three hours from Kent to Bath and he had had all afternoon to recover. Well, she would not accept being slighted by her brother and she had no intention of being slighted by Darcy either. She would accept his absence tonight but by tomorrow if he refused to come into company she would have Charles roust him out. She had not agreed to come to Bath to spend time at provincial balls and with the detestable Bennets. She was here because Darcy was here.

Darcy really was fatigued. He was having a monstrously bad time trying to sleep. Every time he dozed off he heard himself castigating Miss Bennet and Anne and worse of all Elizabeth and then heard Richard's stern tones chastising him for being wrong and he would jerk awake and remind himself that no matter how reasonable it sounded Richard was not necessarily right and ruthlessly suppressed the small voice in his head that said Richard was right, he was wrong, and he had thrown horrible accusations at the beloved sister of the woman he was infatuated with.

As dawn finally broke Darcy gave up on sleep. Ringing for his valet he prepared for the day in silence, drinking the cup of coffee his valet supplied without tasting it, wanting only to remain alone with his thoughts. Striding out to the stables, he checked himself. This was not the country, he could not ride as he wished, but perhaps he could walk off his anxiety.

Unconsciously striding toward Sydney place, he found himself walking rapidly through the gardens that were part of the draw of living in that location. He moderated his pace then, walking more slowly, though his mind was still churning. Rounding a small bend, he stopped abruptly: there she was. Standing with her back to him, gazing over the gardens laid out before her, her bonnet in her hand and her glorious curls teased by the early morning the breeze, she was everything that was lovely, everything he wanted and could not have.

He strode toward her, deliberately making some noise in his progress so he would not startle her, and she turned as she heard him approach.

"Miss Elizabeth," he bowed.

"Mr. Darcy," her voice was cool and withdrawn. Her eyes were shadowed, not joyful this morning but thoughtful, and he understood how a man could drown in the depth of his love's gorgeous eyes.

They gazed at each other in silence, then Darcy knew what he had to do. It would not be completely true, but this needed to be said. "I owe you an apology Miss Elizabeth. I am sure you were not trying to take advantage of Anne."

Lizzy nodded silently.

"I bear you no ill-will for your sister's actions and I forgive you for your intemperate words."

Now her eyes changed, coming alive, flashing fire. "You forgive me? How magnanimous sir. And what of your intemperate words sir? What of your unjust accusations against my sister?"

"I do not believe the accusation was unjust," he replied stiffly, "or do you truly deny that she was trying to entrap my friend?"

"I completely deny it sir," she snapped. "Jane was certainly not trying to entrap your friend; she was never more bored than when in his company. Can you explain to me the propriety of your friend attaching himself to someone on first acquaintance to the exclusion of others? Of so distinguishing a young woman with his puerile attentions that it appears he is going to offer for her then abandoning her at a moment's notice for someone new? How many young women have had their hearts broken, their expectations raised only to have them shattered in a moment by your friend's inconstant and reprehensible behavior? Jane did everything she could within the bounds of courtesy and propriety to discourage Mr. Bingley's attentions, but he persisted. Is it not the part of a gentleman to withdraw when his attentions are unwelcome?"

As Darcy looked at her astonished, she continued, her voice rising with anger. "And what of you sir and your behavior? What is courteous about refusing to exchange even the most simple of greetings to those you are meeting, of standing with your back to the company and refusing to engage with them at all? How is it the proper behavior of a gentleman to take an estate and never once visit any of the tenants? How can you call yourself a gentleman when you insulted me repeatedly?"

Darcy looked at her in shock. Surely that could not be right? He always remained apart from his company; everyone knew that. And Bingley fell in love often, yes, but was his behavior truly so reprehensible? Visiting the tenants? It was a leased estate, why would they do that?

Before he could formulate a defense of himself or his friend she continued, her voice raising as her ire increased.

"What, silent still Mr. Darcy? Have you no explanation of your improper behavior? Can you explain the propriety of your cruel insult to me before we had even met? How proper was it for you to tell me that I had neither experience nor education? How proper is it for you stalk the boundaries of the dance floor at each ball you attend, refusing to dance and glaring at everyone? We were told you were to tutor your friend in estate management, so tell me Mr. Darcy where was he during harvest? What plans has he in place for spring planting?"

"Perhaps Bingley should have paid more attention to harvest, but it is a leased estate I am sure no one expected more of him. I will admit I should not have been so blunt in my statement prior to our meeting, but since then I see no impropriety in my actions. I am reticent in company it is true but stating facts cannot be objectional. The people in Hertfordshire, the people here in Bath are below me in every way, so for me to acknowledge that cannot be a fault."

"Really, below you in every way? Many may be below you in wealth, but they are not below you in birth and certainly they are well above you in those things that truly matter, like kindness, courtesy, compassion, character."

Lizzy drew a deep breath, trying to force herself to speak calmly, but she could not keep the passion from her voice. "I can think of no instance, Mr. Darcy, where you have comported yourself as a true gentleman. Before we had even met you had impressed me with your conceit, your arrogance and your selfish disdain for everyone not connected to you. You bear the title of gentleman by birth but by your words and actions you fall short of the title in every way. Now if you will excuse me, I find the peace of the morning has been broken and I will return to my family."

She turned then, the footman who had been watching from a distance falling in behind her as she walked briskly away from him, leaving Darcy standing stunned behind her.

Darcy quietly entered the house hoping to reach his room unnoticed. He could hear Miss Bingley shrilly demanding of her brother where their guests were. He sighed and approached the dining parlor.

"How can you not know what is happening with your friends? They arrived here yesterday but we have seen nothing of them."

"The Colonel's missive was quite explicit. He was up early and decided to go to his lodgings to see what correspondence is there and to arrange for the rest of his wardrobe to be sent here. That is surely understandable Caroline so kindly be calm. I have always asked Darcy to consider our home as if it were his own and I extend that courtesy to his sister also. They are free to join us or not as they choose." Darcy nodded his agreement and slipped quietly to the stairs, ignoring the voice in his head that said Bingley had sounded weary and that as a good guest he should make an appearance. He simply was not up to it right now, he needed to be alone, needed to try to come to terms with what Elizabeth had said to him.

Leaving his sister behind, Bingley decided that he could excuse an extra visit to Miss Bennet by pointing out that he had not really had a chance to speak with her. As he came toward the house in his carriage he saw his angel in the side garden, clipping the few late blossoms and dropping them into a basket. So instead of presenting himself at the front door, he left his carriage and walked quickly toward her.

"Miss Bennet, how lovely to see you, you are more beautiful than the blossoms you pick," he said in a tone he hoped conveyed his admiration and adoration of his angel.

Unfortunately for him, Lizzy had wasted no time in relating her confrontation with Mr. Darcy to Jane. While she was of an equitable nature she could not help being exasperated by the accusation that she had been chasing Mr. Bingley. To have him come upon her spouting his inane compliments to her just as she was trying to regain her equanimity stuck her in precisely the wrong manner.

"Mr. Bingley are you able to read sir?"

"To read? Of course I can read."

"And you can count?"

By now thoroughly confused Bingley admitted that yes he could also count.

"Then what are you doing here? You received a letter from my father and I assume you understood the contents. It explicitly stated that you would visit no more than once per week and yet here you are for the second time. Since you can read and count I do not understand what you are doing here."

Bingley gaped at her. "You are aware of the letter?"

"Of course I am aware of it Mr. Bingley. Despite your insistence on treating me as a brainless fool, I am a competent adult, and my father would not have taken such a step without my knowledge and agreement. You however do not seem to be able to understand. So I am forced to listen to you blathering on about my beauty as if it were some kind of an accomplishment and no doubt you will leave here thinking I am throwing myself at you. Well I am not. I have never asked for your company; I have never encouraged your attentions and you are a complete ninny if you cannot discern that. Leave Mr. Bingley. Leave now and do not attempt to circumvent my father's wishes again sir."

Jane turned back to the house and stalked in the side door closing it firmly behind. And for the second time that morning a gentleman returned to the Bingley household hoping to gain his room unnoticed.

The Colonel returned in time for lunch and was unsurprised that Georgie was keeping to her rooms. He did wonder where Bingley was, but the Hursts were present along with Miss Bingley. That Darcy was avoiding him was not completely surprising. Richard hoped he was seriously thinking about all that had passed between them.

Meanwhile he taken the opportunity while vising his lodgings to call for reinforcements. His parents would be receiving his express about now and he hoped to hear by return express that they would be arriving on the morrow.

For now, he was going to exaggerate his concerns for Anne's health to explain why he wished for his parents to stay here and not with Anne. He had sent a quick note to her also asking if he could invite himself to tea to speak with her this afternoon and had heard back immediately with a tongue and cheek invitation. Knowing Miss Bingley's curiosity, he waited for her to provide the opening.

"Was there any important correspondence, Colonel, or was your trip in vain?"

"It was not in vain; Miss Bingley for I have discovered my parents are coming to Bath probably tomorrow. I am waiting to hear for certain. I assume they will stay with Anne though I am unsure if she is truly strong enough for company at this point. A year from now I believe I would have no concerns, but she has been directed by her physician to guard her energies."

"Oh that poor dear," cooed Miss Bingley. "I completely understand your concern. Please ask your parents to consider our home as theirs, we would gladly welcome them for as short or long a stay as they wish."

"Are you certain, Miss Bingley? I do not wish to inconvenience you and you have already kindly agreed to host me and my cousins."

"I am quite certain Colonel. We are all such good friends I could do no less."

"Then I thank you kindly Miss Bingley and will let my parents know that they are welcome here."

After the Hursts retired and Miss Bingley departed with the housekeeper, Richard slipped out of the house and rode to Anne's residence.

Once seated in her drawing room he thanked her for the invitation.

"Richard you know you are always welcome. But tell me, why did I invite you today, cousin?"

"Well, you wanted to discuss some family concerns with me."

"Did I? What am I concerned about?"

"Darcy and Georgie."

"Well, I am perfectly willing to be concerned about Georgie, but I have no interest in being concerned about Darcy. He is a rude officious boor and I have told him he will not be welcome in my home until he apologizes to me and to both the Miss Bennets."

"So what exactly happened?"

"I had gone up to fetch a shawl that I wished to send to Miss Lucas and Jane and Elizabeth were waiting for me here. When I came in I heard Darcy ordering them out of my house and telling them that they could never return and to stay away from me. I was furious and told him in no uncertain terms that they were more than welcome. So he said they were fortune hunters and were taking advantage of me and then he forbade me to see them." Anne nodded in satisfaction at Richard's appalled expression. "I truly do not know that I have ever been so angry in my life. I knew he could be taciturn to the point of rudeness but I had no idea that he could speak to two gentlewomen in such a cruel manner. And he may be used to being able to order everyone in his sphere and they obey but if he thinks for one moment he can order me around he is wholly mistaken!"

"I do not know what to say Anne. I have thought for some time that he was becoming too high in the instep but with all the ton fawning on him, I understood it. I did not like it, but I understood it. But this kind of behavior? I do not know what to say."

"Well, you should know it is nothing new. You are aware that Darcy insulted Elizabeth before they met?" At Richard's nod she continued, "I have just learned what he said. They were at an assembly and Bingley offered to introduce him to Elizabeth because of course Darcy refusing to dance and he said that Elizabeth was not handsome enough to tempt him to dance and that he would not give consequence to young ladies who had been slighted by other men."

Richard sat as if turned to stone. He had to remind himself to breathe. In all of his worries that his cousin was becoming too full of his own self-importance he had never thought his cousin would stray completely from the tenets of his upbringing, had never thought he could be so little the gentleman.

"Richard?"

Anne's soft voice recalled him to his surroundings. "I am sorry Anne I was simply so surprised I did not know how to react. But now I am more glad than ever that I have asked my parents to visit."

"Uncle Henry and Aunt Audrey are coming to Bath? Oh that is wonderful. Will they stay with me then? Is that why you are wanted to talk to me?"

"No, I wanted to talk to you because I have manipulated Miss Bingley into inviting them to stay with us. I did not want you to feel slighted but I want my parents to see what is happening with both Darcys. I wanted their advice."

Anne nodded. "Well it makes sense then for them to stay where they will be in company with them. What is your worry with Georgie?"

"Anne, she is six and ten and behaves as if she is no more than two and ten. She plays and she works at lessons as if she is a schoolgirl instead of a young woman soon to make her come out. She knows nothing about running a home or being mistress of an estate and what is more she shows no interest in it at all. When she meets someone she refuses to look them in the eye and mumbles so softly that one has no idea what she has said. She has cocooned herself in childhood and is determined to stay there."

"And Darcy does not demand that she learn these things, that she work on at least learning to properly meet someone?"

"He encourages her to remain as she is, insisting she is a child and has time to learn these things later. But she is not a child, and she should come out in two years though in her case it may be best to wait one extra year. But even then, that is not a lot of time to prepare her for the adult world."

"Well Darcy has certainly mucked everything up has he not? He has developed an overbearing and obnoxious personality, he is keeping his sister forever a child, he has insulted my two best friends and myself, his only real friends who are not family are awful people who encourage the worst of his traits, and he has shown all of his poorest characteristics to a woman I believe he cares for."

"You see it too then? That he is besotted with Miss Elizabeth?"

"I believe the only two people who do not see it are Darcy and Elizabeth herself. She is convinced he despises her, and his behavior has been so wretched that it has been easy for her to be angry with him and to convince herself that she despises him in turn."

"Yes, that makes sense from her point of view. Well, I think they would do very well together. She would remind him that while there is duty in life there is also joy; he would revel in her intelligence and wit as much as her beauty. But first Darcy has to become the man he was and should be. No woman of character would have him as he is. And she needs time to see the man he is under the façade he wears to appease the ton."

Assumed Virtue

38

"Something is wrong with Darcy."

His mother looked at him surprised. "Darcy? Is he ill? What can have happened in so short a time?"

"I do not know. I know he is having to do some serious looking at the man he is and the man he thinks he is. He took his evening meal above stairs yesterday; he made a brief appearance this morning and looked truly ill. He has gone to his rooms again and has not been out and I do not believe he is eating anything that is sent to him. Something is wrong with Bingley too; he has said almost nothing to anyone and usually you cannot think for all the chattering he does. And I am truly worried about Georgiana. I am glad you are here for something must be done."

The Countess asked for more details and when Richard finished his tale she shook her head at him. "I will gladly lend a helping hand with Georgie my dear, but I will not interfere with Darcy. I do not think he could possibly be comfortable confiding in a woman, son. Even with those of us ladies he respects and cares for there is an awkwardness about him in female company. I believe you and probably your father are the only people in whom he might confide."

Richard knocked twice on Darcy's door before simply opening it and walking in. There he found his cousin with a glass of brandy in his hand, sitting listlessly in an armchair, gazing at nothing.

"Darce? Will? Are you alright?"

His cousin regarded him solemnly then said, "Richard, does your mother visit the tenants at Matlock?"

"What? Visit the tenants? She used to certainly, but I would guess Marjorie has taken on the duty now since she and Hill are managing the estate. She probably still goes to visit at least some of them when she has been gone for the season. Why? What has that to do with anything?"

"Elizabeth."

"Who?"

"Miss Elizabeth Bennet," replied Darcy, enunciating each syllable carefully. "She hates me you know."

"Does she? Why would she hate you?"

"Because I am not a gentleman. Neither is Bingley. We are both bad men."

Richard eyed his cousin then glanced at the table where a formerly full decanter of brandy had rested. It was close to empty. Deciding to take advantage of his cousin inebriety, Richard disposed himself in another chair and invited Darcy to explain.

"Remember I told you Miss Bingley told me they were fortune hunters and then I heard about how small the estate was and the entail and I did not put it together until now that the person who told me was also Miss Bingley. And I know she loves malicious gossip. But I believed her. So I tried to protect Anne from bad people, but she says it was me."

"What was you?"

"That I am the bad one, I am the one at fault. And Elizabeth says I am rude and not a gentleman and she hates me."

"She said that did she?"

"Well she did not actually say she hated me, but it was clear. She said I was not a gentleman. Mr. Bennet said he was a good friend of my father, and he disapproves of me, but I do not think he is my father's friend."

"Actually, Will, I believe Mr. Bennet did know your father. He knows my father too. Apparently they were friends in school though my father was not as close to him as your father was. My father actually called Mr. Bennet 'good old Tommy Bennet' when they saw each other in Hertfordshire which I think is a pretty good indication that they knew each other."

Darcy leaned his head back on the seat and moaned. "Why not? Why should that not happen since nothing else good has happened. She heard me insult her at the Assembly, Richard. I said something rude to make Bingley leave me alone and she heard me."

"What did she say when you apologized?"

Darcy regarded him with an owlish look. "I did not apologize. I am Fitzwilliam Darcy, I never apologize. I especially do not apologize to young ladies. You never know what they could be thinking if you apologize."

Richard regarded his cousin thoughtfully. He doubted if he could get the full story out of Darcy in his current condition; since his cousin only rarely drank to excess, he was no doubt going to be sick and unconscious shortly. But he rather felt he had enough to go on for a frank discussion once his cousin's head cleared the next day. For now, he would be best served getting Darcy's valet here and getting his cousin packed off to bed.

Once he had accomplished that mission, Richard went searching for Bingley. He found his host staring out the window in his study, except that he was fairly certain that Bingley saw nothing.

Deciding on a direct approach he simply asked, "What happened?"

Bingley fixed him with a sad, puppy dog look and said, "She called me a ninny."

"Miss Elizabeth called you a ninny?"

Bingley shook his head. "No, Miss Elizabeth was not there, it was only Miss Bennet, Jane. My beautiful angel. She said I was a ninny and then she said that she never encouraged me and that she tried to discourage me, but I never saw it and now I do not know what to do."

Richard gave a silent whistle. Whatever the two men had done, it was far worse than he had imagined. He knew Jane Bennet well enough to know that it took something quite egregious to make her speak so bluntly to someone.

Half an hour later, a confused Richard Fitzwilliam made his way back to his mother's sitting room. "Well, did you discover what is wrong?"

"I am not sure. Neither is particularly coherent right now, though in fairness I do not think Bingley is ever all that good at relating a story. Darcy will not be available today, he is indisposed."

"Is he foxed?" demanded the Countess.

"Mother—"

"Do not patronize me Richard. Do you think I have never seen a man in his cups? I have been a politician's wife for decades if you will remember. Did he tell you why he felt the need? Because he is not one to overindulge."

Richard sighed. "I am not certain, mother. I am not certain, but I believe both gentlemen received a harsh lesson in how they are viewed by others; a lesson administered by ladies they esteem, no less, and neither liked the results. There is nothing to be done today but tomorrow I will visit Mr. Bennet; I may be able to get a more coherent story at the source."

Assumed Virtue

39

Richard arrived at early at the Bennet household and asked to be shown directly to Mr. Bennet's study. He found a warm fire, an offer of tea and a welcoming Mr. Bennet.

Said Mr. Bennet. "It good to have you here Colonel. My daughters have had some difficult dealings with your cousin and your host lately."

"Anne told me about her confrontation with Darcy. I know he was upset but I believe something more happened. I saw my cousin yesterday and it is apparent that he is greatly distressed. And so is Mr. Bingley. Neither could give me a truly coherent version of what had caused their distress. I thought perhaps you might be able to enlighten me."

Mr. Bennet regarded him thoughtfully. "I know that you and my Jane are close to an understanding, but I fail to see why would you feel that you are entitled to a story they will not tell you?"

"Well, I think Bingley cannot tell me because his mind jumps from place to place too easily; my cousin cannot tell me because he is indisposed."

"Got foxed did he? I cannot say I blame him. I have rather thought he was attracted to my Lizzy, and she did not give him any reason to hope when they met yesterday morning."

"Ahh one of the missing pieces. Darcy kept talking about Miss Elizabeth and Bingley made it clear that she was not involved. So we have two separate dressing downs."

"Well, I can give you quite a good idea what was said each time. With five daughters it was necessary to teach them to relate conversations as closely to verbatim as possible, otherwise when listening to several overexcited little girls all trying to tell a tale at once, one never actually found out what was said. They are quite good at it now and since I have spoken with Jane and Lizzy I can tell you much of what happened."

Richard listened attentively as Mr. Bennet related the confrontation sparked by Darcy's cold attitude then Lizzy's condemnation of his; then Mr. Bennet related Jane's confrontation with Bingley. "Jane is quite distressed that she lost her temper and I would not be surprised to find that Lizzy is too though she would not admit it. She may not regret the sentiments, but she will regret speaking with such heat."

"Bennet, could I ask you, does Bingley indeed have such a poor reputation?"

Thomas Bennet hesitated before replying, "You must realize that we have a vested interest in who leases Netherfield. We investigated those interested before we agreed to lease the estate to the Bingleys and it turns out your friend has quite the reputation in the ton. Were his reputation that of a rake, he would not have been allowed to lease the estate; neither Gardiner nor I would be willing to put my daughters at risk. But he is a cad not a rake. Even here in Bath prudent parents were already aware of his lack of serious attentions; I did write to him when he first arrived about the amount of time he was allowed to monopolize my daughter. This is not Meryton, and I would not have her reputation tarnished by him. I would guess in another year or two there is no matchmaking mama who will be desperate enough to allow Mr. Bingley to have more than a casual acquaintance with their daughters."

Bennet sighed and rose to pour each of them a small tot of brandy. "I wrote to Darcy also, letting him know that his behavior is extremely poor. And just as I will not risk Jane's reputation I will not risk Lizzy's. Darcy dances with the two ladies of his party. And no one else. Except my Lizzy. Our neighbors understood and cared not but this is not Hertfordshire, and I will not see my daughter's name bandied about the ton. And it would be."

"Yes, I can see that. I confess I have not spent enough time in company with Darcy in the last years, my profession did not allow it. I was dismayed by some of the behavior I saw but I do not think I realized how bad it was."

Bennet chuckled at him. "As I understand it you were on a mission, and you inherited an estate during your short stay in our county. Perhaps there is a reason you were not as observant as usual."

Richard gave a faint smile. "I am glad to understand why Darcy brought up the tenants. And surprised by his attitude. I doubt if either he or Bingley are aware of what an estate's mistress does, but they would not have visited the tenants except in the fields. Still, Darcy should have made sure that the harvest was supervised, and spring planting arranged. I think that his infatuation with Miss Elizabeth was so disconcerting that he never even thought of it." Richard shook his head at his cousin's attitude. "And unfortunately, he appears to be in the habit of deflecting any criticism by finding a way to justify his own poor behavior."

"You know that you have my approval, son, and that I have enjoyed the company of your parents and Miss Anne and even Maude Jenkinson. But Darcy has not made it easy to find pleasure in his company and the Bingley family is not worth the time to get to know, though lately Mr. and Mrs. Hurst have shown signs of being more social and pleasant that I had previously found them."

Assumed Virtue

40

Richard may have resigned his commission but one did not lose the habit of command simply by changing one's coat. He used the time returning to Laura Place in determining his best course of action. Plan in place, he decided there was no time like the present to begin changing the direction of his cousin's life and possibly everyone else under his hosts' roof also.

Gaining his chambers in his usual fashion, by way of the back stairs, he changed then sought his hostess, who he found complaining to her sister in the front drawing room.

"Miss Bingley, you will do me the courtesy of speaking with me in the garden please. We will remain in sight of the windows."

Too surprised to question his demand, Caroline called for her wrap and rose and walked out the French doors with him. Once far enough from the house to ensure their privacy but close enough for propriety he turned to her and asked imperiously, "What do you think you are about?"

"I am sorry, I do not believe I have the pleasure of understanding you, Colonel."

"It is no longer Colonel, Miss Bingley, I have resigned my commission. I am speaking to you as the son of the Earl and Countess of Matlock, as an estate holder in my own right and as a member of the first circles of the ton. I am asking you what in the world you think you are doing constantly complaining and pretending to be above your company?"

"Pretending? I am not pretending. I am accepted in the best circles, I am above the company here, in every way."

"No you are not. You are accepted in the ton by virtue of your brother's friendship with Darcy, not for yourself. You are below them and you are below nearly every person here Miss Bingley. The people here are gentlemen and their wives and sons and daughters. Most of them would be readily accepted in London, they are in Bath by choice, because they do not enjoy the London season. In trade wealth is all important, in society, birth trumps wealth Miss Bingley. They have it, you do not. More, your manners are atrocious, you have no idea how to behave. Are you aware that a lady waits for a gentleman to approach her and offer an arm? Do you know how amusing it is when it is time for the gentlemen to rejoin the ladies after dinner and we watch you practically sprint across the room, even shoving other women out of your way so you can clutch at Darcy in a most forward and improper manner?"

As Miss Bingley flushed with anger and embarrassment, Richard continued in that same matter of fact tone. "You complained the entire time you were in Hertfordshire, and I am sure you do the same about the residents here. But you are the one who does not know how to behave. You are the spinster daughter of a tradesman, perilously close to being on the shelf despite your fine dowry. If your brother had any vestige of spine at all he would have either forced you to learn proper manners or sent you away."

He spoke over her briskly as she tried to interrupt, "My family has been content to ignore your pretentions and your fawning behavior as a favor to Darcy. But I will warn you now Miss Bingley, do not give the Earl and Countess a disgust of you, you will not like the results."

Bowing to her, he strode away, and locating a passing footman asked if Bingley had come down. Discovering that Charles had not come out of his room yet that day, Richard took the stairs two at a time; arriving at the sitting room attached to the master suite Richard rapped sharply at the door and strode in.

"Bingley, I have just had words with your sister. It is time she learned how to behave, and it is past time that you acted the part of a man and dealt with her."

"What? Why would you anger Caroline? Do you know what she is like when she is displeased?" Bingley looked both distressed and appalled.

Richard waved his objections away. "As far as I can tell she is always unpleasant, so how would I know the difference between when she is pleased or displeased? Since she is never agreeable company what matter if she is angry? If she starts to rant and rave send her to her room. If she refuses to go have her escorted by a footman. Good lord man you are supposed to be the head of your family and as far as I can tell, she is more likely to be issuing edicts than you. Grow a spine, man."

"I do not care for confrontations Richard, I never have."

"Yes, well I have never been overly fond of killing my fellow man and yet that was my task, and I did it. It is called being an adult, Bingley and it is about time you reached that stage of your life; you are a man grown and it is high time you began acting like one. As for your obsession with Jane Bennet, it is time to let it go. First, you never inspired anything more than boredom in her and second she is about to enter into a courtship with someone else."

Bingley's face took on a morose look. "She called me a ninny, she said I blather."

"She is right. You have been behaving like a blathering ninny. How can she respect a man whose sister rules him? Who cannot make any decision, no matter how important, without canvassing the opinions of everyone around him? More, your reputation in the ton is that of an inconstant flirt. And that reputation preceded you. No one in the ton takes you seriously, no one in Hertfordshire took you seriously and no one here in Bath takes you seriously. Behavior characterized by an improper amount of attention by an inconstant flirt is not the kind that engenders a good reputation."

Bingley stared at him dumbfounded. "I do not understand how that could be?"

"Can you not? You meet some young woman, shower her with attention then walk away from her as soon as another catches your eye. No one wants that kind of treatment for their daughters. More than that, think man. How do you think the women you so carelessly abandon feel? How many hearts have you broken because you spent weeks hanging on a woman's every word then appeared to forget her very existence because someone else appeared more attractive?"

"You mean I have hurt these women? I never thought of that, I just lost interest and moved on, I did not mean any harm."

"I believe that you meant no harm, but that does not mean you did not do any harm. There is a reason that propriety dictates that you do not shower a woman with such attentions unless you are seriously thinking about marriage. It is a supreme act of selfishness to treat women in such a manner. It is a supreme act of selfishness to refuse to confront your sister because it would make you uncomfortable."

He spoke even more sternly then, determined to make his point no matter how much it might offend. "The fact is that none of your family behaves well. You have gained a reputation as an inconstant cad, not to be taken seriously; your unmarried sister has a reputation as a malicious social climbing harpy, your married sister is considered to be a completely vacuous woman who is married to a drunken sot. This is your family, and you are the head of that family. Take hold, man. If you do not, you will find the Bingleys are unwelcome at any level of the ton and it will be your fault because it is your responsibility, and you are failing it."

Richard strode out of Bingley's chambers without giving him a chance to answer and charged down the hall to his cousin's rooms.

Again, rapping sharply at a door, and again walking into a sitting room without waiting for an invitation he found his cousin sober, brooding and unwelcoming.

"Go away Richard, I do not wish to talk."

"You do not have to talk; you need to listen. And pay attention because I am only going to be saying this once. You have become everything you have always abhorred about society cousin. You are rude, haughty, disdainful, puffed up with selfish disdain for others and overflowing with conceit."

Darcy stared at him aghast. "Richard!"

"Do not look so stunned, Darcy, you know it is true. I heard the insult you leveled at Miss Elizabeth before you had even met her. How dare you? How dare you say such a thing and still consider yourself a gentleman?"

"I was in a bad mood, Richard."

"This is your excuse? A gentleman does not take out his poor mood on a lady. It. Is. Not. Done." Richard spoke coldly, giving every word weight. "If you are a gentleman, William then you know this is true."

He continued relentlessly. "You are so used to considering no one's feelings to be of importance except your own that you offend constantly. Who are you to be so disdainful of other people? You are equal in birth with the residents here, no more than that. There are people here who surpass you in education, people here who are closer to you in wealth than you know, and virtually all of them are far above you in their behavior which is more important than either of those things. I never thought I would speak these words, but I am completely ashamed of you Darcy. Your behavior is everything abhorrent. Instead of sitting here brooding over what you consider wrongs done to you, maybe you should instead take some time and think about how you would feel if someone treated you as badly as you have treated them. Do you know the last time we went to visit the Bennets when we were all in Hertfordshire, I was worried something was wrong with you? You walked in the room, curtly nodded, then turned your back on the room and refused to engage with anyone there. And then I found out that this was how you always behaved there. If someone did that to you in your home what would you think, Darcy? Would you consider that the behavior of a gentleman?"

"What has come over you Richard?"

"I have discovered your behavior; cousin and I am appalled. You have been my cousin, my brother, my friend but I cannot like the man you have become."

"And throwing orders at Anne? Forbidding her to do something? What in the world would make you think you have that right Darce? She is a grown woman; she needs neither your support nor your approval and yet you demanded she do as you wished without even considering that if you had concerns you should have discussed them with her privately."

Richard turned as if to leave, then paused. "You might ask yourself why the only people you thought of to inveigle into inviting you here are the Bingleys, cousin. Your good friends are a spineless, inconstant puppy who is rapidly gaining the reputation of being a cad, a fortune hunting shrew, their sister who is the only adult I have ever known who can entertain herself for an entire evening playing with her bracelets and her husband, a drunken glutton capable of neither conversation nor courtesy. If a man is known by the company he keeps, what does that say about your character sir?"

Richard strode out of the room leaving Darcy gaping after him, then, satisfied that he had offended and outraged everyone and went to his sitting room, rang the bell and asked for a tray for lunch since he was quite certain no one in the house would be in a good mood for quite some time. Then he ran down the steps, collected his hat and went to visit his cousin Anne.

"Well, Richard, you are looking far less fraught," said Anne.

"I have not yet dealt with Georgie, but I have a plan. And meanwhile I have spoken to Mr. Bennet, and I plan to ask Jane Bennet for a courtship as soon as I have wrangled some sense into Darcy and Bingley, and I have outraged and offended most of the people who have more business being in the house than I do. I do not expect much change from the Bingleys because they appear to be an uncommonly stupid bunch, but Darcy is not stupid, and I believe he might change for the better if he gets over being angry and starts to think."

"Tell me all, dearest Richard. I am still angry at Darcy but perhaps I will forgive him if he turns back into the Darcy he used to be."

Richard promptly started with his cousin's and his hosts pitiful states, his discussion with Mr. Bennet and then, with great gusto, related his conversations with Bingley, Miss Bingley and Darcy. By time he was through, Anne was holding her sides and gasping with laughter.

"Oh Richard, I am so proud of you. It is hilarious in its way but so very needed. I do not know the Bingleys well enough to know if they will take your words to heart, but I am so very hopeful that Darcy will. He has always been quiet and serious, but it has indeed become far worse in recent years. Until our confrontation I had hoped it was only the effect of Lady Catherine because heaven knows she could drive anyone to their limits of patience, but his behavior must change. And even if it does I do not know if Elizabeth will have him. She is as outraged for Jane as she is for herself and that will be harder for her to forgive."

"He may have ruined any chance he had with her. He has insulted her, her family and her friends in every way possible while they have treated him with every courtesy. Then he left her without so much as the courtesy of a farewell call. Then he discovers her in Bath and continues to insult her, glare at her and behave in a most unbecoming fashion. He really needed to hear their criticisms and mine because he is on the verge of ruining both is life and Georgie's, and I cannot stand by and watch that happen."

He rose then and favored her with a smile. "My dear, I am going to return and see if there has yet been a reaction to my words. Meanwhile, I will be about; there are still balls to attend and concerts to enjoy and I did not come to Bath to stay at home."

41

The next morning was notable for several changes in behavior. The Bingleys were uniformly quiet, speaking pleasantly when addressed but initiating no conversation with the Fitzwilliams. Richard occasionally noted a look of thoughtfulness from both Miss Bingley and Charles but neither addressed the conversations he had had with them.

As for Darcy, he was punctiliously polite to Richard, but he initiated no confidences and Richard did not push the issue. He let it ride for now, he had a very important mission this morning. He had already spoken with his parents about courting Miss Bennet, and they would accompany him when he went to see her today. He knew they enjoyed the Bennet's company so it was no hardship for them, and it would make it be easier for him to request a private conversation with Jane.

The visit to the Bennet family was most comfortable. And as soon as Hill brought in the tea tray, Richard softly asked Jane if he could speak with her in the side garden. Jane looked at him with shining eyes and flushed cheeks and quietly assented.

They slipped out of the room, while everyone remaining pretended not to notice. Richard, whose easy facility with words had never failed him, suddenly found that no words seemed ready to leap off his tongue. After several moments of silence, Jane finally prompted him. "You said you wished to speak with me Colonel, but you seem not to have anything to say."

He smiled down at her, his heart in his eyes. "I have never said what I need to say and so somehow it seems impossible to find the right words. Miss Bennet, Jane, my dear, would you consider entering into a courtship with me?"

Jane's eyes filled with happy tears and her voice trembled with shy joy as she responded, "I would be delighted, Richard."

Richard beamed at her, feeling the tension leaving his shoulders. "I would ask for a betrothal, Jane, but I want you to know me. There is much for us to speak of, and I will not push you to come to a decision faster than is comfortable for you. But please know that it will take only one word from you to have me asking for your hand."

He took that hand then, kissing it tenderly and led her back into the house. They had barely made it into the room before Lizzy was on her feet, exclaiming, "Jane, oh Jane you are glowing my dear sister."

"I had heard that joy does that for a woman, Lizzy and am glad to know that it is true."

The next half hour was a blur for Jane. Everyone was wishing her the best, but she had eyes only for Richard. Finally, as the Countess rose, indicating the visit was ending, she slipped her hand into his and walked to the front door with him. "I am going to write to Mama. She enjoyed your company and that of your parents and I know she will be so very pleased we are courting."

"My dearest Jane, I enjoyed her company also and now you will have something more in common with her." He gave her an impish smile. "I understand your father was besotted with your mother's beauty but fell in love with her when he discovered she spoke Latin and read Greek. I can honestly say I was besotted by your beauty but fell in love with you when you explained to me the intricacies of plumbing."

Jane gasped in surprise then began to laugh. "Dearest Richard, that may be the single most romantic thing I have ever heard."

Richard's deep chuckled joined her laughter, then kissing her hand once again he turned and offered his arm to his mother.

On their short journey home, the Countess requested that Richard come to her sitting room. "You did not have a chance to do more than take a quick sip of tea, my son. We will have a second tea and talk." Settled in her sitting room, she smiled over at him. "I like Jane Bennet a great deal, Richard. I believe you and she will do well together."

"I hope I can be a good husband to her, mother, and yes you do not have to ask, I fully believe we will marry. I have ghosts, mother, some hard things from years of battle and she needs to know enough of what I face to determine if she can accept them, accept me. But I believe she will. She is no fragile, fainting miss."

His mother nodded. "Yes. She has spine. She will not wilt at the first sign of trouble, Richard. You are well matched." She sipped her tea, frowning slightly, then said, "You have not told me what was going on with Darcy and Bingley. Nor have we discussed Georgiana fully. And I believe I would like you to do so now please."

"Well, let us start with the least important, Bingley. Mr. Bennet wrote a somewhat scathing description of his behavior and demanded he drastically limit the time he spent with Jane. Then Jane gave him a solid dressing down about his behavior. And I followed up on it. Well actually first I took Miss Bingley to task for her ridiculous pretentions, *then* I took Bingley to task. I told him exactly how disgracefully his whole family behaves and placed the blame squarely on him for being the head of the family in name but allowing Miss Bingley to be the head of the family in fact."

"Ahh, so that is why they were both very quiet today."

"I also told Bingley that Jane was going to be entering into a courtship though I did not mention that it was with me."

"She was never going to give him more than bored courtesy, he was the only one who could not see it. Who next?"

"Well next I will say Georgiana, not that she is less important than Darcy, but she is younger and though she has me completely frustrated right now I do believe that we can get through to her."

"I asked to see her but was informed she is ill."

"I think she probably has made herself ill, I do not believe it is possible to spend hours of the day crying and not suffer some ill effects." And he began the tale of his trials with his ward.

His mother listened in attentive silence, weighing what he said carefully. When he finished she put her teacup down with a sigh. "So we have another Miss Bingley in our midst."

Richard stared at her in surprise. "She is not viscous and manipulative."

"Not vicious but definitely manipulative. She is using tears and timidity to get her own way as surely as Miss Bingley uses vitriol. Different means, same results. She does not do what she does not wish to do, in fact she does only what she wants, and she controls those around her with the threat of tears. In her defense, she may not even realize that is what she is doing, but whether deliberate or unknowing the results are the same. How much did you actually accomplish with her? She admitted no fault, she agreed to no changes. And right now, I do not believe either you or Mrs. Annesley can force a change in her. The only one who can is Darcy. You will need to get to him before he sees her, if she relates to him that you are questioning her behavior before you speak with him he will automatically defend her, and it will be harder to make him understand what she is doing and that he cannot give in to her no matter that it hurts him to deny her."

Richard wholeheartedly agreed. "I do not know if we can force her to change but I agree that she is using her youth and timidity to control the situation. It is particularly effective because she looks so frail and so very young that one cannot help but see her as a fragile child. I found it incredibly difficult to hold firm, because once she was crying and looking like a strong wind would blow her over, I had to keep a tight control on myself not to simply tell her I was sorry and that I would not ask her to do anything she did not want to do. It appears she has not the courage or the strength to do more than she is already doing. But she cannot continue as she is, mother."

"You are right. It goes against everything you are to be unkind to a young woman in distress. And even though you are determined to see her change, I know you find it incredibly difficult to remain firm in the face of her tears."

"Well, I will give my cousin a day or two to recover. I do not believe Darcy is in a place to deal with her right now. He needs time to come to terms with himself and with the damage he may have done to his own happiness."

"Elizabeth Bennet."

Richard gave her a glance of amused affection. "How long did it take you to figure that out?"

"I have known him since childhood. It was not hard to discern. I have not, however, seen him in company with her as most of our time together was in London. So, I repeat, what has he done about it?"

"Well, so far he has insulted her, her family, her friends and pretty much everyone else he has come into contact with; he has stared at her in a disagreeable and forbidding fashion and he has ignored her."

"Dear heavens, what is wrong with him? Never mind, I know what is wrong with him. He has pushed the boundaries of courtesy to the limits, perhaps past the limits. And I have noticed his arrogance also. No doubt he feels she is not good enough for him?"

"That is exactly what he has done. I think he did not realize he was in love with her until he left her in Hertfordshire; I think he decided he was not going to pursue her and regretted it. I believe he was delighted to find she was here and is now devasted that her opinion of him is so poor, but I do not know if he has yet reached the point where he realizes that her opinion is justified by his behavior."

"Of course, I could be wrong," he added thoughtfully. "I am not sure because with all the insulting, ignoring, and generally bad behavior it is difficult to judge. But when I spoke with him he was quite depressed that she dislikes him. So perhaps there is hope for him. Except that quite naturally she is not particularly enamored of him right now and may never be. I do not know how forgiving she is as I do not know her so well as I do Jane."

"I believe she is affected by him also, or at least she could be affected by him, though whether she can forgive him enough to allow him into her heart is open to question. I assume that you have concocted some kind of plan?"

"Well, it is somewhat vague, and it depends on Darcy learning to be the gentleman he once was again. Mother his behavior truly has been abominable. You have not been in company with him much but let me tell you about my one visit to the Bennets at Longbourn with him." Richard related Darcy's antisocial behavior in short blunt sentences. Lady Fitzwilliam closed her eyes as if in pain. "Oh dear heavens, he cannot go on like this any more than Georgiana can. He will ruin his life if he does so. No woman of character will have him as he is and what kind of life will he have if he is married to a fortune hunting harpy?"

The Countess huffed her displeasure. "I knew that he was rude and taciturn in London, I did not know that behavior extended to everywhere he went."

"It certainly won him no friends in Hertfordshire. He has not been out much in Bath but the one evening he was I believe he asked Miss Elizabeth to dance, was refused because her card was full and so he spent the evening stalking the sides of the ballroom and glaring." Richard frowned then, and added, "I do not think the Bingleys have been good for him. Charles depends on his advice too much, to the point where Darcy has begun to feel he is always right and between that and Miss Bingley agreeing with everything he says no matter how ridiculous, he has come to believe whatever he says should be accepted without question. Mrs. Annesley pointed out that Georgie feels she cannot make a mistake because he never does so. And mother, he really does feel that way."

"Well, that is ridiculous, he cannot possibly think that."

"It is ridiculous, but I really think it is true. Look at what happened here. He decided that the Bennets were fortune hunters on Miss Bingley's say-so, then decided to order Anne to drop their friendship and ordered the two ladies to leave a house that did not belong to him, where he was an unexpected visitor. It honestly never occurred to him that if he had any objections to them he should speak to Anne privately or discuss his concerns with you and father. When I tasked him with it, when I related the facts of their situation, he never actually admitted he was wrong."

"I do not believe he has apologized to Anne either."

"Almost certainly not. When I asked him what Miss Elizabeth said when he apologized for insulting her, he replied that he never apologized, he was Fitzwilliam Darcy."

"Well, it is a good thing he was talking to you and not to me for I would have been forced to box his ears. What a stupid thing to say."

"It is even a more stupid thing to think. And he really does think it."

"And your campaign to bring him into Miss Elizabeth's good graces?"

"As I said, it has to start with Darcy. My plan is to let him stew for a day or two. No more than that though because then he will just brood himself into a corner. I laid out for him exactly how abhorrent his behavior has been. He needs to spend a little time looking at it. Then…well, I think I will hint, just hint mind you, that he talk to father. I think he may be the only one who can break through to Darcy."

The Countess mulled this over in silence, then nodded. "Yes, I think it is a good plan. Henry loves him like another son and Darcy knows this. And the generational difference, the respect he has for your father could turn the tide."

"Now back to Mr. Bingley for a moment. He is foolish, but I think he is good hearted. He has no idea how to be an adult any more than Darcy or Georgiana do. I believe that Bingley needs someone like his sister only better tempered. He will never rule his own household, he is not strong enough or smart enough. A nice, intelligent, managing woman would suit him well. If he could overcome his tendency to look only at the surface, Miss Lucas would be perfect for him."

"Miss Lucas?"

"Yes, Miss Lucas. She is not beautiful, but she is not as plain as she appeared in Hertfordshire. She is at a disadvantage because of the Bennets; they are so lovely that everyone in their vicinity seems bland, but in fact now that she is well dressed she presents an elegant appearance. She is eminently practical, and exactly the kind of no-nonsense sort of woman he needs. She would run his household, his budget, his sisters and him with kind firmness."

"I do not think he would consider her. Which is odd now that I think on it because from just little bits of conversation here and there it appears that they have at least spoken seriously about a number of subjects."

"I think I shall have her to tea. Mr. Bingley is very easily led; it is quite possible I can at least set him off in that direction."

Assumed Virtue

42

The Countess wasted no time in setting her plan for Bingley in motion. The next morning at breakfast she asked Miss Bingley if it would inconvenience her if she invited a young lady of her acquaintance to tea. From the tightening on Miss Bingley's features, it was clear that she was not pleased but she had no desire to anger the Countess and so agreed that it would be a fine idea but begged to be excused as she and her sister already had plans for the day.

"I understand completely Miss Bingley and I would not like you to trouble yourself over it. I would like to get to know Miss Charlotte Lucas a little better, and as Henry and I will be returning to London shortly I thought speaking with her over tea would be pleasant. You know Miss Lucas, do you not, Mr. Bingley?"

"Yes, I do know her. I have danced with her in Hertfordshire and here in Bath. She is quite nice and easy to speak with too. She is great friends with the Bennets, particularly with Miss Elizabeth Bennet I believe."

"Yes, I have heard that also," replied the Countess as if she were unaware of the close friendship between the two ladies. "Perhaps you would be good enough to greet her with me when she arrives. I do very much wish for her to be comfortable."

"I would be delighted, Lady Fitzwilliam. Just let me know the arrangements and I will be here to greet her. I am sure we can ensure a most enjoyable visit."

When Charlotte arrived, intrigued that the Countess wished to see her without the Bennets, Charles was indeed there to greet her and shepherd her into the drawing room.

"Unfortunately, my sisters had other plans and cannot join us, but I am sure we can still have a lovely tea, Miss Lucas."

The Countess nodded and asked Miss Lucas to pour, knowing from experience that a woman such as Charlotte Lucas was always more comfortable with something to do. Once she had served them both, preparing Mr. Bingley's cup precisely as he preferred without asking, the Countess ask Charles an easy question about the estate in Hertfordshire. Within a few minutes Miss Lucas and Mr. Bingley were chatting like old friends. The Countess deliberately remained in the background, inserting a comment or directing the conversation unobtrusively. When the polite half an hour had passed, Miss Lucas thanked them, and Charles escorted her to the door.

As he was turning away the Countess called him back to her.

"Do you see what happened here, Mr. Bingley?"

"I am sorry, I do not have the pleasure of understanding you?"

"Mr. Bingley, you focused your attention exclusively on Miss Bennet in Hertfordshire and again since your arrival here in Bath. It has led you to ignore other worthy young women; this is foolish."

Surprised, Charles allowed that this might be true.

"No, not might be true, it is true. Jane Bennet has entered into a courtship and even though you do not know her well, you must realize that she would not have done so if she did not have serious intentions with the gentleman. You have just spent half an hour in company with a young woman of uncommon good sense. She found you interesting and you enjoyed your time with her because you were not trying desperately to impress her. You could speak as friends. Miss Lucas obviously has a working knowledge of how to be mistress of an estate. She is kind, but firm in resolve. She would be an admirable partner for any man wishing to be a successful landowner. More than that, as I said, the two of you spoke easily together; have you never wondered what you would do with one of your beauties if you did capture their attention? You lose interest in the women you so assiduously court because you have nothing in common with them."

Charles looked at her, astonished at the direction the conversation had taken. "Are you suggesting that we should suit as a couple? Miss Lucas and myself?"

"In fact, I am not suggesting it, I am stating it." The Countess sighed. "Mr. Bingley you are friends with my beloved nephew. It would pain him to think you were in a marriage that brought you no happiness; I would like to help you. Please, sit a moment and discuss this seriously with me."

Once Charles was comfortably seated, the Countess continued. "How would you and your wife, whoever she is, be happy given the way your sisters behave? Miss Bingley is unlikely to ever marry you know. She is one season away from being on the shelf and her reputation for being unpleasant is too firmly established for any but the most desperate of fortune hunters to seek her hand. The Hursts do not seem to be in any hurry to support themselves and no doubt assume they will continue to live with you, and I do not see you denying them. You are perhaps too used to them to see them clearly, but they need to be taken in hand. What woman would want to marry into such a situation?"

Charles appeared stunned. "Are they so very bad?"

"Yes, they are that bad. Richard told you so. Now I am telling you so.

They are very bad. As I see it, you have two choices. You can demand that the Hursts remove themselves and force your unmarried sister to behave or you need to marry someone who can be kind to them but is strong enough so that they do not rule you. Do you see yourself able to control them?"

Charles blushed and hunched his shoulders. "I do not like confrontations. They have always made me most uncomfortable."

"Not everyone is well suited to debate, Mr. Bingley. There is no shame in that. But it would be a shame to have your whole life be an unending misery because they are not taken in hand. You do not seem to be able to do it; in fact, you do not want to do it. Again, this is not a criticism, it is just how things are. But tell me, does it not make sense to marry someone who can do so for you? Miss Lucas would be an attractive and elegant wife; she is a strong young woman and while she would be unfailingly kind to your family, she also would not allow them to cause you discomfort. Think on this: she is used to living within a set budget. Can you see her allowing your sister to overspend her allowance each quarter?"

Charles looked much struck by that. "No, I can see that she would not allow it. But would she not then be arguing with my sister?"

"Perhaps, but as long as you make it clear to everyone that you will not interfere with Miss Lucas' decisions, then allow her to handle your family issues, you would not have to be involved. Gentlemen have so many options of being somewhere else, do they not? Is this not one of the reasons for your clubs? To allow you to escape when needed? And should you have to be out of town on business on quarter day, well then a letter can always be unanswered."

Charles mulled this over a moment. "I do not believe I have ever really considered life after marriage in such a way. But I do know that very few people seem to be able to tolerate Caroline for any length of time. Even Darcy, who is very controlled, has come to a point where he is obviously not comfortable in her presence."

The Countess nodded her agreement. "She is a difficult young woman as she is used to always getting her own way; your habit of giving in to her is well established and she knows this. But Miss Lucas has younger siblings and her mother, if you will forgive my bluntness, has taken little interest in bringing them up properly. I understand that Miss Lucas has handled them with kindness but also a firm hand. I believe it is too late for you to take charge of your sister, but the correct wife could do so. How much happier would you be if she were not demanding more money from you all time? How much happier would you be if she were not allowed to cause unpleasant scenes almost daily in your home? How much happier would you be if you did not always have to take into account what she wants even if it is not what you want?"

The Countess fell silent then, quietly sipping her cool tea and waiting for the young man to consider what she had said.

"Do you know, I never once thought of what kind of life I could have if Caroline's wishes were not always having to be taken into account?" he said, his voice a dazed whisper. "It would be a wonderful thing if this were so."

"And it could be so," responded the Countess briskly. "You just need to make the right choice. A wife can be more than an ornament on your arm you know; she can be a partner. And in a good marriage, each partner is allowed to play to their strengths. You could bring a light heartedness to her that she has never known and a sense of security and safety that would enhance her life. She could bring you a peaceful home, one without constant tension always underlying everything you do. And while she would not bring you a dowry, her experience running an estate within a budget would translate into such savings for you that it would matter not."

The Countess rose then and Bingley, still looking dazed, automatically rose with her.

"Young man, no one can be happy, or see their way clearly forward, when someone second guesses everything they do; your wants, your needs, your contentment have always had to take second place to your sisters' demands. But it does not have to continue that way. You have the means at hand to change your life in a meaningful way that does not place you in a position of having to fight with your family. And forgive me for adding this one last bit of knowledge: a common license is easy to obtain and means you can marry someone immediately. Miss Lucas is of age and is not the kind of woman who would demand a lavish celebration. A quick and quiet wedding and the deed is done before your sisters can cavil."

43

Thomas Bennet was taken by surprise the next day when Charles Bingley called alone at the earliest polite time for visiting and requested a private audience with Charlotte. And Charlotte was completely stunned when Mr. Bingley asked for her hand.

"I believe I would enjoy being married to you very much Mr. Bingley. But I must ask you why me? You have not distinguished me with your attentions; indeed, I thought your inclinations were quite firmly with another."

Charles nodded. "And you would be correct. But after our tea yesterday I had a long conversation with the Countess. Until she pointed it out I never really thought that with you I can comfortably converse, that we have actual discussions about things that matter. It is in my mind that we would be very well suited." He drew a deep breath. "You know my family situation Miss Lucas. You should know that it seems likely that my family will be living with me for some time. I do not like arguments. I will give in just to end a quarrel. I realize now that what I need is a wife who is a friend; not just a friend, but a strong one who is on my side always. I can fight battles in business. I cannot do so at home; I simply am not built that way. The Countess pointed out that the right wife, a woman who is more than an ornament on my arm but is in fact my partner in life, could give me the kind of peaceful home I have always dreamed of having, one where there are not daily arguments and dramas, one where what

I want is considered to be of importance."

Charlotte nodded thoughtfully. "Your sisters will object to me, you know this. Can you stand against them long enough to see us wed?"

Charles blushed, embarrassed but determined to be honest. "I do not think I can do so if I simply announce I have plans to ask you to marry me. That is why I am here, before they have even risen for the day. I can get a common license today; we can wed as quickly as we wish and then it will not matter what they say because the deed will be done."

To his surprise Charlotte laughed at that. "What a good idea. Sly, but good. When would you like this to take place?"

"If I purchase the license today we can marry on whichever day you would choose."

"Well then, go purchase the license Charles. I have an idea of how to arrange this and will begin at once. Can you return for tea this afternoon?"

"I will be here."

Charlotte saw him to the door then went to her room to think; then she sought out her good friends and their father.

"So Charlotte, what did our friend Mr. Bingley have to say."

Lizzy drew her friend to her side. "You seem big with news dear friend. What has happened?"

Charlotte shook her head and waited for the tea tray then spoke to her dearest friend's sister directly. "Jane, I do not wish to cause you any pain, but I want you to know that Charles Bingley has asked me to marry him."

"Mr. Bingley? I did not know you had more than a passing

acquaintance," gasped Lizzy.

Charlotte, watching Jane anxiously saw no distress, just surprise. "Jane?"

"My dear Charlotte, if you are worried about me, please do not be. My heart was untouched by Mr. Bingley even before I had met Richard. But I agree with Lizzy, I did not know you knew him well enough to marry. When did this come about?"

Relieved Charlotte relaxed. "Just a short time ago; I think it is actually the Countess' doing. She invited me for tea, and it was just the three of us. Then this morning Charles said that they had spoken after I left about what he really wants his life to be like and I believe she recommended that he offer for me."

"And you accepted him? Just like that?" demanded Lizzy.

"I am not romantic, Lizzy. I never was. I only ask a comfortable home and the chance for children; Mr. Bingley can give me that. I am six and twenty years old, and there is no one in Hertfordshire who is going to offer for me. And, I am afraid with my lack of dowry, there is no one else in Bath who will offer for me either. This is my one chance to marry so yes, I said yes, just like that."

"But Charlotte, I know you have spent a small amount of time with him, but you do not really know him."

"I know enough, Lizzy. He is, I believe, a basically good man if a little weak. That is not something that will deter me; the same could be said about a great many of the husbands in our home neighborhood; I will be blunt and point out that it includes my own father. We talked honestly about this. He cannot stand against his sisters, particularly Miss Bingley. He needs someone who can take her in hand, who will not be afraid to stand up to his younger sister. She dominates him and his home; her dramatics keep everyone on edge constantly. But if he has a partner who will be the mistress of his home, in fact and not just in name, then her power over him is at an end. I can do this; I can force her to mend her ways; he is uncomfortable with unpleasantness, but her displeasure means nothing to me. I know you do not understand but I truly believe that for me this is the only chance I will ever have for a home of my own and I am determined to take it."

Before Lizzy could protest further, Mr. Bennet intervened. "Congratulations my dear. And Lizzy, while this is not the kind of match you want, I do believe that it will do very well for both Charlotte and Mr. Bingley."

"Papa? You agree with this?"

"I do not have to agree child, it is Charlotte's decision, but yes I do agree. I can see exactly what Lady Fitzwilliam was thinking. Mr. Bingley is not a strong man. He is kind, I believe he is honest in his business dealings, but he has never truly grown up and he has no liking for confronting his family. Charlotte is kind and honest also, but she is not afraid to confront someone if needed. Mr. Bingley knows that she will stand up to his sister; I do not believe he yet realizes that she is going to manage more than just his sister," he added with a twinkling glance at Charlotte, "but I also do not believe it will matter to him once she has taken charge; in fact, he will be a great deal more comfortable and that is what he really wants after all. Charlotte, I would give you this advice: use Miss Bingley's funds to control her."

Charlotte nodded. "Yes, I had already thought of that. I will let her know at once that I am going to be in charge of her allowance. And while I am willing to try to work kindly with her to start, I am not afraid of using any means necessary."

She paused then and said diffidently, "I have to ask for your aid."

Mr. Bennet nodded. "You have it my dear. What can we do?"

"Charles is going to get a common license today. We can marry whenever and wherever we want. He wishes to marry as quickly as possible, and I agree with him. Will you help me?"

"Of course. When will you see him next?"

"He is coming to tea this afternoon."

"Then you will send him to me before tea. You may be marrying quickly by common license but that does not mean you should not have a settlement in place. Should you like to have the wedding here, my dear?"

"That would be wonderful! When do you think we can be ready?"

"Well, we will give Mr. Bingley tomorrow and the next morning to arrange the settlement. That should be enough time. So Thursday afternoon. Now you three should go and raid the trunks that you received from Anne. Surely there is something that will work as your wedding dress; I know that you do not have a great deal of time, but I also remember Mrs. Bennet's flutterings that she have precisely the right dress."

When Charles arrived for tea he was first shown into Mr. Bennet's study.

"Mr. Bingley, I understand you and Charlotte wish to marry and to do so by common license. But Sir William has entrusted her care to me, and I will not see her wed without a proper settlement. We can work out the details now and tomorrow morning have a local solicitor do clean copies for you, for Charlotte and for me to send to her father."

"It is an excellent plan. I have sketched out the basics for the settlement to bring with me and wished to discuss this with you sir. I want Charlotte to be comfortable with the settlements and to know she will never be in want."

"Do you wish your sisters to attend your wedding?"

Charles thought about it then said firmly, "No, I do not believe so. I will tell the Countess and ask if she and the Earl will grace us with their presence. I would like Darcy to stand with me and I would invite Richard and Anne and Mrs. Jenkinson. But my sisters will add nothing but tension and unpleasantness to what should be a happy occasion. They will know soon enough."

"Very well then. You will need to see the vicar after tea today and request his presence, but that should not be a problem."

Bingley arrived back at the house at Laura Place in a buoyantly good mood. When they separated after dinner that night, Charles waited only until Hurst was on his way to being thoroughly intoxicated before quietly confiding to the other gentlemen that he was to marry Charlotte Lucas on Thursday afternoon at the Bennet's home in Sydney Place and they were all invited.

"My Lord, I know Charlotte would be delighted if you and Lady Fitzwilliam would attend; and you of course Richard. I plan to invite Miss de Bourgh also, but my sisters and brother Hurst will not be informed until after the ceremony. Darcy, would you stand up with me?"

Darcy was looking at him in consternation. "You are marrying Miss Lucas? You do not know her!"

"I know enough Darcy. She is exactly what I need. I want a peaceful home, Darcy. I want my sisters to behave. I want to know that when I come home I will have a warm welcome and not a litany of complaints before I have had a chance to take off my gloves. She is so strong, Darcy. Caroline's displeasure means nothing to her. The Countess suggested I consider it and the more I thought on it, the more I went over our conversations, the more sure I became."

"She does not love you," stated Darcy bluntly.

"No, I do not believe she does. But she knows my faults and respects me anyway. You have had respect automatically bestowed all your life due to your position and wealth. I have plenty of people who like me, but respect is not something I have seen a lot of in my life. Certainly not in my own family or even in my closest friend." Charles held a hand up as Darcy opened his mouth to protest. "No, my friend, you like me, you enjoy my company but do not pretend a respect you do not feel. But Charlotte understands the problem I have with my family. Her own father is a man much like me. It has not made her respect him any less, nor does it make her respect me any less. I will have a peaceful and comfortable home and that, my friend, is what I want more than anything. If you feel you cannot stand up with me I will understand but I would hope you will do this."

Darcy regarded his friend somberly a moment, then nodded. "If this is truly what you want then yes, I will stand up with you, my friend."

"And the Countess and I will be there to wish you joy, Bingley. I believe you have made a wise decision, one that will stand you in good stead. My wife has spoken to me of her admiration for Miss Lucas and I believe you will do very well together, very well indeed."

Charles beamed at the Earl. "Thank you sir, I am grateful for your support. Richard, I cannot see Miss de Bourgh privately; would you be so good as to accompany me tomorrow afternoon so I can proffer the invitation to her?"

Richard nodded. "Of course, and I will escort her there myself. I wish you joy Bingley."

"I do not know about joy, but I will have a peaceful and comfortable home. You know I never thought about what my daily life would be like once married until her ladyship brought it up. I never stopped to think what will we speak of; how will we live with my family? Once she brought it up I have not ceased to think of it."

Thursday morning Charlotte slipped quietly down the stairs and made her way directly into the sitting room where Lizzy and Jane were putting the finishing touches on a lush bouquet made up of beautiful hothouse roses.

"Oh my goodness, that is so beautiful!" Charlotte's eyes welled with tears. "Oh dear, I am being a watering pot, but it is just what I have always wanted."

"You have been a part of our lives forever Charlotte. We could do no less than our best for you. Come upstairs now. You need to try on your gown so we can make any last minute adjustments."

Once she was bathed and perfumed their maid to work on her hair, braiding and curling until it was beautifully arranged in a soft crown, then delicately placed baby roses around it to complete the crown effect. The re-worked gown, a lovely dusty rose silk, was carefully donned and then Lizzy clasped a beautiful and delicately wrought necklace of gold, rubies and pearls around her neck. "Your groom sent this for you my dear, once I told him what colors would go best."

Charlotte reaches up to touch the jewels. "I have never seen anything so fine," she whispered.

Lizzy drew a deep breath. "I received an express from mama this morning. She had something she wished most particularly that I relate to you. Mama said to tell you there are those who will say that felicity in marriage is a matter of chance. But she does not believe that. Felicity in marriage is a matter of choice not chance, of work, of patience and understanding. When two people are good-hearted and are willing to strive for a happy marriage, that is when it becomes one. And she said that you and Mr. Bingley will do well together, very well." She kissed Charlotte's cheek.

Charlotte eyes filled with tears. "Are you disappointed in me Lizzy?"

Elizabeth shook her head. "I am not, Charlotte, truly I am not. I was shocked at first but as I thought on it I realized that just because you chose something I would not, does not make it the wrong choice for you. We are very different people though we have been close as sisters. I agree with Mama and Papa that you will be happy, Charlotte, though probably not at first." At Charlotte's questioning look, she favored her with an impish grin, "you will have to face the dragon first my dear, but I have every faith that you will be victorious."

Charlotte laughed then drew a deep breath. "Well then, I am ready. Shall one of you see if all is in place?" Jane wished her joy once more and left to let the small number of guests know the bride was ready.

Downstairs, Bingley bounced from person to person, holding half conversations and then bounding off to speak with another, his nerves and excitement palpable. If anyone had worried about him still being attracted to Jane Bennet, they could be reassured by his exuberance and smiling countenance that he seemed to have no regrets.

Jane had been determined to set him at ease, so once she came downstairs she crossed to him immediately and wished him joy with obvious sincerity. He accepted her congratulations cheerfully; thanking her and her family for all their help.

As Darcy came to take him to his place in front of the makeshift altar in the garden, Mr. Bennet murmured to Jane, "I truly believe he has forgotten all the attentions he bestowed on you Jane."

She nodded. "It is what we said of him from the beginning: that once his attention is turned he forgets completely that he was besotted with someone. I hope that he will be constant in his affections with Charlotte."

"I rather think he will. He is not besotted with her, he never was. He has, I think, a genuine appreciation of her and in his case that may be a more reliable gauge of his constancy. He was dazzled by you, but he never knew enough about you to develop any depth of feeling so it is easy for him to move on. I believe he has had more conversations of meaning with Charlotte in the last three days than the two of you had in the entire time he was swooning over you."

Jane laughed softly. "You are quite right. We never discussed his family situation or what he wanted or how he felt. My only worry is that it seems very selfish, for while I am glad there is no awkwardness between us, how could he know that I would not be hurt by his desertion? I do not wish to see Charlotte hurt."

"Jane, I love the Lucases like family, but I am not blind to their faults. They have used Charlotte to ensure their comfort for years and I do not think she ever heard much of gratitude from anyone, certainly not from her mother. I doubt if anyone other than Sir William actually knows how much she has done for them. She has lived her life surrounded by selfishness; she already knows how to make peace with it." He left Jane to cross to the stairs and await Charlotte, allowing Jane to go to Anne and Richard, graciously offering to lead them to their places.

As Thomas Bennet stood in the place of his friend of a lifetime, his thoughts turned somber. Only a man with daughters could understand his joy and sorrow, could realize that for the first time he was feeling fully what it would mean to give a daughter to another man in marriage. He had been the only man in his daughters' lives all these years, but he knew his time with them was growing shorter and Charlotte's wedding only underscored that point.

He hoped he had judged Richard Fitzwilliam correctly, that he would a good and steady husband to his dear first born. Darcy's obvious attraction for his Lizzy was clear to his eyes but he had no worries there. Unless he changed radically his girl would not have such a man. But where there was one, would not another follow? Was that not why they were in Bath after all? How much longer would his Lizzy be his daily companion? His youngest was already five and ten. In other half a dozen years they could all be gone, and he wondered how he would handle the grief and the silence.

Shaking off his introspective mood, he turned toward the stairs where Lizzy was descending in front of Charlotte, with Sally behind them making sure the dress was not dirtied on the stairs or her hair mussed by her passage. He walked over to Sir William's daughter, gave her a fatherly kiss on the forehead and offered his arm to escort her to the garden and to the start of her new life.

Assumed Virtue

44

Charles and Charlotte returned to Laura Place ahead of the rest of the company by choice. Avoiding his sisters had become so commonplace for him that Bingley was astonished when Charlotte asked where they could be found.

Still dressed in their wedding finery they joined the rest of his family in the front parlor.

"Miss Lucas," sniffed Miss Bingley, "how unexpected."

"Mrs. Bingley," corrected Charlotte calmly.

"No, I am Miss Bingley, not Mrs. Bingley," said Caroline in the tone of voice one would reserve for someone who was painfully stupid.

"That is correct. You are Miss Bingley, and I am Mrs. Bingley. Your brother and I were married this morning. As mistress of his household, I will expect to be addressed properly and courteously Miss Bingley."

Dead silence greeted this announcement, then Caroline began to shriek wordlessly.

"Charles, perhaps you would be good enough to speak with the housekeeper and ensure that my trunks have been unpacked in our suite? I will join you there in just a few moments."

Relieved, Charles rushed from the room.

Charlotte turned back to her new relatives, fixing herself a cup of tea and ignoring the still shrieking Caroline.

"Well at least now I understand why you have been unable to find a husband for your sister even with her generous dowry. Has she always been subject to fits?"

Louisa's lips twitched in spite of her shock at both the marriage and Charlotte's comments. "I do not know that I ever thought of her temper tantrums in quite that way, but yes, she has always shrieked and been subject to fits of rage is she does not get her own way."

"Well, I know it is difficult to dispose of a relative who is mad, but we will do what we can to either get her married off."

"I am not mad," cried Miss Bingley.

"Of course you are not," replied Charlotte in a soothing tone of voice. "All well-bred gentlewomen shriek regularly."

She turned then to the Hursts. "I wish to tell you that there are going to be some changes, even above the fact that I am now mistress of this home." She did not bat an eye or pause as Miss Bingley shrieked again. "I will be looking over the budget as I understand that besides having fits your sister is apparently challenged by mathematics and unable to learn to budget. For the two of you, I am going to ask you to change some behaviors if you would. Mr. Hurst if you will moderate your drinking, please? It would be a boon to all of us if you were to be awake and conversable in the evenings. Mrs. Hurst, let us speak tomorrow, you and I, about what you might be interested in learning. I do not care what it is, but it would be most appreciated if you were to be able to hold a conversation on more than fashion. I realize that having Caroline as your primary company has made it difficult, but I hope that together we can make evenings at the Bingley household enjoyable and relaxing."

She sat her cup on the tray and rose. "There are going to be other changes, but we will discuss these in the coming days. For now, it is enough for you to know that Charles wishes a peaceful home; I wish to ensure that is what he has, and I am sure you both wish to do your part also. I will wish you all a pleasant day now. I will expect to see all of you at breakfast tomorrow morning."

As soon as Charlotte had left the room, Caroline Bingley reached for the china teapot and hurled it at the fireplace.

"Caroline, do you know what that costs?" cried Louisa.

Miss Bingley stared at her sister. "How would I possibly know that?"

"I do not know but I guarantee you, Mrs. Bingley will know, and it will be taken out of your allowance."

"Do not be ridiculous," Caroline scoffed, "she cannot do that, Charles will never allow it."

Hurst snorted. "Oh yes he will. Did he stay when you began howling? She sent him away and he ran like a scared rabbit. She has the upper hand now Caroline and she will simply send him away while she does as she likes; he will not gainsay her."

Caroline's eyes had grown wider and wider as Hurst spoke.

"But she cannot—"

"She can," interrupted Hurst. "Louisa, you will do what she asks, as will I." As Caroline began to protest, he interrupted her again. "My pitiful allowance from my father will barely support Louisa and I; we need your brother, Caroline but we do not need you. Louisa will not support you in any attempts to undermine the new Mrs. Bingley; more than that she will support her in any way she can. As will I. There is no doubt that she will begin as she means to go on and I will not live only a pence above poverty because you have dragged Louisa into some fool scheme." Hurst rose then and extended a hand to his wife. "Best come with me now Louisa, we need to talk."

"I need my sister, Hurst, you can talk later," fumed Caroline.

Hurst fixed her with a look of intense dislike. "What you need no longer matters Caroline. Your brother has staged a coup, sister, and you are no longer his hostess, you are simply the younger spinster sister who has nowhere else to go. You had best learn your new place quickly because Mrs. Bingley is not going to accept any interference from you."

On her way to the Mistress' suite Charlotte stopped and had a word with the butler. No letters from Miss Bingley were to be posted, but she was not to know this. Any outgoing mail would be given to Charles, and he would determine if they were to go out or not. The housekeeper was to inform her of any damages done by Miss Bingley and any mistreatment of the staff.

The butler, who had disdained the Bingleys from the moment they arrived, bowed his consent, fully aware that it would be Charlotte who determined what was sent and what was tossed into the fire. And about time too, he thought, going to let the housekeeper know the new edicts. The harpy was no longer a power in the house and the servants were all going to be pleased.

Charlotte retired upstairs to greet her new husband with a warm and affectionate embrace and the knowledge that she had informed the staff that they would ring for dinner when they were ready as they would be dining in their suite that evening. The new Mr. and Mrs. Bingley spent a most enjoyable evening together.

45

Richard looked around the breakfast table with barely veiled amusement. Not only were the Hursts there, something that rarely happened, but Caroline Bingley was at the table and wonderfully silent. Darcy, as was his wont at breakfast, was buried behind a newspaper. Charles and Charlotte Bingley looked cheerful and were engaged in a soft conversation at the far end of the table.

His father was sharing the paper with Darcy, while his mother was speaking to Mrs. Hurst about fabrics and laces. It was, surprisingly enough, a normal house party breakfast, something that had not been the case when Miss Bingley was the hostess. He wondered what other changes were going to be happening. No doubt they would be hearing about it soon enough.

"Gentlemen, I am going to be riding this morning, after I take care of some correspondence. If anyone would like to join me I would guess it will be around ten that I will be leaving."

Darcy looked up from behind his paper. "I would be happy to join you Charles." The other gentlemen all agreed to join them, including Mr. Hurst. Charlotte was going to join her husband directly after breakfast and asked after the ladies' plans for the day.

"I believe I will visit with Anne and the Bennets this afternoon. I will be returning to London shortly and I would like to spend a little time with my friends. I would be happy to have anyone who wishes accompany me," replied the Countess. Charlotte and Louisa immediately agreed to accompany her.

An hour later Darcy knocked lightly at the study door to see if their morning plan with Bingley still held. He found Charles pacing and muttering while Charlotte calmly penned a letter at the desk.

"Are you alright Charles?"

"No. No Darcy I am not. I have finally truly realized what a fool I have been to allow Caroline free reign all these years. Yesterday she was told that Charlotte would be going over her budget. This morning she sent out six letters--SIX, Darcy, all of them ordering vast quantities of items she is expecting me to pay for since the orders would normally have reached the merchants before we have had a chance to speak of her overspending."

"I am sorry to say this does not actually surprise me, Charles. I had not given it any thought of course but if I had known what was said to her, then yes, I would expect something of the sort. I will admit to some surprise that you thought to check her mail."

"Well I did not. Charlotte thought she would do something of the sort. I am appalled at the lack of respect she is showing for my wishes."

"What are you going to do?"

"I am going to hold her letters, Darce. I am going to send to all of the merchants and clearly inform them that I will not be covering her bills; then two days hence hers will be sent. It will do her good to be told that they cannot honor her orders since they have no authorization from myself or Charlotte to do so."

Darcy hesitated a moment then asked, "Did you check her personal mail also?"

"Why no, why would I do that?"

Darcy sighed then said, "I am sorry to say that if she is this angry she is likely to be unwise in other ways. It would not surprise me that she would send letters denigrating the new Mrs. Bingley," and here he gave a slight bow to Charlotte. "She would not stop to think that any scandal touching you would also impact her, she would want to vent her vitriol somehow."

Charles nodded slowly. "Yes, you are right. She did not pen any personal notes, no doubt she was up half the night deciding how she would spend my money and had no time for that. The butler knows that all her mail is to come to me, and I will authorize what is posted and what is not. I hate to invade her privacy but if there are letters going out to her so-called friends in the next few days I will intercept them and read them. If they are what you fear then they will not go out and we will decide what to do about her."

Charlotte finished the letter she had been penning while listening to the gentlemen and rose then. "We will deal with it if it happens, Charles. Let us not borrow trouble. Sign this last letter and then go riding with the gentlemen as planned. There is no need to dwell on this; enjoy your time with your friends."

After the gentlemen left Charlotte had the butler take the letters she had penned, and Charles had signed and hand them to one of the grooms who could read to take them directly to the London addresses. By nightfall, Caroline's access to Charles funds would be severed. Seating herself on a small sofa in the study she called for tea and the housekeeper.

"Mrs. Penn, what has been destroyed by my sister?"

"She threw a teapot at the hearth in the receiving parlor, destroying the pot and damaging the hearth. She also destroyed two vases and the mirror in her dressing room."

"Has the mirror been replaced?"

"Yes ma'am."

"If she breaks another do not replace it. Please get with Penn and have someone come in and give me an estimate on the cost of repairing the hearth. Do you know what the other items cost?"

"Yes, ma'am. I have a copy of the inventory that is always done before each lease." She handed Charlotte a folded piece of paper. "Here are the figures."

"Have there been issues with the servants?"

"No ma'am, she has not been particularly unpleasant, nor has she attempted to countermand any of your orders."

Charlotte nodded thoughtfully. "Thank you, Mrs. Penn. If I need anything I will ring."

46

Caroline felt she had spent a productive day. She had joined the company at breakfast but declined to spend time with the ladies while they visited Anne and those awful Bennets. Who cared about that plain spinster? Caroline, brooding and self-absorbed, had dismissed Anne de Bourgh as soon as she realized that she was a friend of Miss Elizabeth Bennet. She might be the granddaughter of an Earl, but she was no one in society, she had not even had a London season. She knew nothing about Anne giving her estate to Richard and assumed that Anne would be leaving for Kent soon.

No, Caroline had her own plans, and they did not include pandering to either Anne or to her brother's wife. She had spent hours last evening penning epistles to make purchases of fabrics and lace, of jewelry and bonnets and feathers and shoes, in short, everything she would need to have her new season's wardrobe started before she even returned to London and of course, at her brother's expense. Let the new Mrs. Bingley deal with that!

And today? Well today was for penning some letters to some very good friends to tell them, in the strictest confidence of course, what a sad mesalliance her brother had made; how he had been on the verge of offering for a gentleman's daughter and instead had been trapped by the spinster daughter of a former tradesman. Since this was all to be told in confidence, no one could possibly blame her if somehow rumors were started. After all she was not even in London; how could she have anything to do with his wife not being accepted in the ton?

Darcy would not have called his time productively spent. He had, in turn and all at once, been angry at Anne, Mr. Bennet, Miss Bennet, Miss Elizabeth, Richard, Lady Catherine, all of the Bingleys, his father and Wickham. When he was not angry he was in agony because he desperately wanted to see Elizabeth and he was painfully aware that she despised him. And when he was not angry or in agony, depressing scenes played out in his head. Mr. Bennet dressing him down, Elizabeth dressing him down, Anne dressing him down, Richard dressing him down.

He was not able to get a decent night's sleep, he had no appetite, and he was certain if this continued much longer he would go mad. Then Georgie would be left alone in the world. Alright not actually alone in the world as she would still have Richard. And the Earl and Countess. And Anne. And the Viscount and his wife. Dear heavens he had become as overdramatic as Caroline Bingley.

The ride with the gentlemen had helped. It had at least distracted him somewhat and had tired him physically enough that maybe he could sleep. But he had his doubts. He brooded through dinner, barely noticing what was set before him, speaking only enough to escape a reproof of more rudeness. It was as the ladies left the gentlemen to their port that inspiration struck. Richard had mentioned going to his father for advice this morning. He could do the same.

When his father had died the Earl of Matlock had been an unfailing source of strength and advice to Darcy. Grooms from his estate and from Matlock had ridden the road between their estates so often they could have done it in their sleep, and in fact probably had done so. He was not a fanciful man, but there had been times when he had actually felt as if the Earl were standing at his shoulder, solid and dependable and completely confident that Darcy could do this.

It had been years since he had gone to him for advice. He had taken up his inheritance and had gone his own way. Maybe the time had come for him to talk to his uncle about everything that was plaguing him. As they rose to rejoin the ladies, Darcy asked his uncle if he could speak with him privately.

Mere minutes later, in the privacy of Bingley's study, the Earl studied Darcy and Darcy studied his glass of brandy. Now that he had someone to talk to, he had no idea what to say.

"I do not even know where to start. Everything is muddled in my mind," he finally muttered.

"Well, just talk then. Do not worry about a coherent tale, if I have questions I can ask them later. Just talk, son."

And he did. The words came tumbling out, jumbled and out of order but it was such a welcome relief to get them out of his head that once he started he could not stop. He spoke of Wickham and the fight between his head and his heart, the present and his memories, the relief he had felt when Wickham was hanged, the guilt he felt for feeling relieved.

He spoke of Miss Elizabeth and his insult to her and his subsequent attraction. His decision to leave her behind, his desperate fight to forget her, his equally desperate desire to marry her. He spoke of his confusion between the man he thought he was and the man everyone appeared to think he was. He spoke of big things and little, of his questions about Mr. Bennet and his father and what did an estate's mistress actually do? Were the Bingleys so awful and if so why had he never seen it? His anger came out at times, especially when he related the criticisms leveled at him. His despair came out too when he spoke of Wickham and Georgiana and how Miss Elizabeth hated him.

For almost an hour he spoke, circling back, going forward, taking a side road here and there until all his confusion and pain and anger was laid bare to his uncle.

The Earl heard him out in silence, recognizing that something was being lanced here and that the wrong word could stop the flow, bottle everything back up again for his nephew. Veteran of a hundred skirmishes in Parliament, he filed away pertinent bits as they flew past and concentrated not just on the words but what was behind them. By the time Darcy had finally fallen silent he had a pretty fair idea of what had been taking place, at Netherfield, in Bath and even for the last several years of the young man's life.

Darcy let his head fall back against the chair back, closing his eyes and just breathed for a few moments and the Earl allowed him the time to collect himself.

"Well," he finally said quietly, "that is rather a lot to contemplate. I think I will start with the ones that seem clearest to me. Your father did not wish to leave you William and he both loved you and was proud of you. It is perfectly fine to be angry with him; sometimes I am still angry at my own father for not being here, even after all these years. It is part of being human, Will and is nothing shameful."

Darcy sighed, feeling something ease inside him as the Earl continued. "Your father was a good man, but he was not perfect any more than you or I. It is easy to hero worship someone who is not here, whose mistakes are long in the past. He made them. We all make them. Respect him, honor him but do not make him someone he was not."

The Earl stopped then to pour them each a bit more brandy. "Wickham was not loved more than you by your father. It was easier for him to be with Wickham precisely because he did not really care that deeply for him. Your mother's death hurt him badly and he did not handle it well for his children. Do not blame him for that but do recognize it Will. And your father would have hunted him down and shot him dead for attempting to seduce Georgie. I have to agree with Richard that it was past time for him to be hanged. He has hurt too many people for too long."

The Earl stretched his legs out comfortably before him. "Your father and Tommy Bennet were great friends. After your father married they did not see each other often. George was busy at Pemberley and then Bennet's father and brother were killed in a carriage accident, and he had to leave Oxford and take hold there. But they wrote regularly, and George would often mention what was happening in the life of his good friend Tommy. There were differences in standing and in demeanor between them certainly, but they were oddly similar. Both were studious young men, interested more in their studies than in the other entertainments to be had as young men away at school. I believe they first bonded as friendly opponents over a chessboard. They played by mail for many years, you know."

"No, I never knew that."

"Well, it probably would not have been something your father thought would be of interest to you Darcy. But yes, they were friends, close enough that distance and time did not dim their affection for each other. Even once they left school, there would have been much to base a friendship on. Despite the differences, both men married, started families, worried about crops and tenants and the future of their children. I am sure Bennet was most delighted to meet you as he would have wanted to extend a warm welcome to the son of his friend."

The memory hit Darcy then with the force of a blow: the night of the Assembly and Mr. Bennet walking up behind his family to be introduced and of himself wordlessly turning his back on the two younger Bennet daughters and Mr. Bennet and walking away. The man had come to welcome him, his father's friend wanting to welcome him, and Darcy had considered himself so far above his company that he had cut the man. In all the thinking he had been doing, how had he missed that particular act of rudeness? Was there no end to his abhorrent behavior?

Seeing the Earl's compassionate gaze on him, Darcy haltingly told him the story. His uncle shook his head sadly. "Ah William, that was not well done. Even had this not been a friend of your father it was not well done. Son, you must realize that the measure of a gentleman is how he treats the common man. Everyone is polite to royalty, there is nothing to recommend you in that. You know better than to honor the title and not the man. It is how you treat the servants, your tenants, the people here who are not of the ton, that determines if you are deserving to be called a gentleman."

"And I am not?"

"Judging by what you have told me this night I would have to say no. I do not know what kind of a response you hoped for from me, but I cannot tell you the easy lie, Will, and say you are behaving as a fine upstanding gentleman. And I believe the problem with your manners is based in being so absorbed in your own feelings that you never take the time to think about what others feel. When no one else's feelings matter it is easy to be rude and disdainful.

"You walk into a room with a dozen people and ignore them and stare out the window, you actually turn your back on them, well what are they to think but that you are not a gentleman? You have mentioned Miss Elizabeth Bennet several times. Apparently you have gone round and round about marrying her. But now you say she despises you. I do not know if that is true, my boy, but I do know this: if you want her you cannot go on as you have. You are in the unique position of being able to marry without regard to connections or wealth because you have plenty of both. But whether Miss Elizabeth or someone else, when you find the woman you want to marry, you need to respect her. You need to show her every courtesy. You need to treat her with kindness. You need to get to know her and let her get to know you. And you have failed at all of these things with Miss Elizabeth."

"I have always been uncomfortable with those I do not know well."

"That is an excuse Will. A tired and worn one that you need to stop using. It is not serving you well. You cut a man who was your father's friend because you never once gave a thought to his feelings; you were uncomfortable and so you behaved without thought to any feelings but your own. You were cruel and rude to a young woman you had never even met because you wanted Bingley to cease importuning and cared not who might be hurt by your words. You visited your cousin and were so rude and officious that she will not welcome you into her home. You would condemn that kind of selfish behavior in others, but you do not apply the same standards to yourself. It is as if you want everyone else to behave a certain way, but you allow yourself to behave poorly and then justify it afterwards by blaming them for the way you behaved or by saying you were uncomfortable or in a bad mood. But you would not accept that as an excuse from anyone else. In fact, there is one family member who does precisely that: your Aunt Catherine and you know how everyone feels about her."

Darcy shook his head, dismayed by the comparison. "My faults by this measure are very great indeed."

The Earl gave a soft laugh. "Everyone has faults, Will, we are all flawed, we are all human. You have had a great deal to handle over the years. But now you have taken hold in so many areas of your life, it is time for you to take hold here. You are not a ten year old boy in company of adults to be made uncomfortable because of it. You are a successful, productive, admirable man in many ways. But it is past time that you address your childish inability to see beyond your own feelings."

Darcy was silent.

"So, what are you going to do about it? It does no good to simply wish you were a better man, son," the Earl pointed out gently. "You did not become self-centered overnight. You will not become a caring man overnight either. You will need to practice new skills if you want them to become habit. There is no other way. You are in a house with the sister who has looked to you as a parent most of her life. You were told she was feeling ill. Have you asked after her again? Have you gone to her? Or have you been so caught up in your own feelings that you have not had time to think of hers?"

"I do not believe I have ever been so neglectful of her as I have been of late."

"You need to give weight to the wants and wishes and feelings of those around you. I am not chastising you, but I want to ask you how you would feel if you if I simply told you that you were to accompany me to Bath, then told you we were going to Rosings, then dragged you back here and never once asked if this was something that you would like to do. All has to be arranged for your comfort and everyone is expected to bow to your will. That is Lady Catherine's attitude in a nutshell. You had to take charge of your inheritance, to make decisions that affect many lives and you have gotten into the habit of making decisions for everyone around you, including ones that are not truly yours to make. Being responsible does not mean running roughshod over others. Your aunt tells me that Georgie needs to make some major changes in her life also and that one of the things that is inhibiting her is that by your actions you have promoted the idea that you are always right. No one is always right. Apologies may be difficult, but you need to learn to admit your mistakes, admit them and apologize for them and then work to correct them or you will never be the man you want to be."

The Earl was silent a moment, allowing Darcy to digest his words, then continued. "I know you have always been reticent; I will tell you now I spoke with your father about this more than once, telling him he needed to aid you in overcoming your shyness in company and your self-absorption. Being the only son and for many years the only child, you had no one to force you to place importance on any feelings but your own. With Hill and Richard, each would be most vocal if the other ignored their wishes and feelings, so they learned young that their feelings were not the only ones that mattered.

"So, are you going to become a true gentleman? It is the place of a gentleman to be aware of the feelings of those around him, to put others at ease. It is not their job to make you comfortable, it is your responsibility, William to draw them out, to make them at ease with you. That is what a gentleman does."

The two were silent for a moment and then Earl changed to cheerful tones. "By the by, you mentioned that you had some curiosity about the role of the mistress of an estate and tenant visits. I can understand that, you were very young when your mother died and besides a good estate mistress seems to do her job effortlessly. If you really want to know, ask your Aunt. No one could give you a better idea of what is needed to do the job well."

To his surprise, Darcy did sleep well that night. Getting all his confusion, all his hurt and anger, all his faults and his dreams and his failures out in the open air had been exhausting but it had been cathartic too. Now that he had spoken them all he could take them out one at a time, look at them, sort them, analyze them.

So, in the early morning hours, he went for a walk so he could wander and think without interruption. He had never faced that he was angry with his father for leaving him; he had buried that at first out of pain and worry and guilt; buried it later out of habit. He had never really looked past the surface of his hurt feelings about Wickham's relationship with his father. He could see both so clearly now. Forgiving his father for leaving might not be easy but now he could work on it. And with Wickham, well he could understand that. The thought of losing Bingley was hurtful; losing Richard would be agony and so who did he spend more time with? Bingley. Richard was harder on him, he demanded honesty and compassion and real conversation. Bingley was easy; Darcy's presence was enough. There he was certainly his father's son.

His selfishness was something that shocked him to his core. He was a generous master, he was a kind brother, he helped the people he loved any way he could. But in return did he not expect them to defer to him, to accept his help in whatever form he chose to give it even if it was not what they might choose?

And did he know them? He knew Georgie was hurt by the whole Ramsgate situation but since he had no experience with helping people heal he had fled her presence when she did get over being hurt fast enough to suit him. How kind was that? Richard said she had made herself ill and he had been so involved in his own misery he had not managed to check on her. He knew she was safe, and that Mrs. Annesley would tend to her so he did not step up and do what he should do to show her the love and compassion she needed. He knew his tenants' names and he helped when someone brought something to his attention, but did he know more than their names and their family history with Pemberley?

What about Anne? He had ignored her for years. She was his cousin, she had apparently been a virtual prisoner at Rosings, and he had not once made an effort to talk to her, to help her. She had escaped by endangering her health, arriving at Matlock House barely able to stand and what had he done for her since his arrival? He had treated her as badly as her mother, ordering her about as if her opinion must give way to his own simply because he said it was so.

Even Elizabeth. He would say he loved her but did he? Did he know her? Did he respect her? Did he treat her and her family well? No and no and no. He knew he wanted her. It had never once crossed his mind to wonder what she wanted. What did she look for in a husband? And could he provide that to her? He could give her wealth and position but even the little he knew of her informed him that she would not consider that enough to build a future with him.

So. Selfish. Unaware of the feelings of others. And uncaring when he was aware. There was the problem in a nutshell. The question his uncle posed to him remained: what was he going to do about it?

Assumed Virtue

47

By the time he returned to the house for breakfast Darcy felt he had least defined the problems even if he did not know the solutions. When his aunt left the table, he gave into an impulse and followed her, deciding there was no time like the present to ask one of the questions that had been nagging at him. He waited as she spoke with Mrs. Penn, then asked if she would take a moment to discuss with him the duties of the mistress of an estate. By the time she had told him, in exuberant detail, about staffing and the stillroom, the kitchen gardens and the dairy, the making of small beer and vinegar, the needs of the tenants and the villagers, the inventories and purchasing and budgets, Darcy's head was spinning.

An hour later Richard found Darcy sitting in the garden staring into space, a decidedly odd expression on his face.

"Darce? Will? Are you alright?"

"Did you know that housekeepers all over England write to each other?"

"What? No. Why?"

Darcy shook his head as if to clear it. "Richard we men have no idea what goes on in our own homes. Your father told me to talk to your mother about what the mistress of an estate does. It is unbelievable." Darcy went on to briefly relate what he had learned from the Countess. By the time he was through Richard looked as dazed as he felt.

"How in the world do they do it?"

"I do not know all, but part of it is they have an entire communications network of which we men are unaware. After breakfasting this morning your mother spoke with Mrs. Penn. I saw it, I thought nothing of it. Now I know it was deliberately done and that your mother knew precisely what would happen next. Within half an hour of their talk, an express rider would be on the road to Matlock House with a letter from Mrs. Penn letting them know when to expect your parents to return. And not because Aunt Audrey requested it, just because Mrs. Penn is an experienced housekeeper, and your mother knows what an experienced housekeeper does. All the details of getting the house ready for them will be in hand because the housekeepers communicate."

"I did not know any of this. You know, that also explains Mrs. Black; for some reason I assumed she simply handled my mother's social calendar."

"Your assumption was closer to reality than mine. Your mother was kind enough not to laugh at me when I told her I had always assumed she traveled with two personal maids. She could never accomplish all she does without a secretary, and one who handles a great deal more than keeping track of invitations, and yet it never occurred to me she would even need one. Apparently my mother had one and my father had two, one at Pemberley and an assistant to him who remained at the London house. After my mother's death, naturally her secretary left, and my father eased his grief by throwing all his energies into the estate and no longer had need of even one secretary much less two since it was all he did. At any rate, all of the housekeepers write to each other all of the time. Mrs. Reynolds probably knows more about what is going on at my other estates than I do."

"Now I also understand why your mother has been suggesting that I marry for the last few years. An estate needs its mistress as much as its master and I had no idea. She told me too that I need to get at least two secretaries trained as quickly as possible because once I wed I will want to spend less time on correspondence and training a good secretary takes time. And that my wife will need a secretary too. Without them my future wife and I will have no time together because our duties will take all our energy and focus. I had given no thought to any of that." He paused then and met his cousin's eyes. "I owe you an apology. More than one. For so many things, Richard."

"Accepted, Will."

Darcy huffed out a soft laugh. "You are the brother everyone should have. You know that I talked to your father last night for hours? And then he talked to me. I found out so many things I never knew. Do you know why my father spent more time with Wickham than with me or Georgie? It was not, as I have long thought, because he loved him better. It was because it was easier. Which brought me back to your question of why I spend so much time with the Bingleys. They require nothing of me Richard. You, who I love as family, as my brother, you require me to be a better man. How much easier on me to spend time with those who ask so little of me, for whom my presence is enough. I have been quite my father's son there even if I knew it not."

Darcy stood and stretched then, pacing a little but in a relaxed manner. "You were so right in your estimation of the man I have become. After I spoke with your father I thought of Elizabeth. I have thought on her for countless hours but in all that thinking I never once asked myself the question 'what would she want in a husband' nor ever wondered what kind of a husband I would make. Not once, Richard. It was all what I wanted, what I needed, but never once about her wants or needs. So, I ask myself, is that truly love? Do I have any idea how to love the woman who I would make my wife? I objected to Bingley's marriage plans because he did not know the woman. Was I any better? A week ago, if you had suggested that Elizabeth would refuse me if I asked for her hand I would have scoffed at you. What woman would refuse Fitzwilliam Darcy? Well, I know now that Elizabeth Bennet is the one woman who would indeed refuse me. As she should. I have shown her no respect, I have not even shown her courtesy. How do I become the man I want to be, Richard? I know who that man is, but I am so far from him that I cannot fathom how to bridge the distance."

"Darce have you never asked yourself why the military trains endlessly? It is to make something unnatural so much a part of you that it becomes natural, so that you react without thought in the way you have been trained. My answer to you is that you practice. You do not jump to make judgements about others; you stop and ask yourself if you might be incorrect. Better yet, you actually listen to people. You take a minute and try to imagine what other people might be feeling. You go to balls and to concerts and you engage with the people around you no matter how uncomfortable you feel. And all of this will be uncomfortable. It will not feel natural. But if you work at it, if you do it and do it and then do it again, it will become easy, it will feel normal and natural."

Darcy looked at him in amusement. "I might have guessed that the answer would be one I do not like."

"I did say you would be uncomfortable," Richard pointed out. "and I am going to add to your woes. Georgie needs to grow up Darcy, she needs to start mingling. You have pampered her shyness, so have I. But I asked you to think about how others feel when you treat them with disdain. So now I will ask you to think on this: how do you think people feel when your sister greets them in a near inaudible whisper then stands staring at her feet, refusing to so much as look at them? She is a gentlewoman and with the advantages of that position come the responsibilities. She must not use her shyness as an excuse to be withdrawn or to be rude to others. It seems odd to think this but in its own way her shyness and yours are a selfish sort of behavior. She is not thinking of those whom she is meeting, she thinks only of herself and her discomfort. My thought was to help her start as soon as we arrived here but that did not work out as I planned."

"Tell me, then, what I need to know about my sister."

The conversation was every bit as difficult as Richard had expected.

"You cannot be serious, Richard. She is not trying to control anyone. How could she, she is a child."

"But she is not a child. She is a young woman. And she knows almost nothing that will help her transition into the adult world. Mother and I spoke of this, and we believe that she may not even be aware that this is what she is doing but she is using her fragile appearance and her timidity to control us, to get exactly what she wants. And if we allow it to continue Will, we are setting her up to fail."

"What? No, we are doing nothing of the kind. We are protecting her Richard."

"Which is why she fell so easily into Wickham's schemes." He spoke over Darcy's protest, "No Will, I am not placing the blame on others for his perfidy, but if she had known what kind of scoundrel he had become would she not have been more wary? Keeping her ignorant does not protect *her*, it protects *us*. We do not have to have the difficult conversations with her, we do not have to do violence to our own feelings by forcing her to learn and grow. By allowing her to remain as a child we abrogate our responsibility to her, and it does her no favors. Your father had his faults, but one thing he did right, he made you learn, Will. He made you do the hard things and when you lost him it served you well. We must do the same for your sister. And you are the key. She looks to you as the ultimate authority; I have been too long away for her to bow easily to my wishes, but you are the one constant in her life. She needs your approval; she needs to hear from you that her childhood is ending and that she must begin to choose what kind of an adult she will be; and Will, she needs to know that you make mistakes."

"I do not know how to do this, Richard."

"I know my friend; I am not sure exactly how to do this either, but for her sake we must try. As hard as it will be we must not become Bingley, weakly giving in to our young charge because it is easier than taking a stand."

Darcy gave a short bark of laughter. "Low blow, Richard. Amazingly accurate, but low. I had not thought in terms of Bingley and Miss Bingley, but I do see the similarities; if we do not take her in hand now will she spend the next two or three years crying every time we wish her to move forward? And what kind of future would that be for her? I will do this, I *can* do this, though it pains me deeply. I will go to her now. Could you give Mrs. Bingley and your parents our apologies?" He stopped then and shook his head at himself. "I am doing it again am I not? If you have no plans, I would like for you, Georgie, Mrs. Annesley and myself to take dinner in my sitting room. Tomorrow we will all be in company, but I feel we need to do this today or my resolve will weaken."

Richard clapped his cousin on the shoulder. "In fact, I did have plans, but fortunately for us both I am courting the kindest woman in the world. I will drop a note to Jane explaining a little of what we are trying to do and ask her to forgive me for not be able to see her this evening. Tomorrow, though, I will not want to make any excuses."

48

The door to Georgiana's sitting room flew open at Darcy's knock and his sister hurled herself into his arms, sobbing. "Will, oh brother, I missed you, I have needed you so. You cannot know how glad I am to see you," she cried.

He held her close, rocking her slightly, soothing her as he always had. He loved her so deeply; when he looked at his faults, at all the times he had failed to be kind, she was his one success, the one person whose feelings had always mattered to him, and his heart ached at the thought of her distress, but years of discipline, of doing the hard thing came to his aid then and he gently set her aside and stepped fully into the room, closing the door behind him.

He looked at her as she sat across from him, tried to look at her as if she were a new acquaintance. She was young, certainly, but her figure was womanly, her bearing was that of a young lady and he needed to be strong enough to help her mature emotionally as she had already done physically.

"Tell me, Georgie," he invited, as he always had when she had come to him.

Her words tumbled over themselves as she poured out her anguish and fear. Mrs. Annesley and Richard wanted her to do things she could not do, she could not. They felt it was her fault she had been taken in by Wickham. They wanted her to run Pemberley and Darcy House. They said she was weak at one minute then demanded she be strong in the next. They had made her unhappy. He had to make them stop.

He desperately wanted to tell her he would stop them, that she was perfect as she was, that there was no need for her to trouble herself any longer. But though it would be painful to deny her, he knew that agreeing with her now would be exactly the wrong thing to do.

When she finally finished, looking at him with damp hopeful eyes, he steeled himself to disappoint her. "They are right."

"Brother! No, no they are not right."

"This is hard for you, dearest. It is hard for me too. But they are right. You are not a child any longer. You must grow up and that means you are going to have to do things that are difficult, that you do not want to do. Only a short while ago you felt you were prepared to be married but think Georgie, what do you know about running a household? About budgeting? About tenants and staff? Can you wisely choose a housekeeper? Can you help a tenant solve a problem? What do you actually know, Georgie, what can you actually do?"

She looked at him, shocked, wide-eyed and frightened. "I—I do not know how to do those things; how could I know?"

"You could *not* know because no one has taught you. But you must learn, you must apply yourself and learn all these things. I am much to blame for your lack of knowledge and skill, wanting to keep you by my side, seeing you as the child you were not the young woman you are."

He spoke with regret in voice, ruing his failures that had brought her to the verge of adulthood with no notion of how to be an adult. "Oh Georgie, there is a place in my heart that simply never wants you to grow up, to grow away from me. But my dearest girl, that is not possible, I know this even if I have not wished to admit it. In two years, three at most, you are going to go into society, and I have failed to prepare you for that; in fact, I have failed to prepare you to be an adult. You are frightened now, but knowledge and skill, these things will sooth your fears. You will not have to be frightened because you will know. But it takes time to learn, time and work. And still, though I should have begun sooner, it is not too late if you are willing to accept that there is much to do, much to learn and that you must work hard to make up for lost time."

She burst into tears again then, but he stiffened his spine, and kept his voice firm, kind but unyielding. "Now, my dear, we are going to begin, and we are going to begin at once. You will dry your eyes; you will rest a short time and then do whatever you need to do to make yourself presentable and you will join me in my sitting room for dinner. I will not take no for an answer. We have much to accomplish but we are Darcys, nothing is beyond us."

He kissed her forehead then, and stepped back, bowed slightly and left her there, stunned and still sobbing and scared in her sitting room while he went to his own room and fought against the tears that blurred his eyes. He could do this. He had to do it. But he did not have to like it.

Richard, Mrs. Annesley and Darcy were gathered in his sitting room, waiting for Georgiana, but to Darcy's surprise when there was a knock on the door it was not his sister but his hostess. "Mrs. Bingley, I was not expecting you."

"I asked her to join us for just a few moments, Will," supplied Richard. "I spoke to you about how selfish it was for Georgie to meet someone and refuse to look at them or speak. I do not believe this can be explained to her, I want to make the point to her in a way she will understand. Mrs. Bingley has kindly agreed to assist. And Will, not a word, do not speak. The silence will get awkward, but I do not want anyone to speak until the point has been made."

Georgie's knock sounded then. She nodded at the occupants she knew and then Richard introduced her to Mrs. Bingley. As always, she mumbled a virtually inaudible response and stared at her feet. Unlike all the other times, Mrs. Bingley made no effort to engage her. In fact, there was no sound in the room at all. Georgie glanced up briefly to see Mrs. Bingley staring firmly at the floor. She dropped her eyes, glanced up again, down then up again and finally she threw a glance of pure panic at her brother. Satisfied, Richard quietly thanked Mrs. Bingley who gave Georgie a gentle smile and told her they would see each other on the morrow, curtseyed gracefully and left.

"Well, sprite, that was certainly uncomfortable, was it not?" said Richard cheerfully.

"It was awful," Georgie whispered. "Why did she not say anything? Why did no one say anything?"

"Good question. You are someone. Why did you not say anything?"

"What? Me? I never know what to say."

"And so, you stand and stare at your feet and wait for someone else to make you comfortable," he said in that same cheerful tone. "If I had said to you that you are being rude, you are creating an awkward situation for those around you, you would not truly have realized what I was saying. Now you know. What you were feeling is how you make others feel, Georgie. It is rude and it is selfish; it makes the other person uncomfortable. And no, shyness is not an excuse. Shy or no, it is still rude and selfish. This is one of the reasons you must begin to learn to be a true gentlewoman, cousin. It is your responsibility to make others feel at ease, to reach out to them, to be the someone who says something."

Georgie was silent, thinking deeply, and she remained silent as the servants entered and set up their dinners. She was silent through the first minutes of their meal, then she asked shyly, "Is that really how it feels to others when they meet me? I did not think of that, I never really tried to see what others saw when we met. I only thought that perhaps they would not like me, and that I did not know what to say to ensure that they were kind to me."

Mrs. Annesley answered her charge quietly but firmly. "This is why the Colonel said it was not just rude but also selfish, Georgiana. Because you never gave a thought to how your behavior was affecting others, you saw it only from your own point of view. Part of becoming an adult is to learn to try to see things in the way other people perceive them. This is some of what we are going to teach you. Along with the skills to make meeting people much more pleasant. And that will not be so very hard my dear. We will practice, you and I; you will meet with your cousin Anne and her companion Mrs. Jenkinson and with their friends, the Miss Bennets. We will work on what you can say, how you can create an opening for others to speak easily with you. Then, when you are ready, we will meet someone new, and you will use what we have practiced, and it will be far easier than you currently imagine."

The adults allowed her to process that, then Darcy spoke. "I am perhaps the only one here who truly understands you when you say you are too shy to converse, for I have suffered from that myself. And I am having to practice now what you are going to be learning. Believe me when I say that I wish very much that my father had listened to our Uncle Henry when he told him that he needed to help me overcome my reticence in company, that it was no favor to me to allow this to continue. I have offended and hurt a great number of people, Georgie. I did not mean to do so. But that does not change the fact that it is what I did. What is needed, for both of us, is to learn to see beyond ourselves. We need more than just the skill to make conversation with strangers, we need the ability to recognize that others also have their opinions, their feelings and wishes and that these are as real and as important as our own are to us. I am working hard at this."

He hesitated a moment, then decided that she needed to know how bad it could be if she did not learn.

"Our father had a very good friend, from his schooldays, a gentleman with whom he corresponded for years, all his life in fact. When I arrived at Bingley's estate in Meryton I went to an assembly and as ever I was uncomfortable. I was in a poor mood to begin with as I always am in Miss Bingley's company. And before I had done more than refresh myself, I was at a country assembly, there were so many people, and I knew none of them all of which added to my discomfort. I was being introduced to a family, I met the mother and one daughter. There were two other daughters waiting to be introduced to me and I saw a gentleman come up behind them and I simply felt I could not do this any longer, so I just turned away and left. The gentleman was our father's lifelong friend, Georgie, and the young ladies were his daughters. A good gentleman who was coming to welcome the son of his friend to his neighborhood, no doubt anticipating that we could speak of my father, that perhaps we could even be friends. And I cut him, cut them, because I was not comfortable and never once thought of how they would feel."

Georgie listened to him with her mouth actually hanging open in shock. "Oh Will, how horrible, for them and for you. What happened then?"

He sighed, ashamed but determined not to hide from his sister.

"Nothing good, my dear. I insulted one of the daughters even more egregiously later that same evening. I was rude to everyone without even realizing it. And I deeply regret that I still have not apologized. It shames me how little I have ever considered the feelings of anyone not connected to me. I do not know if they can ever forgive me. I do not know if I can forgive myself. I know that you felt I was cruel earlier, but Georgie I do not want you to have to face yourself in the way I have had to do; to suddenly realize that your behavior reflects poorly on you, on us, and have a lifetime habit to overcome as I have done. If you can do this now, it will be your habit to be kind, to be the woman that our parents would have wanted you to become. This is what I wish for you, and I know not how to accomplish it unless we begin now."

Georgie mulled that over for a time, allowing the conversation of the others to play in the background as she thought. Finally with a determined set to her chin, she looked at Richard and Mrs. Annesley.

"I see now that I need to apologize to both of you. I know I made you uncomfortable, particularly you Richard, but I was frightened, and I only saw that you were asking me to do things I did not wish to do, did not think I *could* do, and that I wanted you to stop. This was very wrong of me. I will try not to make such a horrid mistake again; I will try to take into account what those around me are feeling. And, Richard, you asked me why I agreed to elope with Mr. Wickham even though I knew it was wrong and I refused to answer, I put all the blame on Mr. Wickham and Mrs. Younge. But I do know why, I just was ashamed to say it but if Brother can confess his wrongs, then so can I."

She paused a moment to gather her courage, then blurted out the shocking truth: "I was bored. That is why I agreed to elope."

Richard's fork clattered on his plate as he dropped it, staring at his ward, appalled. "Bored? You decided to throw all propriety to the winds, to risk social ruin and a damaging scandal because you were bored?"

"I am afraid so." She fiddled with her own fork, aimlessly pushing the food on her plate. "Oh, there were other reasons I could give you to be sure. It was such a very romantic notion to contemplate, like something out a novel. And he was very handsome and charming, and he said such nice things to me you know. But if I am to be honest, he did not convince me I was in love with him, I convinced myself. And yes, I knew even at the time that it was wrong of me. But my life was so boring, and I did not see that it would ever change. Year after year after year of embroidery and reading and playing the pianoforte. I love those things but if this is all my life was to be then I was going to have an adventure, now when it was it before me. Something I could look back on and say, well, once I did something. Once I had something more, I *was* something more."

"But Georgie, if that was the case, why did you object when we told you we wanted you to do more, learn more?"

"I have just been thinking of this and I think I know why." She blushed bright red, and her tone was embarrassed, but she met Richard's eyes bravely. "This will sound as bad as my reason to elope, but I cannot hide what I think. What you were asking of me, those things would all require such effort from me. Eloping was not something difficult. I would not handle the arrangements; I did not have to work at it. I simply had to go along with it. It was an adventure and one that took no work or even any thought on my part. Everything Brother and you and Mrs. Annesley want from me is going to take all kinds of work and effort. I kept thinking that I would have to change so much, and I do not know how to change, and it all was so very frightening. Well, I might have been afraid, in fact I am still afraid, but Brother is right, I am a Darcy, and it is not beyond me. I will work hard to become a true gentlewoman."

After the ladies retired, Darcy and Richard sipped their port and talked or were silent in turn, comfortable with each other, each deeply thinking over the evening. Once committed Georgie had been eager to discuss some of the upcoming changes, how they would work on things and what she would be doing. They had been hard pressed to keep up with her, but both felt a deep gratitude that the worst seemed to be over, though Mrs. Annesley had quietly pointed out that all rebellion was not likely at an end.

"Well, all in all, that went far better than I had hoped," Darcy finally said. "I was not happy about it at the time but asking Mrs. Bingley to come in was inspired."

"I thought so too. She is a very understanding woman, she had a great influence in the raising of her younger sister and brothers, so when I explained what I was trying to show Georgie she agreed at once. Our ward has not had your experience in the world, I did not think words alone would necessarily work. I needed her to feel what it was like so she could relate to it."

"And do you think that Mrs. Annesley has the right of it too? That there will be rebellions in our future?"

"Perhaps, though I think none will be as bad as this first one. Hour after of hour of non-stop wailing, Darce. I would not have thought she had the stamina! And I truly wondered if poor Mrs. Annesley would lose her mind. But now Georgie is determined to see this through, and she has the Darcy stubbornness; it was telling I think that she agreed to an elopement for the adventure of it, because she was bored. With all she has to learn, I do not think that will be a problem for her. When she does rebel, I am thinking it will be short-lived, that she will come around because likely it will be based in weariness not actually that she does not want to do this. She knows now that we are not trying to be cruel or heartless, but really do wish for her to be her best self and that will count for a lot I think."

Darcy nodded then frowned into glass. "You are content with your courtship of Miss Bennet?"

Richard laughed. "Content? No Darce I am not content; I am over the moon. She is a treasure and if I did not feel it would be unfair to her I would ask for her hand tomorrow."

"She was not chasing Charles was she?"

"No, she was not. He latched on to her and would not leave her alone. She tried to talk about things that might interest him, from crops to the war to plumbing but he would not do anything but speak of her beauty. It was boring and uncomfortable, but Jane also admits she could have discouraged him more. She is hesitant to hurt others and she also did not want him to transfer his attentions to one of her friends and then have him leave that friend heartsore. She was in no danger of being hurt and certainly she never encouraged him. And obviously he was not hurt as he has married another."

Darcy nodded. "And they are not mercenary women looking to marry for fortune. And Mr. Bennet was a friend with my father. I am finding that I have to take everything I have been certain of and turn it on its head."

Richard nodded. "Yes, but in the end Darce you will be a better and happier man. Because as hard as this might be you can always remind yourself that whatever else you have had in your life, happiness as eluded you."

49

The day prior to the Matlocks departure Mrs. Penn brought Mr. and Mrs. Bingley two letters written by Caroline. They had each read one in silence then traded them. Charles had been devastated. This was his sister. How could write such lies? How could she betray him like this?

But to her credit, Charlotte was both wise and steady. "Charles, put this out of your mind for the day."

"How can I do that? She has behaved in the most abominable way. I do not understand this, Charlotte."

"And there is no need for you to do so, my dear. Enjoy your last day with the Matlocks. Do not worry about this. Nothing has left this house; nothing is going to harm us here. I will think on this, for it does not harm me or cause me distress. It is much as I expected. Let it go, my husband. There is no need to worry about this now."

Charles' relief was great. The Countess had been correct in advising him to marry such a wise and wonderful woman. Anyone else, he thought, would have been angry or hysterical or demanding that he do something at once. His wife, however, had simply calmly placed the letters in a drawer, locked them away and counseled him to let it be. Which was exactly what he wanted to do but had feared he would not be allowed to do. Really, this whole marriage thing was working out very much to his advantage.

What he had not expected was his reaction to seeing his sister later in the day. When he had watched her pretense of courtesy to his wife, when he had seen in her self-satisfied smirk that she thought she was deceiving them, he experienced such a revulsion of feeling that he had been forced to briefly emulate Darcy and stand looking out a window with his back to the room until he could regain his composure. He had done so; it had cost him pain to do it, but he had treated her as much the same as he could. He thought she detected no difference. And to his complete surprise, he found that he did not want to leave this entirely to Charlotte to handle, that he wanted to be there even if it was just to be silently supportive. It would be a long time before he marked that day as the one in which he finally took the Colonel's advice and began to become an adult.

He had enjoyed parts of his day. Darcy was becoming more talkative, more approachable and he had felt more comfortable in his presence then he ever had. The Matlocks, while busy, had been cheerful and courteous guests. To his surprise, he had even enjoyed the company of the Hursts. The day had gone well, and he had risen to farewell his guests with real regret that they were leaving. He would miss their congenial company.

Mrs. Penn brought another letter that day. He read it, feeling curiously calm. His sister's reprehensible behavior did not surprise him now, though he dimly felt some shock that she would behave in such a manner. And he had listened to Charlotte's counsel with a sort of detached admiration. Really, she was quite wonderful, thinking of details he would surely have missed.

She disagreed utterly with his first thought, to send Caroline to their Aunt Mathilda in York. "We are just pushing the problem onto someone else, Charles, by sending her away. In the end, if we cannot teach her to be a better person, then we may have to resort to that. But no matter how badly she is behaving she is still your sister. You do not like her right now, I understand that; I do not like her very much at the moment either. But that does not mean you do not still love her, do not still want a relationship with her. Let us try and see if we can manage this. We can handle this harshly, but I think instead we try to handle it gently."

When Miss Bingley was called to her brother's study, she went with no expectation that her duplicity had been discovered. Charles had never read her letters; he respected her privacy even though she had sometimes snuck into his den and read his correspondence.

Charles handed her the three letters she had written.

"Charles, these have been opened. Did you read my correspondence? How dare you?"

"Sister, I am sorry, but your behavior has reached a point where you are in danger of damaging the Bingley family reputation. I cannot let you do that."

"I do not understand why you would say that."

Charlotte spoke then, her voice gentle. "Miss Bingley, any scandal involving me, or your brother will damage your reputation also, you know this, you have been a member of the ton long enough to know how quickly people turn on each other. You handed these young ladies a damaging scandal and they would have run to the ton with it; no consideration of past friendship would stop them from blackening your name along with your brother's and mine."

Miss Bingley sat a moment, quivering with rage and the desire to throw something at this upstart, this woman who had usurped her position, who was determined to reduce her role as the power in the Bingley family. Then she stood and strode out of the room, rushing to the stairs and was practically running by the time she reached her room. Louisa, who had witnessed her fleeing to her room, was torn. Caroline was her sister. She did not like her, but she did love her as family. Her first impulse was to follow her, to try to comfort her.

Then she did something that she would not have thought to do in the past: she knocked on the study door and asked her brother and Charlotte if she could speak with them.

"I saw Caroline flee the room. Can I ask you what caused her distress?"

Charlotte considered her a moment, then handed her the letters. Louisa read them in silence, handed them back with a resigned sigh. "Oh Caroline," said she, softly. "I cannot apologize enough Mrs. Bingley. Anyone can see that the two of you will do well together."

"Thank you. Do you think you would be comfortable calling me Charlotte?"

"I would be honored. Please call me Louisa. My husband is Reginald, Reggie or Hurst whichever you would prefer. Can I speak with you honestly about our situation, Charlotte? My brother knows this, but I would like you to understand something of what we are dealing with."

"Of course, I would welcome a frank discussion."

"Reginald and his father have never gotten along. There was an older brother who died at only two years of age and for some reason my husband's father has always seemed to resent that Reginald lived to adulthood. He has been treated as a usurper, as if he had stolen his brother's place, even though he had not even been born when his brother died. There is an estate that will come to him upon his father's death, but he has been given no training in running it, his father's resentment has been too strong; I think his mother would welcome teaching me to be mistress, but she will not gainsay her husband, which I understand, but it has made things difficult for us. Reggie's father gives him a small allowance and the use of the Hurst townhouse in London, but the allowance barely covers the basics of the servants and the expenses. Living with my brother is a godsend to us, as it allows us to have some of the elegancies of life." Louisa paused, watching her new sister closely but could read little in her expression.

She forged on, determined to try to make Charlotte understand. "Caroline has always been difficult. She mastered the art of the tantrum at a very young age, and we have all given in to her to avoid the scenes she seems to revel in. Reggie is not really a fool or a drunkard; he drinks to avoid Caroline, often playing the part of more inebriation than is real. I stare at the wall or play with my bracelets, hoping to avoid her notice. Charles would give in to her, and please believe me brother when I say I do not blame you one bit; we have perfected the parts we have played to keep the peace. Your advent has been a blessing, not just to Charles but to us. To be able to converse amiably with another woman, to have an evening's entertainment that is not filled with malicious gossip and vicious innuendos is such a relief. Hurst and I will support you in every way we can."

Charlotte had begun listening to her new sister with a certain wariness, but the explanation caused her immense relief. She was not without allies; she could be friends with Louisa and perhaps even with Mr. Hurst. She smiled in genuine pleasure at her new sister.

"Louisa, my father is a good man, but he is not a strong man, not when it comes to family. Until I was old enough to take hold in the house, my mother was running us into financial ruin and kept the entire family and the staff at Lucas Lodge in a constant state of turmoil and emotional upheaval. I understand the turmoil your sister can cause. I am very sorry that your husband's family is not willing to support you and I have no hesitation in continuing my husband's welcome to you. I would be pleased to help you learn to be mistress of an estate. I have run Lucas Lodge for many years, but I will need to learn all the ins and outs of handling an estate the size of Netherfield and I would be most pleased to have your company."

"So we will return to Netherfield?"

Charles nodded at his sister. "I had not realized until Charlotte and I were talking that I should have stayed through harvest. The owner came in and the neighbors helped, but I should have been there. She has suggested I speak with Mr. Bennet about spring planting, and I definitely need to be there for that. And honestly Louisa, I enjoyed the country lifestyle. I liked how easy and honest our welcome was. And we are now related to those very people by my marriage, and I look forward to knowing them all better."

"And what are we going to do about Caroline?"

The Bingley's shared a glance then Charlotte turned back to her new sister. "We are going to hire a companion for her."

"A companion?"

"Yes, one who has handled difficult young ladies in the past. She has no experience with someone of Caroline's age who needs to learn how to behave, but I believe that is our best course. I have spoken with Mrs. Annesley, Georgiana's companion, as she has some concerns about her charge. During that time, she informed me that her sister is looking for a position and she seemed to think that Mrs. Madison would have no problem dealing with Caroline. We are trying to treat your sister with kindness but when all is said and done, what she needs is to learn how a gentlewoman is supposed to behave."

Louisa favored Charlotte with wry smile. "I will confess I am in favor of it as I agree she needs to learn some manners. Ideally she would learn to care about someone other than herself but that may be too much to ask. For now, I will go to my younger sister and see if I can help her to see the error of her ways, though I have little hope of success. I believe I can face her now from a position of strength and perhaps that will make a difference. Maybe simply knowing that you have the support of all of her family will begin to turn the tide with her."

Louisa entered Caroline's room quietly, unsurprised to find her sister lying on the bed crying angry tears. It was her pattern if she was denied something. She pulled the bell for a maid and quietly asked for a bowl of water and a cloth, some tea and some headache powders. Once her requested items had been supplied, she pulled a chair to the bed and began to bathe her sister's face.

"Oh Louisa, that woman Charles married is horrible, she is an awful woman who will ruin all our lives."

"No, she is not, Caroline."

Caroline sat up, pushing her sister's hand aside. "You do not know; you cannot imagine what she has said to me."

"I read the letters Caroline."

That stopped Caroline. "She showed them to you," she said resentfully.

"She did. Caroline, how could you do something so unwise. Do you not know that any scandal involving Charlotte will involve our whole family? That any disgrace you brought on her would reflect on all of us, on you? If she is not accepted, it will damage you also you know this is true."

"No, no, it is only she that would be disgraced."

"No, Caroline, that is not true. And you know this if you will stop to think calmly about it. Any disgrace to Mrs. Bingley is a disgrace to the entire Bingley family and that includes you. You may rail at her as you like, but not allowing those letters to be received has saved you from social ruin as much as it has saved her."

Caroline was silent a long moment then sighed. "Well, then, I suppose that is true enough; I did not think it through."

"No you did not. And it was not just unwise, it was wicked."

Caroline's eyes flashed with anger. "How dare you? I did nothing wrong."

To Caroline's surprise Louisa snapped back at her. "You are a fool, Caroline. You think you are so much above everyone including your own family, but you are simply a spoiled and wicked child. What you did was entirely wrong. You hurt Charles, Caroline. You hurt him badly, so badly I do not know if he will ever recover."

Caroline gasped in shock at that. "That cannot be true, Louisa, you take that back, take it back at once do you hear."

"I hear you, sister, but I cannot and will not take it back for it is true. I saw it in his eyes after you left the room Caroline. He is devastated. He may eventually forgive you, for he is a gentle and kind soul, but he will never trust you again Caroline, he will never feel the same for you. He has been blind to your machinations, blind to the way you have manipulated him, but he sees it now and it has hurt him deeply, more deeply than you can imagine. He has loved you as his baby sister, forgiven your airs and your bad manners and your vicious conversation. He has given and given and given to you. And you repaid him in the most injurious of fashions. You have damaged your relationship with him, perhaps beyond repair."

Louisa handed her a glass of water with the headache powder stirred into it. "Drink this for your headache Caroline, and when you wake tomorrow think of what you are doing to the family for once."

50

The next day, Caroline dressed carefully, donning what she thought of as her prettiest day dress, though it was overelaborate for a day at home with family and too garish to really compliment her coloring. She had gone in search of her brother, only to be told he was busy and could not attend to her. She carefully controlled both her fear and her temper and simply asked that a message be conveyed to him that she would like to see him when convenient and returned to her room. It was some hours before he had knocked on her sitting room door and by then Caroline was in a state of such nerves she jumped and almost stumbled at the sound.

She had forced cheer into her voice and invited him in but then had no idea what to say. His visage was calm and grave; there was no censure in voice or manner but no welcome either and she was pushed even further into uncertainty. She expected him to be furious, she knew what to do when he was angry. She was confused and all her carefully prepared speeches fled from her mind.

"You wished to see me Caroline?" he asked, his voice calm and courteous.

"I did Brother. I have not seen much of you these last days."

"Well, I am here now. What is it that you want of me?"

"Can I not simply wish for you company?"

He thought about that for a moment then answered bluntly, "No."

"No?" she gasped.

"No. You have never asked to see me just for the pleasure of my company Caroline. Not once that I can recall. You have asked to see me to tell me you need funds or to order me to buy you some piece of jewelry that has caught your fancy. You have asked to see me to complain about everything from the servants to the weather to whatever action I have taken that you are currently abhorring. But you have not once, not ever, asked to see me for my company. So I will ask you again, what is it you want from me?"

In spite of her resolve, Caroline's eyes filled with tears. "I did not mean to hurt you, Charles. I was angry and unthinking. Please, forgive me."

"I do not know if I can," he answered in that same grave, measured tone. "Since our parents' deaths, I have cared for you to the best of my abilities, Caroline. I have placed your wishes above my own time and time again. I have done everything in my power to give you a good life, to make you happy. And you repaid me with a betrayal of such magnitude that even now I can barely think of it without pain."

"I know, I know, I am so very, very sorry Charles."

"So you said. Well, I am sorry for your actions too, but that does not really change anything does it? I do not know that I can forgive you. I do know that I cannot trust you. I cannot trust you to be kind, I cannot trust you to be generous, I cannot trust you not to betray me again if I anger you and you are so very often angry Caroline. It seems to be your natural state. I cannot accept an apology that I do not believe is sincere and I do not trust your sincerity any longer."

"Will you never forgive me Brother?"

"Never is a long time, Caroline. Perhaps one day I shall. But it will not be today or tomorrow or even next week or next month. If it happens, it will be because you have proven yourself over time to be a caring sister to me. I will not ask you to leave, though I will be honest and say it was my first thought. Charlotte argued against it so for now you can remain a guest in my home. I will be hiring a woman to act as your companion Caroline. I am not going to be available to escort you any time you wish any longer and Mrs. Madison can, perhaps, help you learn more of how to behave in a way that does not distress your family."

Caroline had cried for hours after that. Cried until she thought there were no tears left in her, then cried some more. She had not truly believed that she could destroy Charles' love for her, had not believed that he would not accept her apology and simply beg her once again to moderate her behavior, had not believed that everything would not be resolved, and they would go on as before.

This quiet and hurt Charles, she did not know him, did not know how to talk to him, to convince him she had not meant to injure him. She had meant to hurt Charlotte, yes, but it had truly never crossed her mind that hurting Charlotte would be seen as a betrayal by Charles. She was his baby sister; she had always come first in his life. That she did not hold that coveted place any longer was a dagger to her heart.

She did not go down to dinner, not that night or the next or the next. She stayed in her room, hurt and confused and unable to believe that her life had taken such a turn. The conversation with her brother had played over and over in her mind and with each retelling she moved further into depression, until she began to refuse to eat. She had taken off the day dress she had so carefully chosen and gotten into her night dress and for three days refused to get out of bed. She did not look at it directly, but there was a portion of her mind that was convinced that if he knew how she was suffering he would come to her, he would comfort her and accept her apology and all would be as it was. But he never came.

Louisa came, finally, obviously reluctantly. But there was little sympathy or comfort to be had from the sister she always had callously dismissed as worthless and a fool, little more than a willing tool for her to use. Louisa held out no hope for a true reconciliation with Charles.

"I told you, Caroline that you had hurt him beyond reason. I do not understand why you are now pretending to be sorry. You certainly were not sorry when I last spoke with you."

"I did not believe you. I did not believe that anything I could do would turn Charles away from me like this. I am not pretending to be sorry; I am truly sorry. I did not mean to hurt him. Why has he not come to see me? He must know how much I am suffering now too. Does he truly care nothing for me any longer? I am his sister."

"But you have never been a true sister, not to him and not to me. So no, he is not going to come to you, Caroline. Are you really this blind? Do you not see your true self at all? Even now, you are not thinking about how you have hurt him, but how you are suffering because he did not immediately forgive your betraying us all. He has not forgiven you nor have I and I do not know his mind, but I doubt that I can do so. You have made our lives a misery for years Caroline. Always angry, always wanting everything and returning nothing."

As Caroline began to cry once again, Louisa snapped at her angrily, "Oh stop it. Your tears do not mean anything to me anymore. When have you ever dried my tears Caroline? When have you ever stopped thinking about yourself long enough to try to ease someone else's troubles? You have brought this upon yourself. How many times have you been asked to moderate your behavior? How many times have we pleaded with you to behave like the gentlewoman you aspire to be? And never, not once, have you paid any attention. You have behaved badly for years, and we have allowed it because we did not want to be the subject of your bitter, vitriolic temper. Well you will have a companion now and hopefully she can teach you how to behave well enough to finally find someone who will marry you and leave your family in peace."

And Louisa had stormed out of the room, leaving Caroline stunned and ashamed, alone once again.

She had gotten up then and discovered that three days in bed with little to eat had left her shaky and weak and moving like she had been physically injured. But she had rung for a bath and had dressed again, though she took little thought to her dress or hair. How could those things that had once mattered most to her have lost all meaning? She could not bring herself to care, could not even meet her own eyes in the mirror.

She had eaten dinner in her room, unable to face her family yet. And slept fitfully, unable to get comfortable or find peace in sleep. And the next day she had asked for an interview with Charlotte Bingley.

Charles was not unaware of Caroline's plight, and he was not entirely untouched. But he had Charlotte now, to anchor him, to discuss how he would handle this. Caroline's betrayal had had an unexpected benefit for the newlyweds. They had become closer, affection becoming deeper for both of them. Charles had known he could depend on Charlotte; she had made that clear from the start that she would be on his side. What he had not expected was that he wanted to be on her side too. That he wanted to protect her.

His sister's betrayal had shifted his loyalty from Caroline to Charlotte and with that came a desire to be a husband she could be proud of, a good landlord, a master who was as caring and capable as the mistress of the estate would be. And that meant that if Caroline were to be part of their lives she would have to cease trying to control them all with her temper and her ceaseless demands that she be given her own way. For Charlotte, she had not expected that she would see him begin to demonstrate the strength of character needed to withstand his sister's demands. Respect and gratitude were becoming true affection and he felt that and returned it.

So, when Caroline had asked to see him, he and Charlotte had discussed what he would say, how he would act. He had never won an argument with Caroline so he would not argue with her. He would control his tendency to give her what she wanted and focus instead on what he wanted, on how he truly felt. He had only really told Caroline his feelings when her behavior was so egregious that he was furious. And his anger engendered a loss of control that made it easier for her to control him, so he would not lose control, would not lose his temper, would not give in to the impulse to berate her. He would, at least outwardly, show her nothing but calmness. He would not shout, nor demand an explanation when they both knew there was no acceptable explanation.

And he had walked away from her proud that he had seen it through as planned, elated that he appeared to have gotten through to her and slightly sick to his stomach from the confrontation.

When Caroline remained in her room, when her maid reported she was not eating and was remaining in her bed, he would have gone to her. If not for Charlotte he would have given in by the third day. He did not trust Caroline any longer but a lifetime of taking care of her did not equip him to ignore her distress. But Charlotte had talked him through it, gently, never ordering or demanding. She had asked him questions, what he really wanted, what was it that worried him most and she had helped him to see that Caroline was not really hurting herself with her withdrawal.

It was not her usual pattern, she was not screaming and raging, but it was another side of the same coin. It was a silent demand for his attention, and he was done giving in to her demands. If he went to her now, if he gave in to her now then he would never rule his household, she would have won again. With Charlotte's support he would hold firm.

When she received the request for a meeting, Charlotte decided to see Caroline in the study, the scene of their last confrontation.

When Caroline had entered, Charlotte greets her with the same calm gentleness she had shown her from their first meeting. "Miss Bingley."

Caroline had curtseyed, "Mrs. Bingley."

"You wished to see me, Miss Bingley. What is it that you need?"

Caroline forced herself to not allow offense to color her tone. "I want to know what you want me to do."

"I could give you a list I suppose but it all comes down to one thing Miss Bingley: you need to develop some kindness. If you cannot do that you can at least learn to behave courteously and as a gentlewoman. Charles told you that we would be hiring a companion for you. Mrs. Madison will not only be available as an escort when Charles and I are not, she will teach you how to behave in a more acceptable manner."

"I do not think there is a need for that," Caroline protested.

"Perhaps you do not but Charles and I have decided this is the course we will pursue. Mrs. Madison will be here within the week. Perhaps you can think of a way to make her feel welcome."

Caroline was silent for several moments, ego warring with her resolve to repair her relationship with her brother; for perhaps the first time in her adult life, ego lost. "I will try to do so."

Charlotte nodded. "Your brother and I have spoken of this, Miss

Bingley. We will not be available to escort you until you have spent some time with Mrs. Madison. You may dine with the family but if we have guests or are going out we will ask you to remain above stairs."

As Caroline opened her mouth to protest, Charlotte held up a hand to stop her. "This is not a decision we have lightly made, Miss Bingley. You came perilously close to ruining your entire family only days ago. Your behavior in Hertfordshire was such that we do not believe you are able yet to discern what is proper behavior to enhance the Bingley reputation or at least not to damage it. Therefore, until Mrs. Madison informs us that you are prepared, we will insist that you remain withdrawn from society. You are, I think, an intelligent woman. I am sure you can quickly learn what changes need to take place in order for you to resume a place in society."

51

The morning after the Matlocks left to return to London, Darcy asked Richard if he could accompany him on his visit to the Bennets that morning. He was anxious and nervous but if he were to become the man he wished to be, if there were ever to be a chance for him to win Elizabeth's approbation, this visit was necessary.

Once in the parlor Richard and Jane retired to a corner to talk softly, leaving Elizabeth alone with Mr. Darcy.

"Miss Elizabeth, I owe you an apology, indeed I owe you several apologies. My behavior has been shameful, I cannot think of it without abhorrence."

Lizzy's eyes widened in surprise at his statement, and she was honestly at a loss of how to answer. Fortunately, he took her silence as at least a willingness to hear him out.

"I know that I have no right to ask anything of you, but I should like to explain something of my situation to you."

Lizzy nodded, her curiosity overwhelming her lingering anger at him.

"As a child I was given good principles, but I was never taught to regulate my temper, I was allowed to apply those principals in pride and conceit. Being the only son and for many years the only child of my parents and coupled with the isolation of Pemberley from our neighbors I am afraid I never developed the skills that you and your sisters have in abundance, that is the ability to be empathetic. My uncle pointed out to me that his two sons were close in age and therefore they bumped up against each other all the time. They had to adjust to someone else's opinion, or at the very least, take it into account. For me, I was alone most of the time so there was no one for me to be concerned about except for myself."

Darcy looked at her searchingly and could see that she had moved from completely closed off to him to at least interested and continued.

"Then I entered the ton. I am wealthy and well connected and with the death of my father when I was just two and twenty I became so sought after for my fortune that I developed a cynical disregard for others, an automatic assumption that whoever I was meeting would want something from me. Everywhere I went I heard whispers of my estate and my fortune. 'Ten thousand a year' has been my introduction over and over again."

"I can see how discouraging that would be," Lizzy said thoughtfully, remembering clearly that more than one matron at Meryton Assembly had loudly said exactly those words.

A faint smile lifted his lips as he continued, "Well it has been. That does not excuse my behavior, however. I was rude to you and your family multiple times the evening we met and after. And I had decided against your sister, labeling her a fortune hunter, when in truth all I knew of her was her name. I have no excuses; the ones I have always used in the past I now realize were nothing more than a way to convince myself that my behavior was correct, when in fact it was in every way unacceptable for one who would profess to be a gentleman."

Lizzy flushed a little then. "I should not have spoken to you with such heat sir. While I did indeed disapprove of the way you were acting, my unregulated speech was not that of a gentlewoman and I do apologize to you that."

Darcy shook his head. "What did you say that I did not deserve? I had indeed proven myself to be no gentleman time and time again. I know that you have little reason to accede to any request of mine, but I should like us to begin again if we can. Your sister is to marry my closest friend and cousin and I would like it if we were to be friends."

Lizzy studied him carefully. He certainly seemed to be sincere. "I would be willing to try Mr. Darcy."

"Thank you, I cannot tell you how much I appreciate your generosity, Miss Elizabeth. My cousin tells me the only way to become the man I would like to be is to practice. I am going to be going into society here and I will attempt to be a welcoming gentleman, a man others find pleasant company. Having a friend among the crowd of strangers will help me I think."

Elizabeth laughed softly at him. "Ahh, I see sir. So you have an ulterior motive in asking for my friendship."

Darcy's chuckle answered her laughter and she found herself blushing at the difference his amusement made to his face. Where before she had considered him coldly handsome, she found the warmth of his smile and twinkling eyes made him even more attractive. "I suppose that is truth. When I think of it, I would appreciate your help very much. You are so at ease in company, so welcoming and joyful that others are drawn to you like moth to flame. I have no hope of ever being able to reach those heights, but I hope to become the kind of gentleman that others welcome on his own merits and not only because of wealth and connections."

"Mr. Darcy, if this is truly your mission I will be more than happy to aid you sir. And I will begin by saying that you must smile more often. You look far more approachable. I think you will be surprised at how much of what you wish to accomplish can be done with that one adjustment. It will allow people to speak more easily with you and that in turn should allow you to be easier with them."

"Then that is the first thing I will practice," replied Darcy, feeling amazingly lighthearted at having her acceptance of his request. "I will ask another favor from you: I would like to speak with your father please. I owe him my apologies also. I have treated him shabbily and I know I must ask his forgiveness."

"I will go to him now and see if he can see you. I believe he will appreciate your apology very much, Mr. Darcy. He has voiced his regret that he has not had the chance to speak of your father with you."

Darcy rose as she did, regarding her gravely once more. "I can understand that. One of my many, many regrets is that I may have lost forever the regard of someone who knew my father well and with whom I could have had a friendship. I am hopeful that he has your generosity of spirit and will also allow me to begin again."

Seeing Lizzy leave, Richard excused himself to Jane and came toward Darcy. "Is all well, cousin?"

"It is, Richard. Miss Elizabeth has kindly accepted my apologies and is going to ask her father if he will grant me a few moments of his time." He paused a moment, then spoke somewhat hesitantly to Jane, "Miss Bennet, I want to apologize to you also. I have been so rude and ungentlemanly, and I condemned you as a fortune-hunter when I had no rational reason for doing so. Please forgive me."

Jane gave him her sweet smile. "Of course I forgive you Mr. Darcy. As for assuming I was a fortune hunter, your cousin Anne told me that there was actually a certain amount of excuse for this, that almost all of the women of the ton were after your fortune so that you perhaps became a little jaded in that regard."

Darcy nodded gravely. "She is correct, but that does not excuse my behavior. Just because there were many who were seeking my fortune, that is no excuse for my assuming it was true of everyone."

Lizzy returned then and nodded to Mr. Darcy; he followed her down the hallway then paused a moment in front of the closed door to Mr. Bennet's study to draw a deep breath and calm his nerves as much as possible. Then he knocked firmly and, upon being invited in, strode in like a man facing a firing squad.

Lizzy who had accompanied him into the room sighed, looking at his haughty expression which she now assumed hid nerves and was not an accurate representation of what he was feeling.

"Mr. Darcy."

"Miss Elizabeth?"

"Have you forgotten already my suggestion sir?"

Darcy looked at her blankly then gave a faint smile. "I had yes. My cousin tells me the only thing I can do is practice until it feels natural. Did I look so forbidding then?"

Lizzy nodded emphatically. "You looked haughty and somewhat angry."

Darcy sighed. "And I was neither, simply nervous and uncertain."

"I would never have thought to describe you as either, Mr. Darcy," interjected Mr. Bennet.

"I know and I am sorry for it sir. Perhaps I would not feel either emotion now if my behavior had been in line with the principals my father tried to instill in me so long ago."

"You feel you have not done so?"

"I *kno*w I have strayed sir. I understand you knew my father well so you are aware that he would have been rightly disappointed in my behavior of late. I have let myself get as cynical and haughty as the worst of the ton, people I have always thought were abhorrent in their behaviors. And, as I explained to Miss Elizabeth, as an only child on an isolated estate I had little opportunity to learn empathy or to consider the feelings of others. But these are excuses only, for I know that there can be no good reason for my poor treatment of others beyond a selfish disregard for the feelings of any outside a very narrow circle of family and friends. I owe you multiple apologies sir, for my rudeness to you and to your family. I hope you will consider beginning anew."

Mr. Bennet looked at him searchingly for a moment, then motioned to a chair. "Lizzy, please have tea sent in. Mr. Darcy please be seated."

Once his daughter had left Mr. Bennet relaxed into his own chair and gave Darcy a faint smile. "Do I assume correctly that being taken to task by Miss de Bourgh and then by my daughter Elizabeth has wrought a change of thought, Mr. Darcy?"

"They certainly were the catalysts, yes. Then Richard thoroughly verbally trounced me, the Earl expressed his disappointment in me, and I discovered the sister to whom I have stood as parent since my father's death was showing many of the same poor behaviors that I had been modeling for her. Her view of me was of a man who never made a mistake, who had no faults and thus she felt she could not make a mistake and could not own to any faults."

"An impossible standard to live up to then," commented Bennet softly.

"Impossible. Unrealistic. And false, of course. I am afraid that becoming a parent of a ten year old girl when I was but two and twenty myself caused me to feel I must be perfect in her eyes."

The gentlemen paused their conversation as tea was brought in and poured, then Bennet commented, "While she may have needed the comfort of seeing you thus when she was ten, as she matured she needed to see you as human and flawed. My girls are aware of many of my faults; I rather believe they love me as much because of them as in spite of them."

Darcy nodded. "I should not be surprised, sir. I also was shy as a boy, having little experience in being with large numbers of people. I was something of a loner in school, having only a small circle with whom I felt comfortable, and I did not find the ton conducive to forming friendships based on mutual esteem."

"And once you lost your father, the ton would have come at you like wolves on the hunt."

That surprised a genuine laugh from Darcy. "You could not be more correct, Mr. Bennet. And being young, single and already possessing an estate and a fortune allowed me to demonstrate my contempt for them with no diminution of their so-called esteem. Thus, what began as reserve and a certain shyness became haughtiness and contempt. And it bled over into everything I did, every relationship I had."

Thomas Bennet nodded thoughtfully. "I do understand. I will let you in on a secret only my family knows. I am a lazy man."

At Darcy's look of surprise, he continued, "I do not appear lazy, I know; I administer my estate, have been active in educating and raising my daughters, I have invested my funds and through all these years I have had to fight a running battle with the side of me that wishes to do nothing more than sit in my study with a good book and a fine cognac and retreat from the world. The battle has admittedly become easier as time has passed. Hamlet had the right of it you know."

"May I ask sir, what your catalyst was?"

"The birth of my first child, Mr. Darcy. My wife and I were busily living our lives, and while we are both intelligent beings at that time we were not particularly practical ones. Then Jane was born. When I held that tiny miracle in my hands for the first time, I realized that I would need to change, would need to become a man she could be proud to call her father. So I assumed the virtues I needed to demonstrate to become that man. I became actively involved in my estate and my children's future; I became frugal and invested wisely with my brother Gardiner. I was fortunate in my wife, she has supported my efforts and supplemented them with her own efforts and together we have done well indeed for ourselves and for our children. And, as I said, the battle has indeed become less fierce over the years."

"You give me hope, Mr. Bennet. I told my cousin that the distance between the man I am and the man I wish to be seems unbridgeable. His advice was much the same as yours and as Hamlet's though it was couched in military terms." At Mr. Bennet's questioning look he explained, "He told me this is why soldiers train. So that something that is unnatural becomes so much a part of them that it becomes an automatic reaction."

"You may call me Bennet, Mr. Darcy."

The words were balm to Darcy's troubled spirit. "Thank you sir. Please call me Darcy. I appreciate all you have said to me. And I will not trouble you further this day. But if you would permit me to return I would very much appreciate talking to you about my father."

Bennet nodded and rose from behind his desk to see the younger man out. "I will certainly welcome that chance. Your father was a wonderful friend to me, and I would like some of the memories I have of him to live on with his son."

Upon leaving the Bennet residence, the gentlemen walked the short distance to the de Bourgh town house. The butler greeted Richard cordially but looked askance at Darcy. "Do not worry that I am here to trouble your mistress," said Darcy. "I do request you take her my card. If she does not wish to see me I shall not stay."

The butler nodded, took the card and went into the parlor, closing the door firmly behind him. "Good move Darce. I thought you might go all haughty on him."

"I am trying, Richard. On the walk over I did as you advised and thought of what Anne might feel. And though I had not considered the butler's feelings, once here I realized that I have put him in a difficult position. Becoming haughty would not have helped the situation."

"Miss de Bourgh will see you both," said the butler as he returned from the parlor and then turned to escort them in.

Anne nodded to the men, returning Richard's greeting warmly, then looked sternly at Darcy. "Why are you here cousin?"

"To offer my abject apologies Anne. You were entirely correct. I know I was mistaken in the motives I assigned to the Miss Bennets and, as Richard pointed out, even had I been correct I had no right to make demands of you. If I had concerns I should have voiced them to you privately and then accepted whatever decision you made. I have no right to make any decrees about your life."

"Have you apologized to my friends?"

"I have and also to their father."

"Then I gladly accept your apology William. Let me ring for tea and we will talk."

Before leaving Anne's home Richard tendered an invitation to dine at the Bingley's to his cousin. "Mrs. Bingley particularly wished to host you this evening if you are not engaged, Anne. She asked me to assure you the invitation is also for Mrs. Jenkinson."

"I should be delighted," beamed Anne. "I believe Maude would enjoy it also. We have been going to so many balls and concerts and I truly enjoy them, but dinner with friends sounds like a wonderful change for me."

52

Jane rushed through her toilette for dinner then hurried down the hall to Lizzy's bedchamber. "We do not share a room here, Jane. Have you lost your way?" said Lizzy mischievously.

Jane laughed at her and said, "I will echo your words back to you: I am exactly where I planned to be Lizzy: sitting in your room until you tell me what you talked about with Darcy."

Lizzy's laughter joined her sister's. "Jane, I was never more astonished." She sighed then, turning pensive. "I will admit there is a cynical side to my personality that cannot help but wonder if he is playing some game with us, that he is pretending to a change that is only on the surface."

"But what would be his purpose, Lizzy? I know he has been unpleasant, but do you truly know any ill of him? There was much said of his poor manners and if he had been unscrupulous in any dealings it would have been whispered in every drawing room in the county in a matter of minutes."

"That is true. And I cannot name a purpose. But why would he so suddenly wish to change?"

"I do not believe Richard would object to my relating some of our conversation to you Lizzy. Richard said that your anger with Mr. Darcy, along with Anne's had a profound effect on him. There were other reasons and one in particular he would want me to relate to you, but I believe that he truly wishes to change." She directed an impish look at her sister and ended with a tease, "and do not tell me you did not notice his dimples for I should hate to disbelieve my dearest of sisters."

Lizzy could not help the giggle that escaped or the accompanying blush. "I will admit that perhaps I noticed a little bit."

Laughing the two entered the dining room and each sister bent to kiss their father's cheek before seating themselves. "Is Cousin William not to join us?"

"He will be here momentarily my dears. He was engrossed in a book of sermons I happened upon while at the bookseller and lost track of time."

Although there was always much to talk about between them, naturally this night the conversation centered on Mr. Darcy.

They all listened with keen interest as first Lizzy then Mr. Bennet related their conversations with the gentleman. "Jane, you were struck by something?"

"I was, papa. Richard told me that he and Mr. Darcy have been worried about their ward, Miss Georgiana Darcy. She is painfully shy but is striving to overcome it. Richard asked if we would be agreeable with an introduction."

"That would accord with what Darcy described to me. If she begins now at six and ten to learn how to be at ease in company she will not be in danger of going the way of her brother and having reticence turn to rudeness and avoiding others by ignoring them."

"I agree Cousin," said Mr. Collins. "She has far fewer years of habit to overcome and it is to her credit and to his that they are willing to try to change."

"But can someone change so very much and have it be a lasting change?" wondered Lizzy.

"I know one can, my dear. I have done it myself," replied her father. "I think there are many factors involved but one thing I know, he will need encouragement. Anyone attempting such a change needs to know that others see and appreciate it."

"Indeed," approved Mr. Collins. "I know that we are to improve ourselves for the good of the soul and the glory of our Maker, but we are only human after all. There are few indeed who can sustain such an effort without support."

Dinner at the Bingley's was surprisingly lively and interesting. The loss of Miss Bingley's company, for she once again was suffering from a headache, could only improve any atmosphere. Charles and Charlotte created a relaxed and welcoming table and the Hursts contributed their opinions often. Anne, Mrs. Jenkinson and Mrs. Annesley were excellent company. And both of the Darcys made a real effort to be conversable, though they both seemed easiest conversing with Richard.

It was midway through the final course that the subject of business was broached. "I have been thinking that after spring planting next year we should go to York, Charlotte. I wish to introduce you to the rest of my family and while I can carry on much of my business by correspondence, there are some things I must attend to in person."

"Are you still active in business then, Mr. Bingley?" asked Anne, intrigued. "Somehow I was under the impression that you were going to purchase an estate."

"I am almost certain to do so. I enjoyed the experience very much, but I know I have a lot to learn. Charlotte will be an amazing help in this as she was raised to it as I was not. But that is part of the reason

I need to travel there. If I am going to be spending more of my time managing an estate I need to turn some of the decisions I have been making over to others." He gave them a somewhat wry smile. "It feels very odd to be thinking of my father's business, of the family business, in terms of an investment only and yet I believe that is the course I will need to pursue."

"You will maintain the investment though, will you not?" asked Louisa anxiously.

"Of course I will," he reassured her. "I have other investments as you know. Father believed in diversifying and so do I. There will always be a place for our family business. But for myself I think I need to focus on learning what is needed to manage an estate. I understand the basic mathematics of it, of course, but there is a lot more than that involved, and I will need to spend my time wisely."

"I would join you in learning, brother," stated Mr. Hurst, surprising them all except Louisa. "It would be a great boon to me to learn as much as possible before I inherit."

Charlotte nodded her approval at him. "I could not agree more. My experience running an estate will be a good foundation for me but wherever we purchase it is going to be a different experience. The size of course is one change, but there will be others and I cannot wait to get started! Louisa and I have already spoken of working together on this. Netherfield will be an excellent place to learn."

"Perhaps I could join you for a part of the time?"

Georgiana's softly voiced request startled the company into silence for a moment, then Charlotte beamed at her. "Of course you may do so. We would welcome your company. And do not forget, when Richard and my friend Jane are wed, Rosings Park will have a mistress who has also been well trained in running an estate."

Georgie's eyes brightened. "That is true, I had forgotten. Richard?"

He laughed. "My dear I have yet to ask Miss Bennet for her hand," he joked, winking at her. "But yes, I will tempt fate and say it too. Once we are wed you will be a very welcome guest. You will find her to be very kind."

Although Georgiana had been retiring to bed when the gentlemen and ladies separated, this evening she remained with the ladies until the company came together again. As she practically skipped up the stairs, Darcy raised an eyebrow at Anne, who smirked at him and said, "Will, you must ask Richard about Jane's other interests, we cannot discuss this now. Mrs. Jenkinson and I must be taking our leave, but we will see each other at services tomorrow morning. Thank you again, Charlotte, it was a wonderful evening."

As Charles returned after seeing them out, he heard Darcy quizzing his cousin and Charlotte's laughing assurance that the ladies would not be offended. Richard explained to Darcy, "Naturally we would not discuss plumbing in company, but we are all family after all; if you have never visited the refreshing room at Bennet house it would be difficult to imagine. There are actually four in the house, the main floor, one for the bedroom level with a separate one for the Master and Mistress chambers and one for the servants. No more hauling water and although the boiler must be lit it takes only a short time to have hot water."

Darcy and Charles both looked intrigued. "I would be very interested in seeing this," exclaimed Darcy. "I have read much on it but have never had the opportunity to see one. Is that why Georgie was so excited?"

"It is," replied Charlotte. "Not just the plumbing though that is interesting, but that Jane Bennet was instrumental in the planning. I think she had a sudden realization that there is a whole world of interesting things she could be studying and not just reading one more history or re-reading Shakespeare."

Richard nodded thoughtfully. "I never considered that, but you are correct. Like most of us her education has centered on the classics, but that is no reason she should not dip her toes in other waters. She may never develop an interest in archeology or mathematics or the sciences but that is no reason not to have her learn something of each of these things. If she has no real interest she will at least have a basic knowledge of the subject and she just might come across something that she loves to learn or do."

For a moment Darcy almost protested. He felt the words forming, the dismissal of someone other than himself directing his sister's education. Fortunately, before he could say anything the image of his sister's face as she had left flashed in front of his eyes for a moment. She looked happier than he had seen her in years, he realized. Here was something that had caught her imagination and interest and he was ready to deny it to her because he was not the one who had thought of it. Grateful he had taken a moment to think before speaking, he voiced his agreement. "I believe you may be on to something Richard. She has a great deal to learn and if she can find something that captures her interest it will make the other learning easier I think."

53

The next day the friends and acquaintances of all three household met after services and Mr. Bennet tendered an invitation for all the join them for luncheon and an afternoon of conversation. Everyone agreed at once then separated to return to their homes briefly before meeting at the house in Sydney place.

The gathering at the Bennets might have been difficult if not for Richard and Lizzy. Knowing they had a very disparate group, they moved among the company and helped initiate conversations and soon the group was conversing easily sometimes all at once and sometimes in smaller groups. It was while Lizzy was drawing Georgiana into the group that Georgie suddenly rushed into conversation. "I know we are not to speak of this in company, but everyone here knows, and I simply cannot help wondering, Miss Elizabeth, can I see the plumbing?" She then blushed bright red and looked down at her toes, but Lizzy simply laughed and agreed.

"My dear, I know exactly how you feel. It is a wonder and yet we cannot speak of it. I believe I have mostly gotten over blushing when the subject comes up. Come with me then and I shall show you and anyone else who wishes to take a peek. But I will defer all questions to my dear sister who knows far more than I about it."

The conversation that followed did indeed engender some blushes, but everyone was so genuinely interested, and the conversation became so technical that they all ended up enjoying it very much. As they moved toward the dining room Lizzy could not help the gurgle of laughter that escaped her. Mr. Darcy, who was escorting her into the room gave her a questioning look. "But three days ago, if you had told me that I would have an enjoyable afternoon watching you and my sister discussing how to build the proper support to hold a boiler in a refreshing room I should have said you need to be sent to Bedlam at once!"

Darcy's laughed along with her. "I have to agree with you and what a shame that would have been. I am fascinated and I can see that I am going to have to start looking at remodeling both Darcy House and Pemberley. My other estates will need to wait their turn I am afraid."

"Other estates?" Lizzy lifted an eyebrow at him. "I have heard of Pemberley of course. Not only quite incessantly from Miss Bingley but from my Aunt Gardiner who grew up in Derbyshire and has been trying for years to convince us all that is the most wonderful county in the country."

"I cannot say I disagree with her; and yes, I have some other estates, but they are not of the size, or I must say the beauty of Pemberley."

"Speaking of Miss Bingley," said Mr. Collins, "I was surprised she did not accompany you all. I hope she is not unwell?"

There was silence at the table, then Charles answered quietly, "She is not going into company at the moment."

The subject was allowed to die, and the company moved to other topics of interest. But later Charlotte spoke with Mr. Collins and Lizzy about it. "We made the decision that she will not be allowed back into society until we have seen a measurable improvement in her manners. It was a difficult decision and a difficult discussion with her."

"It must have been," said Lizzy thoughtfully. "But how is she to improve if she is not in company?"

"We have hired a companion for her. Mrs. Madison is sister to Mrs. Annesley and will be arriving Tuesday and we are hopeful that she will be able to teach Miss Bingley the proper behavior for a gentlewoman."

Mr. Collins shook his head ruefully. "I believe she may be able to do so if Miss Bingley feels it is the only way to return to society but if there is no corresponding change in her heart I do not see that it will be a lasting change."

Charlotte sighed, resigned. "I know but I do not know if it is possible to teach someone to be kind."

"I think it is," said Lizzy thoughtfully, "but I also think you need to wish to learn such a skill and I do not know that Miss Bingley sees kindness as a trait that she would want to learn."

"She does not," replied Charles, who had come up behind them. "And I cannot say that it was a character trait she ever displayed, not even as a very young child. But Charlotte and I have discussed this, and we feel that if she cannot learn to be kind she can at least learn to be polite and that may be all we can hope for at this time."

The next day found Jane once again hurrying through her toilet and rushing to Lizzy's room. "So, Miss Lizzy, shall I witness you dancing with Mr. Darcy this evening?"

Lizzy's eyes met hers in the mirror. "If he dances with others, then yes you shall." She paused and fiddled with her brush and comb a moment. "Jane, I am confused by him. I enjoyed his company very much yesterday, but the change is too sudden for me to accept yet."

"You do not trust him?"

"I cannot, not yet. It will take some time I think for me to believe this is more than a surface change. What Charlotte fears with Miss Bingley may be also true of Mr. Darcy, that the change is only surface but does not touch the heart."

Jane eyed her thoughtfully. "Why do you think that dearest?"

Again Lizzy fiddled with the items on her dressing table before responding in little more than a whisper. "Jane, I believe that I have been drawn to him from the beginning despite his behavior. And I had to teach myself to ignore all his good qualities to guard myself against him. His deplorable manners made that easy to do. Now, when I see him smiling and laughing and at ease in company, when his sister praises his many kindnesses, when I see papa enjoying sparring with such an intelligent and quick man, I can feel my defenses weakening. What will I do if I allow myself to care for him and then find this change is only of manner and not of the man himself?"

Jane moved to wrap her arms around her sister's shoulders. "I will not tell you not to fear Lizzy. I believe he is truly a good man and that this is what we are seeing emerge, but I had my fears when I realized I was falling in love with Richard. It is wonderful but frightening and we have been able to be friends from the beginning. How much more difficult for you."

"Jane, I do not know if he would feel for me what I believe I could feel for him, even if the change is real. I have seen no signs of particular regard from him."

"Lizzy, I know that there were many factors that contributed to Mr. Darcy's wish to change but I think that your disapprobation was the true catalyst. As much as he cares for Anne as a cousin, I do not believe it would have brought about such a change."

"Perhaps, but I cannot accept this, not yet."

"Then let it go for now, my dear. Let us simply go to the ball and enjoy ourselves, leaving all the more weighty matters behind for the evening."

With her new knowledge of Mr. Darcy's background, Lizzy watch the approach of the Bingley party and found that her compassion was stirred by his obvious discomfort. She remembered when he had approached her father looking disapproving and even a little angry though in fact it was discomfort he was feeling, and she determined again to help if she could.

So, when he asked for a dance later in the evening then looked around somewhat helplessly, she laid her hand gently on his arm and said softly, "Wallflowers, Mr. Darcy."

"I beg your pardon?"

"You should request dances from the young ladies who are being slighted by other men, Mr. Darcy."

As he flushed with the reminder of their first evening, she gave him her brilliant smile. "Mr. Darcy, you are trying to change and that is wonderful, but some things do not change, and you can use them to your advantage. There is nothing wrong with the young ladies who are sitting out; perhaps they are not as lovely as others, or their fortunes are not as great. But have you not come to esteem my dear friend Charlotte Bingley? This was her fate so very often. Not pretty enough or not rich enough to tempt the gentlemen to dance. I will pander to your ego a moment and admit that your consequence is quite enormous in the ton. Use that to help someone Mr. Darcy. By asking some of these young ladies to dance you will give them a presence here and others might well follow suit. You could change lives for the better Mr. Darcy, or if not their lives, certainly their evening."

As Darcy listened to her, his embarrassment turned to astonishment.

"Do you know I never once thought of that? My only question now is what shall I say to these young women?"

"Oh that is easy enough, sir. You will ask them if they are residents here or just visiting. Whichever their answer it is sure to include a family member, for instance, perhaps the answer is 'I am visiting my uncle'. This allows you to ask them about their uncle, is it one their mother's side or their father's? Is he a resident or has he also just taken a house for the season? If they are resident then you say you are visiting for your first season here and ask what they recommend as sights to see or things to do. This will set them ease and once they begin to speak you can choose something they say to respond to. Questions are your friends Mr. Darcy; people enjoy talking about themselves and giving advice to strangers."

Mr. Darcy favored her with a smile of delighted comprehension, his dimples on full display. "I have never had someone explain how to do this in such a simple and understandable fashion. I thank you Miss Elizabeth. I think I can do this and if you will excuse me I shall find the nearest wallflower and begin my education in conversing with strangers."

He bowed and moved away, leaving her quite breathless. Really, the man ought to be more careful with that smile, she thought amused and intrigued and worried all at once. It was altogether too enticing. She tried to push him out of her mind then, greeting her dance partner cheerfully and moving to the dance floor. She was as engaging as ever, chatting with her partners and enjoying herself thoroughly but some part of her awareness seemed unable to leave him. She could have answered the question of where he was at any point in the evening as if an invisible thread tied her to him, and that knowledge made her uneasy. She did not want to lose her heart to him and find that his was not also engaged.

Elizabeth was delighted that the weather, while colder, was still clear and she bundled up for her morning walk with a feeling of relief. She needed to be outside, walking briskly, letting her thoughts arrange and rearrange themselves until they made sense to her. She wished she was at Longbourn where she could stride out for miles, where her feet knew the pathways so well that her mind could roam at will. She would take what she could get though and if the gardens were not the pathways at home, they would be empty and quiet this early in the day.

Some forty minutes later, she sighed and began to think about returning home. No doubt the poor footman trailing her in the cold was ready for a warm drink and a fire, but she had needed the walk and the silence and if it had not brought her any real clarity, it had settled her a little and made her ready to face the day, she thought somewhat ruefully. As she began the walk back she was somehow unsurprised to see Mr. Darcy walking toward her.

He bowed and smiled at her as he greeted her, but he seemed preoccupied to her. Setting aside the thought that she was beginning to read his expression so well to contemplate later, she asked him if something was troubling him.

"I am troubled, indeed, for I believe I have caused harm that is unrecoverable, that no good deed I do in the future can ever repair," he replied sadly. "I have been thinking about the ball last night. Because of your suggestion that I dance with someone who was not being asked, I took the time to watch, and you were correct. In every case, a young woman who I danced with was soon partnered with another. Such a little thing for me to do and yet what a difference it made for their evenings. And I realized how very much damage my former behavior must have done. How it must have dismayed even you, who are lovely and no wallflower, to be so egregiously insulted. What if I had directed that insult to someone like Miss Westmont, who very shyly told me that it was only the second time anyone had asked her to dance? My words could have devastated her so badly she might never have wished to be in society again. My selfishness may have injured others in ways I will never know and can never make right."

"I am very much afraid I have no true comfort to offer you, sir," she replied gravely. "This is a sorrow that cannot be healed for you are correct that you will never know and so cannot make any reparations. But it is still truth and painful as it is to know, it is the kind of truth that will allow you to avoid such a thing in the future. You cannot change the past, Mr. Darcy, but you can change the present and so change the future. I cannot imagine, with this new insight you have had, that you will ever allow yourself to say such a thing again."

Mr. Darcy's expression lightened a bit at that. "Then you are mistaken, and there is a comfort you have offered me. I have made grave mistakes and they are painful to confront, but I see also that I can change and if I cannot repair the damage to someone I have harmed I can at the least avoid damaging another."

"And more than avoiding the damage, you can aid others as you did Miss Westmont. Her evening was brighter for your presence. And who knows, perhaps one of the young men who followed your lead and asked her to dance will be someone with whom she forms a friendship or even perhaps a marriage. It does indeed begin to balance the scales Mr. Darcy."

He gave her a genuine smile then and took her hand to lay on his arm as they walked toward her family's home. "You comfort me indeed, Miss Elizabeth. Only a short time ago I felt as if I were in the depths of despair, that I would never become the man I should be; now when I return to that dark place I will have your words to help draw me back."

Over the next two weeks Mr. Darcy and Miss Elizabeth not only met at the balls and concerts in the Lower Rooms they encountered each other often in the gardens. And while Lizzy thoroughly enjoyed his company during their evenings, it was their morning walks that began to teach her to trust him and to believe that perhaps his feelings were warm for her.

Their meetings were not planned of course, that would have been impossible. And although they met often it was not every day, for sometimes the weather was too unsettled even for Lizzy to chance being out in it. She knew he was walking there to meet her, and that it was not, strictly speaking, proper for her to continue her walks knowing he would be there. She assuaged her guilt for her behavior with the knowledge that they were public gardens after all; she could hardly forbid him to walk there, and she was always accompanied by a footman. It was sophistry but she found she had such a need to speak with him, to understand him, that she could not force herself to stop their meetings.

One morning as they walked and talked, the subject of little decisions causing changes in all the lives around them came up.

"I have always seen this is true when dealing with my estates, but I think it is only recently that I realize the truth of it in people's lives in general."

"Like Anne's decision to give her estate to the Colonel and how it has changed not just her life but his and by extension Jane's life and to a lesser extent the lives of my family."

"Indeed, and that goes back to her decision to accompany her mother to visit my uncle. That one determination on her part set in motion a series of decisions that changed lives. My decision to accept the judgement of those around me and to speak with my Uncle is another. He pointed out the similarities between my actions and those of Lady Catherine's. I wonder how differently everything would have been if someone had taken her to task when she was a much younger woman. Would any of this have come to be?"

"How do you know someone did not do so?" questioned Lizzy. "It was not just that others took you to task but that you decided to change. Perhaps she made the decision not to change."

"That is inconceivable to me. I see so clearly how I was heading down that same path. Do you know that on the journey from Pemberley I was contemplating replacing Mrs. Annesley? She is so good for Georgie, and yet I was unhappy with her because she disagreed with me. How like Lady Catherine I was becoming. If someone who works for me cannot tell me when they feel I am going in the wrong direction then what kind of man would I become?"

He paused then stated abruptly, "Rosings Park would have had to be sold to cover the debts Lady Catherine was incurring in another few years."

At Lizzy's gasp of surprise, he nodded at her to confirm his words. "I looked over her books each year, you know. I estimate five years perhaps a little more and the estate would no longer have been solvent; Richard is able to save it not just by managing it better but because he brought with him an influx of funds from selling many thousands of pounds in jewelry that she had purchased over the years. The estate would have been lost without that. And all because she would not listen to anyone who disagreed with her."

"I had no idea it was that bad," whispered Lizzy, shocked. "What would have become of Anne?"

"She would always have a place with family, of course, and Lady Catherine was unable to touch her dowry, but the London and Bath homes would have had to be sold to meet the debts. It would have been such a waste and it could have been easily avoided if only she had been willing to listen when others gave her advice that she found unpalatable. I could have been the same if not for you. If you had not taken me to task, if you had not given me the dressing down I deserved, would I have followed that path, becoming more disagreeable with every passing year until even my own relatives no longer welcomed me?"

He drew a deep breath then and stopped their progress, removing her hand from his arm and cradling it in his own larger ones. "Miss Elizabeth, I have come to ardently admire and love you. Tell me, please, could you find it in your heart to not just forgive me but to welcome me into your life? Would you consent to a courtship with me?"

Lizzy's eyes filled with tears. Here were the words she had been afraid to hope she would hear; no matter that she had counselled herself to guard her heart, she had had no true defense against him, and her fears dissolved in a wave of joy.

"Yes," she whispered, then more clearly she cried, "Oh yes, I would consent. I can think of nothing that would bring me more happiness."

"Elizabeth," he said softly. "You have been my Elizabeth in my thoughts for many months. Will you call me William now dearest, loveliest Elizabeth? I have dreamed of hearing my name on your lips."

"William," she replied trying out the name tentatively. "Yes, William suits you very well." She raised her brow at him, giving him the impish look that delighted his soul. "And I believe William suits *me* very well also."

Assumed Virtue

54

Thomas Bennet recalled thinking that his ladies were whirlwinds before the Netherfield ball and realized that he had far underestimated the chaos a half a dozen ladies could cause in his life.

In fairness to himself, he had to admit that he had only had his own half a dozen ladies to contend with then. There were additions which, while welcome, no doubt added to the noise and confusion.

He cocked his head, hearing one of the additions and his younger girls giggling somewhat wildly in the garden behind his study. Ahh, and there was his Mary's voice, calming them without dampening their spirits. What were they saying?

"Do you truly think we could?" Georgiana Darcy's voice was breathless with excitement.

"I do not see why not," replied Mary calmly. "In fact, I believe Kitty has hit upon an excellent notion. After the weddings we will talk with mama and with Charlotte and I believe we can carry out your plans."

Unable to help himself, he stuck his head out the window. "Might an old man inquire what plans you young ladies are hatching?" he called.

His girls laughed at him, while Georgiana blushed and ducked her head a little before remembering she was a young lady and she straightened up and looked at him.

"Teas, Papa," cried Lydia exuberantly. "We are all becoming young ladies now you know, and Kitty has suggested that we take it in turns hosting each other and the ladies in the neighborhood who are our ages to tea."

"It would be a good experience I think, Papa," said Mary her eyes twinkling at him. "Mrs. Annesley and Charlotte and I will be there to help and to teach but the planning and the execution of the teas would be in the hands of ladies who are not yet out."

"Hmmm, let me think on this," said Thomas. "You are proposing that our girls host teas for one another; I would have to ask, does this include making sure there are enough cream cakes for others besides the girls? Because if that is the case, I believe I could be persuaded to support your cause."

This engendered much merriment from the girls, though Thomas noted that it was short-lived for Mary and that her face took on a wistful look. Glancing up he saw the two engaged couples walking slowly toward the manor, each couple apparently blind to all except their partner.

He sighed a little then, for he foresaw another season in Bath would be needed; Mary had matured a great deal while her older sisters had been gone. The responsibilities and duties she had taken on had given her confidence and the respect she was given for taking on her tasks with diligence and grace had helped her reach the potential he and her mother had seen in her. It was a great cosmic joke, he thought, that parents were tasked with giving their children all the needed skills to leave them. Catherine too, had matured and she would be eight and ten by the time the season started. Two of his girls were leaving him and these next two were now prepared to follow them.

Lydia's laughter recalled him to the present. At least he would have his youngest yet a little while longer, he consoled himself. And although Georgiana was staying with the Bingleys at Netherfield, he was quite certain she would often be in company with his Lydia. So, for a little while at least there would girls to brighten his days.

He felt a soft hand on his shoulder and turned his head to meet his beloved wife's knowing eyes. "It is hard to let go is it not?" she said, understanding and compassion softening her voice.

"It is. Where did the years go my love? Our girls are leaving us, and I find I am not ready for it."

"My dear, we have been blessed to have them so long. Jane is three and twenty and as for Lizzy, that child has been leaving us in small increments since the day she saw the outside world from Longbourn's windows." She sighed a little then too, for she loved her girls and would miss them every day of her life.

Then she brightened, "But Thomas just think…GRANDBABIES!" Her voice reflected joy and excitement now. "We shall have grandbabies to spoil, my dear husband. Oh Thomas, God has been very good to us."

SNEAK PEEK OF "NETHERFIELD'S DUCHESS, BOOK 1"

Lady Fetton, lavender skirts of her half mourning gown rustling softly as she paced her sitting room, re-read the letter she had received from her oldest friend. With a decisive nod she turned to address her major domo. "Martin, where is my guest?"

"I believe Miss de Bourgh is reading in the conservatory attended by Mrs. Jenkinson."

Her Grace nodded, unsurprised. Anne had fallen love with the conservatory the first time she had seen it and could often be found there, enjoying the scents and greenery.

"Excellent. I shall speak with her then I believe our plans will need to be revised. We will depart for Netherfield in only a day or two and I believe we will be accompanied by Colonel Fitzwilliam and Major Askins." Lady Fetton swept from the room to find her guest.

"My dear Anne," her Grace announced, "I have a change in plan."

Miss Anne de Bourgh smiled as she looked up from her book. "Are we no longer going to the country?"

"No, we will still be going to Hertfordshire. But the plan is to leave sooner and to increase the size of our Netherfield party."

Anne's smile changed to a look of confusion. Ever since her Grace had rescued Anne from her mother's tyranny two months prior, the plan had been for the two of them to summer at Netherfield with some invitations for short stays to be issued to a select few. Indeed, the Dowager's half mourning would not allow for a large party of friends. How had that changed to a "Netherfield party"?

Lady Fetton settled onto the settee next to Anne. "I have just received a letter from your Aunt Elaine, she is worried about Richard's recovery in London, but the doctors do not wish him to travel so far as Matlock." Lady Fetton beamed at Anne. "We shall invite Richard to accompany us, and also his friend who was so sorely wounded."

"If he comes he would certainly want Major Askins to join us," Anne agreed. "But will he consent? He has not wanted us to visit, has not wanted to be in company since he was injured."

"I believe I can convince him it is the right thing to do."

"You can convince anyone of anything I think."

"Good, I'm glad you agree, I shall set my new plan in motion." Her Grace quitted the room to return to her sitting room and pen a missive to her dearest friend, Lady Elaine Fitzwilliam, Countess of Matlock.

Anne's smile widened as she reflected on the Duchess' energetic exit. No one, she thought, could be more kind, more sensitive or more determined and Anne felt that blessing daily.

After a long bout of childhood illness, Miss Anne de Bourgh's life had been completely curtailed; over the years, boredom had become depression then despair as every aspect of her life was constrained and controlled by her mother. What had started as real concern over possibly losing her only child, her mother's care had devolved over the years into Lady Catherine's determination to completely dominate her daughter. No protestations of better health from Anne, no request to further her education or to travel away from Rosings was ever met with a positive response from her mother; care had become control. Finally, in desperation, Anne had appealed to her maternal uncle, Henry Fitzwilliam, Earl of Matlock; her dear companion Mrs. Jenkinson had smuggled the letter out for her, a necessary deception as Lady Catherine demanded to see anything written by her and, indeed, opened and first read anything addressed to her daughter. Unfortunately, the timing could not have been worse for the Fitzwilliams. They had just received word that their younger son, Colonel Richard Fitzwilliam, had been badly wounded and was even now returning to them to recover. For Anne, the smuggled response explaining the complication had been cause for further despair; her dear cousin being badly wounded had shocked her deeply; that her uncle wrote that they would find a way to aid her seemed to Anne nothing more than a polite fiction.

The unannounced visit two days later by her Grace, Lady Fetton, the Dowager Duchess of Langsley, had astonished both de Bourgh ladies. While the Matlock and Darcy branches of the family had long been close with the Fettons, in truth the de Bourghs had never been part of that close association. The visit from her Grace had thrown the household into turmoil. Having spent the last couple of months with Lady Fetton, Anne was quite certain the lack of prior notice and ensuing chaos had been deliberate.

In a completely astonishing exchange with Lady Catherine, Lady Fetton had announced that she was suffering from the sadness of the Duke's demise, now a year past, and it was no longer to be born; she had then informed her mother that only Anne would do as a companion in her half mourning, as Anne's quiet nature was just what she needed and in no time at all Martin had Anne and Mrs. Jenkinson bundled into the carriage, departing Rosings for London in her Grace's carriage and six.

Once enroute Anne had discovered that her aunt, Lady Elaine Fitzwilliam, had appealed to the Duchess on behalf of her niece. "For you know my dear, your Aunt Elaine is quite my dearest friend. She has a great fondness for you and so did not hesitate to enlist my aid," her traveling companion had confided, patting her hand. "Now, here is my plan." And with that the Duchess had laid out an ambitious schedule. Anne would see Her Grace's physician to confirm her good health ("*not* one of those quacks your mother employs"), and once that was accomplished there would be choices for Anne to make, ranging from what books to read to what activities would best be suited for her. First, though, was her wardrobe. "Really my dear," the Duchess had sighed, "I don't know what your mother is thinking. Not only has she no sense of style or what colors would best suit you, but Anne, we do not dress for a London soiree' for a morning at home in the country."

"Mama likes to preserve the distinction of rank," Anne said dryly.

"Yes, that's what I counted on," Her Grace had returned smugly.

Anne's life since then had become a source of wonderment to her. Going from never having any choices to an abundance of them had been a most welcome shock. Would she like to take vigorous walks for her health, or would she like to learn archery? Her Grace had learned fencing as a girl, would Anne like to learn? Would she like to peruse the extensive library Fetton House boasted or learn the pianoforte or the harp? Art lessons? Floral arranging? Riding lessons? A new wardrobe of pretty frocks and gowns had been acquired, in fact two wardrobes for they would summer in the country and less formal wear would be the order of the day. Smiling in appreciation of the Duchess, Anne returned to her book, satisfied that whatever plans were formulated she would be consulted, and no doubt approve.

Years of military experience had trained Colonel Richard Fitzwilliam to be instantly alert upon waking—the last months had turned it from a blessing to a curse. He lay wide awake, taking silent inventory of his aches and pains, gently easing his body into movement. The wounds were healing but slowly, so slowly. He tolerated the physical ache better than the mental weariness, the effort to heal feeling more and more like an unending battle.

Two hours after waking, having broken his fast with Major Askins in his sitting room, he finally made his way slowly down the stairs of his parents' London home, favoring his right leg. The shoulder wound had healed well, no longer requiring the careful maneuvering that the still healing leg demanded. As he neared the foot of the stairs, a footman approached; the Countess requested his attendance in the smaller, family sitting room. Richard had nodded and made his way down the hallway to see his mother.

Lady Eleanor Fitzwilliam sat comfortably on a settee, looking perfectly groomed and composed as always. Only someone intimately familiar with her would have seen the concern in her eyes as Richard entered the room.

"Richard, how well you look," she lied with aplomb, "I am so pleased you are here, come, have tea with me."

Once Richard was settled with tea and lemon tarts his mother studied him closely a moment. "I heard from your godmother this morning."

Richard smiled at that. He could not help it; people seemed always to smile when thinking of his beloved godmother.

"Does she have a plan?" he teased.

"Of course she does, and it concerns you and the Major. She wants you and Major Askins to escort her and Anne to Netherfield Park; and to stay for the summer."

Richard blinked in surprise. "Netherfield Park?"

His mother nodded and settled in to explain. "When the Duke became unable to manage the Duchy, Marianne was suddenly faced with finishing training Jonathon and Theresa to become the next Duke and Duchess; she was still managing her properties that she had brought with her to the marriage and now the properties of the Duchy became her responsibility also. She decided it was too much so except for one property she sold them all; I don't know all the ins and outs, but she kept Beechwoods, and she purchased Netherfield Park." For moment Elaine's smile faltered. "At the time we all still had hope that Lucius would recover enough to leave Langsley and live quietly for at least several more years so having something closer to London seemed a good idea."

She looked at her son, both concern and affection in her gaze. "Richard, the three-day trip to Matlock is out of the question for you. But Netherfield is only a three-hour journey from here. You really cannot continue to convalesce here in the summer, it is too awful. And, according to her Grace, she needs a gentleman to escort Anne and herself there and then stay to act as host for her."

Richard nodded thoughtfully. It was true his parents needed to be at Matlock. Though the spring planting as far north as

Derbyshire was later than for those in the south by now it had already begun; he knew that the Earl wished to be there to oversee it; this year they had tarried in London due to his injuries. Sadly, his brother the Viscount had already left them in no doubt of his plans to leave London to travel from estate to estate in his usual summer round of parties, gambling and ladies of easy virtue. Richard's injuries were not important enough to keep Andrew from his dissipated lifestyle.

He had resigned himself to staying in London until he could tolerate the journey to Matlock and had been trying to convince his parents he would be fine in London with little success. On the surface Lady Fetton's idea a good one, but a lifetime of experience with his godmother made him wary. She always had a plan, and they were mostly far more complicated than this.

"That's not an Aunt Marianne plan, it's far too simple; I wonder what more she has decided."

His mother laughed softly, "Truly my dear, that is all I have been privy to so far." The Countess directed a long, thoughtful glance at her beloved youngest son. "I think it is a generous offer; we would never leave you here at such a time, Richard; but Matlock needs our presence. Knowing you were recovering in the country with your godmother would give both your father and me enough peace of mind that we could, in good conscious, see to the estate. How do you feel about it?"

"Yes, mother you are correct, it is a generous offer indeed. I will have to discuss this with Thomas of course." Major Thomas Askins, fifth son of a baronet, had chosen a career in the army to support himself. He had saved Richard's life but at the cost of his left forearm. He had been recovering, along with Richard, at

Matlock House since their return. If Richard was disinclined for company, the matter was more complicated for the Major. It was one thing to move stiffly and to limp a little, it was another to pin up one's sleeve and go out in company again. Still, Richard could see this was the best choice for both for now. He would simply have to convince Thomas.

/////////

Fanny Bennet opened the conversation with breathless enthusiasm. "My dear Mr. Bennet, have you heard that Netherfield Park is to be occupied at last?"

Mr. Bennet replied that he had not.

"But it is," returned she; "for Mrs. Long has just been here and she told me all about it."

Mr. Bennet made no answer.

"Do you not want to know who will be arriving?" cried his wife impatiently.

"You want to tell me, and I have no objection to hearing it."

This was invitation enough. "Why my dear you must know, Mrs. Long has the Duchess returning and she is bringing with her several single young men of large fortune. What a fine thing for our girls!"

"How so? How can it affect them?"

"My dear Mr. Bennet," replied his wife, "how can you be so tiresome! You must know that I am thinking of them marrying our girls."

"Is that their design in settling in here for the summer?"

"Design! Nonsense, how can you talk so! But it is very likely they may fall in love with our girls and therefore you must visit them as soon as they come."

"I see no occasion for that. You and the girls may go, or you may send them by themselves which will perhaps be still better, for as you are as handsome as any of them, they may like you the best of the party."

"My dear, you flatter me. I certainly have had my share of beauty, but I do not pretend to be anything extraordinary now. When a woman has five grown-up daughters, she ought to give over thinking of her own beauty. But my dear, you must indeed go and see them as soon as ever they are settled."

"It is more than I engage for, I assure you," replied Mr. Bennet, sardonically amused. "Really my dear, do you think it proper for me to rush out and demand the attention of the Duchess?"

"Perhaps not at any other time. But remember, she is not unknown to the entire family. She wrote you a very fine letter, praising our girls, when last she was here."

Mr. Bennet admitted it was so. In fact, there had been a meeting besides the letter, but of this Mrs. Bennet was unaware. "That was because of their care for the Netherfield tenants during the time of leaseholders when no one was seeing to their needs. It was a business letter, not an invitation to intrude on her privacy. No, Mrs. Bennet, if the company there wishes to engage with us, no doubt they will know how to do so. It is not for us to make the first overtures."

"But consider our daughters. Only think what an accomplishment to have one, or dare I say, several of them established."

"A lovely thought indeed my dear, but whatever schemes you may have in mind will have to proceed without my aid" replied Mr. Bennet, folding his newspaper and quitting the room directly.

Mrs. Bennet sighed, then cheered again, surely she could eventually convince her recalcitrant spouse to support her in this; after all, according to Mrs. Long it would be at least a week before they would see their august neighbor arrive.

Victoria Lynn

Made in the USA
Monee, IL
29 May 2023

34929618R00243